CLEAN
KILL

STEPHEN LEATHER

CLEAN KILL

HODDER

First published in Great Britain in 2023 by Hodder & Stoughton
An Hachette UK company

This paperback edition published in 2024

1

Copyright © Stephen Leather 2023

The right of Stephen Leather to be identified
as the Author of the Work has been asserted by him in accordance
with the Copyright, Designs and Patents Act 1988.

All rights reserved. No part of this publication may be reproduced, stored in a
retrieval system, or transmitted, in any form or by any means without the prior
written permission of the publisher, nor be otherwise circulated in any form
of binding or cover other than that in which it is published and without
a similar condition being imposed on the subsequent purchaser.

All characters in this publication are fictitious and any resemblance to real
persons, living or dead, is purely coincidental.

A CIP catalogue record for this title is available from the British Library

Paperback ISBN 978 1 529 367454
ebook ISBN 978 1 529 36743 0

Typeset by Palimpsest Book Production Ltd, Falkirk, Stirlingshire

Printed and bound in Great Britain by Clays Ltd, Elcograf S.p.A.

Hodder & Stoughton policy is to use papers that are natural, renewable
and recyclable products and made from wood grown in sustainable forests.
The logging and manufacturing processes are expected to conform
to the environmental regulations of the country of origin.

Hodder & Stoughton Ltd
Carmelite House
50 Victoria Embankment
London EC4Y 0DZ

www.hodder.co.uk

The first prayers of the day came to an end and the two men collected their shoes and left the mosque. It was one of the biggest mosques in the country, built of red brick with a green dome and four towering minarets, and the streets were soon filled with worshippers, on their way home or off to work. Most of the male worshippers wore traditional Islamic clothing, tunics or long robes, but Nazim Hussain and Mohammed Tariq were wearing jeans and black bomber jackets. They were both in their late twenties, skinny with neatly trimmed beards and styled hair that glistened in the sunlight. A third man was waiting for them in the street. He was Mizhir Khaliq, a few years younger than they were, wearing a long black puffer jacket and a red beanie hat. He was clean-shaven and wearing round-framed glasses. His left eye was lazy and would often wander inward of its own accord.

Hussain and Tariq stood back to allow four women clothed from head to foot in black to pass, then joined Khaliq. He took turns hugging them and kissing them on both cheeks, muttering a greeting in Arabic.

'You have it?' asked Tariq.

'I do,' said Khaliq, patting his pocket. 'So who is this Tony Swinton?'

'He's a screw we've got working for us,' said Tariq. 'He started at Bradford nick about three months ago. He's got a gambling problem and always needs cash. His mum is in a nursing home in Listerhills and he visits her several times a week, so we've got leverage if we need it. We've used him a few times to take contraband in already.'

'And he's taken phones in before?'

Tariq nodded. 'Twice. Good as gold.'

Khaliq nodded. 'Let's go, then.'

Parking close to the mosque was almost impossible at prayer times so they had to walk several hundred metres before they reached Tariq's car, a grey Prius. Hussain climbed into the back. Khaliq dropped into the front passenger seat while Tariq started the engine.

'Is it true, he's coming back?' asked Tariq.

'That's what they say,' said Khaliq.

'I'll believe it when I see it,' said Hussain.

'No, it's happening,' said Khaliq. 'That's why we need to get that phone in today.'

'I always thought he would die in America,' said Tariq as they pulled away from the kerb.

'He has friends in high places,' said Khaliq. 'Powerful friends. Here and in the US.'

Tariq banged on his horn as a white van pulled out in front of them, and the van's horn blared back. 'Wanker,' he muttered.

Swinton's house was a thirty-minute drive from the mosque, a terraced house in a row of fifty or more identical homes, two up, two down, the front door opening directly on to the pavement with a small yard and an alley behind it. They managed to park close by and climbed out. A woman in a full burkha walked towards them pushing a double stroller with two toddlers in it. She was holding a phone to her ear and shouting in Urdu and they all moved out of her way.

Tariq took them over to a house with a black door and rang the bell. It was opened by a man in his late forties, frowning as he held a mug of coffee. He was wearing a white shirt with epaulettes and black trousers and tie. His eyes hardened as he saw who was on his doorstep. 'What the hell do you want?' he said.

'We want to come in,' said Tariq.

'Yeah, well I don't want you here. If you want to arrange a meet, you've got my number. You can't just turn up unannounced. And I'm just off to work.'

He tried to close the door but Tariq put up a hand and pushed it open. 'You don't have to invite us in, Tony, we're not vampires,' he said.

'So you're coming in whatever I say, is that it?' said Swinton. He took his hand off the door.

'Got it in one,' said Tariq. He pushed his way in and Hussain and Khaliq followed him.

'Please, make yourself at home,' said Swinton sourly. He closed the door and followed them into the cramped front room. There were grubby net curtains over the windows which overlooked the street, and an old fireplace that had been boarded up with a sheet of plywood. The only furniture was a grey plastic sofa and a green fabric armchair, the back stained from years of dirty hair rubbing against it and the arms fraying through, and a pine coffee table covered in water ring marks. There were several copies of the *Racing Post* and the *Racing Paper* open on the floor.

'So to what do I owe the pleasure of this visit?' said Swinton, his voice loaded with sarcasm. He bent down to put his mug on the coffee table. 'I don't have time to chat, like I said, I'm on my way to work.'

'One of our brothers was sent to solitary yesterday,' said Tariq. 'We need to get a phone to him.' He nodded at Khaliq who put his hand into his pocket and took out a miniature mobile phone, about two and a half inches long and an inch wide. It was black with a small screen and a full keypad. He gave it to Swinton.

'His name's Javid Mir,' said Khaliq. 'He's on B Wing. He got into a fight and now he's in solitary.'

'You say solitary,' said Swinton, slipping the phone into his pocket. 'Do you mean solitary or do you mean cellular confinement, or is he in the segregation unit or the Block?'

'The Block? What's the Block?' asked Tariq.

'He means the Close Supervision Centre,' said Khaliq. 'It's where they keep the troublemakers.' He glared at Swinton. 'We were just told that he was in solitary and that someone needs to talk to him.'

'There's a big difference,' said Swinton. 'If he's in solitary in his own cell, I can just go and see him. It's a lot harder if he's in the segregation unit and it'll be virtually impossible if he's in the Block. That's a prison within a prison and there's no way I can get a phone to him if he's there.'

'This isn't up for discussion,' said Khaliq. 'You'll do as you're fucking told.' He nodded at Tariq who reached inside his jacket and took out an envelope. He tossed it at Swinton. Swinton fumbled and the envelope fell to the floor. It opened and fifty pound notes spilled out on to the threadbare carpet. 'There's five hundred quid there,' said Tariq.

Swinton knelt down, gathered up the notes and shoved them back into the envelope. 'Look, I'll do my best,' he said, as he straightened up. 'But I can't promise anything.'

Tariq pushed him in the chest and he fell back on to the sofa. 'This isn't a fucking discussion,' said Tariq. 'You'll get a phone to him and you'll do it this morning. If you don't, we'll pay your mother a visit in her nursing home.'

'Guys, come on, there's no need for this,' said Swinton.

'We know what room she's in, we know exactly how to get to her. Easiest thing in the world to send a couple of brothers. And I know a couple who really get turned on by old flesh . . .'

'Okay, okay,' said Swinton. 'I'll do it.'

'Damn right you'll do it,' said Tariq. 'Because you know what'll happen if you don't. First your mother, then you.'

'Just stop threatening me,' said Swinton. 'I've said I'll do it.' He pushed himself up off the sofa. 'Just let me get ready for work and I'll do it first thing.' He shoved the envelope into his back pocket.

'We'll take you,' said Khaliq.

'I can get the bus,' said Swinton. It was unnerving speaking to the man because his left eye seemed to have a life of its own.

'We'll drop you,' said Khaliq. 'We don't want you having a change of heart on the way.' He held out his hand. He was holding a condom. He offered it to Swinton.

'What the fuck?' said Swinton, holding it on the flat of his hand.

'For you to . . . you know . . .'

Swinton looked at him in disgust. 'Are you stupid?' He looked across at Tariq. 'This idiot thinks I'm shoving the phone up my back passage?'

Tariq chuckled. 'It's a possibility, innit?'

Swinton shook his head. 'No,' he said. 'It isn't.' He tossed the condom on to the floor in disgust.

'How you get the phone to him isn't the issue,' said Khaliq. 'But you need to get it to him this morning.'

Swinton shrugged. 'Okay, okay,' he muttered.

Khaliq pointed a warning finger at Swinton's face. 'Say it like you fucking mean it.'

'Okay,' said Swinton, louder this time. 'I'll do it.'

'That's more like it,' said Khaliq. 'And just remember, you give him that phone the moment you set foot in the prison or your life changes forever, and not in a good way.'

Swinton put on his anorak and picked up his backpack. Khaliq pointed at Swinton's mobile phone, which was sitting on the coffee table. 'Don't forget your own phone.'

Swinton shook his head. 'We're not allowed to take phones into the prison. It's a sackable offence.'

Khaliq laughed. 'But the prison's full of mobiles, innit?'

'Yeah,' said Swinton sourly. 'You could say that it's ironic.' He looked at his watch. 'We should be going.'

∙   ∙   ∙

Liam Shepherd stood on the end of his bed and thumped the side of the air conditioning unit with the flat of his hand. It was an old unit and periodically something inside would start whirring with the sound of an angry wasp. A good solid thump often did the trick. This time it took three slaps before the noise stopped. He stepped off the bed, picked up a water bottle and took a long drink. Even with the aircon on full blast it was still over twenty-five degrees in the Portakabin that he had called home for the past four weeks.

The Portakabin was in the West African country of Mali, specifically in Camp Roberts, just outside Gao, a sprawling town some 750 miles east of the capital Bamako. Camp Roberts was home to the UK's Long Range Reconnaissance Group and Liam was there to fly the three Chinook helicopters that had been sent to support the UN's peacekeeping forces. Camp Roberts was part of Camp Castor, a Dutch-built camp that at its peak had been home to more than 1,100 peacekeepers.

When he had first been told that he was being sent to Mali, Liam had googled the country to find out more about it. He learned that it was landlocked, with its borders to the north deep in the Sahara Desert. According to Wikipedia, Mali had once been one of the wealthiest countries in the world, with rich gold deposits and endless supplies of salt that it exported around the world. But that was nine hundred years ago. Present-day Mali still had its gold, and was also rich in lithium and uranium, but the country was in a mess, its glory days a distant memory. Child and infant mortality rates were among the highest in the world. Yellow fever, cholera and malaria were common. Twenty per cent of the country's children still had no access to primary education and only one third of the population could read. Much of the country's problems were exacerbated by various Islamic terror groups who had been wreaking havoc across the country. Al-Qaeda were active in the region, as were their arch rivals ISIS. When the jihadist groups weren't fighting each other, they were carrying out terror attacks against the local population and the UN peace-keepers. Thousands of lives had been lost and hundreds of thousands of people had been forced from their homes.

One of Liam's colleagues who had done a tour in Mali the previous year had described it more succinctly than Wikipedia.

'It's a shit hole, mate,' he had said. 'An absolute shit hole.'

But Liam was actually enjoying his time there. The locals were friendly and happy to chat to him, testing his schoolboy French to its limits. To his surprise he found himself enjoying the local food, especially the different types of bread the women cooked in earth ovens usually found at the entrance to their homes. The national dish of Mali was Tigua Degué, basically rice with peanut sauce, to which was added chicken, beef or lamb, if any was available. Liam couldn't get enough of it, and had even scribbled down the recipe so that he could recreate it on his return to the UK.

Liam dropped down on to the wooden chair at the end of the bed and picked up the dog-eared French phrase book that had been left by the room's previous occupant. He had just started trying to memorise the French for 'How many brothers and sisters do you have?' when there was a loud knock on his door. 'Are you decent, Skills?'

It was Liam's next-door neighbour, Harry 'Mobile' Holmes. Mobile was six months younger than Liam but had been flying Chinooks for more than two years. The door opened and Mobile popped his head around it. He was a tall, gangly Geordie with a shock of unruly red hair and a sprinkling of freckles across his cheeks and nose.

'We're up, Skills,' shouted Mobile. 'Grab your gear.'

'Skills' was Liam's nickname, picked up in his early days of helicopter training. An instructor had suggested that he needed to work on his hovering skills. One of Liam's colleagues had helpfully chipped in with a Liam Neeson impersonation, saying he had a particular set of skills but hovering wasn't one of them. The nickname had stuck, which was a relief as the other possibility had been 'Sheep-shagger', courtesy of his surname.

Liam got to his feet, zipped up his flight suit and picked up his helmet. 'What's the story?' he asked as he followed Mobile out of the Portakabin.

'A UN convoy has run into problems about thirty-five clicks out on RN18,' said Mobile. 'One of the vehicles has lost an axle, we need to bring it back.' RN – Route Nationale – was a hangover from the days when Mali had been a French colony.

'Anybody hurt?'

'Apparently not,' said Mobile.

'Couldn't they call the RAC?'

Mobile laughed. 'Joking apart, they were out there to quieten down some al-Qaeda activity, so it's a bit of a hot spot. At the moment they're sitting ducks.'

They walked over to their Chinook. The British Chinooks were used to ferry around troops and equipment for what the United Nations called its Multidimensional Integrated Stabilisation Mission in Mali, or MINUSMA, which was set up in 2013 to back foreign and local soldiers battling Islamist militants. Camp Castor was sandwiched between a joint civilian-military MINUSMA supercamp and the south-eastern edge of Gao International Airport.

Gao was the Wild West – not exactly lawless, but close, despite the efforts of MINUSMA. Most of the MINUSMA troops were from Chad, Bangladesh and Egypt. British troops had been in Gao since 2020, but they would soon be leaving. The French had already pulled out of the country, and the Germans would be following the Brits. Western troops were pulling out in response to the military government's request for assistance from the Wagner Group, Russian mercenaries who had close links to the Kremlin. The Wagner Group had carried out atrocities in Ukraine and across Africa, and had started employing the same terror tactics in Mali. Liam figured that the situation was going from bad to worse with no hope of things getting better. The British contingent were simply arranging deckchairs on the Titanic; all Liam could do was to carry out the orders he was given as best he could until it was time to go home.

Mobile had the laminated checklist in his hand and he called out the checks as Liam carried them out. They started by examining the condition of the main rotors, then the forward and aft pylons, then the transmission and engine oil levels. Then they went inside the cargo area to inspect the generators, hydraulic pumps and fuel levels. Pilots always carried out the preflight checks themselves. Their lives depended on the heli being airworthy, so the job was never given to anyone else.

Once they were satisfied, they climbed into the cockpit. Liam took the right-hand seat. Mobile was the more experienced pilot, but he was happy to let Liam take the hours as pilot in command. They saw the two other members of the crew jogging over: crew chief Michael Smith – a fifteen-year veteran of the RAF – and gunner Gerry Fowler. Both were wearing green flight suits and helmets with integrated ear muffs.

'Thanks for waiting, lads,' said Smithy in his heavy Shropshire accent, all clipped consonants and extended vowels. The crew chief was responsible for anything to do with the non-flying functions, including any fetching and carrying the Chinook would be called on to do. He climbed into the back and strapped himself in. 'What's the story?'

'Armoured personnel carrier has lost an axle,' said Mobile. 'Sounds like it's not budging so we'll need the sling to airlift it back to base.'

'Roger that,' said Smithy.

'They taking fire?' asked Fowler. He was the weapons system operator, responsible for the Chinook's two 7.62mm M134 Miniguns and one 7.62mm M60D machine gun. Like Liam, he was a relative newcomer to the Chinook. The Miniguns were mounted at the Chinook's port and starboard firing ports at the front of the helicopter. They could fire up to 4,000 rounds a minute, using a design similar to the old Gatling gun. The high rate of fire could be used for landing zone suppression and to support troops on the ground. Tracer rounds were slotted into the linked ammunition feed at regular intervals so that the gunner could get a clear view of where his shots were going, allowing him to walk the stream of rounds on to a target. The M60D was a standard NATO M60 machine gun that had been modified for use as a door gun. It was link-belt-fed and air-cooled with a firing rate of close to 650 rounds a minute. A canvas bag clipped to the gun caught all the ejected links and cartridge cases so they wouldn't end up in the engine intake or whirring rotor blades.

The firepower was impressive but standing orders were that the guns were only to be used defensively, if the Chinook itself was under fire.

'We're told not,' said Mobile. 'Just a breakdown. But we're tasked with getting them out ASAP, the top brass don't want them exposed any longer than necessary. Things could change.'

There had been a recent upsurge in terrorist attacks against the blue helmets in and around Gao. The previous week, three Egyptian peacekeepers had died when their truck ran over an improvised explosive device some sixty kilometres north of the city. The IED had been detonated remotely by wire and the bombers had allowed three armoured cars to drive over it before detonating it under a less-well armoured truck. And only two days earlier, eight Bangladeshi peacekeepers had been injured when their logistics convoy was attacked on the RN19 highway from Tessalit to Gao, north of the camp. Islamists had attacked with AK-47s and machine guns but the peacekeepers had fought them off.

Liam and Mobile started the two Lycoming T55 turboshaft engines which were mounted on either side of the helicopter's rear pylon, then did a final check over their shoulders that Smithy and Fowler were ready. They both gave the pilots the 'okay' sign.

Mobile finally put the checklist away and nodded at Liam. 'Good to go,' he said.

Liam pulled on the collective with his left hand and eased the cyclic forward. The turbines roared and the helicopter lifted into the air. He took the helicopter up to 800 feet and then put it in a slow bank to the left, heading west, the airfield behind him. Camp Castor was spread out below him, lines and lines of containers, warehouses and hangars, plus a football field, a running track and an outside gym, all surrounded by razor wire-topped chainlink fences.

Dutch engineers had built Camp Castor, initially using tents and shipping containers. The original plan had been to build a camp that could be dismantled and taken back to Holland when the peacekeeping mission came to an end, but over the years the facility had become more permanent. The Dutch had built paved roads and imported concrete from Holland to build a helipad. They'd installed sewage, water, electricity and telecommunications pipes and cables underground, and brought in solar panels to supply the camp with electricity.

Within seconds the Chinook had passed over RN17 and they were flying over the city of Gao. Gao was built in a grid layout, mainly two-storey sandstone buildings, dotted with mosques, schools and the occasional French colonial building. Ahead of them was the River Niger. The Niger was the third longest river in Africa, beaten only by the Nile and the Congo River. The Niger began in the Guinea Highlands, close to the border with Sierra Leone, then wound its way in a crescent shape through Mali, then through Nigeria until it emptied into the Atlantic Ocean. The soil was lush and fertile close to the river, but after a kilometre or so the vegetation gave way to dry, barren dust.

The RN17 joined the RN18, which ran north to south, parallel to the river. As they continued to climb, Liam put the Chinook into a slow turn to the right. He flew over the RN18 and stopped the turn when he was heading due north, the highway directly below them.

Liam took them up to a thousand feet and levelled off. They followed the highway as it cut through the desert. They were flying at just over 500 kilometres an hour so it would be less than five minutes before they reached the convoy.

Mobile was peering ahead while Liam concentrated on flying the helicopter. When he was first offered the chance to switch from flying the single-rotored Wildcat, Liam had been apprehensive to say the least. He had assumed that flying a helicopter with two rotors would require twice the work, but in fact the Chinook came with a flight computer that reduced the workload considerably. The biggest difference was that with a single rotor, the pilot had to constantly use the foot pedals to counter the torque. But the Chinook had two rotors which counter-rotated and cancelled out the torque. One of the first things his Chinook instructor had told him was to take his feet off the pedals and rest them on the floor, something that would almost certainly end in disaster if he'd tried it while at the controls of the Wildcat.

Liam started climbing again, taking the Chinook up to 2,000 feet.

'I see them,' said Mobile, pointing at his one o'clock.

'Roger that,' said Liam.

In the distance were five white UN armoured vehicles. The first was at an angle to the rest of the convoy. Blue-helmeted peacekeepers were standing in the highway, keeping the traffic moving.

There was sandy wasteland either side of the road, but to the east was a small village of stone cottages and barns.

Liam started a slow descent towards the road.

Several pick-up trucks were working their way past the convoy. Two peacekeepers were stopping traffic on the same side of the road as their vehicles.

'What do you think?' asked Liam.

'We need to land to the left of the road, attach the sling and then lift,' said Mobile. 'We need to talk to the soldiers, see how many they can take with them. The rest we'll take with us.'

'Any problems, Smithy?' asked Liam.

The crew chief was peering out of the doorway on the starboard side. 'Piece of cake,' he said.

Liam levelled off at a thousand feet and started circling above the convoy. Mobile frowned and looked over at him.

'I just want a look-see,' Liam said.

'It looks okay,' said Mobile.

'Yeah, looks can be deceiving,' said Liam.

'If it was an ambush, they'd have used an IED and gone in with guns blazing.'

'Maybe,' said Liam. 'It's just that my Spidey sense is tingling.'

'Better safe than sorry,' said Mobile. 'Let's keep looking.'

Liam did a slow circuit at a thousand feet. There wasn't much traffic on the highway and the peacekeepers were dealing with the bottleneck around the stalled convoy. He eased back on the power and started descending again. He levelled off at five hundred feet and this time did a figure of eight flight path centred on the convoy. 'Eyes peeled, guys,' he said.

All four of the crew scanned the highway and the surrounding area.

Two goat herders were moving a large herd of goats across the road to the north of the convoy. A small group of men were squatting on the ground outside one of the cottages, smoking cigarettes. Three small girls in white shirts and blue skirts were playing with a skipping rope.

'Everything looks cool to me,' said Smithy from the starboard door.

'Me too,' said Fowler, who was peering down the barrel of his machine gun.

'What do you think they drove over?' asked Liam.

'Some sort of pothole,' said Mobile.

'And it just happened to cripple the convoy?' said Liam. 'All those pick-up trucks and farm vehicles drove over it with no problems? And how come they didn't see it? Was the driver asleep?'

'It could have been a drain under the road,' said Smithy. 'They collapse all the time out here.'

'But this one just happened to collapse under a UN convoy?' said Liam.

'It's a heavy vehicle, what with all that armour,' said Mobile. 'These roads just weren't built to take the weight. You're over-thinking it, Skills.'

Several of the peacekeepers were waving up at the helicopter. They were all carrying carbines but they had them on their slings. They didn't seem to be worried about anything.

Liam levelled the Chinook, then went into a slow descending turn that took them over a clump of flat-roofed stone cottages. The schoolgirls were still skipping, and the group of men were still squatting and smoking. Four hundred feet. Three hundred feet. His turn took them back over the road. Two hundred feet.

The downdraft began to swirl the sand below them. Liam and Mobile scanned the area, looking for any obstructions that might impede their landing. There was a line of poles carrying power cables off their starboard side but they were too far away to be an issue. The ground was dotted with small rocks but nothing large enough to cause a problem. Liam started to flare the rotors as he prepared to land. A hundred feet.

'RPG!' shouted Fowler.

Liam's heart pounded. His breath caught in his throat as he tried to shout 'Where?' and Fowler beat him to it.

'Starboard!' screamed Fowler.

Liam thrust the cyclic to the left and pulled the collective up, putting the Chinook into a climbing turn. Mobile twisted around, looking over his shoulder. 'Shit!' he shouted.

Liam kept pulling on the collective and the engines roared. Then the Chinook shuddered and there was a flash of light and deafening bang that assaulted his eardrums even through the helmet and ear defenders.

The cyclic went loose in his right hand and the nose dipped down and he heard the ripping of metal. The nose lurched to the left and he kicked hard on the right pedal but it didn't make the slightest difference.

All he could see now was the ground spinning towards him.

His body was biting into the nylon harness and his feet slipped off the pedals. He pulled on the collective to try to get some lift but the engine note was now just an angry roar. He tried to get his feet back on the pedals but his legs felt too heavy.

Mobile was screaming at the top of his voice as he wrestled with the cyclic but it was clear to both of them that the controls were useless. Nothing they did was going to change the outcome, but they continued to struggle with the controls all the way to the ground, when everything went black.

. . .

D an Shepherd climbed into the back of the Prius. He was wearing a black anorak over his prison officer's uniform and carrying a small Reebok backpack containing a packed lunch and a flask of tomato soup. Hussain, Tariq and Khaliq had stood over him in the tiny kitchen as he had prepared his lunch.

Initially he feared that they had discovered that he wasn't Tony Swinton, prison guard, but was actually Dan Shepherd, MI5 officer. But he decided that was paranoia kicking in. If they knew who he really was they wouldn't have hung around while he prepared his lunch – he'd be dead on the lino floor by now.

There was a smoke detector in the kitchen ceiling containing a concealed camera that recorded everything that happened, sound and vision. There were similar cameras throughout the house. Everything that happened inside the house was recorded, and Shepherd and his team already had more than enough evidence to put Hussain and Tariq, and any of their collaborators who had visited the house, behind bars for a long time. But MI5 was after bigger fish. Shepherd had been under-cover as Tony Swinton for three months already and figured he had another two or three months to go. The woman that Hussain and Tariq thought was Shepherd's mother was actu-ally a retired MI5 officer who had moved into the home with two armed guards close by. Shepherd visited her three or four times a week for tea and a chat about the way things used to be. He had grown fond of the lady and planned to stay in touch when the operation was over.

Khaliq was in the front passenger seat and Tariq was driving. Hussain sat next to Shepherd in the back. The car doubled as a taxi, and when Tariq wasn't threatening prison officers he was ferrying customers around Bradford.

The phone was in Shepherd's right shoe. It wasn't the first time he had taken contraband into the prison. He wore thick-soled boots and he had hollowed out a small compartment under his arch, just big enough for the phone. All visitors to Bradford Prison, including staff, had to pass through a metal detector, but unlike airport security they did not have to remove their shoes.

The prison was a fifteen-minute drive from the house. They dropped him around the corner from the prison's main entrance. 'Don't fuck this up, Swinton,' said Hussain as Shepherd climbed out of the car.

'I won't.'

'You'd better not,' growled Tariq. 'And call me as soon as it's done.'

Shepherd climbed out and headed towards the prison. There was a public phone box ahead of him and he made sure that the Prius had gone before popping in and calling Diane Daily, who was handling surveillance for the Bradford operation. Daily had served five years in the Royal Corps of Signals before joining MI5. She was sharing the work with Donna Walsh, who headed up MI5's London surveillance operations, and they had agreed to twelve-hour shifts, Daily covering 8 a.m. to 8 p.m. and Walsh handling the night. There was always at least one of them based in a city centre hotel.

'Diane, did you get all that back at the house?'

'We did indeed, Dan,' said Daily. 'Donna was here too so we both saw it live. And idea who that guy is? The new one?'

'They didn't tell me his name. He's young but Hussain and Tariq deferred to him and he rode shotgun in the Prius. He has a lazy eye. The left one. Can you pick up the condom from the floor? He wasn't wearing gloves so we should be able to get prints and DNA.'

Daily chuckled. 'You teaching your grandmother to suck eggs, Dan? We're picking it up as we speak. Probably with tweezers.'

'Excellent, thank you.'

'And what about the guy you're delivering the phone to? This Javid Mir?'

Shepherd had memorised the details of the prison's 1,124 inmates, 315 prison officers and 363 civilian staffers before he had gone undercover, and Javid Mir wasn't on his radar. Mir had no terrorist connections that MI5 were aware of, though he worshipped at a mosque where more than a dozen young men were known to have gone to Pakistan, allegedly for religious studies but in fact for three months at an ISIS training camp. Mir was serving a two-year prison sentence for marijuana dealing and had been a model prisoner. He worked in the prison kitchens and according to his file was hoping to follow a career in catering when he was released. 'Nothing known,' said Shepherd. 'But they were very keen that he gets the phone today. First thing, they said.'

'It would have been nice to let Amar have a look before you handed it over.' Amar Singh was one of MI5's top technical experts. It was Amar who had rigged up the house with cameras and microphones. On the two previous occasions Shepherd had been asked to smuggle phones into the prison he had managed to show them to Singh first, giving him time to install a surveillance program so that calls and messages could be monitored.

'I know, but they didn't give me a chance, they drove me straight to the prison and my shift starts in five minutes.'

'Maybe switch it on and check if there are any contact numbers or messages.'

Shepherd laughed. 'Now who's teaching who to suck eggs? Give me a second.' He took the small phone out of his pocket. He pressed the button on the side to switch it on and within a few seconds it had powered up. There was just one number in the contacts directory, with no name attached. According to the phone's internal record only one call had been received, from the number in the directory, presumably just to load the number. There were no messages. He read out the number so that Daily could make a note of it.

Then he switched the phone off, opened the back and took out the SIM card to look at the integrated circuit card ID number. The number was unique to the SIM card, as individual as a fingerprint. The ICCID was made up of nineteen or twenty characters, but as was the case with the one in the small phone, often just the last thirteen characters were printed on the card. Reading the code was simple enough. The first two digits on SIM cards were always 89, to differentiate them from other types of chip cards. The second two characters were for the country code, followed by a number that identified the network that had issued the card, followed by an account number. He gave the number to Daily, ended the call and reassembled the phone before tucking it into his sock.

He left the phone box and continued towards the prison. As he turned on to the main road he saw two more prison officers about to start their shifts: Sarah Hardy, a redhead who had done six years in the army including two tours in Afghanistan, and Stephen Underwood, who had transferred from HMP Wakefield, nicknamed the 'Monster Mansion' because of the large number of high-profile, high-risk prisoners held there. Underwood had a host of stories about serial killers such as Robert Maudsley, Sidney Cooke and John Cooper and was happy to relate them to anyone who would listen.

'Not on the bus today, Tony?' asked Hardy as he drew level with them.

'A friend gave me a lift.'

She grinned. 'Girlfriend?'

'Just a guy I know.'

'Have you got a partner, Tony?' asked Underwood. He was in his thirties, with jet-black hair and gold-rimmed glasses. Like most prison officers he wore a coat over his uniform before he came on duty. The prison service was fine with its people wearing uniforms in public, but suggested they keep them covered to avoid confrontations. 'You never mention anyone.'

'Married to the job,' said Shepherd.

Hardy laughed. 'Me too,' she said. 'But I'd get a divorce in a heartbeat if I could find a job that paid better.'

Ahead of them was HMP Bradford. It was a Category B prison, which meant that it held local prisoners serving their sentences and men on remand who had yet to face trial. The brick building was grim and forbidding. It had been built in 1852 and Victorian prisons were designed to intimidate, to keep the population in a state of fear. Behave, or this is where you'll end up. The walls were high and topped with razor wire, the windows were small and barred, the brickwork stained by years of pollution.

They reached the main entrance. Signs directed visitors to the left and staff to the right. The staff entrance was a single black door. Jim MacLeod was on duty, a gruff grey-haired Scotsman who signed them in and watched them place their bags on a baggage scanner's conveyor belt along with their wallets, keys and loose change. Hardy went first, followed by Underwood. MacLeod looked at the screen and pressed a button to eject their bags and to pass Shepherd's backpack through the scanner.

'What have you got today, Tony?' he said as he looked at the screen.

'Cheese and Branston pickle,' said Shepherd.

'Nice. But I'm a piccalilli man myself.'

'Yeah, I've heard that,' said Shepherd.

'And the soup?'

'Tomato.'

'Heinz?'

'Of course.'

Hardy and Underwood walked through the metal detector arch. Shepherd followed them but he stopped in his tracks when a buzzer went off. MacLeod raised an eyebrow. Shepherd went through his pockets and found his keys. 'Sorry, Jim,' he said, holding them up.

'Toss them in with your bag and try again,' said MacLeod.

Shepherd did as he was told and this time the alarm stayed silent as he walked through. The detector was great at picking up most objects but it had a blind spot below ankle level.

'Have a great day, guys and gals,' said MacLeod. 'And be careful in there.' He pressed the button to open the sliding door that allowed them into the staff rooms. The women's changing room and toilets were to the left, the men's to the right. Underwood and Shepherd went right. It was a cramped room with lines of grey lockers, many with padlocks. Shepherd unlocked his locker, shoved in his backpack and hung up his anorak next to the fleece that he wore on cold days.

'Who's running the control centre today?' Shepherd asked.

'Neil Geraghty,' said Underwood.

Shepherd nodded. Geraghty was a custodial manager with almost twenty years of service, a big bruiser of a man who was a rugby referee in his spare time. He was one of life's complainers, and would tell anyone within earshot the changes he would make if ever he was given the chance to run the prison – changes that pretty much involved taking the institution back to the Victorian days.

Shepherd took his belt from his locker and strapped it on. His extendable baton was attached, in a small holster, as were his rigid bar cuffs and a canister of PAVA spray. PAVA was the incapacitating spray favoured by the prison service and the police; it was banned for civilian use and was much more effective than either mace or pepper spray. One squirt in the eyes would stop someone in their tracks for several minutes.

Once Shepherd's belt was on he went over to a charging rack filled with radio sets. He pulled out a radio, signed for it on a clipboard on the wall, and attached it to his belt before clipping the handset on to his right shoulder.

Bodycams were charging on another rack. They were made of black plastic and had a single lens, with fluorescent yellow stickers showing an image of a camera and the words 'SOUND AND VISION'. Shepherd noted the registration number of the device and signed for it. The bodycams had to be activated to start recording, and it was up to the officer if he or she felt it was necessary. The inmates knew this and were constantly looking to see if the little red recording light was blinking. It wasn't unknown for an inmate to verbally abuse an officer right up until the point when the officer activated his or her bodycam, at which point the prisoner became all sweetness and light. There were a number of reasons for the bodycams not being on all the time. Some were technical – battery life and data storage issues – but it was more down to the fact that the union didn't want their members being recorded throughout their shift. It would be a breach of their human rights to be filmed in the bathroom or discussing personal matters with a colleague.

Shepherd and Underwood went over to the key collection point. In the old days they would have handed over a metal key tally in exchange for a set of prison keys, but Bradford Prison had installed a hi-tech fingerprint recognition system. It was supposedly more efficient but in fact was quite temperamental and subject to frequent breakdowns. Shepherd pressed his thumb against a reader and a flap flicked open. He reached in, took a set of keys and clipped them to a long chain attached to his belt, then closed the flap.

Underwood had less luck and had to try half a dozen times before a flap opened.

Hardy came out of the women's locker room swinging her keys and joined them as they walked down the corridor to the control centre.

Bradford Prison followed the standard Victorian design, with an octagonal central control centre off from which were five wings, like spokes on a wheel: A, B, C, D and E. It meant that the guards in the control centre had a clear view down all of the wings, which were also monitored by CCTV. In terms of manpower, the wings were generally understaffed. There was a wing governor, based in an office on the ground floor of each wing, a senior officer super-vising, and sometimes just two officers to do the locking and unlocking. That meant four men in charge of as many as a hundred and sixty inmates. It was a recipe for disaster, Shepherd knew, but the government had been resolute in reducing the number of prison officers in the country. There were fewer than 15,000 front-line prison officers country-wide – a drop of more than a quarter in the last ten years. And there were no signs of the decline being stopped, despite a steady increase in the number of people being sent to prison.

The control centre had a couple of dozen officers, some dealing with admin, some walking around checking on the wings, others scrutinising the CCTV monitors. The control centre was three storeys high with gantries running all the way around so that the officers could see down all the landings. It reminded Shepherd of a cathedral with its vaulted ceilings, though there was no ornate artwork, just painted bricks and metal gates.

Bradford Prison was a typical Victorian prison. The cells were small and the doorways were low and narrow. After all, people were smaller back then. There were candle alcoves set into the wall to provide light at night but the windows were small, barred and set high up in the walls. Between 1842 and 1877, ninety prisons were built across the country, all following the same design. Many had never closed. Though the cells remained small, they now had electric lights and toilets. But they now usually housed two prisoners, cramped into the space designed for one. A prison that had been designed to hold almost 600 prisoners was now home to more than a thousand.

There were up to 120 cells on a wing, spread across three landings. The ground floor landing was always referred to as 'the ones', the first floor was 'the twos' and the top floor was 'the threes'. The showers were in the basement of each wing, along with a makeshift gym, generally just a few sets of weights and a couple of running machines and exercise bikes.

A sixth building, between B Wing and C Wing, housed the prison workshops, skill centres, classrooms, medical centre and admin offices. That was where the number one governor, Jonathan Blunt, the man in overall charge of the prison, was based. There was a walkway jutting off to a newer building, the Close Supervision Centre, effectively a prison within a prison, where the most dangerous prisoners were kept, surrounded by its own razor-wire topped fences and where guards with dogs regularly patrolled.

The kitchens were housed in another building, with covered walkways linking them to the various wings so that meals could be delivered no matter the weather. When the prison had first been built, the prisoners ate together in communal dining rooms, but a growing prison population meant that was no longer possible so meals were transported to the wings on heated metal trolleys and eaten in the prisoners' cells.

There were walkways criss-crossing the grounds, and no signs, so newbie prison officers were forever losing their bearings. It was the height of embarrassment for a prison officer to ask for directions from an inmate, but it wasn't unusual for them to get lost, much to the amusement of the men they were supposed to be controlling. Shepherd had never had that problem; one look at a map of the prison and his eidetic memory had kicked in.

The control centre was never quiet. There were always prison officers moving around and during the day prisoners were constantly being escorted through the hub.

Custodial Manager Geraghty, with three silver stripes on his epaulettes, was standing behind a counter looking at a computer screen and rubbing his chin when Shepherd walked up. 'What's the story with Javid Mir on B Wing, Mr Geraghty?' he asked once he had the custodial manager's attention.

Geraghty frowned. 'What do you mean?'

'I heard he was in solitary.'

Geraghty picked up a clipboard and flicked through several sheets of paper. 'Oh, yeah, that was a fracas on the landing. Him and Ricky Morgan had words and Ricky threw a punch.'

'What was it about?'

'Football, I think. Six of one, half a dozen of the other. They're both up before the governor today. What's your interest?'

'I was just surprised to hear that he'd been in trouble, that's all. Generally he keeps his nose clean. Am I on B Wing today? I wouldn't mind a word with him.'

Geraghty picked up another clipboard and studied it. 'You are, yes with Stephen Underwood. You're going to be short-handed but I don't think there's anything I can do, not with this flu doing the rounds.'

'Thanks, Mr Geraghty.'

'And see if you can get Javid to open up about what happened. At the moment they're both claiming they tripped.'

'Sure.'

Underwood was already heading towards the gate that led to B Wing, so Shepherd hurried after him. 'I'm with you today,' he said.

'Anyone else?'

'I'm afraid not.'

'Two officers taking care of three landings, they're taking the piss.'

Underwood unlocked the gate, they went through and he relocked it. They were on the ground floor so there were two landings above them, visible through the metal netting that was supposed to prevent inmates from throwing themselves from the upper floors. As always, his ears were assaulted by the noise of a crowded wing. Stereos and televisions were blaring, a guitar was being strummed, badly, video games were being played at full volume, men were shouting and even screaming and doors were being kicked or banged shut. Prisons were never quiet, even in the middle of the night there'd be shouting and screaming and banging. Always banging. It was as if the men felt that the only way they could make their presence felt was by making sound, and the louder the sound, the better. Like most prison officers, Shepherd had learned to blank out the noise, otherwise it would have driven him crazy.

Often when he left the prison after a shift, the silence outside the building would hit him like a cold shower.

Ahead of them was a pool table with blue baize, and beyond that a table tennis table. To their right was the wing governor's office. The door was open but Shepherd knocked on it anyway. The wing governor was Maria Crowley. She had light brown hair and a cheerful smile and she waved them in. She had been studying her computer and she took off her wire-framed glasses. 'Good morning, gentlemen,' she said. 'I suppose you've heard it'll just be the two of you this shift.'

'It's outrageous,' said Underwood.

'It's been that way all week, I'm afraid,' she said. 'I've mentioned it to Mr Blunt but it's like talking to a brick wall.'

Two prison officers appeared at the door. One was Mary Garner, who had worked at Bradford Prison for the best part of twenty years. She was a tough, no-nonsense officer who could stand her ground against the most violent of prisoners but was equally capable of offering a hug and a shoulder to cry on when necessary. With her was Sonny Shah, a young British Asian man with glistening black hair and a five o'clock shadow. There were very few British Asians in managerial roles in the prison service, so university-educated Shah was being fast tracked. He and Garner were both finishing their shifts. A third officer appeared behind them, Ed Blackhurst, bearded and wearing glasses. He had two silver stripes on his epaulettes denoting his status as a supervising officer. He had an office next to the governor's but spent most of his time on the threes, looking down to check that was all was right with the world. His hawk-like presence had earned him the nickname Eddie the Eagle.

'Anything Mr Swinton and Mr Underwood need to know?' Crowley asked Blackhurst.

'Mr Mir and Mr Morgan are confined to their cells,' said Blackhurst. 'There was a ruckus yesterday evening during association and they're up before the number one governor today.'

'Any idea what it was about?' asked Shepherd.

'They both say they tripped, but the CCTV shows them trading punches.'

'But we don't know what started it?'

'They're not saying,' said Blackhurst.

'Anything else we should know?' asked the governor.

'There's a smashed window in the cell of Vullnet Haka and Ibrahim Bezati on the top floor,' said Shah. 'They say it was an accident but I think the Albanians have got a drone delivery planned.'

The governor nodded. Haka and Bezati were two of a dozen Albanians on the wing, both serving long sentences for rape. The Albanians had formed a tight group and were responsible for much of the spice that was smuggled into the prison. Spice, also known as K2 or Black Mamba, was synthetic cannabis, usually a mixture of herbs and spices sprayed with a compound that was chemically similar to THC, the psychoactive ingredient in marijuana or cannabis. It wasn't picked up by most drug testing and didn't have the familiar smell of cannabis. On the outside, a gram of spice would cost about five pounds. Inside, it would fetch a hundred pounds.

The latest hi-tech way of getting contraband into the prison involved using sophisticated drones, costing upwards of two thousand pounds, which could carry a few ounces of drugs or tobacco. Dropping the contraband on the ground was hit and miss as the guards might well get to it before the prisoners, so they tried to deliver it to the cell if possible. The windows were sealed shut but were made of regular glass and easily broken. A skilled drone operator could fly a drone from a nearby golf course and get it to the prisoner's window in less than a minute or two. At any one time there were more than two dozen cells with broken windows in the prison, but repairs were carried out by an outside contractor and it often took more than a week to get the glass replaced.

'Mr Blunt has been looking at the possibility of covering the windows with netting but is having budget problems,' said Crowley. 'I'll add it to the repair list.'

Shah looked at the governor and gestured at Shepherd and Underwood. 'Are you short-handed today, ma'am?' he asked.

'Every day,' said the governor. 'Why, are you okay for a double shift?'

'I could do with the overtime, if there's any going.'

'After what happened yesterday I'd feel happier with three on the wing, so yes, I'll sign off the paperwork and speak to Mr Geraghty. Do you want to take a quick break before we open the cells up?'

'I might just grab a cup of coffee, ma'am. Thank you.'

'Right then, let's get to it,' said the governor, looking back at her computer.

Shah headed to the control centre with Garner.

Blackhurst tilted his chin at Shepherd. 'Quick little job for you, Mr Swinton,' he said. 'I've got six guys waiting to use the shower.' He nodded at six inmates who were standing by the gate that led down to the showers and gym. They were all wearing flip-flops and carrying wash bags. 'I didn't have anyone to take them down, can you do that now?'

'Will do.'

Shepherd really wanted to get the phone to Mir as quickly as possible, but Blackhurst was the senior officer on the wing. He went over to the group as Blackhurst disappeared back into his office. 'Are you the guys who need to shower?' He stopped and sniffed. 'No need to answer that.'

'Very funny, boss,' said the man closest to the gate. 'This is the third time this week I've been stopped from showering.' His name was Willie Macdonald, an expatriate Scot who was awaiting trial for passing off fake twenty pound notes in a succession of Bradford pubs. He was wearing a red polo shirt with a large gold polo player on his chest and blue Adidas tracksuit bottoms. He was holding his shower things in a blue net bag. The clothes looked fresh but Shepherd could smell the man's body odour and it wasn't pleasant. Bad hygiene was always an issue inside, but that was because many of the inmates had mental health issues and struggled to take care of themselves. Macdonald clearly wasn't in that group, and Shepherd sympathised.

'I'm sorry, we're just understaffed at the moment.'

'You've been understaffed since the moment I got here,' said Macdonald. 'I'm entitled to a shower. That's a basic human right.'

'Mr Macdonald, I hear what you're saying and I sympathise. Let's get you under running water without further ado, shall we?'

Shepherd unlocked the gate and opened it and the men streamed through. There was a short flight of concrete steps that led to a second gate and the men gathered there, shifting from foot to foot like marathon runners waiting for the off. Shepherd relocked the gate and walked down the stairs. The men parted to let him through. He unlocked the second gate and the moment it was open the men rushed through. Shepherd smiled but really it wasn't funny – just because they were in prison didn't mean they shouldn't be allowed to stay clean.

There was a corridor to the right that went by the gym. The lights were on but the gym was empty. Presumably there wasn't an officer available to supervise as the gym was always popular. The shower room was at the end of the corridor and the men hurried through. In between the gym and the shower block were three toilet cubicles with two-foot gaps between the bottom of the door and the floor, and a row of foul-smelling urinals.

The shower room was all tiled, blue tiles on the walls and white tiles on the ceiling and floor. It clearly hadn't been cleaned in a while and the floor was covered with empty sachets and shampoo bottles and streaked with soap scum. The men stripped off their clothes and put them on hooks above a bench. They all left on their underwear. Most inmates did when they showered. Shepherd was never sure if it was because of modesty or they thought that they were safe if they weren't fully nude. There were six shower heads set into the wall, each with their own controls. There were wooden boards with green paint peeling off fixed to the wall to separate the shower heads, but offering little in the way of modesty protection. The men began showering and Shepherd stood back to give them some privacy.

There was a locked gate at the end of the corridor, and beyond it was darkness. Shepherd had studied the plans of the prison and knew that the basements of the wings were all connected by a series of corridors. In Victorian days they had been used to move prisoners around when there was bad weather outside but after covered walkways were constructed in the seventies, the tunnels were no longer needed. They could still in theory be used as escape routes in the event of a fire and the locks were regularly checked, but as far as Shepherd knew there was no lighting system and the only people who went into them were the pest control people.

Macdonald began singing 'Flower of Scotland' but he was soon shouted down by the rest of the men. One by one they switched the water off and towelled themselves dry, still wearing their underwear. Macdonald was the last out. 'I needed that, boss,' he said, grabbing a towel. Shepherd realised that the man was wearing tartan boxer shorts, and he couldn't help but smile.

'Glad to be of service,' said Shepherd.

When the men were all dried and dressed, Shepherd took them back to the ones. He had to escort them all back to their cells and lock them in. All the landings were painted in the same colours: cream walls and bright blue doors. For some reason all the pipework was painted the same blue colour. There were twenty cells on the right, twenty on the left, facing each other across the metal safety net. The only way of telling the doors apart were the numbers stencilled on them in white letters. Each door had a lockable hatch and a long, thin window so that officers could get a view of the cell and its occupants from the landing.

The last one to be locked away was Macdonald, whose cell was on the threes. He thanked Shepherd profusely for his shower before he closed the door.

Underwood was on the twos now, walking around and whistling to himself. Shepherd walked along the landing to Mir's cell and unlocked it. He pushed open the door. Mir was lying on his bunk, hands behind his head, staring at the ceiling. Shepherd slipped inside and closed the door behind him. He took the phone from his pocket. 'Your pal Tariq said I should give you this.'

Mir sat up, took it and slipped it under his pillow. He was in his early twenties and had a neatly cut beard. His right eye was bruised and there was a cut on his lower lip. He was wearing a pale blue tunic and baggy tracksuit bottoms.

'He said you need to call him. ASAP.'

'Is that what he said?'

'Something like that. He said you needed it first thing.'

'Okay. Thanks.' He frowned and the frown deepened as Shepherd made no move to leave. 'You expecting a tip or something?'

'Some gratitude would be nice.'

'You got paid, didn't you? Or are you doing Mo a favour out of the goodness of your heart?'

Shepherd put up his hands. 'Javid, I'm just trying to help you, that's all. If you've got a problem on the out, maybe I could help.'

Mir looked at him for several seconds and then shook his head. 'No problem,' he said. 'I'm good.'

'It's nothing to do with what happened with Ricky Morgan yesterday?'

'What? No.'

'From the bruises on your face, it looks serious.'

'Just a bit of rough and tumble.'

'Was it racial?'

Mir looked down at the floor. 'I'm taking the fifth.'

'I'm not asking you to grass, Javid. But the way it stands, if you both keep shtum, you'll both be punished. That means losing your privileges. Is that what you want?'

'Of course it's not what I want.'

'If I knew what happened, I could put a word in with the governor. You've been a model prisoner, why spoil it now? Do you want to lose your job in the kitchen?'

Mir looked up sharply. 'What the fuck, man? Why would they do that?'

'You were fighting. A few punches on the landing is one thing, but a fight in the kitchens where there are knives and boiling water, well that's a whole different ball game.'

'But I wasn't fighting in the kitchen, was I?'

'No, you weren't. But it's about minimising risk. Health and safety.'

'I'm not a risk. He just pushed me, that's all.'

'Literally?'

'I was talking to a brother about football. Morgan went by me and said that Pakis didn't know anything about football. He said we should stick to cricket. I told him to go fuck himself, he shoved me, I shoved him back, he threw a punch, I smacked him in the mouth, he nutted me and then we went at it until the screws pulled us apart. But he started it.'

'So you can tell the governor that.'

'I already said, I'm not a grass. Look, it'll get sorted.'

'Sorted how?'

'Don't you worry about it.'

'Okay, fine.' Shepherd pointed at the pillow. 'Two things,' he said. 'Do not let that be found,' he said. 'And if it does get found, say you've had it for weeks, say you found it, say what you want but do not say that I gave it to you.'

Mir nodded. 'Okay.'

'I'm serious,' said Shepherd.

'All right, all right, message received,' said Mir. 'Now piss off and leave me alone.'

'You need to watch your tone with me,' said Shepherd coldly. 'I'm trying to help you here.'

Mir's eyes narrowed. 'You're on Mo's payroll, kafir, you do as he says. I don't need to watch nothing with you.'

Shepherd let himself out of the cell and locked the door. Underwood was walking down the landing towards him. 'Everything okay, Tony?' He asked.

'Just having a word with Mr Mir.'

'Yeah, he's in front of the governor at three.'

'Were you here when it kicked off?'

'Nah. I was on A Wing yesterday.' He pointed at a closed door on the other side of the landing. 'Ricky Morgan's confined to his cell, too. Why are you interested?'

'Just wondered why it kicked off. Javid's on enhanced privileges, he's got a job in the kitchen, with him it's always yes sir, no sir, three bags full, sir. He doesn't seem the type to get into a fight.'

'You can never tell when it's going to kick off,' said Underwood.

Their radios crackled, then they heard Crowley's voice, telling them to open the cells. Shepherd looked at his watch. 'Do you want to do the threes?'

'Sure.'

'I'll do the twos. If Sonny gets back he can do the ones, if not we can do it together.'

Shepherd went down the stairs to the twos. The doors were all opened at eight o'clock in theory, but with only two officers on duty it could take almost half an hour to unlock all ninety cells. The men would bring out their rubbish and dump it into black plastic bags before gathering at the gate to the control centre to be taken to either work or education classes.

There were close to 200 prisoners on the wing that day, and more than a third of them had to be moved by Shepherd and Underwood, which meant that Shepherd would be responsible for up to forty men, any one of whom could be carrying a shank and intent on causing him harm. Moving the prisoners from the wing was one of the most stressful parts of the day.

He began opening the doors. Most of the inmates were keen to get out and would be on the landing the second the door was open. Almost all of the cells were two-up. They had originally been designed for single occupancy but those days were long gone and most cells had bunk beds and two cabinets for personal belongings. Sometimes the cells were so cramped that only one occupant could stand up at a time.

Several of the men ran to the phone at the far end of the wing. There was one phone per landing. Inmates were issued with a PIN and a phone account and could make as many calls as they could afford. That was the theory, but most of the time there would be a queue and it wasn't unusual for fights to break out.

Most of the prisoners filed down the stairs to the ground floor. Shah had reappeared and was opening doors there. Once all the doors were open, Shepherd headed down to join him. Inmates heading for education stood on the right side, those who were working lined up on the left. Some of the inmates had work to do around the prison, including in the kitchen, cleaning the wing and in the library. Others had 'real' jobs, such as packing plumbing parts, compiling mailing lists for magazine companies, and even answering customer queries for a high street bank. There was a workshop sewing children's clothes, and another making furniture. Prisoners were paid fifty pence an hour for their trouble. There were also vocational training courses including bricklaying, plastering, hairdressing and motorcycle repairing, which were all very popular and oversubscribed. Some were run by prison staff, others by the prisoners themselves. A former butler to the Prince of Wales, before he became King Charles, was serving a seven-year sentence for fraud and had starting giving lessons on how to be a butler. Shepherd couldn't help but smile at the thought of some of the inmates being let loose in the country houses of Europe. Not all of the prisoners who had signed up for the course were looking to better themselves, and it was obvious that more than a few saw it as a way of widening their target base.

Shah returned just as Underwood and Shepherd were unlocking the final doors on the ones. A least one officer had to stay on the wing at all times so Shah stayed behind while Shepherd took the education inmates and Underwood took the workers. The control centre was already buzzing with the inmates from A Wing, and they waited for them to pass before Underwood unlocked the gate. 'Right, working inmates with me. Stay close and keep the noise down please, otherwise I can't hear myself think.' He opened the gate and the men filed through.

'So you're all education, right?' Shepherd shouted at the remaining men. 'Anyone working needs to be with Mr Underwood.'

No one responded. 'Right, wagons roll!' shouted Shepherd. He waited for the men to file out before locking the gate, then he walked quickly towards the gate that led to the admin wing. Underwood had already locked the gate and was taking his men to the education block.

'Come on, we haven't got all day,' growled one of the older inmates as Shepherd weaved his way through the crowd to get to the gate. He was one man trying to move forty others, and it was tiring and frustrating. A sheepdog wouldn't have any trouble controlling that many sheep, but prison inmates weren't sheep. They were more akin to feral cats who took pleasure in adding to the prison officer's stress levels.

'I'm going as fast as I can,' said Shepherd. 'It would make it easier if you stood in a line.'

He unlocked the gate and stepped aside to let the men stream through. They all knew where they were going and split up. Some were carrying Open University textbooks, others GCSE handbooks, but most were just there to get out of their cells and had no intention of studying.

It was up to individual tutors to take roll calls. Shepherd was supposed to do a head count of the men leaving the wing and do another when they arrived at the education block, but that was asking the impossible. He clicked on his radio and spoke to Geraghty back at the control centre, confirming that all the inmates were present and accounted for. Geraghty or one of the control centre team would have followed their progress on the CCTV feeds.

It was up to Shepherd whether he stayed at the education block or went back to the wing, so he decided to hang around for a while. He took the stairs to the top floor. There were a dozen rooms on each floor, some large enough to take up to fifty men, others not much bigger than a cell. Each door had a glass panel set into it, and a blackboard sign on which the name of the course was written in white chalk.

There were two large men in robes and skullcaps standing outside the door to one of the larger rooms, arms folded and faces sullen. Shepherd walked down the corridor towards them, his boots squeaking on the highly polished linoleum floor.

He passed a sign saying 'GCSE ENGLISH', and another

that said 'OPEN UNIVERSITY LAW'. Law was always a popular choice, for obvious reasons, and there were a couple of dozen inmates earnestly studying their textbooks under the watchful eye of an elderly man who looked the spitting image of Leo McKern, the actor who for many years had played Rumpole of the Bailey on the TV.

As he approached the two men in the corridor, they stiffened and raised their chins. 'ISLAMIC STUDIES' had been written in capital letters on the blackboard and through the window Shepherd could see more than thirty men, all of them wearing Islamic clothing, sitting cross-legged in a circle around a white-haired man with a bushy beard and thick-lensed spectacles. Holding court was Malik Abid Qadeer, the emir of B Wing, who had become one of the main targets of the MI5 investigation that Shepherd was involved in. He was wearing a long white robe and was peering over the top of his glasses as he addressed the room. The men listening to him nodded in agreement with whatever he was saying.

The two men moved together, blocking Shepherd's view of the room. The one on the right, the bigger of the two, sneered at Shepherd. 'Muslims only,' he said. 'No kafirs.'

As Dan Shepherd, or even as a regular prison officer, Shepherd would have read the men the riot act and reported them, but he was Tony Swinton, and Tony Swinton was in the pay of the emir's people so he just smiled, nodded and said 'No problem, gentlemen' as he walked on by.

There were more stairs at the end of the corridor and he took them down to the ground floor. There was a gate to be unlocked on the ground floor to get to the corridor. To the left was the workshop block and he heard the sound of a motorcycle engine being revved up.

He headed back towards the control centre. The corridor was deserted. He could hear the squeak of his boots but the prison was never silent – in the distance he could hear the shouts and sometimes screams of the prisoners still in their cells, and the clanging of doors being slammed shut. The smell was always there too, no matter where you went, bleach and sweat and stale cabbage. The smell of cabbage had always confused Shepherd, because they rarely serve it at the prison. And always in the air was the smell of decay, of a Victorian building that was poorly maintained, of damp and rot and dust. It was a soul-destroying place to be confined to for any length of time, as an inmate or as a prison officer. Shepherd would be glad when the operation was over.

· · ·

S hafiq Ali Rafiq said his final prayer, touched his forehead to the floor one last time, and got unsteadily to his feet. The pain in his stomach was debilitating, but he had no choice other than to bear it. The guards delivered his painkillers every eight hours in accordance with the prison doctor's instructions. It didn't matter how much pain he was in, he was entitled to two tablets every eight hours and that is what he was given. No more, no less.

USP ADX Florence had been Shafiq Ali Rafiq's home for almost twelve years. The prison was on a thirty-seven-acre compound, a hundred miles south of Denver. He was currently one of 346 inmates. The facility had been designed for 490 inmates but had never been at full capacity since the day it opened in January 1995.

No one had ever escaped from ADX Florence, and no one was likely to. It was as close to escape-proof as a prison could be. All the facility's 1,400 steel doors were opened and closed electronically from a central control centre and inmates were monitored 24-7 by CCTV. If an escape attempt was even suspected, pressing a single button would close and lock every door. The perimeter was surrounded by twelve-foot wire fences topped with razor wire and patrolled by armed officers.

Shafiq Ali Rafiq was confined to his cell for twenty-three hours a day. Once a day he was handcuffed and shackled and taken to the exercise area, a concrete pit much like an empty swimming pool that he could walk around in thirty-two steps. Not that he did much walking. These days he just stood and looked up at the sky until they took him back to his cell. Walking was painful. Standing was painful, too. In fact everything caused him pain.

The guards brought him his food three times a day. He was given the kosher option. His lawyer had demanded Muslim food in line with his beliefs but the authorities would not budge and he was kept on the kosher menu. Not that it mattered. His appetite had all but gone and all he could manage was a few mouthfuls of bread or rice and a few gulps of soup.

He walked slowly over to the sink and looked at the polished steel mirror above it. His cheeks were sunken and there were dark patches under his eyes. He bared his yellowed teeth and stuck out his tongue, now coated with white fur. He looked like shit. When they had first put him in the cell, his hair and beard had been jet black, his lips had been full and his eyes had burned with a fierce intensity. No longer. Twelve years in confinement had left him a dried husk of his former self. His hair and beard were grey, his lips had shrunk to thin slits, his skin was wrinkled and as dry as paper.

He walked slowly over to his concrete bed and sat down. His cell was seven feet wide and twelve feet long. There was a single window, four feet tall and four inches wide, angled so that all he could see was the sky and the roof of a neighbouring building. To his left was a stainless steel sink and toilet. There was no tap, just a button to press for water, and another button to press to empty the toilet. The flush was on a timer so that he couldn't flood his cell, even if he had wanted to. His bed was made from poured concrete, as was the small stool and table next to the toilet. To his right was a small metal shower. The single fluorescent light was buried in the ceiling and there was no switch in the cell. The light was operated remotely.

He heard footsteps outside his cell. Then muffled voices. Then the click of the lock mechanism, followed by the rattle of the door opening. Four guards stood in the corridor.

'Stand in the middle of your cell,' barked one of the men.

Shafiq Ali Rafiq did as he was told. He always did. There was no point in resisting. He stood up and held his hands out. One guard fitted handcuffs to his wrists, another fixed shackles to his ankles. His arms were seized and he was taken out into the corridor. The guard who had spoken led the way, a guard either side held his arms, and the fourth guard followed behind. They said nothing as they walked him down the corridor. They never did. No matter what he said to them, they would never respond. The only time a guard would speak was to issue an order.

They reached the end of the corridor. The lead guard looked up at a CCTV camera and the door rolled open. They walked through into another windowless corridor lined with more cell doors. They reached another door and it too opened. That led to a corridor running left and right. The exercise pit was to the left but they took him to the right, which meant that he had a visitor. In all the years he had been imprisoned at ADX Florence no one from his family had come to see him. Most were on the no-fly list, and visiting him wasn't an option. Not because they had ever broken the law – it was just another example of American vindictiveness. He had insisted that those who could fly should stay away because he didn't want them distressed by seeing how the infidels were treating him. The only visits he had were from his legal team.

They stopped in front of another locked door. It opened and they took him along to a door with a sign that said 'MEETING ROOM'. There was a CCTV camera above the door. A red light was blinking underneath it. The door rattled open to reveal a windowless room with a table and four plastic chairs. The room was one of the few in the facility not to be covered by CCTV. Despite the brutal regime, the authorities still respected lawyer–client interactions as sacrosanct.

There was a man standing next to the table. He was a Pakistani American, who had been on Shafiq Ali Rafiq's legal team for the best part of seven years. His name was Anis Qadri. He had been to Harvard and was a good Muslim with six children and a detailed knowledge of the Koran that rivalled Rafiq's. Qadri was tall and good-looking, with slicked-back glossy hair and a thick moustache that gave him the look of a Bollywood movie star. His aluminium briefcase was on the table.

He smiled at Rafiq, revealing a wall of gleaming white teeth, but didn't say anything until the guards had seated their prisoner on one of the chairs and gone back into the corridor.

The door rattled closed. It would stay that way until the lawyer pressed the button to signal that the meeting was over.

'I have good news, Shafiq,' said the lawyer.

'I'm going home?'

The lawyer nodded. 'Yes. You are going home.'

For the first time in many years, Shafiq Ali Rafiq smiled. '*Alhamdulillah*,' he said. Praise be to Allah.

. . .

S hepherd walked around B Wing with Sonny Shah for a couple of hours. They checked on Morgan and Mir, and two other prisoners who were confined to their cells, peering at them through the glass slits in the doors. Shah wanted an early break so he headed for the staff canteen at eleven o'clock. Underwood was down in the wing governor's office filling out paperwork, leaving Shepherd to patrol the landings. Blackhurst was at his favourite post, up in the corner of the threes, leaning over the rail and looking down.

Several inmates were still in their cells, doors open. Not everyone went to classes or work, some stayed put watching television, playing video games or reading. Some would nod as he walked by and he'd get the occasional 'How's it going, boss?' but generally he was ignored. A good percentage of the men were vaping, and the landing reeked of it. Smoking tobacco had been banned in all prisons since 2018, but the authorities knew that they faced riots if they prohibited nicotine completely, so they had permitted vaping. In fact they had promoted it, selling vape devices and products through the prison shops. They had even offered payment plans for those inmates who were short of funds. The shops sold the vape devices, refillable capsules and USB charging plugs. Clearly no one had bothered to ask the prison staff what they thought of the new regulations. The refillable capsules could be refilled with cannabis and spice, in fact any drug to hand. And the USB charging plugs could be used to charge any illegal phones on the premises. Before vaping was allowed, USB chargers would be confiscated. Now they were in plain view in most cells and there was nothing the officers could do about it. Inmates were only supposed to vape in their cells, but that rule was rarely enforced. Not that it would have made any difference – the fumes billowed out of the cells whether the doors were open or not.

At eleven thirty, Shah returned to the wing. Shepherd watched from the twos as Shah walked a slow circuit of the ground floor. Three prisoners wearing tracksuits came out of a cell and gathered around the officer. Shepherd tensed as he looked down on them, wondering if it was going to be a problem, but the men seemed relaxed and made no threatening gestures. Shah was nodding and replying but the men started waving their arms around, clearly getting agitated. Shepherd headed for the stairs, but before he reached them Shah's voice crackled over the radio. 'Mr Swinton, this is Mr Shah. I have three prisoners who need to go to the gym. They were supposed to have been collected but their escort hasn't turned up. I'll take them now, I'll be back before you and Mr Underwood leave.'

'No problem, Mr Shah.'

Shah and the three inmates headed down to the basement as Shepherd walked down the stairs to the ground floor. Having only three prison officers on the wing was ridiculous. Six would be a more reasonable number considering all the moving around that had to be done. But even six officers controlling close to 200 men was laughable. It could only be done because the inmates agreed to be controlled. If at any time they refused en masse to obey instructions there was nothing the prison staff could do. In the same way that the police on the outside depended on policing by consent, discipline behind bars also required the cooperation of the inmates. The officers knew it, and so did the prisoners.

Shah was back within ten minutes and Shepherd and Underwood headed to the admin block to bring the B Wing inmates back for their lunch. There were three meals a day, all eaten in the cells. Lunch and dinner were served on the ground floor and taken back to the cells on blue plastic trays.

Breakfast was served the night before: a small carton of milk, one of orange juice, a yoghurt, a piece of fruit, a slice of bread, and a pack of butter and jam. It was sealed in a plastic bag, delivered at the end of the association period before the inmates were locked up for the night and eaten before the doors were unlocked at eight.

Lunch was served at noon and the evening meal at five. The trolleys were brought from the kitchen by trusted prisoners, known as 'red bands' because of the bands they wore on one arm. They served the food and collected the dirty plates and cutlery once the men had finished eating. There were five choices at each meal, including a halal option, a vegetarian option and a 'healthy heart' option.

Inmates were already gathering on the ground floor of the admin wing. It was barely controlled chaos with inmates from all five wings mixing together. It was one of the most dangerous times of the day. Moving prisoners from one wing to another was a way of diffusing disputes and rivalries, so when wings mixed there was always the possibility of scores being settled. There were more than four hundred prisoners in the classes and workshops, and just ten officers to get them in order and take them back to their wings. The one thing that worked in favour of the officers was that the men were hungry and didn't want to be last to get their lunch. Meal orders were placed the previous day, but it wasn't unusual for popular dishes to run out.

A Wing were already being led out as Underwood and Shepherd walked down the corridor, so they kept to the right. Shepherd saw Kamran Zaidi heading towards them. Zaidi was wearing a long pale blue shirt over baggy black pants. He made the briefest eye contact with Shepherd and rubbed his nose with the back of his hand. Shepherd had arranged signals with Zaidi and Sayed Khan, who was on D Wing. If everything was okay, they rubbed their noses, if there was a problem then they would tug at an ear. If they needed to be pulled out immediately they would rub the back of their neck. Zaidi and Khan were undercover MI5 officers, and they were Shepherd's responsibility. He was their protection and their lifeline if anything were to go wrong. Shepherd rubbed his own nose as he walked by Zaidi and followed Underwood to the gate.

The B Wing inmates were keen to get back and had formed into two groups. 'You want to go first, Mr Swinton?' asked Underwood.

'Hey, fuck that!' shouted one of the older inmates, at the head of the workshop group. 'We were here first.'

'Language, Mr McBride,' said Underwood. Jimmy McBride was a Scottish coach driver who was serving seven years for a road traffic accident. That's what he called it, though the truth was that he had been surfing porn sites on his phone as he drove his packed coach along the M1 and had smashed into a Ford Fiesta, killing a housewife and her three toddlers.

'I'm just saying, boss, we did the decent thing and got here first, and now you're punishing us.'

Underwood sighed. 'Fine. We'll go first.'

McBride grinned at the minor victory and puffed out his chest. There was an immediate outcry from Shepherd's group. Shepherd raised his hand. 'Plenty of time, guys, we'll get you all back in time to be fed.'

There were more grumblings and several of the men pushed their way into the workshop group. Shepherd didn't try to stop them. The important thing to do was to get them back on to the wing without incident.

Underwood led his group out into the corridor and then stood to the side to carry out a head count as they walked past. Shepherd's group followed and he did a head count, coming up short because several members of his group had merged with Underwood's.

'I have forty-seven,' said Underwood.

'Thirty-five,' said Shepherd. That was a total of eighty-two, so all the men were accounted for. A miscount would have meant locking everyone in the corridor and carrying out a recount, which wouldn't have gone down well with the hungry inmates.

They took the men down the corridor, through the control centre, and on to B Wing, unlocking and locking doors and gates as required.

As the first men filed on to the wing, the first of two lunch trolleys appeared at the far end of the landing, pushed by two red bands. Several of the men broke into a run to get to the front of the queue.

'Walk, don't run!' shouted Shepherd, but he knew he was wasting his voice.

• • •

Ricky Morgan was lying on his bed playing FIFA on his PlayStation, one of the perks of having the highest ranking on the Incentives and Earned Privileges scheme. Harry Kane had just scored his third goal of the match when Morgan heard the rattle of a key in his lock. He continued to play as the door opened.

'Good afternoon, Mr Morgan,' said the screw. Morgan knew the voice. Sonny Shah.

'How's it going, boss?'

Prison officers had to refer to inmates as Mister whatever their name was, and inmates had to do the same for the officers, though they were also allowed to say 'Boss' or 'Sir', or 'Miss' for the female officers.

'You're up before the governor in ten minutes, so make yourself presentable.'

'Will do, boss,' said Morgan. His food tray was on the table on the other side of the cell. It had been delivered by one of the red bands, the tray pushed through the hatch in the door. Morgan had gone for the healthy heart option, a piece of grilled white fish and a salad, a plain yoghurt and an apple. He'd eaten the fish and salad and was saving the yoghurt and apple for later. He had heard the buzz of inmates carrying their trays to the cells, then fifteen minutes of quiet as they ate their lunches. Then the wing was buzzing again as the inmates gathered to go back to classes or work. That was about fifteen minutes ago. He was due before the Number One Governor at three o'clock. He continued to play as the prison officer left the cell and walked down the landing. Morgan knew that he was almost certainly going to lose his enhanced privileges as a result of the fight with Javid Mir, which meant that he would almost certainly lose his PlayStation and possibly his television. It had been Mir's fault, he'd taken a joke the wrong way and started throwing punches. It had all been over in a matter of seconds but the screws always came down hard on fighting and a price would have to be paid. Morgan wouldn't be saying anything, he'd stick to his story that he'd tripped on the stairs. If Mir knew what was good for him, he'd say the same and accept his punishment like a man. Snitches got stitches, that was the golden rule.

He heard footsteps at his door but his eyes stayed on the screen. Kane was coming up for his fourth goal. 'Be right with you, boss,' he said as his fingers tapped on the controller.

The door opened and a figure appeared at the side of his bed. Morgan looked away from the screen. There was a blur of movement and something raked across his throat. His mouth filled with blood and he began to choke. He dropped his controller and clutched at his neck, blood trickling through his fingers as the cell door slammed shut.

● ● ●

Shepherd ate his lunch in the staff canteen after the inmates were back at work or in classes. The men had carried their trays to their cells to eat, then Shepherd, Shah and Underwood had carried out a roll call before Shepherd and Underwood had taken the men back to the admin block.

There was plenty of hot food available in the canteen but Shepherd stuck to buying fruit or a sealed yoghurt. He was wary of anything that had actually been prepared by the inmates. Most of the staff didn't appear to have any such misgivings and tucked into their meals with relish.

He opened his flask and poured tomato soup into the cup, then opened his Tupperware container and took out a sandwich. The other reason for bringing his own lunch was to add credence to his story that he was short of money. His precarious finances coupled with a gambling problem meant that he was marked as an easy target from the first day he set foot in the prison.

It had always been planned as a long-term operation, and Shepherd had been far from happy at the prospect of spending months behind bars, breathing air tainted with bleach and sweat and spending up to ten hours a shift with a group of men who might take a pop at him at any moment. But once it had been explained to him how high the stakes were, he had agreed to the assignment.

Bradford Prison had popped up on MI5's radar after an analyst on the agency's Pakistan Desk noticed that a growing percentage of former inmates were travelling to the country for terrorism training. Several had returned to the UK and been apprehended planning terrorist attacks with targets including MPs, Jewish leaders and civilians. Disaster had narrowly been averted when a terrorist cell was found to have infiltrated the baggage handlers at Leeds-Bradford Airport. The cell had obtained explosives, detonators and timers and were assembling them in a storage locker on the outskirts of Leeds when they were arrested by armed police. Of the eight men arrested, three had served sentences at Bradford Prison. Another group was arrested in the final stages of planning a mass machete attack on the Manchester Arndale Centre. Four of the eleven men arrested had done time at Bradford Prison.

Once the links between Bradford Prison and terrorism had been flagged, MI5 sent in an agent for a preliminary assessment. The agent was Terry Thompson, a former drug dealer from Essex who had begun giving information to MI5 when he was a year into serving a ten-year sentence for importing hundreds of kilos of cocaine on a yacht from St Lucia. He had been serving his sentence in Pentonville Prison when he had overheard two prisoners discussing a friend who was planning a terrorist attack on Waterloo Station. Thompson had contacted his solicitor who arranged a meeting with an MI5 officer. Thompson's intel proved to be gold and within days a major terrorist incident was thwarted and half a dozen conspirators were arrested in Ealing. All ended up being convicted and sentenced to an average of fifteen years in prison.

Thompson was given a 50 per cent reduction in his sentence as a reward for the tip, but was also offered a deal by the agency. If he agreed to continue acting as an agent, he'd be given further reductions in his sentence, and in addition he'd be paid handsomely. As a sign of good faith, he would be paid £20,000 for the information he had already supplied.

Thompson was given an MI5 handler and moved from prison to prison to gather intel. He proved to be so successful that once he had served his sentence – reduced to just three years because of his tip-offs – he was persuaded to stay on as an MI5 agent. He was on the MI5 payroll and spent most of the year in one prison or another, paid £1,000 for each day he was inside plus extra payments for any tip-offs that bore fruit.

Shepherd had met Thompson several times over the years. He was in his late forties and planning to quit for good when he hit fifty, by which time he hoped to have several million pounds in the bank. His plan was to head for Spain, buy himself a luxury villa by the sea, and enjoy himself to the full.

Living in a prison as a professional grass was a precarious profession, but Thompson had the advantage of the perfect cover story. He was Terry Thompson, a tearaway who had stolen cars across Essex as a teenager, graduated to robbing building societies in his twenties, serving two prison sentences as a result, before graduating to large-scale cocaine importation in his thirties. Anyone who checked into his background would have no problem confirming who he was, and he had done time in half a dozen of the country's Cat A and Cat B prisons long before he started working for MI5. Anyone who had ever served time with him would say the same – nice guy if you leave him alone, minds his own business, never farts and never uses the toilet when the door is locked. The perfect inmate.

Thompson had just been coming off an investigation in Durham Prison where he had exposed a spice and tobacco smuggling ring that was operated by an Albanian gang who were also running a people smuggling operation across the Channel. He had been briefed on what they suspected was going on at Bradford, and he was transferred straight from Durham.

What Thompson found had set alarm bells ringing all around Thames House. According to Thompson, the prison was virtually being run by a group of Muslim godfathers. Muslims generally were over-represented in British prisons. They made up about 5 per cent of the population of the country, but accounted for more than 15 per cent of the prison population. The percentage was much higher in Bradford Prison as one in four of the city's population were Muslim, mainly from Pakistan.

According to Thompson, nothing happened on the wings without the approval of the godfathers. They decided on which cells were assigned and which jobs the prisoners got, and were behind the smuggling of most of the contraband into prison, especially phones, drugs and tobacco. And they had organised terrorism training courses in the prison, under the guise of language and culture classes.

Thompson had been told that several of the prison officers had been coerced into working for the godfathers, and that at least one of the governors was on their payroll.

There was a limit to how much intel Thompson could gather and much of the information he had was second hand, gleaned from other non-Muslim prisoners. But what he heard second hand was more than enough for MI5 to mount a major intelligence-gathering operation. Two British Asian MI5 officers had been selected: Kamran Zaidi and Sayed Khan. Both had joined MI5 through the graduate entry programme and had spent most of their time in Thames House working in the surveillance division, studying and translating CCTV footage and phone taps. Both men had been born in the UK but were fluent in Urdu.

Shepherd had been brought in at the start of the operation. Neither men had worked undercover before so they needed Shepherd's experience. Shepherd wasn't keen on the idea of using undercover virgins, but knew that their youth would be an advantage, plus there was no chance of them being recognised. The downside, of course, was that an inexperienced undercover officer could make a slip, and in a prison a simple mistake could be fatal. He spent a week with them in South London, filling them in on what they needed to know about life behind bars, and running them through various exercises. Several times a day he'd take them to a pub or a fast food restaurant and watch as they struck up a conversation with a total stranger. The idea was to get as much information about the target as they could while at the same time giving the target their own cover story, exchanging the truth for lies. Both passed with flying colours, which was encouraging, but Shepherd knew there was a world of a difference between chatting in a pub and being interrogated on the landing of a Cat B prison.

Eventually the time came for them to be put into Bradford Prison. Only two people in the prison knew the real reason for them being there: the number one governor, Jonathan Blunt, and the head of security and operations, Liz Maguire. They were transferred from different prisons – Zaidi from Wandsworth and Khan from Liverpool – and on different days. Zaidi's story was that he was being bullied and had requested a transfer, and Khan's was that he wanted to be closer to his family. They were placed on separate wings. Shepherd had been sent in as a prison officer to keep an eye on them and to offer any support they needed. Again it was only Blunt and Maguire who knew what Shepherd really was doing in the prison, and they were only included after they had been positively vetted by MI5. Thames House had carried out similar checks on all the governors and prison officers and, while Blunt and Maguire had passed muster, the investigators had turned up red flags on more than a dozen members of staff, including unexplained deposits of cash, property and car purchases, and one governor who had paid off his mortgage early. That suggested that corruption was rife in the prison, but Blunt and Maguire had been told only that it was a terrorism investigation that was being carried out.

Zaidi had been put on A Wing and Khan on D. Their brief was to keep their heads down and take it slowly. Softly softly.

Shepherd had been put in place two weeks before they arrived. His cover story as Tony Swinton was that he had transferred to be closer to his elderly mother and that he had previously worked in HMP Liverpool, one of the biggest prisons in the country. The advantage of choosing Liverpool was that even if he was unlucky enough to cross paths with someone who had worked there at the same time as he had supposedly been there, there were so many staff there it was perfectly possible that they wouldn't remember him.

Shepherd had been amazed at how quickly he had been approached by one of the smuggling gangs. He had made a point of complaining about how he was short of cash when inmates were in earshot, and he would carry a copy of the *Racing Post* with losers circled. He regularly asked for overtime, and again he made sure that inmates were in the vicinity. He knew that it was the Muslim godfathers who controlled most of the smuggling in the prison, but the initial approach had come from a non-Muslim inmate. Tommy Warner was a heavy smoker, had been for almost thirty years, and while smoking was illegal in British prisons, the change in the law had only forced the habit underground. As a result, prices had skyrocketed. Rolling tobacco that cost less than twenty pounds in a supermarket could sell for a thousand pounds behind bars. A match could sell for several pounds, and even a single sheet of Rizla paper could be sold for five pounds. As a pack of fifty sheets cost less than a pound on the outside, there were huge profits to be made. The tobacco smuggling racket was so profitable that when some prisoners were released they committed crimes so that they could be sent right back.

Warner had sidled up to Shepherd one day, and had begun complaining about how he couldn't get any cigarette papers. Shepherd had half-heartedly tried to persuade Warner to give up the habit, but Warner was adamant that he had tried and failed many times. 'Boss, if I can't give up when a smoke costs me close to twenty quid, it ain't ever going to happen.'

The conversations continued over several days, and eventually Warner offered the carrot. He'd happily pay a hundred pounds for a pack of Rizla. Shepherd had feigned disbelief but Warner had been adamant. Shepherd had asked about payment and Warner had said he could be paid on the out. Cash would be dropped through his letterbox. Shepherd had laughed it off, not wanting to appear to be too keen, but a couple of days later he had visited Warner in his cell and tossed a pack of cigarette papers on his bunk. Warner had asked for Shepherd's home address. Shepherd had expressed reluctance but obviously the cash wasn't going to be paid in the prison so he'd eventually given it to him. The next day an envelope containing two fifty pound notes had been put through his letterbox.

MI5 had the house under surveillance and had filmed and identified the motorcyclist who had dropped the money off. He was on their watch list and had been reported several times to Prevent, the government's flagship counter-extremism policy which aimed to identify potential terrorists.

A few days later, Warner asked for a box of matches, and

again Shepherd was rewarded with two fifty pound notes in an envelope delivered by the same motorcyclist.

The tobacco papers and matches were a clever way of drawing him in. They could be walked in through the metal detector, and in the unlikely event he was found with them, they could easily be explained. Warner asked for several other Rizla deliveries, and each time an envelope was delivered within twenty-four hours.

Warner then raised the stakes and suggested that if Shepherd could bring in just an ounce of rolling tobacco, he could earn two hundred pounds, cash. Again there was next to no risk, it wouldn't set off the detector and even if he was unlucky enough to come across one of the prison's drugs dogs, they were trained to spot cannabis, cocaine and heroin, not tobacco.

Shepherd had turned down the offer, but Warner kept on asking and eventually Shepherd had brought in an ounce, wrapped in clingfilm. The next day the envelope contained four fifty pound notes.

Warner made it clear that he would take as many deliveries as Shepherd could make, but Shepherd said he would only do it once a week. The risks of getting caught were just too high, he'd said.

After his third delivery, Tariq knocked on his door one Sunday morning, accompanied by two heavies. They had pushed their way into the house and laid down the law. Now he was working for them and if he didn't do as he was told, he'd be reported to the governor and the police. If exposed, he'd lose his job and get sent to prison, and former prison officers didn't fare well behind bars. Shepherd had run through the gamut of emotions expected of him – anger, fear, shock, resentment – but eventually he'd agreed to do whatever they wanted.

It didn't take MI5 long to identify Tariq and his associates, and surveillance teams were put in place to track his movements. Within a month they saw him visiting prison officers and a governor at their homes, and phone records showed him contacting another half-dozen members of staff. It seemed that the more they looked for corruption at the prison, the more they found it.

But the prime focus of the MI5 investigation was terrorism, and that was down to Zaidi and Khan. Both were making progress. The emir of A Wing was Wajid Rabnawaz, born in Pakistan but granted British citizenship when he had moved to the UK with his parents in the early eighties. Rabnawaz was serving four years for VAT fraud, but had been on the MI5 watch list for almost a decade before he was sent to prison. He was an imam at a small mosque in south Bradford that was known to be a hotbed of jihadism. MI5 had tried to get agents close to him but always failed. Rabnawaz was an expert at anti-surveillance. He never used his own landline and never carried a mobile, and was always accompanied by two heavies. He had continued to preach in prison and was a regular at Friday prayers, which could be attended by any Muslim in the prison and which was always a logistical nightmare for the prison officers.

Zaidi had signed up for Rabnawaz's Islamic Culture course and was also a regular at Friday prayers. Zaidi was picking up lots of intel about the emir, but so far it was all second hand. He had spoken to Rabnawaz several times but was taking it slowly. Zaidi was debriefed two or three times a week by Donna Walsh, who would pose as his solicitor. Shepherd rarely spoke to him, but kept an eye on him whenever he was on A Wing.

D Wing's emir was Sarfraz Addalat, who at twenty-four years old was the youngest of the emirs. British-born, he had never appeared on MI5's radar until the prison investigation. He was young and headstrong and made his contempt for non-Muslims clear, referring to the prison officers as kafirs behind their backs and often to their faces. Kafir literally meant disbeliever, someone who rejected the tenets of Islam, but when used as an insult it was as racist as insults go.

Addalat's sentence was relatively short, just two years for stealing a car and driving without a licence or insurance and resisting arrest, but his reputation had preceded him and he had taken over the wing within days of arriving. He had led several riots, protesting about the food, about the drugs dogs, about Friday prayers being cut short, and latterly he had been trying to get the governor to keep women officers off the landings on D Wing. Khan was close to Addalat's age and they were both keen Aston Villa fans. The two had grown close and Addalat had started opening up about his release plans, plans that included flying to Pakistan for terrorism training and returning to the UK to wreak havoc. Diane Daily was running Khan, posing as his solicitor for regular visits, and she reported that Khan was sure Addalat was serious. He was definitely one to watch.

Addalat was also funnelling recruits to various education classes and had promised to find a place for Khan. He had hinted that there was more on offer than culture and Koran studies. The MI5 analysts had discovered that a high percentage of graduates from the classes ended up in training camps in Pakistan and Afghanistan.

Shepherd's thoughts were interrupted by his radio. It was

the B Wing governor. 'Code Six on landing number two,' said Crowley. 'Code Six. Code Six.'

Shepherd stood up and hurried out of the canteen, leaving his food and flask on the table. A Code Six meant a death on the wing and that all available officers were needed. As he hurried to the control centre he met up with Underwood. 'This isn't good,' said Underwood.

They hurried into the control centre where half a dozen officers were standing around Neil Geraghty, waiting to be briefed.

'Could be a suicide,' said Geraghty. 'It's messy.'

'Who?' asked Shepherd.

'Ricky Morgan. Sonny Shah's up there now with SO Blackhurst. Get everyone banged up now, I'm calling for an investigation team.'

Shepherd and Underwood hurried to the gate. Underwood unlocked it, they both went through and Underwood relocked the gate as Shepherd hurried up the stairs to the second landing. Half a dozen prison officers followed them.

Blackhurst was hurrying down the landing towards Sonny Shah, who was standing outside Ricky Morgan's cell. There was a pool of vomit on the floor by the door. Several dozen inmates were crowded on the landing outside the cell and two inmates were actually standing on the threshold peering around the door.

'Move away from the cell please!' shouted Blackhurst. 'Back to your own cells, now!'

There was a chorus of moans and expletives from the inmates as they realised they were going to be banged up.

'It won't be long!' shouted Blackhurst. 'But we need the landings clear.'

More officers ran up the stairs and began gently pushing the inmates back to their cells. Underwood joined Shepherd next to Shah. 'Are you okay, Sonny?' asked Underwood.

Shah shook his head. He looked close to throwing up again.

Blackhurst pushed open the door. Shepherd peered over the supervising officer's shoulder. Morgan was definitely dead, his throat had been slashed open. There was a large pool of blood on the floor and his pillow and sheet were soaked with it. Blood had spurted up the wall across Morgan's posters and photographs and had dripped down the painted concrete.

Shepherd backed away, but Blackhurst stayed where he was. Geraghty came up the steps, followed by Crowley. Most of the inmates were heading back to their cells, complaining loudly. Several were shouting that their human rights were being abused. 'How bad is it?' asked Crowley.

'Bad,' said Shepherd. He made a cut-throat gesture with his hand.

'What the hell happened, Sonny?' asked Crowley.

'I don't know, ma'am, I told Mr Morgan he was to get ready to see the governor, he said okay, then when I went back ten minutes later . . .' He shrugged, unable to finish the sentence.

'You left the cell door unlocked?'

'I was taking him to see the number one governor. He's on report, for that fight yesterday.'

Blackhurst came out of the cell. He caught Crowley's eye and shook his head.

'I know he's on report,' said Crowley. 'He's on cellular confinement which means his cell door stays locked at all times.'

'I was taking him to see the governor,' repeated Shah.

'No you weren't. If you had been, you'd have been there

when he was attacked. In fact, if you had been there he wouldn't have been attacked, would he?'

'This isn't my fault.'

'Then whose fault is it, Sonny? Did somebody else walk away and leave his door open?'

'I was letting him get ready. I wasn't away for more than a few minutes. There was a ruckus at the pool table. A couple of lads were getting rowdy, I went down to help sort it out and when I went back he was dead.'

'He was with me, Miss Crowley,' said Underwood.

'What happened?'

'Like Mr Shah said, there was a ruckus. Lots of shouting and waving pool cues around. Mr Shah helped me calm things down.'

'Where were you, Mr Swinton?'

'On my break. Canteen.'

The governor looked at Blackhurst. 'Were you on the threes?'

'Sorry, guv. I was catching up on my paperwork.'

Crowley sighed. 'Right, well get the doc out to call the time of death. Keep everyone in their cells until the body has been removed. Then give them their dinner. The investigation team is on the way, along with the doctor.'

'What about association?' asked Blackhurst.

'They can have association tonight but any sign of trouble and they're all back in their cells.' She looked at her watch. Dinner time was only an hour away. 'Open the cells once the food arrives,' she said. 'They're always quieter on a full stomach.'

• • •

L iam Shepherd tried to sit up but he was lying on his side and his hands were tied behind his back so he could barely move. There was a hood over his head made of something rough that scratched against his skin when he moved. He couldn't remember the impact, or being dragged from the wreckage of the Chinook. The last memory he had was of struggling with the controls as the desert rushed towards him. 'Is there anyone there?' he whispered. His mouth was bone dry and he could barely manage to get the words out. He licked his lips and took a deep breath. 'Mobile, are you there?' he called, louder this time. There was no answer. 'Mobile? Talk to me? Anyone?'

'I'm here,' said Smithy, off to Liam's right. 'Smithy.'

'Smithy, thank God you're okay. What about Gerry and Mobile?'

'There's someone next to me,' said Smithy. 'I can feel his chest moving. I dunno if it's Mobile or Gerry. But Gerry got sucked out when the heli broke up so . . .' He left the sentence unfinished.

'What about you, Smithy?'

Smithy snorted. 'I feel like I got hit by a train. It hurts when I breathe, I think I've cracked a few ribs. What about you?'

'Sore all over. But I think I'm okay.'

'Where the hell are we?' asked Smithy.

'Your guess is as good as mine,' said Liam.

'Have you got a hood over your head?'

'Yeah.'

'Me too.'

'I always heard that was a good sign.'

Liam snorted. 'Say what now?'

'It means they don't want us to recognise them. Which means they're not going to . . .'

Liam knew Smithy was going to say 'kill us' but his voice tailed off. It was nonsense, of course. If they were being held prisoner by jihadists – their captors wouldn't care less if Liam and Smithy saw their faces. But it was definitely a good sign that they weren't dead already. Whoever their captors were, they surely had something planned. Liam screwed up his eyes as he tried to remember what had happened after the RPG had hit them. He hadn't made a mayday call, but had Mobile done it? As co-pilot it would have been Mobile's responsibility, but it had all happened so quickly and Mobile had been fighting with the controls. That probably meant no mayday call had been made. The UN peacekeepers would have seen the Chinook go down so presumably they would have called in the attack. But why hadn't they helped? Why hadn't they rushed over to the crash site and rescued them?

'Do you remember anything?' asked Liam. 'After we crashed?'

'I remember the explosion, and I remember Gerry screaming as he got sucked out, but that's it. I only came to a few minutes ago. You tied up, too?'

'Hands and feet,' said Liam.

'What do you think's happening?'

'We're being held prisoner, that's for sure,' said Liam. 'But as to who's got us, your guess is as good as mine.' He slowly rolled over on to his back and tried to sit up, but he didn't have the strength and he fell back, gasping.

Liam heard voices, off in the distance. He strained to hear what was being said, but it was just a dull murmur. The voices got louder and then he heard grating metal. A door being unbolted? His guess was proved right when he heard a door squeak open.

He heard the brush of sandals across stone and then a foot kicked into his ribs. Liam grunted.

'Are you awake?' a voice grunted in French.

'*Oui*,' said Liam.

'Ah, good, you speak French.'

'A little. Who are you? What do you want?'

The man kicked him again. 'No questions,' he barked in French. 'Are you hungry?'

Liam wasn't in the least bit hungry but he knew that they needed to eat to keep their strength up. And they needed to communicate with their captors on as human a level as possible. '*Oui*,' said Liam. '*Merci.*'

'I will return with some food.'

'My friend, is he okay? He isn't talking.'

'He is sleeping.'

'I don't think he's sleeping, I think he's . . .' Liam struggled to remember the French word for unconscious. '*Sans connaissance*,' was all he could come up with.

'*Il dort*,' repeated the man. 'He's sleeping.'

'Do you have water? I'm thirsty.'

Hands gripped Liam's shoulders and lifted him into a sitting position. His hood was loosened and the neck of a plastic bottle was forced between his lips. 'Drink,' said the man. Liam drank greedily.

Eventually the man took the bottle away. 'Please, *monsieur*, can you give my friend some water?'

Liam heard him go over to Smithy followed by the sound of Smithy gulping down water.

'Excuse me, sir,' said Liam, in halting French. 'Can I please check on my friend?'

'You are a pilot, not a doctor.'

'I have had some medical training,' said Liam. It wasn't exactly a lie, he had been on several first aid courses over the years.

'Later,' said the man.

Liam heard muttering in French, two men talking to each other, maybe three. Then he heard footsteps, then the door being opened and closed, and the bolt being drawn back. Then they were alone again.

'We're screwed, aren't we?' said Smithy.

Liam ran his right hand along his left and felt the watch on his wrist. His captors must have missed it under the sleeve of his flight jacket. 'Maybe not,' said Liam.

. . .

The two food trolleys rattled down the wing to a chorus of shouts and whoops and calls from the inmates to be allowed out of their cells to collect their evening meal. Shepherd was up on the top landing, waiting for the signal from Crowley down below.

'Open doors, all landings,' said Crowley over the radio. Shepherd walked down the landing, opening the doors one by one. Each time he opened a door the occupants rushed out holding their plastic plates or Tupperware containers and dashed towards the stairs. No one wanted to be last in line for their food. They all filled in meal requests but it was still first come, first served and there was no guarantee that those at the end of the line would get what they wanted.

'Don't run!' he shouted, to no avail. The men ran down to the stairs and lined up in front of the trolleys.

Down below he saw Mir join the queue. Two other men joined him and patted him on the back. He said something and they all laughed.

Once the inmates were served their food they headed back to their cells to eat. Once they had finished and the trolleys had been wheeled back to the kitchen there was a roll call where the prisoners had to stand in their cells while they were counted. After roll call they were on association, which meant they could walk around the wing, visit other cells and play cards, table tennis or pool on the ones.

The door to Malik Abid Qadeer's cell was open and the emir of B Wing was holding court. Two big men in long robes and skullcaps stood guard either side of his cell door and half a dozen men had already formed a line outside.

Shepherd walked slowly along the twos, studying the faces of the men in the queue. Two of them were on MI5's watch list. And one of the men guarding the door was on remand for terrorist offences. The offences were of a low level – possession of videos and ISIS handbooks – but it didn't make sense to Shepherd that the man was being held in a Cat B prison. He should have been in Belmarsh high-security prison in South London, which knew how to handle prisoners who posed a threat to national security.

As Shepherd walked along the landing he saw Mir playing pool with one of the guys he'd been laughing with as he had queued for his food. Shepherd frowned and called up the wing governor on his radio. 'Miss Crowley, this is Mr Swinton. Is Javid Mir out of solitary?'

'There's no point in keeping him banged up now that Morgan is deceased,' said Crowley. 'He's sticking to his story that he tripped on the stairs so the governor says just let it slide.'

'No problem,' said Shepherd.

'He's back in the kitchen tomorrow.'

'Understood.'

Shepherd continued to watch Mir play pool. He seemed a lot happier than when Shepherd had visited him in his cell to deliver the phone. Shepherd wondered what he had done with the phone and who he had called. He had an uneasy feeling that the phone had something to do with Morgan's death.

He walked along the landing, looking into the cells as he went by. Some were minimalist bare, with no personal possessions other than clothing and toiletries, others were packed with televisions, stereos, books and had walls covered with posters and photographs. Several of the inmates had guitars and one, a lifer in his sixties, had managed to convince the authorities to let him have a violin. He was actually a talented violinist who in a previous life had played with some prestigious orchestras, including the London Philharmonic. He was a quiet man, small and bald with a kindly smile. It was hard to believe that twenty years earlier he had killed his neighbours – a family of five – by setting fire to their house. The old adage that you couldn't judge a book by its cover was certainly true in prison. Men who looked as if they wouldn't say boo to a goose could be serving life for murder, fresh-faced youngsters who barely looked out of their teens could be running huge drug empires, and quiet bookish types could be planning terrorist outrages that would kill dozens of civilians.

He walked all around the landing and found himself looking down on Malik Abid Qadeer's cell again. The line of men standing outside had grown. As Shepherd watched, a young man in a grey sweatshirt and joggers came out, his head bobbing back and forth like a metronome. As he headed towards the pool table, an older man in a long tunic went inside.

Malik Abid Qadeer had a cell to himself. It was lined with expensive rugs and there were silk tapestries on the walls. Qadeer's meals were brought to him in his cell in a separate delivery from the kitchen, and he was allowed to use the showers and gym whenever he wanted. For one hour each evening, usually between 6 p.m. and 7 p.m., he held a surgery, where anyone on the wing could seek an audience. Any Muslim, anyway. Everyone in the queue was wearing Islamic clothing – baggy tunics and long robes – and most had skullcaps on their heads. Several were holding prayer beads.

Shepherd had been surprised the first time that he'd seen the queue outside the cell. Underwood had explained to him how it worked – Qadeer resolved issues and solved problems before they were made official. He settled disputes, made sure that debts were paid and, in some cases, ensured that punishments were carried out. Some six months before Shepherd had started at the prison, a drug dealer serving a three-year stretch had been caught stealing food from another inmate's cell. It was the third time he'd been caught, and as punishment his right hand was stamped on so hard that most of the bones were broken. The injured man had staggered to the wing office and been taken to the infirmary where they patched him up. The man would say only that he had trapped his hand in his cell door and no member of staff had queried his account.

Governor Crowley seemed perfectly happy with the arrangement as it made her look good. Over the past two years incidents of violence on the wing had dropped by 50 per cent and reports of theft and bullying were down by almost 70 per cent. The only official complaints being made were by non-Muslim prisoners, and even they were well down. From a cursory look at the wing spreadsheets, the governor was doing an awesome job. Except, of course, she wasn't. Qadeer was maintaining order and imposing discipline, and the wing governor was taking the credit.

'Ironic, isn't it, boss?' murmured a voice at Shepherd's shoulder, interrupting his thoughts.

Shepherd turned to see who had spoken. It was an inmate he hadn't interacted with before, but he recognised him from the prison files. It was Mick Walker, a former Para who was serving nine years for GBH. Shepherd had checked the man's service record but their paths had never crossed. Walker had done three tours in Iraq and two in Afghanistan, and had served with distinction, rising to warrant officer. He had been one of the first Paras into Basra in 2003 and three years later was in Afghanistan as part of Operation Herrick. But he was made redundant in 2013 when the government had slashed more than 5,000 army jobs, cutting the army back to just 80,000 soldiers – its lowest level since the eighteenth century. Walker was almost a decade younger than Shepherd, but he looked much older with unkempt steel grey hair and a face lined from several years living on the streets.

'What do you mean?' asked Shepherd.

Walker nodded at the queue outside the cell. 'It wasn't that long ago that I was being paid to kill men like that, and now they're practically running the place.'

'You were in the army?' asked Shepherd, feigning ignorance.

'Bloody right I was. Iraq and Afghanistan. Now I ask myself what the hell I was fighting for. First chance they got, the army dumped me. Yet these guys are fed and clothed and will probably get a council house as soon as they're released.'

Shepherd didn't say anything. If he was reported for saying anything even remotely racist or homophobic he'd be up before the governor himself. It wasn't unknown for inmates to try to get officers to say something controversial, and then to immediately report them to the governor.

The lack of a response didn't deter Walker. 'I was sleeping rough before I got sent down,' he continued. 'I was literally begging on the streets. I had a dog. Butch. Alsatian. Butch would sit with his paw up, asking for money. My only friend.'

'Didn't you have a pension?'

'Got made redundant before my full pension kicked in,' said Walker. 'Fucking scandal it was. They did it to thousands of us, kicked us out before they had to pay us decent pensions. Then my wife divorced me and got the kids and the house and most of the pension that there was.'

'Sorry to hear that.'

Walker shrugged. 'Yeah, it was my own fault. I was a bastard to her. PTSD, the works. I'd lash out at the slightest thing. Serves me right. Anyway, I was sleeping rough, I had a den outside of Trinity Leeds with my own shopping trolley and all. I'd sleep there at night and go begging around the centre with Butch during the day. But here's the thing, boss. There were two four-star hotels in the city centre, not far from the Trinity, and they were packed with illegals, most of them from Afghanistan and Iraq. They had four-star rooms, three hot meals a day, they had swimming pools and fitness centres and the government gave them cash and mobile phones. You know what they gave me? Sweet FA, boss. Sweet FA. I fought for this country, put my life on the line fighting for Britain, and yet I had to beg on the street.' He took a breath as if calming himself down, then forced a smile. 'Mind you, if I thought all

I had to do was so sail a dinghy across the Channel to France to get a free house, mobile phone and money in my pocket, I'd probably be the first one to start paddling. C'est la vie, right?'

Shepherd still didn't reply.

Walker grinned. 'So what's your name, boss?'

'Mr Swinton.'

Walker grinned. 'No first name?'

'You know how it works. You call me Mr Swinton. Or boss. Or sir.'

'And what do you call me?'

'Mr Walker.'

His eyes widened. 'Ah, so you do know me?'

'I looked at the roster.'

Walker held out his hand. 'Mick Walker.'

Physical contact with inmates was discouraged – a handshake could quickly turn into an assault – but Walker seemed genuine so Shepherd shook. 'Mr Swinton,' he said, with a smile.

Walker chuckled. His grip was firm but relaxed and he soon let go of Shepherd's hand. 'So still no first name?'

'That's not how it works here, Mr Walker, and you know it. And besides, if the rest of the cons hear us using first names, they'll mark you down as a grass.'

Walker laughed out loud. 'You know why I'm in here, right?'

Shepherd did, but he feigned ignorance again. 'I don't. To be honest, I don't care.'

'Butch picked up a skin condition. Kept scratching and that only made it worse. One day this RSPCA bastard said he was taking Butch away. He said I wasn't fit to keep a dog. He pushed me in the chest and I hit him. Not too hard, just a tap. But he was all wind and trousers and went down. Cried like a baby and called the cops on me. Half a dozen turned up with batons drawn and tasers out and didn't even give me a chance to explain myself. They literally just rushed me, swinging their batons. I took four of them out before they tasered me.' He grinned, showing grey, uneven teeth. 'They had to taser me three times before I went down. I hate cops. So no one's ever going to think I'm a grass.'

'And what about prison officers? How do you feel about them?'

Walker grinned. 'Some I hate, but most are all right. Like you Mr Swinton. I can see your heart's in the right place. You served, right?'

'Why do you say that?'

'You've got the look. I'd say you were a Para, too. In a previous life.'

'Sorry to disillusion you, I was in the building trade before I became a prison officer. I was a plasterer.'

'Well you live and learn,' said Walker.

They stood in silence for a while, watching men go in and out of the emir's cell.

'How long has this been going on?' asked Shepherd eventually.

'Today you mean?'

'No, long term. Is this a recent thing?'

'It wasn't like this when I first came here, three years ago. Back then maybe one in eight was Asian. Now it's what, one in three? I heard it's fifty-fifty on some wings. But they started taking control about two years ago. That's when Qadeer moved in. He was given a single cell almost immediately, which was weird. I mean, I've been here three years and I've always doubled up. He went on enhanced straight away, and it took me six months.'

'Any idea why he got special treatment?'

'I know exactly why. Not long after he was on the wing a group of Asians kicked off. The screws lost control of the wing for about three hours and they were going to send in a Tornado team but Qadeer offered to mediate and he calmed everyone down.' He grimaced. 'If you ask me, it was a power play. Fake as fuck. But it worked. Look at him now. He pretty much runs the wing.'

'That's an exaggeration,' said Shepherd. Tornado teams were specially trained officers who operated in groups of up to a hundred, dressed in black boiler suits and equipped with American-style PR-24 sidearm batons with side handles. They wore heavy-duty riot helmets and carried large riot shields and had access to smoke and flashbang grenades. They were available country-wide and were called in whenever the regular officers lost control of the landings, but only as a last resort. If prison officers were having problems the governor would send in a Rapid Reaction Team who would use sheer brute force to quell any unrest. But if the Rapid Reaction Team failed to maintain order, the Tornados would be sent in.

'No, it's not,' said Walker. 'The governors just want an easy life, and they get that by cooperating with the emirs.' He shrugged. 'No skin off my nose.'

'What happened to Butch?' asked Shepherd.

'They killed him.'

'They killed Butch?'

'He was put down when I was on remand. The cops had it done. It was payback for me kicking the shit out of them.' He grimaced. 'Fuck them.'

'Sorry about that,' said Shepherd. 'That was out of order.'

'Tell me about it. When I get out, I've got some scores to settle, that's for sure.'

'You know the Chinese proverb, right?' said Shepherd. 'He who seeks revenge digs two graves.'

'It's not about revenge, Mr Swinton. It's about vengeance. There's a difference. Revenge is an act of passion, vengeance is an act of justice. You're a prison officer so you're a big fan of justice, obviously.'

Shepherd couldn't help but smile. 'So you're a philosopher?'

'I have a code,' said Walker. 'Most soldiers do. And I suspect you live by a code, too. Right?'

Shepherd wasn't about to give Walker an insight into how his mind worked so he nodded over at Morgan's cell which still had 'DO NOT ENTER' tape across it.

'You didn't by any chance see who went into Mr Morgan's cell, did you?'

Walker threw up his hands. 'Hear no evil, see no evil, Mr Swinton. I ain't no grass.' He walked away, chuckling to himself.

∙ ∙ ∙

Diane Daily sipped her coffee as she studied the screen in front of her. There were two red dots moving across a map of Bradford. One dot was an MI5 surveillance operative driving a Deliveroo motorbike. The other was an Openreach van. They were front and back of the vehicle they were tailing, a grey Prius being driven by Mohammed Tariq. The Openreach van was Foxtrot One, the motorbike was Foxtrot Two, and Tariq was Tango One. Target One. With Tariq was Nazim Hussain, Tango Two, and Mizhir Khaliq, Tango Three. The Prius was Victor One.

'Foxtrot Two, can you overtake and keep eyes on?' said Daily through her headset.

'Foxtrot Two, roger that.'

Daily watched on the screen as the dot at the rear overtook the other dot. The bike was now ahead of the Prius. The Openreach was at the rear. They had tried to get a tracking device on the Prius but when it wasn't being driven it was parked in the driveway of Tango One's house, covered by a CCTV camera. Without a tracker they had to go back to basics. Eyes on.

Tango One's visits to prison staffers were interspersed with hours spent working as a minicab driver, criss-crossing the city with the occasional long distance trip. Those days were the worst as Tango One could easily take on a couple of dozen jobs with frequent stops. Today had been much easier. Tango One had left his house at midday before collecting Tango Two from his house and picking up Tango Three outside a coffee shop in the city. This wasn't a taxi day, they were on a mission.

They had driven to the city centre and as usual Tango One appeared to be oblivious to the fact that he was being followed. The followers had never once seen him carry out anything in the way of anti-surveillance or counter-surveillance.

'Foxtrot One, Victor One is heading into the Bradford NCP car park.'

'Can you follow him, Foxtrot One?'

'Roger that.'

Daily sipped her coffee as she watched the red dot that was Foxtrot One come to a halt on Thornton Road. Foxtrot Two drove on for a hundred yards and then came to a halt.

'Shit!'

'Is that you Foxtrot One?' asked Daily.

'Some arsehole has just pushed in front of me,' growled Foxtrot One. He was Jamie Donaldson, a Scot who had decided on a career change in his thirties, moving out of IT and becoming an MI5 surveillance operative after a short spell as a cab driver. He worked mainly north of the border but had been brought down to Bradford at short notice and was finding the city tough going. 'Shit. Victor One has now entered the car park.'

'Can you follow him, Foxtrot One?'

'Negative. Sorry. This moron has stopped in front of me. I don't know what he's playing at.'

'Foxtrot Two, can you enter the car park?'

'Foxtrot Two, affirmative.'

Daily sipped her coffee as she watched Foxtrot Two backtrack to the entrance of the car park.

'Foxtrot Two entering the car park.'

'Foxtrot One is still blocked. Wanker.'

'Foxtrot Two, I don't see Victor One on the ground floor. Heading up.'

'Finally,' said Foxtrot One. 'Foxtrot One is heading into the car park.'

Daily grimaced. With Foxtrot Two already inside, there was no need for Foxtrot One to follow. It would make more sense for Foxtrot One to wait outside. 'Stay on the ground floor, Foxtrot One.'

'Roger that.'

'Foxtrot Two is on the second floor. Still no sign of Victor One.'

Daily studied a large scale map of Bradford on the wall to her left. There were no obvious places nearby that they would be visiting. The Leonardo Hotel. A cinema. The magistrates' court was a short walk away.

'Foxtrot Two is on the third floor. I have eyes on Victor One. It's parked up.'

'Any sign of the occupants?' asked Daily.

'Negative.'

'Foxtrot One, any sign of them on foot?'

'Negative,' said Foxtrot One.

'Are you parked, Foxtrot One?'

'Affirmative.'

'Get on foot and see if they've exited the building,' said Daily.

'Roger that.'

'Foxtrot Two, can you exit the building and check Thornton Road?'

'Roger that.'

Daily sat back in her chair. In all the weeks they'd been following Tariq, nothing like this had ever happened before. Hopefully they had just parked the Prius and were now on foot and the two Foxtrots would find them. What worried Daily was the possibility that they had switched vehicles. If they had planned a vehicle switch, that suggested they were moving to another level.

. . .

Shepherd's shift ended after the inmates had finished their evening meal and the kitchen staff had wheeled the trolleys out of the wing. Inmates were on association, playing pool and table tennis, or just chatting and playing cards. Most stayed in their cells, playing video games or watching television. Shepherd, Underwood and Shah headed to the wing governor's office. There were three prison officers already there, waiting to start their shift. 'I was just bringing everyone up to speed on what happened to Ricky Morgan,' said Crowley. 'We've been quiet since, which is a blessing. Anything else worth flagging?'

'There are two guys passed out in their cell on the second landing,' said Shah. 'Jackie MacLean and Martin O'Leary. They didn't come out for their food. They're okay, just out for the count. There's the end of a joint on the floor so I'm guessing spice. They're not bothering anyone so I've just left them to it. If you want, I can write them up, but . . .' He shrugged and left the sentence unfinished. If they took disciplinary action against every inmate who was high on drugs, there'd be no time to do anything else. A comatose inmate wasn't a problem, it was when they kicked off and started abusing the staff that it became an issue.

'Anyone else seen any spice problems today?'

Shepherd and Underwood shook their heads. 'There's still a smell of cannabis in and around Sake Nazir's cell,' said Underwood.

Crowley nodded. 'I'll have a word with the emir,' she said.

It wasn't the first time that Shepherd had heard the governor say that she would seek assistance from Malik Abid Qadeer. The emir could solve a problem with a few words in the right ear, whereas if the guards got heavy a clampdown on cannabis smoking could easily spill over in to a riot. The problem, of course, was if the emir wanted a quid pro quo.

'What's happening with Ricky Morgan's cell?' asked one of the newly arrived prison officers.

'It's sealed off until further notice,' said Crowley. 'There was a lot of blood so we need a deep clean and the contractor we normally use is backed up.'

'And Mr Mir is out of his cell now?' said the officer.

'Now that Mr Morgan is dead there's no point in punishing Mr Mir, who anyway is sticking to the story that he tripped.'

'And we still don't know who killed Morgan?' said another officer. 'No sign of a weapon?'

Crowley grimaced. 'I'm afraid not.' The fact that there was a deadly weapon on the wing was the last thing a prison officer wanted to hear. She looked over at Shepherd, Shah and Underwood. 'Before you head off, Mr Blunt wants a word with you,' she said.

'With us?' said Shah. 'Why?'

'I'm assuming it's because of Ricky Morgan,' said Crowley.

'Is he seeing everyone on the wing?' asked Underwood.

'You're the ones he's asked to see,' said Crowley.

'Are we getting the blame?' asked Shah. He looked over at Underwood. 'They're going to try to hang this on me, aren't they?'

Crowley put up a hand. 'Don't overthink it, Sonny, I'm sure Mr Blunt just wants to know what happened.'

'We know what happened,' said Shah. 'Someone slipped into Ricky Morgan's cell and topped him. And I left the door open. So it's down to me.'

'I wouldn't jump to conclusions,' said Crowley. 'He's asked for all three of you, and I know he's already spoken to Neil Geraghty. I think this is about understanding what happened. It's the first killing we've had at Bradford since he took over so it's a big issue for him.'

'I hope that's it,' said Shah.

'You'll be fine,' said Crowley.

Shepherd, Shah and Underwood left her office and headed for the admin offices. There were six gates and doors to get through. Underwood did the unlocking and Shah did the locking. A large part of their shift was spent locking and unlocking doors, literally hundreds of times a day. The number one governor's office was on the third floor of the admin block. There was no lift and they headed up the stairs.

The governor's secretary was a grey-haired woman in her sixties, Mrs Derbyshire, who waved them to a row of plastic chairs and said that she would let the governor know they were there. Shah and Underwood shifted uncomfortably in their chairs.

Eventually the door was opened by Liz Maguire, the prison's head of security and operations. 'Mr Swinton,' she said. She was wearing a grey suit over a blue polo neck sweater and had pulled her chestnut hair back in a ponytail. Shepherd had only met her once but she had impressed him with her no-nonsense approach to the job. 'The governor will see you one at a time, you first.'

Shepherd walked into the office and she closed the door behind him. The governor was sitting behind a large oak desk that looked as if it was a century old. Most of the furniture in the office was of a similar age, all of it weathered over the years. The bright green carpet was new, as was the green and cream striped wallpaper, and there were two large computer monitors on the desk. On the wall behind the desk was a large framed aerial photograph of the prison.

Blunt was a big man, six foot six in his bare feet. He was in his fifties. He had started in the prison service on the Isle of Wight, walking the landings of Albany and Parkhurst prisons, in the days before they were merged into the super prison HMP Isle of Wight.

He had worked his way up to governor and had been in charge of HMP Bradford for a little more than three years. MI5's vetting procedure had shown that he was as honest as the day was long, and had been married for almost twenty-five years, father of a son and a daughter, grandfather to three boys. He was sitting on a large straight-backed leather executive chair that would have dwarfed most men, but it looked almost too small for him. He had taken off his jacket and hung it over the back of the chair. His sleeves were rolled up, revealing a selection of naval tattoos including a spectacular mermaid and a sea serpent twisted around a trident, relics of five years spent in the merchant navy after leaving school at sixteen. He looked at Shepherd and wagged a finger at him. 'Right, Mr Swinton, or whatever your name is. I had a murder in my prison today, or at the very least an unlawful killing. It's the first such death since I took over, and I'm obviously not happy about it.'

Shepherd nodded but didn't say anything. Better to wait for the man to run out of steam.

'Inmates kill themselves, we've had our fair share of suicides here and as regretful as they are, they are a fact of life in a prison like Bradford. But when one inmate kills another, that's when people start looking to pin the blame on someone, and more often than not it's the governor who takes the flak. The story is going to be all over tomorrow's papers and I'm going to have to explain what happened.' He leaned across his desk. 'So I have to ask you, officially and on the record, if this death has anything, anything at all, to do with your investigation?'

Shepherd looked the man in the eye. He wasn't actually

going to lie, but there was no way he could tell the governor the truth. 'I can assure you, Mr Blunt, Ricky Morgan was not being looked at in any way. He was totally off our radar.'

'And what about Javid Mir, the inmate that Morgan was fighting with yesterday? Was he off your radar?'

'Mir has no terrorism links that we are aware of. He's just a guy who made a few bad decisions.'

Blunt's eyes narrowed. 'So it was coincidence that you were on the wing when it happened?'

'I was actually in the canteen when Morgan was killed,' said Shepherd.

'I didn't mean I think that you killed the man, I meant that you were obviously on the wing for a reason because the two undercover officers of yours are on wings A and D. Or has that changed without my knowledge?'

'No, they are on A Wing and D Wing.'

'So what were you doing on B Wing?'

'Gathering intel,' said Shepherd. 'Malik Abid Qadeer is very much on our radar and as we don't have a man on B Wing, I figured I'd have a look around.'

'And that's the only reason you were on B Wing?' Blunt leaned towards Shepherd, his jaw tense. The questioning was going somewhere, and like all good interrogators, the man seemed to be asking questions that he already knew the answers to.

'I'm not sure what you want me to say, sir.' Shepherd's mind was racing, trying to work out what Blunt knew, or thought he knew.

'What I want is for you to be straight with me, Mr Swinton.' He sat back in his chair and grunted in frustration. 'I hate dealing with you people,' he said. 'You wouldn't tell the truth if your life depended on it. I'm damn sure that Swinton isn't your right name but I'm not allowed to ask you for your real identity, I'm supposed to give you free rein. When the home secretary personally rings you up and tells you that he wants you to cooperate with MI5, well, you don't really have much choice. Well, I've done as I was asked and now I have a dead inmate on my hands and you're sitting there as if your shit doesn't stink. Well it does, Mr Swinton. It stinks to high heaven.' He leaned forward again and clasped his hands together so tightly that his knuckles whitened. 'According to Mr Geraghty, you specifically asked to be assigned to B Wing this morning. What do you have to say to that? And you seemed very interested in what had happened between Javid Mir and Ricky Morgan.'

Shepherd held the governor's look. 'Yes, I wanted to see what was going on, I'm gathering intel on the prison as a whole. We don't have anyone undercover on B Wing but we need to keep eyes on Malik Abid Qadeer.'

'And your interest in Javid Mir and Ricky Morgan?'

'Just conversation. I had come across Javid Mir in the kitchens and I was surprised to hear that he'd been involved in an altercation, that's all.'

'So were you on the wing to see Malik Abid Qadeer or Javid Mir?'

Blunt's eyes narrowed again. The man was definitely only asking questions that he knew the answer to. So what did he know and where was he heading? If he caught Shepherd in an absolute lie then he would be within his rights to bring the investigation to an end, no matter what the home secretary had said. Shepherd's mind continued to race. Did he know about the phone that Shepherd had given Mir? Almost certainly not because they wouldn't have found it without searching the cell, and so far as Shepherd knew there had been no search. So what did Blunt know? Then it hit him like a bolt from the blue. CCTV. Blunt – or more likely Liz Maguire – had checked the CCTV and seen that Shepherd had gone into Mir's cell that morning. They were waiting to see if Shepherd would mention it, and if he didn't they would want to know why. He had to raise it first. 'Six of one,' he said. 'I've been on all the wings at some point, the rota will show that. I'm not just here to keep an eye on my two guys, I have my own intel-gathering role. So I mentioned to Mr Geraghty that I'd heard what had happened to Javid Mir, and that I knew him. That would give him a reason to put me on B Wing today. If he hadn't, I would have tried another day. I'd rather it happened organically rather than asking you or Miss Maguire to pull strings. Now, having been assigned to B Wing I thought I would also check in on Mr Mir. I know he was in cell confinement but I thought I'd just pop in and see how he was. Truth be told, I had sort of earmarked him as a possible agent down the line.'

'You mean you were planning to use him?'

'Not planning. Just testing the water. See where his loyalties lie.'

'And how did it go?'

'When I saw him in his cell? He was polite enough but wouldn't go into any details about what had happened between him and Morgan. I got the feeling it might have been racially motivated, but he wouldn't say, he was sticking to his story that he tripped.'

Blunt looked across at Maguire who gave him an almost imperceptible nod. Blunt leaned back in his chair and for the first time seemed to relax a little. It looked as if he had bought

Shepherd's explanation. Blunt sighed. 'This is happening at the worst possible time,' he said.

'Why? What's happened?'

'I'm surprised you don't know,' said the governor. 'I thought you MI5 types knew everything. We're expecting Shafiq Ali Rafiq tomorrow. Special delivery from the United States of America.'

Shepherd's eyes widened. 'They locked him up and threw away the key,' he said. Shafiq Ali Rafiq was a Pakistani who had moved to the UK as a teenager with his parents. His parents had embraced the British way of life and had turned a corner shop in Leeds into a supermarket empire that had stores across the north-west. But Shafiq Ali Rafiq had rejected them, returning to Pakistan in his late twenties to fight the Russians alongside the mujahideen in Afghanistan. When the Russians had left, Shafiq Ali Rafiq had returned to the UK. Still estranged from his parents, he had become a funda-mentalist preacher. MI5 had photographed him celebrating after the 9/11 attacks, and once the Allied forces invaded Afghanistan and Iraq, he began preaching on the streets of Leeds. He eventually began to recruit British Muslims to join ISIS in Afghanistan, and in the winter of 2010 flew there himself. He swiftly moved up the ranks and was the brains behind a number of terrorist attacks in Kabul – his forte was using children as suicide bombers. At a conserv-ative estimate he was responsible for the deaths of forty British and American soldiers and hundreds of civilians. He was eventually caught by American Navy SEALs and sent to Guantanamo Bay. He was sentenced to life imprisonment many times over and moved to a high-security prison in Colorado, which was where he was supposed to live out the rest of his days. There was no way he should be on his way back to Britain.

'That's what we all thought,' said Blunt. 'But I had the home secretary on the phone again yesterday telling me that he's coming here.'

'That makes no sense at all. He got multiple life sentences, he was never going to be released.'

'He's dying. Cancer. He got himself a good lawyer and the Americans are releasing him into our custody so that he can see his family before he dies.'

'That's ridiculous.'

Blunt shrugged. 'Human rights. He has two wives, fifteen children and eight grandchildren. There was no way they could visit him in the US so they're sending him here. You can imagine how thrilled I was to hear this.'

'Where will you put him?'

'Initially in the Close Supervision Centre. His lawyers here will probably try to get him out and into the general population, but obviously that will be too disruptive. A lot depends on the state of his health. If he's bedridden we could keep him under guard in the medical centre. But really it's the last thing I need just now, especially coming after today's death.' He sighed. 'Anyway, we're done for now, Mr Swinton. I called Mr Shah and Mr Underwood here as well, but it was you I wanted to talk to. I'll ask them a few questions and say that we're investigating the death, then I'll send them on their way.' He pointed a warning finger at Shepherd. 'But if I find out that you've been lying to me, if I find out that you were involved in some way with Ricky Morgan's death, you'll . . .' He left the sentence hanging and waved Shepherd away.

Shepherd went out. Underwood and Shah looked up at him expectantly. Shepherd flashed them a thumbs up and mouthed 'All good'. They both smiled in relief.

'Right, Mr Shah,' said Maguire from the doorway. 'The governor will see you now.'

• • •

'I fucking hate Albanians,' said Mohammed Tariq as he watched the two men climbing out of the white van. They were big men with shaved heads that glistened under the overhead fluorescent lights, both wearing boxy leather jackets, tight jeans and heavy boots.

'Everybody hates Albanians,' said Mizhir Khaliq. 'Even Albanians hate Albanians. But, they've got the guns so we've got no choice other than to deal with them.'

'Can we trust them?' asked Nazim Hussain, who was sitting in the back of the Transit van. The van was used by a fishmonger and the stench was almost overpowering. They had left the Prius in the multi-storey car park in Bradford and transferred to the fishmonger's van which had been waiting for them. They had driven to an industrial estate on the outskirts of Leeds and into a modern windowless unit, guarded by two more Albanians.

'We're not giving them any money,' said Khaliq. 'There's no way they can rip us off.'

'They're doing this for free?' said Tariq.

'When did you ever know an Albanian do anything for free?' said Khaliq. 'They're being paid in Tirana through hawala.'

Hawala was a money transfer system based on trust which

used a network of brokers throughout the world to transfer funds. It was cheap and efficient, and the anonymity of the transactions meant that it was often used by money launderers and terrorists. The men who had supplied the guns would pick up cash from a hawaladar in Albania's capital city.

'I still think we should be strapped,' said Tariq.

Khaliq shook his head. 'Guns would just put everyone on edge. This has all been arranged through Qadeer. We're logistics, nothing more.'

'I know,' said Tariq. 'But you know, Albanians.'

'They're Muslims, brother,' said Khaliq. 'We'll be fine.'

He climbed out of the van and walked towards the Albanians, holding his hands up to show that he was unarmed. '*As-salamu alaikum*,' he said. Peace be upon you.

'*Wa-alaikum-salaam*,' said one of the Albanians. And unto you peace.

The two Albanians shook hands with him in turn. Tariq joined them and they all shook hands.

The older of the two Albanians pointed at the fishmonger's van. 'There is someone else in there?'

Khaliq nodded. 'One more.'

'Tell him to show himself so that there are no surprises,' said the Albanian.

He stared at Khaliq's lazy eye as he spoke. The pupil had almost disappeared into the socket. Khaliq was used to being stared at. Most people didn't mention it, they were too embarrassed. He turned to the van. 'Hey, Nazim, step out of the van!' he called in Urdu. 'They want to see everyone.'

'Let's all talk in English,' said the man. 'As I said, no surprises. I'm sure you'd get nervous if we started talking in Albanian.'

'You're right, of course,' said Khaliq, bowing slightly. 'My apologies.' He called over at the van again. 'Just step out and keep your hands visible.'

Hussain appeared at the back of the van, his hands in the air.

The older Albanian nodded. 'Good,' he said. He opened the rear doors of the white van and stepped back so that Khaliq could see inside. There were five grey metal cases and another fifteen smaller black cases. Khaliq picked up one of the black cases and opened it. It contained a Glock pistol and two magazines.

'Most of them are Glock 17s but some of them are Glock 19s,' said the Albanian.

'What's the difference?' asked Tariq.

Khaliq flashed him a warning look. He didn't want them to appear to be amateurs.

'The Glock 19 is a smaller version of the 17,' said the Albanian. 'They call the 17 a compact.'

'But they use the same bullets, right?' asked Tariq.

The Albanian smiled and Khaliq glared at Tariq. Tariq's attention was focused on the gun so he didn't notice Khaliq's annoyance.

'They are both nine millimetre, yes,' said the Albanian. 'But you have to be careful with the magazines. A Glock 19 will accept the magazine from a Glock 17, but a Glock 19 magazine will not fit in a Glock 17 pistol.' He shrugged. 'Best to keep them separate.'

Khaliq nodded and handed the black case to Tariq. 'And the AKs?' he asked.

The Albanian reached into the van and pulled over one of the metal cases. He opened it and stepped back. There were three Kalashnikov assault rifles in the box, with folding metal stocks. 'So five boxes, fifteen AK-47s,' Khaliq said.

'I cannot fault your maths,' said the Albanian.

Khaliq picked one up and checked the fire selector. There were three settings. Safe in the up position, semi-auto when it was down, and fully automatic when it was centred. It was in safe mode. Khaliq sighted down the weapon and nodded. It wasn't new but it was in good condition. 'Magazines?' he said.

The Albanian pointed at a cardboard box behind the metal cases. 'There are thirty magazines there. A mixture of metal and polymer, including a couple of drum magazines that hold seventy rounds. Most are thirty rounds. None of them are new, but they're all in good condition.'

'And ammunition?'

The Albanian pointed at another box. 'Wolf cartridges, from Ukraine. Twenty cartridges in a box, forty-eight boxes.'

'So nine hundred and sixty cartridges?'

The Albanian grinned. 'You are a human calculator,' he said. 'I don't know what you're planning, but that is a lot of fire-power.'

Khaliq waved Hussain over. He picked up four of the Glock cases and took them over to their van. The two Albanians grabbed a metal case each and followed him.

The big Albanian wrinkled his nose as he reached the van. 'What's that smell?'

'Fish,' said Khaliq.

'How can you drive around in that?'

'You get used to it.'

They loaded the guns and ammunition into the back of the van. When they had finished, Hussain climbed in the back too and Khaliq slammed the door. He nodded at the big Albanian. 'Thank you,' he said.

The Albanian nodded back. '*Allah yusallmak.*' May God protect you.

• • •

Shepherd got off the bus and started walking towards his house. The sky was darkening and the street lights had already come on. He wasn't thrilled at the idea of using public transport, or of living on one of Bradford's roughest streets, but he had to play the part of a prison officer down on his luck. If the bad guys saw him driving his BMW SUV and living in a decent apartment, his whole cover story would be blown.

His heart sank when he saw the three teenagers standing under the streetlight, their heads down and hoodies up. They had mugger written all over them. They were about fifty feet ahead of him so he started to cross the road. He kept his head up and his shoulders back, showing no weakness. Muggers tended to pick on the old and the weak and Shepherd didn't fall into either category. Shepherd wasn't dressed as if he had money, but these days even cheaper mobile phones were worth several hundred pounds so anyone could be a target.

The muggers moved across the road towards him, swaggering with their hands in their pockets. Shepherd cursed under his breath. He'd had a long, tiring day and the last thing he wanted was a bit of rough and tumble with three tearaways. 'Hey, mate, got a cigarette?' one called out. White, in his teens, his face pockmarked with acne.

'Don't smoke,' said Shepherd, increasing his pace. In a

perfect world he'd have had his PAVA spray and baton with him, but both had to stay in the prison.

'Got any spare change? We can buy our own,' said another. Older. Mixed race. Facial hair and a gold chain around his neck.

'Guys, I'm flat broke until payday,' said Shepherd. The three men were on the pavement in front of him now, blocking his way.

'Can we borrow your phone?' said the third one. The tallest of the three. He looked as if he worked out. Brand new Nikes.

Shepherd let his hands swing by his sides as he stopped. The only way to get by them was to step into the road so he was going to have to face them, one way or another. He took a quick look around. No police, which was hardly surprising. Beat cops in Bradford were rarer than hen's teeth. And no CCTV either.

Nikes Guy reached for Shepherd's jacket. 'Come on, give us ya phone,' he said.

'I don't have a phone on me,' said Shepherd.

'Bollocks,' said Nikes Guy. 'Everyone has a phone, innit.'

'Well not me, not today.'

Nikes Guy tried to pull Shepherd towards him. Shepherd grabbed his hand with both of his, twisted, and pulled him to the pavement. The guy with the gold chain pulled out a knife. It was what tabloid journalists called a zombie knife, a black serrated blade with a green handle. He stabbed at Shepherd but Shepherd had seen it coming. He took a step back, then lashed out with his foot and kicked the attacker's knee, so hard that he heard it crack. The man cried out and staggered back, still holding the knife. The guy on the ground was getting to his feet so Shepherd kicked him in the stomach, hard, but not too hard. If he did too much damage the police would get involved and that was the last thing that Shepherd wanted. He had to hurt them enough so that they would run away, but not so much that they would end up in hospital. It was a narrow line to tread.

The third one, the one with the acne scars, was bobbing up and down as if trying to work up the courage to attack Shepherd. 'Just go,' said Shepherd. 'Or I'll hurt you.'

The man raised his fists, then had a change of heart, turned and ran down the road, his trainers slapping on the pavement.

Shepherd took a quick look around. Drivers were slowing to watch what was happening but no one had stopped. A family with three kids and another in a stroller were heading towards them but paying them no attention. Shepherd wasn't so much worried about eyewitnesses as he was about being filmed on a phone and having a video posted on the internet. So far, so good.

The guy with the knife regained his courage and moved towards Shepherd, slashing the knife from side to side. His upper lip was curled back in a snarl and he was breathing heavily through his nose. Shepherd was totally relaxed as he faced his opponent. In the hands of a professional a knife was an advantage, often the difference between life and death. But when used by an amateur it was more often just for show. Shepherd knew a dozen or so ways of taking a knife off an amateur, and an amateur attacker was usually so focused on the knife that he forgot all other options.

Shepherd slid off his backpack and held it in his left hand, ready to block any blow. The man slashed again but he was out of range and it was an empty gesture. All he was doing was wasting energy, tiring himself out. Another slash. And another. The man was breathing heavily now, his eyes burning with rage.

'Last chance,' said Shepherd. 'Piss off or I'll hurt you.'

The guy that Shepherd had kicked got to his feet, holding his stomach. 'You bastard,' he hissed, reaching into his hoodie and pulling out a flick knife with a black handle and a shiny chrome button. His thumb clicked the button and the blade sprang out. It was about five inches long, not much more than a toy.

'Suit yourself,' muttered Shepherd. 'Just don't say I didn't warn you.'

One attacker with a knife, especially an amateur, was easy enough to deal with, but two attackers upped the ante.

They moved apart, which was the first sensible thing they had done, and Shepherd knew that he had to take the initiative. He couldn't afford to let one of them get behind him. The guy with the zombie knife slashed again and as the blade went by Shepherd threw his backpack at the man's head. The attacker's instincts kicked in and both his hands went up to protect his face. Shepherd dropped down into a crouch, jumped forward and planted three quick punches in the man's solar plexus. The breath exploded from the man's mouth and the knife clattered on the pavement as he bent double and staggered back before collapsing on the pavement.

Shepherd grabbed his backpack and whirled around. The guy with the flick knife had raised it above his head and was running towards Shepherd. Shepherd swung his backpack and knocked the knife sidewards. The man's momentum carried him forward and Shepherd twisted to the left and swung his right elbow at the man's chin. It was a knockout blow and the man's eyes rolled back in his head as he slumped to the ground.

Shepherd slung his backpack over his shoulder and walked away. He wasn't even breathing heavily. As he reached the corner of his road he looked back. The two men were getting to their feet and no one was giving them a second look.

As soon as he got home, Shepherd kicked off his boots and went upstairs to shower. Walking the landings was physically demanding and emotionally draining. It was hard on the legs to be on his feet all day, and it was never possible to relax. Violence could break out at any moment, as the Ricky Morgan killing had demonstrated. A prison officer could never let his guard down on the wings.

Geraghty had studied the CCTV from the landing. It showed a figure in prison greys entering the cell and leaving a few seconds later. The killer had kept his head down and there was no hope of identifying him. The killing had possibly been in retribution for Morgan's attack on Mir, perhaps a warning to other non-Muslim prisoners not to tangle with the Muslim community. But if that were the case it seemed to be a massive over-reaction, as Mir only had a few cuts and bruises and hadn't been badly hurt.

After Shepherd had showered he changed into a sweatshirt and jeans and went downstairs to the kitchen to microwave a Marks & Spencer ready meal of sausages, onion gravy and mashed potato. He ate it from its plastic tray while watching Sky News and drinking a bottle of lager. He was just finishing when his personal mobile rang. The number wasn't recognised but he took the call anyway.

'Spider? It's Matt.'

Matt. Matt Standing. SAS Sergeant Matt Standing. They were friends but they weren't close so it wasn't a social call. 'What's up, Matt?'

'Where are you?'

'Bradford.'

'Bradford? What the hell are you doing in Bradford?'

'Don't ask,' said Shepherd.

'Have you heard about Liam?'

Shepherd's blood ran cold. 'No. What's happened?'

'Okay, look, it's bad but it's not bad bad. He's in a spot of bother, that's all.'

Shepherd's mind went into overdrive and he had a sick feeling in the pit of his stomach. He had a hundred questions but he held back and waited for Standing to finish.

'You know he's in Mali, right?' Standing asked.

'Yeah. Helping the UN mission out there.'

'Well his Chinook was shot down this afternoon. He's okay, so is his co-pilot and crew chief. His gunner died in the crash, though.'

'So Liam's okay?'

'It looks as if he's been taken prisoner, along with the two other survivors.'

'But he's okay, right?'

'They left the gunner at the crash site, so the assumption is that Liam and the other two are alive. It's probably a kidnap situation, but there's been no ransom demand yet.'

Shepherd cursed. Liam had been out in Mali for almost a month. His son had been excited about the posting, but had been aware of the dangers. They'd had dinner before Liam had left, a fiery curry at Shepherd's favourite Battersea curry house. Over several bottles of Cobra beer, Shepherd had given him what knowledge he had about operating in war zones, because peacekeeping mission or not, that's what Mali was. The fighting had started early in 2012 when several insurgent groups in the north of the country began calling for independ-ence. A few months later the military, annoyed at the way the government was failing to contain the conflict, organised a coup. In the disarray that followed, Islamist rebels seized much of the north of the country and declared independence. The military rulers asked for foreign military help and the French responded, keen to help their former colony. By early 2013 the Mali government were back in control, but fighting continued, and was still going on. The UN had a peacekeeping mission in place, but it wasn't having much success. Liam had made light of the risk, emphasising that the UK Chinooks were mainly in Mali for logistics. 'We're an airborne DHL, Dad,' he'd said. 'There's no need to worry.'

Shepherd pushed the thoughts away. He needed a clear head and there would plenty of time for reminiscing down the line. 'So what's happening, Matt?' he asked.

'We're putting together a team now and there's a Herc ready to fly us from Brize Norton later tonight. There's a seat for you if you want it.'

'Damn right I want it. Who's the head shed?'

'Colonel Davies is in overall charge. He gave me the green light to call you. Though I'd be calling you anyway, green light or not. But with the colonel's backing, there's no problem getting you on the flight. What about your boss?'

'I'll clear it with him. What happened, Matt?'

'Intel is sketchy at the moment. All I know is that his Chinook had gone to RV with a UN peacekeeping patrol and they were shot down with an RPG. The UN peacekeepers bailed out but the British contingent sent out their own people. When they got there they found the body of the gunner but no sign of Liam, the co-pilot or the crew chief. Like I said, there hasn't been a ransom demand but kidnapping is rife out there. Problem is, the government doesn't negotiate with terrorists blah blah blah. So even if there is a ransom demand, it's not going to be resolved anytime soon.'

'Who's responsible for security in the area?'

'Yeah, that's the other problem. The Brits and the Germans are still there but basically it's the Wagner Group who are calling the shots. So they're not going to be in a rush to help.'

Shepherd grimaced. The Wagner Group were Russian mercenaries backed by the Kremlin. They had recently done a deal with Mali's military rulers to take on the Islamic funda- mentalists who had been causing problems in the country. The mercenaries had fought fire with fire and launched a series of offences against the extremists, but were soon committing atrocities on a par with the terrorists, carrying out rape, torture and murder on a daily basis. Once the Wagner Group arrived, most Western countries began pulling their troops out. The French left first, the UK were in the process of withdrawing their forces, and the Germans had announced they too were leaving. The Wagner Group were no friends of the West and Standing was right, they'd have no interest in helping resolve a British hostage crisis.

'So what's the Colonel got planned?'

'It's all up in the air at the moment. Still at the intel- gathering stage. But he wants a team in place so that when we do have a plan we can hit the ground running. Look, I'm gonna have to go, but see you at Brize Norton before midnight, okay?'

'I'll be there,' said Shepherd.

The line went dead.

Shepherd paced around the cramped sitting room as he ran

through what he was going to say to his boss, MI5 director Giles Pritchard. Shepherd wasn't going to ask for permission to go to Mali, but he'd prefer to have Pritchard's blessing so it was important that the conversation went the right way. He was just about to make the call when his phone rang on the coffee table. It was Pritchard.

Shepherd took the call. 'I've just heard about Liam,' said Pritchard. 'Are you okay?'

'Still in shock. I was just going to call you. How did you hear?'

'Julian Penniston-Hill at MI6 called me. There's lots of radio chatter in Mali at the moment, al-Qaeda are taking all the credit for shooting down a Chinook. Julian got the manifest from the MoD and recognised the name. I thought Liam was in the Army Air Corps, flying Wildcats?'

'He was, with 659 Squadron,' said Shepherd. 'But he's on a one-year attachment with the RAF. He retrained on the Chinook and a few months ago he joined the Support Helicopter Force at RAF Odiham in Hampshire. He's with 7 Squadron now and they're out in Mali supporting the UN peacekeepers. Do you have any details?'

'Just that the Chinook was taken out by an RPG. Three members of the crew including Liam are apparently okay but they're being held hostage by extremists.'

'That's all I know, too. The Regiment is putting together a rescue mission and I want to be part of it.'

Pritchard made a tutting sound. 'Dan, I understand that you want to be involved, but . . .'

'But what?'

'Look, there's no easy way of saying this, but aren't you maybe a bit long in the tooth to be doing any action man stuff?'

'Thanks for that,' said Shepherd.

'You know what I mean. Mali is practically a war zone. Maybe you should let the pros handle it.'

'I'm going out there, with your permission or without it,' said Shepherd coldly.

'That's a threat, is it?'

'No, it's not a threat. Look, my son's in danger and I'm going to do whatever I have to. I've been involved in hostage rescue before, my experience will be useful.'

'Okay, Dan. You've got to do what you've got to do. But your current job is entering a critical phase. Kamran and Sayed are depending on you. You'll be cutting them loose.'

'For a few days. And if it's a worry, get the governor to put them in solitary on a trumped-up charge until I get back.'

'And this Javid Mir is a new wrinkle. You gave him the phone?'

'First thing. I didn't get the chance to run it by Amar, but there was a number stored in the contacts directory and I gave it to Diane along with the ICCID.'

'The number belongs to a burner phone, we're trying to track it as we speak but most of the time it's off and the battery's out.'

'So they know what they're doing.'

'Yeah, he wasn't given the phone for social chit-chat so something is going on. The phone records show that he was talking to the burner phone for twenty minutes not long after you gave it to him. It must have been important. And it hasn't been used since. If he does switch it on again we can get a tracker program on it remotely but if these guys are pros that's not going to happen. Chances are he's flushed it already.'

'That's what I thought.'

'Did you also think that the murder of the guy Mir was in a fight with was connected to you giving him a phone?'

'I wondered about that, yes. But that wouldn't make sense, would it? Mir and Morgan were both in their cells, Mir wouldn't have to call outside to put a contract on Morgan. He'd just have to talk to one of the emirs.'

'So it's a coincidence?' said Pritchard.

'I don't know. I really don't know. What about the new guy? Did anything turn up?'

'Condom Man? Yes, there's something going on there, for sure. We're still looking.'

'As I told Diane, the other two deferred to him. He's a big fish.'

'We'll keep an eye on him,' said Pritchard. He sighed. 'There's nothing I can do to persuade you not to do this, is there? We really do need you here.'

'I'm sorry, no. He's my son.'

'Okay. Then all I can do is to wish you well. You're right, of course. He's your son. You have to do what you have to do.'

'Thanks, Giles. I appreciate your understanding.'

'What are you going to tell the prison?'

'I'll call in sick first thing.'

'Just be careful, Dan. I know you've been in more than your fair share of trouble spots, but Mali really is the Wild West. You know the Wagner Group have moved in?'

'Yeah. They're in the territory where it happened. Just outside Gao.'

'They're vicious bastards and won't take kindly to you turning up on their turf.'

'I'll bear that in mind.'

'How do I stay in touch while you're over there? It's doubtful that your mobile will work.'

'Colonel Davies will be running the show from Stirling Lines.'

'Okay, I'll liaise with him,' said Pritchard. 'The Germans are all about surveillance in Mali, mainly using drones. I'll get in touch with my opposite number at the BND and see if they can help.'

The Bundesnachrichtendienst was Germany's foreign intelligence agency, the equivalent of Britain's MI6. 'I'd appreciate that,' said Shepherd. 'And again, I'm sorry about leaving everyone in the lurch.'

'Just get back as soon as you can,' said Pritchard. 'And in one piece.' He ended the call.

. . .

Shepherd had to collect his blue BMW SUV from a multi-storey car park half a mile from the house he was using. He took a circuitous route and doubled back several times until he was sure he wasn't being followed. He had a small backpack with him containing his Dan Shepherd wallet, his phone, a change of clothing and a washbag filled with the essentials.

He climbed into the SUV and tapped Brize Norton into his satnav. It was a 185-mile journey, with a three-and-a-half-hour drive time. He waited until he was on the M1 heading south before phoning Chris Thatcher on hands-free. Thatcher was a former London detective who now worked for an international security firm that included kidnapping insurance in its portfolio. Thatcher was a skilled hostage negotiator who had worked in trouble spots around the world. He answered almost immediately. 'Chris, it's Dan Shepherd. Sorry to bother you so late, but I need to pick your brains.'

'Pick away, Dan,' said Thatcher. 'Just let me pour milk into my coffee and I'm yours.' Thatcher put down the phone. Shepherd glanced at his speedometer and realised that he was ten miles over the speed limit. He eased off the accelerator. He had plenty of time.

Eventually Thatcher came back on the line. 'All right, Dan. What do you need?'

'I'm just about to head to Mali,' said Shepherd. 'Possible kidnap situation. I just wanted to know what I might be up against.'

'Yes, it's a problem area,' said Thatcher. 'Hundreds of incidents a year and kidnapping is on the increase. Is it a Brit?'

'Yeah. An RAF helicopter crew.' Shepherd didn't want to explain that one of the victims was his son. That information was best kept to himself.

'Has a demand been made yet?'

'Not yet. All we know is that the crew are alive and have been taken prisoner.'

'Okay, well it's good news, bad news. The good news is that the vast majority of kidnappings in Mali are about the cash. If the ransom is paid, the hostages are released.'

'And the bad news?'

'Well you know the bad news. The British government never negotiates with terrorists. Unless they're Irish, of course, in which case they can sit in the House of Commons and have tea at Buckingham Palace. But a kidnapping group in Mali, no, there'll be no negotiation. Who do you think the kidnappers are?'

'Not sure,' said Shepherd.

'Almost half the kidnappings out there are carried out by jihadist groups,' said Thatcher. 'The usual suspects. Al-Qaeda, JNIM, Islamic State West African Province, Islamic State Sahel Province, Al Murabitoun, Ansar Dine, Katiba Macina and Boko Haram. Kidnapping for ransom is the main source of JNIM's finance, for example. Then about a third of all kidnappings are the work of criminal gangs, and with them it's all about the money. Usually they take locals, though. In fact there aren't many foreigners taken these days because so many governments advise their citizens to not go.'

'Have you worked out there?'

'Me personally? Yes, a few times. Mostly for clients in the gold mining business. But these days their security is so tight that the kidnappers look for easier pickings.'

'And it's always been straightforward?'

'Pretty much. As I said, it's all about the money. It's not like Iraq or Afghanistan where the jihadists want to score political points or ratchet up the terror. There you can be pretty much sure that the hostages are going to end up dead, probably with their heads hacked off on YouTube. But in Mali, it's money they're after.'

'What sort of sums?'

'That depends on the situation. A few years back, Mali's military government paid two million euros for the release of opposition leader Soumaïla Cissé. But the deal also included the release of more than a hundred convicted jihadists. The French have paid up in the past, too. Tens of millions of euros. But if it's an armed gang kidnapping a local businessman, a few thousand dollars might be enough.'

'I think we're looking at one of the jihadists groups,' said

Shepherd. 'They shot the helicopter down so they definitely have military experience.'

'And how many in the crew? Two?'

'Four,' said Shepherd. 'It was a Chinook. But one of the crew was killed so they'll have three hostages.'

'My guess is that they'll be aiming high,' said Thatcher. 'Ten million euros. Twenty million.'

'Except, as you say, the British government won't pay.'

'In fact they can't pay. Payment of terrorist ransoms is illegal under the Terrorism Act 2000.'

'So how would you see it playing out?'

'The kidnappers will make their demands clear. The British government will say it doesn't negotiate with terrorists. That will take time. But with the government's refusal to pay carved in stone, it only ends one way. I'm sorry I can't be more optimistic.'

'I'm not looking for optimism, Chris. Just a realistic assessment of where we stand.'

'We have a local firm out there, I can you send you their details.'

'That's okay, Chris, I don't think negotiating is going to be an option.'

'Understood, Dan. Take care then, and stay safe.'

Shepherd ended the call.

• • •

Liam wasn't sure how long his captors had been away. It was difficult to keep track of time and he dipped in and out of consciousness, but eventually he heard the bolt rattle back and the door squeak open. He heard the scrape of sandals against stone and then he was gripped by the shoulders and pulled upright. He felt something being placed around his neck, then he heard a click and the rattle of a chain. A few seconds later the chain tightened around his neck and he began to gasp and struggle. 'Please, no . . .' he said in English, and then switched to French.

The chain pulled him backwards but then hands gripped his arms and pulled him along the floor until his back was against a wall. The chain loosened and he gasped for air. The chain rattled and there were more clicks, then his captors walked away. A few seconds later, Smithy began struggling and shouting, swearing at them that he'd kill them if ever he got their hands on them.

'Smithy, relax!' shouted Liam. 'They're just chaining us up. They won't hurt you.'

Smithy went quiet. Liam heard him being dragged across the floor and chained to the wall.

'Smithy, are you okay?' said Liam.

'I'm okay.'

Footsteps headed towards Liam and he flinched, fearing that he was about to be hit. But there was no blow. A hand grabbed his hood and it was ripped off. Liam blinked and coughed. As his eyes came into focus he looked up at the face of the man standing over him. He was dark-skinned and in his early twenties, not much older than Liam, wearing a stained long grey tunic over baggy black pants and holding a small notepad. 'What is your name?' barked the man in French.

'Liam Shepherd.'

'Spell that.' He spoke in French and it took Liam a second or two to understand the question, then he spelled out his name. The man scribbled in his notepad. He looked around the room. It was about twelve feet square, dusty stone walls and a dirt floor. The light came from two windows, one directly above his head, the other in the wall to his left. Mobile was to Liam's left, unconscious on the floor with a chain running from his neck to a thick metal bracket set into the wall. Smithy was directly opposite Liam, sitting with his back to the wall, his knees up against his chest. He was also chained to the wall. To the right was a wooden door, guarded by a man who was twice the age of the man with the notebook. He had a straggly grey beard and wore spectacles that had been repaired with duct tape. He was wearing a brown tunic and matching baggy pants. He was cradling an AK-47 across his chest, his finger on the trigger.

'Don't look at him!' shouted the man with the notebook. 'Look at me.' Liam looked back at him. 'And your army number?'

Liam gave it to him. The man had a burn mark on his left cheek as if a red hot poker had been pressed against it. 'And your date of birth.'

Liam slowly said his date of birth. The man wrote down the details in his notebook, then went over to Smithy.

He shouted at him in French and Smithy frowned, not understanding.

'He wants your name, service number and date of birth,' said Liam.

'Okay, okay,' said Smithy. He gave the details to the man who wrote them down in his notebook before walking back to Liam. He gestured at Mobile. 'Your friend. What is his name?'

'Harry Holmes.'

'Give me his service number and date of birth.'

Liam gave him the numbers and the man wrote them down.

A third man appeared at the door, carrying a tray. He was a teenager, Liam realised, maybe not even that. Small and slight and wearing a Bart Simpson T-shirt and dirty jeans. He had curly black hair and his cheeks were smeared with dirt.

'Give them the food,' said the man and the boy nodded. He placed the tray on to the floor. On the tray were three clay plates of food and three plastic bottles of water. The boy picked up the water bottles and handed one to Liam.

'Good evening,' said the boy.

Liam couldn't help but grin. The lad obviously wanted to practise his English. 'Good evening,' he said. He held up the bottle. 'Thank you for the water.'

The man pointed his pen at the boy and shouted at the boy in French. 'I told you not to talk to the prisoners!'

The boy lowered his head and mumbled an apology.

'Give them the food and water and then go!' barked the man.

The boy hurriedly placed bottles of water next to Smithy and Mobile, then picked up a plate and took it over to Liam. Liam smiled his thanks. He didn't want to provoke the man with the notebook. The boy smiled back and placed the plate next to him. On it was a small piece of white fish and a mound of rice.

The boy fetched another plate for Smithy and put the final plate by Mobile's side. The man with the notebook gestured for him to go and the boy picked up the tray and hurried out of the door.

'Understand this,' said the man to Liam. 'If you try to hurt us, or you try to escape, we will beat you, then we will put the hoods back on and we will stop feeding you. Do you understand?'

Liam nodded. 'I understand.'

'And your friends speak French? They understand?'

'They speak a little, but I will make sure that they understand. Thank you for the food.'

'It isn't much, but we don't have much. We are at war.'

'We are grateful for what you have given us,' said Liam. '*Monsieur,* can I ask you a question?'

The man jutted his chin out. 'What do you want to know?'

'What will happen to us? What is it you want? We're peacekeepers, we're with the UN, we're not part of the war.'

'You are soldiers in a foreign land.'

'We're pilots. We were there to rescue a vehicle that had broken down.'

'Your helicopter had guns on it.'

'For our own protection. We're not here to fight. We're here to help.'

The man shook his head. 'You're helping the army and they are murdering us.'

'We're peacekeepers, we're in the middle.' He held up his hands. 'Please, I don't want to argue. And we are really grateful for the food and the water. I just want to know what's going to happen to us.'

'That depends,' said the man.

'On what?'

'On what your government does,' said the man. 'We will be asking for a ransom. If they pay, you will be set free.'

Liam nodded. 'Okay, thank you.' He forced a smile, and pointed at Mobile, who was lying on his back next to the far wall. A chain led from his neck to a metal bracket three feet off the ground. 'One more thing, please. Our friend. He needs to see a doctor.'

'He's sleeping. You can see his chest moving.'

'No, he's unconscious. He's been like that since you found him. He needs a doctor.'

'We don't have a doctor.'

'Please, he's dying. He could be bleeding internally.'

The man walked over to Mobile and kicked him in the side. Mobile didn't react, but his chest was rising and falling slowly. 'We will see how he is tomorrow,' said the man.

He went over to the door. The man with the AK-47 stood to the side to let him pass.

'Can I ask your name?' said Liam.

The man frowned. 'Why do you want to know my name?'

'Because you helped us. We should know the name of the man who helped us.'

The man shrugged. 'My name is Youssouf.'

'Thank you Youssouf. *Barakallahu Fik.*'

Youssouf frowned. 'You speak Arabic?'

Liam shook his head. 'Not really, just enough to say God bless you.'

Youssouf stared at him coldly for several seconds, then turned and left. The man with the AK-47 followed him, slammed the door shut and bolted it.

Smithy reached for his plate and pulled it towards him. He picked up a piece of fish and popped it into his mouth. 'We're screwed, aren't we?'

'I'm just hoping your theory about not letting us see their faces is crap, because now we've seen all their faces.'

'Being able to identify them isn't an issue,' said Smithy. 'The issue is that the British government doesn't pay ransoms, end

of. As soon as those bastards realise that, we're toast.' He
unscrewed the top from his bottle and drank.

Liam looked at his plate. He wasn't hungry. He looked over
at Mobile. He wasn't sleeping, he was unconscious. Mobile
needed help, and soon.

He pulled back the left sleeve of his flight jacket and held
up his hand. Smithy stopped eating. 'They didn't find your
watch?'

'It was under my sleeve. And they weren't looking.'

'Will it work?'

'I guess we'll find out,' said Liam. The watch was a Breitling
Emergency 2, a gift from his father on his last birthday. It was
a watch favoured by pilots, with a bright orange face, analogue
hands and a digital screen. But what made the Emergency 2
special was that it was equipped with two emergency beacons,
which when activated sent a digital signal via satellite and an
analogue signal on the 121.5 MHz frequency used by search
and rescue teams. His dad had joked that activating the beacons
meant a rescue helicopter would be on the scene within an
hour, and that he'd have to pay a $10,000-dollar fine if there
was no actual emergency. He was only half joking. The watch
came with a twenty-page legal contract and Breitling took a
copy of the owner's passport at the time it was purchased.
When the watch was activated, Breitling knew where the watch
was and who owned it. Liam had been genuinely touched. He
knew that it was a sign that his dad was worried about him.
The watch was big and chunky as it incorporated two batteries,
one for the watch and another for the beacons. Liam had come
in for some teasing when he'd started wearing the watch
because it was so big and the orange dial made it hard to miss,
so he tended to keep it hidden under his sleeve.

'So activate it,' said Smithy. 'The sooner, the better.'

'It's more complicated than that,' said Liam. 'It works best outdoors, being inside cuts down the signal. And I have to pull out the antenna.'

'The what?'

Liam pointed at a cylinder that ran along the bottom of the watch, about the circumference of a cigarette, with a screw cap on one end. 'I have to undo this to activate the watch. It releases a wire antenna and that needs to be hanging as vertically as possible to broadcast the signals. Like I said, outside is best, but if we do it inside they'll see it as soon as they open the door.'

Smithy pointed at the window above Liam's head. 'Hang it out of the window.'

Liam twisted around and looked up. The window above his head was two feet wide and a foot deep, nothing more than a hole in the wall with three-inch-thick rusting bars running horizontally. 'Yeah, that should work,' he said. 'But we don't know what's on the other side of that wall. For all we know there could be a dozen jihadists sitting there. If they see a watch being lowered out, we're screwed.'

'So wait until it gets dark,' said Smithy. 'The sooner you activate that thing, the sooner they'll come looking.'

. . .

The satnav was bang on with its estimate and Shepherd arrived at Brize Norton at just before ten o'clock at night. He showed his ID to two guards at the entrance. They checked his name against a list on a clipboard and waved him through.

Shepherd headed towards the general aviation terminal and saw Matt Standing on the steps outside. Standing waved and Shepherd flashed his lights and parked. Standing walked over as Shepherd climbed out of the SUV. Standing was almost twenty years younger than Shepherd, and only a few years older than Liam. He was a typical SAS grey man, neither tall nor short, no bulging muscles or swagger about him, just a quiet confidence that he could get the job done, no matter what it was. His hair was unruly and looked as if Standing had cut it himself, and the patches of sunburned skin on his face suggested that he had recently shaved off a beard. He had a black backpack slung over one shoulder.

'Any news?' Shepherd asked.

Standing shook his head. 'Sorry. Nothing else.'

'No ransom demand?'

'Not yet.' He patted Shepherd on the shoulder. 'Come and meet the guys, then we'll board. They're all familiar faces.'

'Give me a second, I need to make a call.'

Shepherd walked away and took out his phone. He called the prison and asked to be put through to the control centre. He faked a couple of coughs and told the duty officer that he had come down with a bug and wouldn't be in tomorrow. The duty officer didn't ask any questions. Taking frequent sick days was one of the few perks of the job and all the officers took full advantage of it. On average, prison officers took sixteen days sick leave each year to add to their thirty days annual leave. No one would ever complain or ask for a doctor's note, the rotas would be amended accordingly and life would go on.

'Okay, done,' said Shepherd, putting his phone away as he walked back to Standing. Standing pushed open a door to reveal a waiting room with several grey sofas and a kitchen area with tea- and coffee-making facilities. Half a dozen black kitbags were piled up against one wall. There were four men in the room and Shepherd grinned as he recognised them all immediately.

Jack and Joe Ellis were sitting together, and as always at first glance it was almost impossible to tell which was which. They were identical twins, lanky and tall with soulful brown eyes and drooping moustaches. Both had served with distinction in the Paras before joining the SAS. Jack had passed Selection first and Joe had followed him a year later. They had picked up the nicknames Thing One and Thing Two. Shepherd knew that Jack had a small mole under his left ear, so as soon as he spotted it he grinned. 'Great to see you again, Jack,' he said. Jack was wearing black jeans, a grey turtleneck sweater and his favourite Timberland boots.

They shook hands, then Joe came over and patted him on the back. 'Couldn't keep us away from this one, Spider,' said Joe. He was wearing desert fatigues and from the look of his sunburned cheeks was just back from somewhere hot and sunny. 'Any news?'

'You know as much as I do, Joe,' said Shepherd.

Helping himself to a mug of coffee was Terry 'Paddy' Ireland, who despite the nickname was Norfolk born and bred. He was wearing a dark green quilted jacket and baggy jeans. He raised his mug in salute. 'Do you want a coffee, Spider?'

'I'm good, Paddy, thanks,' said Shepherd.

Ireland's skin was also tanned, and he had a shaggy beard that was greying in places. Like Joe Ellis, he was probably just back from the Middle East, where dark skin and facial hair helped the SAS men blend in with the locals.

The oldest of the group was a long-time friend of Shepherd's, a grey-haired man in his late forties who was wearing a North Face fleece over a blue denim shirt. Andy 'Penny' Lane had joined the SAS six months after Shepherd, but whereas Shepherd had left to pursue a career in law enforcement and then MI5, Lane had stayed put. He was a talented linguist, fluent in several European languages and near-fluent in Russian and Arabic. He was a signals specialist and would probably be handling comms for the mission. Shepherd grinned and shook hands with Lane. 'Great to see you, Penny. I keep thinking you'll retire but there's no stopping you, is there?'

'What else would I do?' asked Lane. 'Nightwatchman on some building site?'

Shepherd knew that Lane was selling himself short. Any one of a dozen security firms would snap the man up if he ever offered his skills on the open market. But Lane wasn't the type to work in the private sector. He'd probably never admit it, but Lane loved the adrenaline rush that came from combat, from pitting his skills against men who wanted him dead. Shepherd understood, because he had felt the same way – when he was younger, anyway. Shepherd had left the Regiment after he had married and Liam had been born, but Lane had remained single and devoted to the SAS. Lane had had more than his fair share of romantic entanglements over the years, but when push had come to shove the Regiment had always won out.

'Sorry about your boy,' said Lane.

'He knew the risks,' said Shepherd.

'Chip off the old block.'

Shepherd nodded. 'Yeah, unfortunately.'

'We'll get him back, Spider.'

Shepherd forced a smile. 'I hope so.'

'Count on it,' said Lane.

'Right, guys, the sooner we're on board, the sooner we're in the air,' said Standing.

They grabbed their kitbags and headed for the door. Standing took them around the side of the building where a Hercules C-130J was parked in front of a hangar.

The Hercules was the SAS's plane of choice for moving men and equipment around the globe. The cargo compartment was forty-one feet long and nine feet wide, enough room for eight freight pallets or 128 combat troops, ninety-two if they were wearing parachutes. The plane had a crew of three – two pilots and a loadmaster. The pilots stayed in the cockpit and the team were greeted on the rear ramp by the loadmaster. He was tall with black hair cut short, the sleeves of his desert-pattern fatigues rolled up to his elbows. Standing gave him a high five, and introduced him to Shepherd. 'Nick Kluge,' said Standing. 'Saved my bacon out in Syria a while back. The pilots were about to leave me and my team high and dry but Nick here persuaded them to stay.'

'Persuaded is one way of putting it,' said Kluge.

'Better late than never,' said Standing.

'Not sure that they saw it that way, not with two jihadists gun trucks heading their way, guns blazing.' He laughed. 'All's well that ends well,' he said. 'So you guys hot-footing it to Mali? This about that chopper that went down?'

Standing nodded. 'This is Spider, his son is one of the pilots.'

'Sorry to hear what happened, Spider,' said Kluge. 'Let's get you there ASAP. Soon as you guys are strapped in, we're wheels up.'

Shepherd saw that there were two large pallets of gear in

the middle of the plane, along with five stripped-down electric quad bikes in desert camouflage livery.

'I didn't have much time so I grabbed what I thought might come in useful,' said Standing. 'I've got six parachute rigs, plenty of guns and flashbangs. Night vision gear, obviously.'

'Comms?'

'Personal headsets and we've got two sat phones for communicating with Stirling Lines. Penny has one and you can have the other.'

'Nice one.'

The SAS team hurried up the ramp, stowed their kitbags and strapped themselves into the seats that lined the fuselage. Shepherd and Standing sat next to each other in the middle of the aircraft.

'I wasn't sure how you were fixed provisions-wise so I grabbed some sandwiches and biscuits and some soft drinks,' said the loadmaster. He pointed at a black nylon kitbag. 'Just help yourselves.' He pressed the button to raise the ramp, checked that it was securely locked and then took his own seat.

The engines roared, the six-bladed propellors began to turn and the plane rolled forward. Within a minute they were in the air.

Shepherd waited until the Hercules was at its cruising altitude and heading south before leaning towards Standing. He had to shout to make himself heard over the roar of the four massive Allison AE2100D3 turboprop engines.

'Who do we have in Mali at the moment?' Shepherd asked.

'The Regiment? No one. The British Army has three hundred troops based there, mainly from the Light Dragoons and the Royal Anglians. Not much in the way of combat troops, unfortunately. There are bomb disposal teams, drone operators and a field surgical team. There's a lieutenant colonel running the show but Colonel Davies said we should link up with a Major Jeremy Jones. They've got a history, he says, and the Major has promised to offer us every assistance.'

'And what do we know about the guys who are holding the crew hostage?'

'No details at all. Jihadists, definitely. But there's a lot of different groups out there.'

'Yeah, so I gather. What about the location of where they're being held?'

'Nothing. Sorry, We're going in blind.'

'My boss has asked for help from the Germans out there.'

'We're going to need all the help we can get,' said Standing. 'Otherwise it's needle in a haystack time.'

'I might have something that can help narrow down the size of the haystack,' said Shepherd.

'What's that?'

'Let's wait until we're on the ground,' said Shepherd. He stretched out his legs. 'I'm going to get some shut-eye. We've got a long day tomorrow.'

· · ·

Shafiq Ali Rafiq looked out of the window of the Gulfstream jet. There were no stars to be seen so he assumed they were flying through cloud. They were somewhere over the Atlantic Ocean, more than halfway through their flight. They had stopped to refuel somewhere on the east coast of America and had spent less than an hour on the ground.

He eased his legs forward and the shackles around his ankles rattled. He was flying on a private jet but Homeland Security had insisted that he be manacled and shackled throughout the flight, even when he visited the bathroom. He was wearing an orange jumpsuit and plastic shoes that were at least one size too large for his feet.

There were two agents from Homeland Security sitting at the rear of the plane. They wore matching dark blue suits and white shirts, though they were wearing different ties. The older one, Bill, who had grey hair and bifocal spectacles, was wearing a red-and-blue striped tie. The younger one, Trey, whose hair was receding fast and threatening baldness by the time he reached thirty, wore a blue tie. Both men were dozing and the older one occasionally snored.

Just in front of them were the medical team responsible for his wellbeing during the flight, a black doctor and an Hispanic nurse. They had insisted on taking his blood pressure and temperature before allowing him to board the plane, a nonsense as the cancer that had spread through his body would kill him in months if not weeks. He hadn't protested and complied with their instructions, keeping his face a blank mask.

Once he had been seated, the nurse came over to take his temperature every thirty minutes and once an hour she took his blood pressure and pulse, noting down the figures on a clipboard. She would smile and tried to engage him in conversation but he refused to interact with her. Her head was uncovered and she had a small crucifix on a chain around her neck. The insult had been deliberate, he was sure of that. The Americans were vindictive to the core, they took every opportunity to belittle and humiliate their captives. After a year at Florence they had allowed him to have a small television, visible behind a toughened glass screen. But the channels were restricted to education programmes and religious shows. Christian religious shows. Shows that a good Muslim like Shafiq Ali Rafiq would never watch. Even a privilege was turned into a punishment by the Americans.

Every prison meal had been served on a metal tray with rounded edges so that he couldn't use it to hurt himself, and he was given plastic sporks that were so flimsy they broke under the slightest pressure. It was so he couldn't kill himself, but that suggestion was an insult to a Muslim. Islam forbade suicide. The Koran was unequivocally clear on the matter. 'And kill not yourselves. Surely Allah is merciful to you. And whoever does that by way of transgression and injustice, we shall cast him into fire.' Suggesting that he might take his own life was an insult, one that was repeated every mealtime.

Still, that was behind him. He was heading home. Not his real home, of course. That was Pakistan. But for more than forty years he had held British citizenship, and it was Britain where his wives, children and grandchildren lived. He was looking forward to seeing them again.

He looked around the luxurious interior of the private jet. It was owned by a Qatari company. The kingdom of Qatar was headed by Emir Sheikh Tamim bin Hamad Al Thani, who oversaw one of the richest dynasties in the world. The royal family controlled assets of close to 350 billion dollars including jewels such as the Empire State Building, Harrods department store and the Shard, the tallest building in the UK. The family had stakes in international giants such as British Airways, Barclays Bank and Volkswagen and lived in a gold-plated palace that cost more than a billion dollars to build. But there were other families in positions of power, not quite as rich as the Al Thanis but still among the richest dynasties in the world.

The man who owned the company that owned this jet belonged to one of those families. Mohammed bin Hamad Al-Attiyah was sitting on the other side of the plane from him, sipping a glass of red wine. How a man who called himself a good Muslim could partake of alcohol made no sense to Rafiq, but he kept his revulsion to himself. Mohammed bin Hamad Al-Attiyah was the man's given name, but in the US he was known as Harry Hamad, the name he had taken when he had attended Harvard University, a year after his father had bequeathed the institution 5 million dollars. Shafiq Ali Rafiq was equally offended by the man's change of name. It was an honour to bear the name of the prophet, and blasphemous to replace it with the name of an infidel. But again he kept his thoughts to himself. If it wasn't for Harry Hamad, Shafiq Ali Rafiq would still be rotting in a concrete box and not settling back in a hand-stitched buttery leather seat in an 80-million-dollar jet.

Hamad looked over at him. 'Would you like some food?' he asked.

'No thank you, I am good.'

'We have Kobe steaks on board. The best in the world.'

'I do not eat beef,' said Rafiq.

'We have fruit.'

'No thank you.' He didn't feel like eating. The cancer growing inside him had killed his appetite in the same way that it was killing his body. When he did eat he always felt nauseous afterwards and sometimes he was hit by cramps so painful that he wept. 'Perhaps just some water.'

'Of course,' said Hamad. He held up his hands and clicked his fingers. A blonde stewardess hurried over from the galley. She was wearing a short black skirt and a tight blue blouse, and her hair was loose around her shoulders. She was wearing bright red lipstick that matched her garishly painted nails. Rafiq turned his head away so that he didn't have to look at her. At the very least the woman should have her head covered, he thought – that was made clear in the Koran. 'And tell the believing women to lower their gaze and be modest, and to display of their adornment only that which is apparent, and to draw their veils over their bosoms.'

'Some water, for my friend,' said Hamad.

'Of course,' said the woman. She went back to the galley, her high heels clicking on the floor.

'You will soon be home, brother,' said Hamad.

Shafiq Ali Rafiq nodded. Yes, he would be. But it was a bitter-sweet return, because he was going back to die. That was the only reason that the Americans had allowed him to leave. And they hadn't done it out of the goodness of their hearts, they had done it because Hamad had employed a team of top Washington DC lawyers to press for his release. The lawyers, and Hamad's personal representations to the White House, had eventually succeeded. They would allow him to go back to the UK, but there were stringent restrictions and he would have to remain in a British prison. He wasn't being freed, just moved. But at least he would be closer to his family, and he would be able to meet them face to face and not through armoured glass as was the case in America. 'I am grateful for everything you have done for me,' said Rafiq. That was true. He was grateful. He had nothing but contempt for the man's morals and the way he seemed to play fast and loose with his faith, but Hamad had managed to do what Rafiq's legal team had never managed to achieve.

The woman returned with a bottle of water and a glass. Rafiq turned his head away so that he didn't have to look at her.

'Would you like ice with your water, sir?' she asked.

Rafiq shook his head. He waited until she had gone back to the galley before sipping his water. He looked over at Hamad. 'Can I ask you a question?'

'Of course.'

'All the work you have done. The lawyers. This plane. Why have you done this?'

Hamad shrugged. 'You were being treated unfairly. I wanted to redress the balance.'

Rafiq frowned. 'That is the only reason?'

'You were being punished for your beliefs,' said Hamad. 'You are a Muslim and an attack on one Muslim is an attack on all Muslims.' He sipped his wine, then held up his glass. 'I see the way you look at me when I drink wine. Yes, I know that alcohol is haram. Forbidden. And that the Koran says that intoxicants are the work of Satan. So does the fact that I enjoy a glass of claret make me a bad Muslim?' He shrugged. 'Maybe it does. But helping you makes me a good Muslim. So there is balance.'

Shafiq Ali Rafiq's eyes narrowed. 'You helped me so that you could break sharia law with impunity?'

Hamad chuckled and waved a languid hand. 'No, of course not. I'm just saying that in my view the occasional glass of wine does not make me a bad Muslim. To me, being a Muslim is more about politics and power than it is about slavishly following the Koran. You think the Pope cares about whether his people use condoms or not? How many Jews work on the Sabbath these days, when their rules prohibit them even switching on an electrical appliance on their day of rest?'

Shafiq Ali Rafiq sipped his water. He vehemently disagreed with the man, but there was no point in voicing that disagreement. The man had his beliefs and it was up to him whether or not he wanted to burn in the fires of hell. Islamic hell was an ever-flaming pit of fire filled with venomous animals where sinners were given only pus, blood and boiling water to drink and prickly thorn branches to eat. If that is where he wanted to spend eternity, then so be it.

Hamad leaned towards Rafiq. He looked over his shoulder to check that no one was paying them any attention, then lowered his voice. 'The British thought they had got rid of you forever. They assumed that you were going to die in America, that you were their problem. I wanted to prove them wrong. I wanted you to be back where you belong. And I wanted to cause the British as much embarrassment as I could.'

'You hate the British?'

'How can you not hate the British? Do you know the history of the British in Qatar? We were practically a colony for almost a hundred and fifty years. Then when the British moved out, the Americans moved in. We are a tiny country, just a peninsula built of sand, and a population of less than a million people. If it wasn't for the fact that Qatar sits on the largest, purest natural gas field in the world, no one would give a shit. Then when Iraq invaded Kuwait, everything changed. The royal family realised that only one country could protect their wealth.'

'The United States?'

'Exactly. The Great Satan. After the Gulf War ended, Qatar spent more than a billion dollars building the Al Udeid Air Base and invited the United States to use it. And after the 9/11 attacks, use it they did. There are now more than ten thousand

US troops there and over a hundred American aircraft. It is the largest US military base in the Middle East. Our rulers have made our country a lapdog for the Americans. The base was used as a jumping-off point for American and British troops to fly to Iraq and Afghanistan where they killed hundreds of thousands of Muslims. And the Americans used the base to launch bombing attacks against Syria in which thousands of civilians died, Muslim civilians. Men, women and children.' He held up his glass. 'Me taking the occasional drink of wine is a very small sin compared to what the Qatari royal family has done to betray our faith.'

'Yet I understand that they also offer financial and moral support to Hamas? Their political leadership is now based in Qatar. And Hamas hate the Americans.'

'Oh, that is true,' said Hamad. 'And al-Qaeda and ISIS are allowed to operate with impunity in Qatar. Much of their funding goes through Doha banks. And the royal family offer support to terrorist groups in Syria. They are happy to play both ends against the middle, though their support for the jihadists comes more from fear of offending them rather than respecting their aims. They have too much to lose if the jihadists wreak havoc in Qatar. But they are in bed with the West, and intend to stay that way.' He sneered. 'Do you think they would have helped you get back to the UK, to be with your family? They care only about themselves and their wealth. Everything they do is about protecting what they have.'

Shafiq Ali Rafiq frowned as he sipped his water. He didn't want to offend the man, not after all he had done for him, but there was so much about him that didn't make sense. He had attended Harvard University, he had Americanised his name, he played fast and loose with the five pillars of Islam, but he seemed to have nothing but contempt for the West.

'I can see the wheels turning, my brother,' said Hamad. 'Why don't you tell me what is troubling you?'

Rafiq studied him with unblinking eyes for several seconds, before finally nodding. 'I am not troubled,' he said. 'I am . . . confused.'

Hamad raised his glass. 'By this?'

'You seem to have embraced the ways of the West, yet you clearly despise them.'

'I am a Muslim first and foremost. I do whatever I can to protect our religion against the infidels. I was in America when the twin towers went down, and I cheered. Finally we were striking back. Finally we were showing the world that we Muslims were a force to be reckoned with. And then when George W. Bush and Tony Blair invaded Afghanistan, I was sure the Muslim world would rise up to defend our brothers. But look what happened. Muslims in the US and the UK stood by as their brothers were murdered in their thousands. More than a million killed in Iraq, Afghanistan, Syria, Yemen and Pakistan. And I felt shame when I realised that my country, my beloved Qatar, was helping the West commit mass murder.' He lowered his voice to a quiet whisper. 'I know what you are planning, my brother. I know what you intend to do in your final days, and I applaud it. Your actions will strike at the heart of the British, and the British are the lapdogs of the Americans. You will hurt them both and they will probably blame each other. That is why I am happy to help you achieve your aims.' He raised his glass. 'And I hope in return, you will not begrudge me the occasional glass of wine.'

Shafiq Ali Rafiq smiled and nodded but did not say anything.

If the man wanted to spend eternity burning in hell, that was his choice.

• • •

The sun went down gradually until Liam's cell was in darkness. No one had come to collect their plates. Liam had finished his fish and rice and drunk half of his water. He was rationing himself because he had no way of knowing when they would be giving him water again.

It had been half an hour since they had heard any sound through the windows and that had been a dog barking. Liam stood up. The window was just above his head and even standing on tiptoe he could only see a strip of night sky.

'Do you think they'll be looking for us?' asked Smithy.

'Of course. You think they'd just abandon us?'

'If it was left up to the UN, no doubt,' said Smithy. 'It's all about protecting their own arses. Why the hell didn't they rescue us when we crashed? They saw us go down.'

'I don't know,' said Liam.

'They abandoned us,' said Smithy. 'Ran away with their tails between their legs.'

'We don't know that for sure.'

'The fact that we're chained up in this bloody cell tells me all that I need to know,' said Smithy. 'The question is, will our mob come out to get us?'

'My dad will,' said Liam quietly.

'Are you serious?'

Liam turned to face him. 'I know my dad, and there's no way he'll leave me here.'

'I thought he'd left the SAS?'

Liam nodded. 'He's got friends. Lots of friends. And they'll move heaven and earth to rescue us. Trust me on that.' He unclipped the bracelet of his watch. 'But first they have to find us.' He slowly unscrewed the cap off the cylinder that contained the antenna. It popped out and unravelled. Liam stretched it out. It was almost three feet long. He knew that the beacons were activated the moment the antenna was released. Any plane within a hundred miles would pick up the signal on 121.5 MHz, and the stronger signal would be received by satellites orbiting the earth and passed on to Breitling's monitoring centres. Liam had no idea how much the fabric of the building would absorb the signals – for the best chance of being heard the watch needed to be outside.

He stood on tiptoe again and carefully fed the watch through the gap below the lowest of the three bars. He allowed the wire to slip slowly through the gap, then when he had just six inches remaining he wound it around the bar and tied it, tight.

'Okay, that's it,' said Liam, sitting down with his back to the wall. 'All we can do now is wait.'

'And hope,' said Smithy.

'Amen to that.'

. . .

Gao International Airport was just short of 4,000 kilometres due south of Brize Norton. At its cruising speed of 540 kilometres an hour, the flight took almost eight hours. Shepherd and the SAS team slept most of the way. Like soldiers the world over, they grabbed sleep and food whenever it was available. There was a flush toilet at the rear of the plane, close to the ramp, but the only privacy came from a curtain that could be lowered and the men had all avoided using it because they knew they'd come in for shouted abuse from the rest of the team.

Eventually Kruge woke Shepherd by shaking his shoulder. 'We'll be starting our descent in five minutes, sir,' he said.

'What's the landing situation, are we going in hot?' asked Shepherd.

The loadmaster shook his head. 'There's no history of attacks on the airport so we're fine.'

'You've been here before?'

'Not personally, but one of the pilots has. He says we're good.'

The loadmaster went back to his seat and strapped himself in.

Shepherd reached over to shake Standing. 'Matt, we're landing.'

Standing groaned and stretched his hands above his head. The rest of the team were awake now. Lane unfastened his harness and went over to the bag of provisions. He undid it, looked inside and grinned. 'Breakfast is served,' he said. He pulled out sandwiches and fruit and shared them out. Shepherd had a ham and cheese and a can of Fanta. He was finishing the last of the soft drink when the wheels of the Hercules touched the tarmac. It was a smooth landing and the plane was soon taxiing off the main runway and heading towards a line of white-painted metal hangars, each with the letters 'UN', large and in black, on its side and roof. Eventually the Hercules came to a halt and the engines powered down. The loadmaster stood up and pressed the button to lower the rear ramp.

Shepherd and the SAS team unbuckled their harnesses, stood up, and stretched. A wave of hot air billowed into the cargo area, along with the sound of aircraft engines and military vehicles.

Shepherd and Standing grabbed their bags and headed down the ramp.

'Thank you for flying Not-So-EasyJet,' said Kruge, giving them a mock bow. 'We live to serve.'

'Where are you headed now?' asked Standing.

'I'm told that we're refuelling and then back to Brize Norton later today. Then I think we're heading to Turkey. What about you guys?'

'Open-ended,' said Standing. 'As long as it takes.'

Kruge nodded at Shepherd. 'Good luck,' he said. 'I hope your boy's okay.'

Shepherd smiled grimly. 'Thanks.'

Shepherd and Standing reached the bottom of the ramp. A big man wearing desert fatigues and brown boots came towards them. He was in his mid to late forties with a square chin and a steel-grey crewcut. He had UN patches and German flags on his sleeve. 'Are you Dan Shepherd?' he asked, with a strong German accent.

'I am,' said Shepherd.

The man held out his right hand, the size of a small shovel. 'Stefan Fischer. Herr Pritchard has asked me to brief you.'

'Excellent,' said Shepherd, shaking the man's hand.

Shepherd nodded at Standing. 'This is Sergeant Matt Standing.'

'Pleased to meet you,' said Fischer, shaking Standing's hand. He looked at the four SAS men coming down the ramp, carrying their kitbags. 'This is all of you?'

'Six of us,' said Shepherd.

'I was expecting more.'

Standing grinned. 'It's quality rather than quantity,' he said.

'Any news since last night?' asked Shepherd.

'There has been no ransom demand, no,' said Fischer. 'Can I ask you, do you plan on using the British forces here?'

'Not unless they are absolutely necessary,' said Shepherd.

'The reason I ask is that the British soldiers are attached to the UN peacekeeping force and so are bound by the UN's rules of engagement,' said Fischer. 'So they will be limited in what they can do.'

'Well, as I said, we'll only be using them if we have to,' said Shepherd. 'I'm confident that Matt and his team have the skills we need to bring this to a conclusion.'

'I hope you're right,' said Fischer. 'So, if it is okay with you I'd like to brief you and your sergeant at our facility.' He pointed off to his left. 'My offices are over there and I have some video to show you. Then I can take you back to your plane, or to Camp Roberts.'

'Camp Roberts?' repeated Shepherd.

'That is where the UK forces are based. We are all segregated here. All the troops wear blue helmets and our vehicles all have UN markings, but when we are not on patrol the various countries keep to themselves.'

The four SAS troopers gathered behind Standing, their kitbags over their shoulders.

'Your men can wait here,' said Fischer.

'If it's okay I'd like them to sit in on the briefing, we tend to act as a unit,' said Standing.

'*Sehr gut*,' said Fischer. 'Maybe you could leave your bags here, I will drive you back when we've finished.'

Standing and his men piled their bags up next to the hangar and followed Shepherd and Fischer over to a white Toyota Land Cruiser. Shepherd took the front passenger seat while Standing and his team piled into the two rows of seats at the back. The interior was uncomfortably hot but Fischer had the air conditioning on full blast and it was soon bearable. He drove between two massive hangars, then turned left towards a line of white-painted containers topped by blast shields, many of which were flying German flags. Most of the vehicles in the area were Mowag Eagles, Swiss-made lightly armoured vehicles which had an armour-protected shell bolted on to a Humvee chassis. They had been specifically designed to protect UN peacekeepers, but didn't offer much in the way of attack capability.

'Can I ask you a question?' Shepherd asked the German.

'Of course, I am here to provide what intel I can.'

'How did you know it was me, when I came down the ramp?'

Fischer smiled. 'Herr Pritchard said you would be the oldest member of the group. So I knew.'

'Spider prefers to think of himself as experienced rather than old,' said Standing, patting Shepherd on the shoulder.

'Spider?' said Fischer, frowning.

'I ate a spider once,' said Shepherd. 'A long time ago.'

'What did it taste like?'

'Like a spider,' said Shepherd. 'I wouldn't recommend it.'

Fischer brought the Land Cruiser to a stop outside a white container. It had a sign showing a 'no entry' logo superimposed on a black figure with the words '*Zutritt Für Unbefugte Verboten*'. Underneath was the same logo with the words in English: 'Access For Unauthorized Persons Prohibited'.

Fischer pressed his right thumb against a scanner and tapped a six-digit code into a keypad, then he pushed the door open. He had left the air conditioning on and it was pleasantly cold. There was a desk at the far end of the container, a row of metal filing cabinets against one wall and a large map of the area on another wall. In front of the map was a metal table with six white plastic chairs around it.

Fischer waved at the chairs. 'Please, sit.'

Shepherd and the SAS team sat down. Shepherd realised that there was no seat for the German so he stood up, but Fischer waved for him to sit down again. 'I'm happy to stand,' he said. 'I spend most of the day on my arse.' He walked over to the map and pointed at an area to the north of Gao airfield. 'The Chinook went down here, about forty kilometres north of the camp. A UN convoy had reported mechanical problems and the Chinook was sent out to recover an armoured car. The Chinook came under attack and was shot down. We had a drone in the area and were able to get video of the whole thing.' He went over to his desk and picked up a laptop. He placed it on the table and the men moved around so that they could all see the screen.

Fischer started the video. It was taken from a drone high in the air. Directly below were five white vehicles. The UN convoy. The lead vehicle was at an angle to the rest. From the look of it, it had driven into a pothole. More than a dozen blue-helmeted UN soldiers had taken position around the vehicles. To the west was the River Niger, the land close to the water lush and green and dotted with houses. The road itself was in the desert, but there were still buildings around, several within shooting distance of the convoy.

'What happened?' asked Shepherd.

'We think a hole had been dug in the road.'

'So it was a trap? An ambush?'

'Most definitely.'

'So why didn't they call it in as an ambush?'

Fischer shrugged. 'It was a Bangladeshi unit,' he said. 'They are not the best trained. They didn't come under fire so they probably assumed there was no danger.'

'Tossers,' said Standing, shaking his head in contempt.

'Here is the Chinook now,' said Fischer.

The helicopter appeared on the bottom right of the screen, heading towards the convoy. Then it banked to the left and gained height.

'It looks as if they were doing a fly-around to check the surrounding area,' said Fischer.

'They probably realised what the soldiers didn't,' said Shepherd. 'It was . . .' He stopped speaking when the plume of white smoke emerged from one of the stone buildings over-looking the road and streaked towards the helicopter. There was no sound on the video but he could imagine the 'whoosh' that the RPG rocket made as it cut through the desert air. It came up behind the rear of the Chinook and slammed into the fuselage, just below the rear pylon.

There was a flash as the grenade exploded. It was almost certainly a HEAT round – high explosive anti-tank – designed to take out tanks and armoured vehicles and more than capable of bringing down a helicopter.

The pylon disintegrated in a ball of orange flame and the rear rotor span through the air. The wounded Chinook immediately began spinning out of control. Shepherd's stomach lurched as he pictured Liam fighting to control the injured heli. His son probably hadn't even seen the RPG hit; one second they were flying normally, the next the Chinook was heading towards the ground in an uncontrollable spin. He knew that Liam had survived the crash, but that didn't make the video any less terrifying.

The rear section of the Chinook broke away and the front section began to spin faster. Shepherd figured that Liam and the other pilot would have still been fighting to regain control but there would have been nothing they could have done.

The two sections of the helicopter hit the ground at the same time, about fifty feet apart. The rear section came to a halt in a cloud of dust. The rotor of the front portion was still spinning and it smashed into the ground. The impact shattered the rotor and sent the fuselage rolling across the sand. It made three revolutions before it came to a halt, upside down. There was a body lying near the wreckage, Shepherd realised, face down in the sand and twisted like a broken doll.

'Shit,' said Standing, under his breath.

Fischer paused the video. 'It was a lucky shot,' he said.

'Not lucky for the heli,' said Standing.

'I meant that if the jihadists had used a MANPAD-type short-range surface-to-air missile or a radar or infrared-guided missile, the Chinook's electronic defence suite would probably have spotted it and dealt with it,' said Fischer.

Shepherd knew that Fischer was right. Chinooks were equipped with state-of-the-art missile defences, including a radar alerter that would tell the pilots when they had been targeted and a laser alerter that would direct a laser at an approaching missile's thermal guidance system. The Chinook was also equipped with chaff countermeasure dispensers and flares to neutralise a missile attack. The problem was, a bog-standard RPG didn't use infrared or radar so none of the sophisticated electronics on board would have seen the rocket coming. And Fischer was right about it being a lucky shot. The operator had pulled the trigger and once the rocket had left the launcher its trajectory couldn't be altered. If the Chinook had simply changed direction, the missile would have missed. But as the shot had come from the rear, the crew almost certainly hadn't seen it coming. The RPG missile had an effective range of no more than 500 metres, and the helicopter had been about that far away from the buildings. Liam and his crew had simply been unlucky.

Fischer pressed a key to restart the video.

As the dust settled around the wreckage of the Chinook, the UN soldiers moved away from their vehicles. Then they suddenly threw themselves to the ground.

'At this point the peacekeepers came under fire,' said Fischer.

A second RPG rocket streaked away from one of the buildings and slammed into the armoured vehicle at the rear of the convoy. It shuddered from the impact but stayed intact.

The peacekeepers began crawling towards their vehicles. It was impossible to see if they were being fired upon, but certainly none of them appeared to have been hit. They reached the convoy and piled into the three vehicles that were still serviceable.

'They ran away?' asked Shepherd as one by one the vehicles lurched forward.

'I'm afraid so.'

'They didn't even check to see if the rest of the crew were okay?'

'UN policy is for peacekeepers only to use force to defend themselves,' said Fischer. 'Once they reached their vehicles, standard operating procedure would be to leave the area.'

'Then what bloody good are they?' said Standing. One by

one the armoured vehicles turned around and headed south. 'Why didn't the drone attack the jihadists? You could have at least taken out the buildings they were hiding in.'

'The drone has no armaments,' said Fischer, pausing the video again. 'It is for surveillance only.'

'What do you use?' asked Shepherd.

'We have the Heron 1,' said Fischer.

Shepherd nodded. He had come across the drone before. It was manufactured by an Israeli company in partnership with a Canadian defence firm. It was originally used by the Indian Air Force but was now flown around the world and the Australian Air Force had used it extensively in Afghanistan. The eight-and-a-half-metre-long drone could take off and land automatically and had multiple sensors and satellite communication systems. It could fly as high as 10,000 metres at a top speed of just over 200 kilometres an hour, with a range of 350 kilometres. But unlike its American competitors – the Predator and the Reaper – the Heron carried no weapons. It was purely for surveillance. 'It's a pity you don't use something that's armed,' Shepherd said.

'We have no choice,' said Fischer. 'The UN refuses to use armed drones, and the Malian government has been making it difficult for us to even fly the Heron. They have been denying overflight permission to Western forces, meaning that most of the time we are not able to operate drones in Malian airspace.'

Shepherd frowned. 'Why would they do that?'

'Presumably they fear that we will see what they do not want us to see,' said Fischer. 'You are aware of the Wagner Group?'

'Unfortunately, yes,' said Shepherd.

Standing nodded. 'Fucking animals,' he said.

'Exactly,' said Fischer. 'It is the presence of the Wagner Group in Mali that persuaded our government to pull out their troops. They can't risk being tainted by Russian mobsters.' He shrugged. 'You can understand why, of course. The alternative would be to go to war with Russia, and they've no stomach for that. Not while we are so dependent on them for energy supplies. The refusal to issue overflight permissions started at about the time the junta did a deal with the Wagner people. I am sure that was not a coincidence. But please, let me show you the rest of the video. Then I will explain why the Wagner Group is an issue.'

He restarted the video. The UN convoy picked up speed as it headed south. A dozen or so men appeared from one of the buildings, carrying AK-47s. They ran to the road.

Three pick-up trucks emerged from a barn. They had machine guns mounted on the back. They kicked up plumes of sand as they drove to the road. They crossed it and fanned out, their machine guns swinging around to cover the downed helicopter.

They stopped about fifty yards away from the wreckage. The fighters got near the helicopter and approached it cautiously, sweeping their guns from side to side. One of the fighters went over to the body and kicked it in the side, several times.

One of the fighters stuck his gun inside the cockpit, then backed away, waving his AK-47 in the air. Four of the fighters slung their weapons over their shoulders and leaned into the cockpit. Two of the fighters pulled out a figure in a flight suit and helmet and dragged him by the feet away from the helicopter. It was Liam, Shepherd realised, and his blood ran cold. Liam looked lifeless but Standing had been clear that the surviving crew were being held prisoner and he held on to that thought as they dragged Liam over to one of their pick-up trucks.

Two more fighters went into the fuselage of the front section and pulled out another unconscious figure, either the crew chief or the gunner. He was dragged over to another of the pick-ups and thrown roughly into the back.

Shepherd looked over at Standing. 'Matt, are we sure these guys are okay?'

'They wouldn't have taken them away if they were dead,' said Standing.

Shepherd looked over at Fischer. The German paused the video. 'Do we know who the casualty is?' asked Shepherd.

'I don't, but the Brits sent out a recovery team yesterday afternoon and they recovered the body. I wasn't given the name but I gather it was the gunner. And there has been radio chatter to the effect that the jihadists have three prisoners.' Fischer started the video again.

The jihadists dragged the second pilot from the cockpit. They threw him on to the back of a third pick-up truck. 'The drone operator at this point decided to use the drone to follow the jihadists who had taken the helicopter crew,' said Fischer. 'Unfortunately they were running low on fuel.'

The drone circled overhead until the jihadists drove towards the highway and headed north. Two more trucks had joined so there were now five, four of them with machine guns mounted on the back. Also in the convoy was a battered SUV and an old Mercedes. The drone followed them, high overhead. The minutes ticked by as the convoy drove north. Often vehicles ahead of them, spooked by the sight of machine guns in their rear-view mirrors, would pull off the road to allow the convoy to pass.

The jihadists drove by several small villages and through a small town. 'This is Dana,' said Fischer. 'About seventy kilometres from here. At this point the drone had reached the point of no return: if they had continued on they would have run out of fuel.' He pointed at a line of numbers running across the bottom of the screen. It gave information on the location of the drone, its altitude, speed and bearing, and how much fuel it was carrying. A red warning light had appeared next to the fuel reading.

'So they abandoned the surveillance?' said Shepherd.

'They had no choice.'

'They could have continued following until they ran out of fuel and landed in the desert,' said Shepherd.

'The drones cost upwards of ten million dollars,' said Fischer. He saw the look of anger that flashed across Shepherd's face and raised his hands. 'Please, Mr Shepherd, do not shoot the messenger. I am only explaining why the drone returned to base. The drone operator was following protocol and he would have been in serious trouble if he had disobeyed protocol and the drone had indeed crashed. If I had been there I could have overruled the protocol, and I would have done, but the drone operator couldn't do that. I'm sorry.'

The drone slowly turned to the left until it was heading south again, about a hundred yards away from the highway.

'The drone flew close to the crash site as it was returning to the airfield, and it recorded something that you need to see,' said Fischer. 'Let me speed up the video.' His hands played across the keyboard and the time marker started to go at double, treble and then quadruple speed. The drone followed the highway south. Fischer kept an eye on the time marker, and then tapped on the keyboard again and the video reverted to normal speed. The drone continued to fly south but the camera tilted to the right to get a view of the crash site.

A vehicle was parked next to the wreckage. It wasn't a UN vehicle, it was in desert camouflage livery and had a machine gun pointing through a turret on top of it. 'That's a Wagner Wagon,' said Standing, beating Shepherd to it.

'Yes, it is,' said Fischer.

The Wagner Wagon was the favoured vehicle of the Wagner Group. It was an armoured vehicle manufactured in Russia and used by the mercenaries around the world. It also went by the name of Chekan, Valkyrie and Shchuka. It had been developed from a six-wheeled truck and was fitted with anti-bullet and anti-fragmentation armour, and had extensive mine protection. Unlike the white-painted vehicles used by the UK peacekeepers, the Chekan was painted to blend in with the surrounding desert.

Half a dozen Wagner soldiers were moving around the wreckage. They were wearing desert camouflage fatigues and matching Kevlar helmets. Unlike the UN peacekeepers who had run away with their tails between their legs, these guys were clearly professional soldiers. One of the men kicked the body on the ground.

'I just see the one vehicle,' said Shepherd. The drone continued south but the camera turned to keep the Chekan in the middle of the screen. 'How active are the Wagner Group out there?'

'They've been capturing and killing jihadist militants in the area,' said Fischer. 'Village by village. They usually torture them for intel, before killing them. They don't even bother moving the corpses, preferring to leave them out in the open as a warning to others.'

As they watched, the Wagner soldiers left the wreckage and climbed into the Chekan. Once they were all on board, the door closed and the vehicle headed north along the highway.

'Do you think they were going after the jihadists?' asked Shepherd.

'It's possible,' said Fischer. 'The Wagner Group use encrypted comms but they were on the radio and there are plenty of their people in the area.'

'What are you thinking, Spider?' asked Standing. 'You think they're planning a rescue mission?'

Shepherd shook his head. 'The opposite, I'm afraid.' He looked at Fischer. 'What do you think, Stefan?'

Fischer looked pained. 'I don't think they have any intentions of cooperating with the Western forces,' he said. 'They are solely here to further Russia's interests, nothing more. We have drone footage of them staging evidence of French atrocities near an army base on Gossi, before the French pulled out. They were arranging corpses in mass graves and posting photographs on social media. It's part of an ongoing scheme to turn West African countries against the French and to get them to embrace the Russians. Unfortunately the Africans are falling for it.' He shrugged. 'What they're doing is blatant but nobody seems to care. The first Wagner Group soldiers moved in just before Christmas 2021, paid for in part by the Mali military government, in cash and in natural resources, predominantly gold. They have surprised even their government paymasters with their viciousness. In the first quarter of 2022 more civilians were killed than in the whole of 2021. In March they were responsible for a five-day siege in Moura, in the middle of the country. They were fighting alongside the army – the Forces Armées Maliennes – and together they rounded up and killed more than three hundred civilians. The worst atrocity since the conflict began.' He shrugged. 'The government describes it differently, of course. They say that all those who died were jihadist militants. But that's a lie. Almost all the victims were civilians. Russia blocked a proposed UN Security Council request for an independent investigation into the killings. No surprises there. Anyway, it's going to get worse once all the European peacekeepers have pulled out.' He grimaced again. 'It's going to end badly.' He went over to a fridge and took out half a dozen bottles of water which he placed on the table. He unscrewed the top off one and drank. It was displacement behaviour, Shepherd realised, a way of distracting himself from bad news, but he thanked him and took a bottle.

Fischer forced a smile. 'Yes, I think the Wagner people will be on the trail of the jihadists. But it'll be a hunt and kill mission. I think they will have zero interest in freeing the hostages. The opposite in fact. I know that's not what you want to hear, but there is no point in giving you intel that is anything less than truthful.'

Shepherd held up a hand. 'Stefan, I appreciate your honesty. You're right, we need accurate intel and you've come through on the score. Thank you.'

Fischer nodded but still looked uncomfortable.

'So what can you do for us now?' asked Shepherd.

'Personnel-wise, not much, I'm afraid,' said Fischer. 'And drone-wise . . .' He grimaced. 'We've been grounded, for the foreseeable future.'

'Say what now?'

'The order came through while you were still in the air. No drone flights until further notice.'

'Whose order?'

'The Mali military. Speaking for the junta, of course.'

'This is because the Wagner Group are involved?'

Fischer nodded. 'No doubt. I can let you have this footage, and I can give you the coordinates, but I won't be able to get you any fresh drone footage.'

'You've given us more than enough,' said Shepherd. 'We'll take it from here.'

Fischer went over to his desk and picked up a small grey thumb drive and two rolled-up maps. He gave the thumb drive to Shepherd, then unrolled the maps on the table. One was a regular map, the other was a satellite image of the area. The regular map had the area where the Chinook was attacked circled in red, with a red line showing where the jihadists had gone, up to the point where the drone had turned back. The satellite image was concentrated on the site of the attack and the route taken by the jihadists. Fischer tapped the satellite image and ran his finger along the highway up to the point where the jihadists had turned off the road. 'They had already turned off the highway by the time our drone turned back,' he said. 'That suggests to me that they were nearing their destination.'

Shepherd nodded as he studied the map. That made sense. There were no towns or villages out there, just small settlements and farms. The haystack was definitely getting smaller.

• • •

Fischer drove the SAS team back to the Hercules. The pallets and quad bikes had been taken off the plane and loaded on to a truck. As Shepherd climbed out of the Land

Cruiser, Kruge waved at him. 'The guy over there is waiting for you,' said the loadmaster, gesturing at a large white Ridgback 4x4 with 'UN' on the doors and roof, which was parked in front of the truck. Shepherd had come across the Ridgback in Afghanistan. It was a PPV – a protected patrol vehicle. He'd seen them mounted with general purpose machine guns and heavy machine guns, but this was the troop-carrying variant, which could carry a dozen men in the back. It was a brute of a vehicle, with mine-resistant armour, that could run at fifty-five miles per hour on flat tyres.

As Shepherd and Standing headed towards the Ridgback, the driver climbed out of the cabin. He was a big guy with a shaved head wearing desert fatigues with sergeant stripes on the arms. 'I'm looking for Sergeant Standing,' he said in a broad Newcastle accent.

'You've found him,' said Standing.

'I'm to take your group to Major Jones. How many of you are there?'

'Just six,' said Standing. Joe and Jack Ellis came up behind him, followed by Ireland and Lane.

'Your guys can ride in the back,' said the sergeant, pointing at the rear door. 'You can ride up front with me.'

Standing looked over at Shepherd, who nodded. 'Sure, go ahead.'

The sergeant took that as a sign that Shepherd was an officer and he stiffened to attention and threw him a salute. 'Sorry, sir,' he said.

'That's all right sergeant, I'm just a consultant on this one. No salute necessary.'

The sergeant lowered his arm, then hurried around to open the armoured car's rear door. Shepherd climbed in and Lane, the Ellis boys and Ireland followed him. They sat down but didn't bother with the seat belts. The sergeant shut the door and got into the driver's seat. Standing sat next to him. The engine roared and they headed off. The truck followed them. Shepherd shoved the maps and the thumb drive into his backpack.

The aircon was on full blast but it was still swelteringly hot in the metal box, and by the time the Ridgback came to a halt the men were bathed in sweat. Lane opened the rear door and they stepped out into the blistering sun. They were parked in front of a shipping container, one of more than a dozen lined up next to each other. There were various UN vehicles parked in front of the containers, all with union flags on the doors.

'You said you had a sat phone for me?' Shepherd asked Standing.

'Sure do,' said Standing. He shrugged off his backpack, took out a sat phone and gave it to him. 'Someone you need to talk to?'

Shepherd nodded.

'About reducing the size of the haystack?'

Shepherd grinned. 'Exactly.' He looked over at the sergeant. 'I just need a couple of minutes.'

'No problem, sir.'

Shepherd walked away from the group and dialled a number from memory. It was a Breitling monitoring centre in Grenchen, Switzerland. It was the main centre for tracking emergency watches that had been activated. Shepherd gave the operator Liam's name, date of birth, his passport number and the registration number of the watch. After a few minutes the operator was able to confirm that the watch had been activated six hours earlier.

'Who did you inform?' asked Shepherd.

'Air traffic control at Gao Airport.'

'And did they say what they would do?'

'Just that they would take the appropriate action.'

'Which would be what?'

'Initially to ask all aircraft in the area to check transmissions on the 121.5 MHz frequency, and to send out search and rescue teams.'

'Are you aware of the situation in Mali?'

'In what way?'

'There's a military junta in power and UN peacekeeping forces trying to keep the lid on various jihadist terrorist groups. Did air traffic control actually say they would send out a search and rescue team?'

'It wasn't me who made the call, sir. But in the event of one of our watches being activated, we notify the nearest ATC and they take the appropriate action.'

Shepherd gritted his teeth. He knew there was no point in getting angry at the operator, he was just doing his job. 'Can you give me the coordinates of the watch?'

'Of course. Do you have a pen?'

'That's okay, I don't need a pen.'

The operator read out the latitude and longitude. Shepherd's trick memory came into play – once heard, he would never forget the numbers. He thanked the operator, ended the call and went back to the group. 'Sorry about that, sergeant,' he said.

'No problem, sir,' said the sergeant. He was standing next to the door of the container. There was a regimental crest on the door, and under it the name of the occupant: Major Jeremy Jones. The sergeant opened the door and cold air billowed out.

Shepherd and the team followed him inside. There was a metal desk at the far end of the container and half a dozen chairs lined up against one of the walls. There was a large noticeboard on the wall facing the door, covered with typed sheets of paper of various colours, and next to it a large map of Mali dotted with different coloured pins.

The Major was sitting at his desk and he stood up as the men filed in. He was young for his rank, probably early thirties, with ginger hair and freckles over his forearms. He was wearing square-framed spectacles and he looked over the top of them as Shepherd and Standing walked up to his desk. 'Dan Shepherd?' he said.

Shepherd nodded.

'And you're Sergeant Standing? You come highly recommended, Sergeant.'

'Thank you, sir.'

The Major looked at Shepherd. ''I'm sorry about what's happened to your son, Mr Shepherd. I can't imagine how you're feeling at the moment.'

The SAS team filed in. If the Major was surprised that they had all crowded into his container he didn't show it. Shepherd figured that the Major knew the SAS operated by their own rules. He waved for them to sit and dropped down on to his own chair. The men grabbed the chairs and arranged them so that they were facing the Major before sitting down.

'Is there any news?' asked Shepherd.

'Nothing has changed since last night, I'm sorry.'

'I gather you sent your men out yesterday? After the UN peacekeepers turned tail.'

'As soon as I heard what had happened I sent out a team from the Long Range Reconnaissance Group, but the jihadists were long gone by the time they got there. We recovered the casualty.'

'The gunner?'

The Major nodded. 'Corporal Gerry Fowler. We're flying his body back to the UK today. In fact it'll be on the Herc that you flew in on.'

'And your guys didn't go after them?'

'They wouldn't know where to go, it was enough of a risk to go to the crash site. Their orders were to pick up any survivors and come back here.'

'Which is what the bloody peacekeepers should have done,' said Standing. 'If they'd stood their ground, they could have brought all the crew back with them.'

Shepherd flashed Standing a warning look. There was no point in crying over spilled milk, plus he'd rather the Major didn't know that the Germans had been giving them intel. 'How much assistance can you offer us, Major Jones?' he asked.

'I'm to offer you every facility, but you understand how it works out here?'

'You're peacekeepers, first and foremost?'

'Exactly,' said the Major. 'It was made very clear to us before we got here that this is not a combat operation, nor is it a counter-terrorism operation,' said the Major. 'We were given the old UN doublespeak, that peacekeepers protect civilian populations, support political dialogue and reconciliation and promote and protect human rights. Oh, and as an afterthought, we were to prevent and reduce conflict.' The Major smiled ruefully. 'I can't remember his exact words, but I remember some UN official parroting that it was in all of our interests to work together to protect civilians and help build a safer, healthier and more prosperous future for the people of the region. I'm quite proud of the fact that all my men managed to keep a straight face.'

'So no combat at all?' said Shepherd. 'That's fighting with both hands tied behind your back, isn't it?'

'We are to avoid opening fire on enemy combatants, unless they fire first. And we are to use equal retaliation force. So if a group of jihadists open fire on one of our convoys – which they do on a regular basis – we can return fire. But once they stop firing, we must do the same. And we cannot call in air firepower. It would be the easiest thing in the world to call up a Chinook to blow them to kingdom come, but we are forbidden from doing that. We have a Long Range Reconnaissance Group that gathers intelligence and engages with the locals, and we can fly non-weaponised drones to gather intel. But that's about it. And then of course the Russians arrived and it all turned to shit.'

'How bad is it?' asked Shepherd.

'The Russians have been carrying out atrocities as bad as or even worse than the ones the jihadists commit, but we are expressly forbidden from engaging with them. You've probably heard that the Europeans are all pulling out. The French have gone, and the Germans and us won't be far behind them. The likes of Bangladesh, Chad, Egypt and Senegal will probably stay, but frankly they're as much use as a chocolate teapot. The Ivory Coast have already said they're pulling their men out. No one wants to get into a fight with the Russians.'

'So where does that leave us?' said Shepherd.

The Major smiled. 'Well from what I've seen of you guys, you're pretty much a law unto yourselves.'

'But what can you offer us in the way of assistance?'

'Mr Shepherd, if it was up to me, I'd give you whatever you

want. But we're here under the UN umbrella so we have to follow their protocols.' Shepherd opened his mouth to speak but the Major held up his hand to silence him. 'Having said that, there is a reason that the lieutenant colonel wanted me to brief you.'

'Plausible deniability?'

'Exactly. Don't ask, don't tell. So far as the lieutenant colonel is concerned, I am briefing you on the importance of following UN protocols while you are in Mali.'

'Sounds like he's getting ready to throw you under the bus,' scowled Standing.

The Major's eyebrows shot up. He clearly wasn't used to being spoken to like that by a sergeant, but he flashed Standing a tight smile. 'He's protecting himself, that's all. As I'm doing. I am telling you officially and on the record that you must follow the UN protocols while you are here, and that means no combat. On the record I can offer you logistics assistance and any intel we have. But that is all. Off the record, you need to do what you need to do and I have no intention of standing in your way.' He grinned at Standing. 'No pun intended. Look, we have three Chinooks here, and one is undergoing maintenance. When the crew of the third Chinook heard that the other had been shot down, they were begging to be allowed to fly out there to help. I had to tell them to stand down. The only thing that placated them was me telling them that a team would be flying out from Hereford. They know that you boys will do whatever is necessary to get their colleagues back. So, they'll be wanting to fly you wherever you want to go, and that's fine by me. So far as combat goes, the UN protocol is that they are not to fire on enemy combatants unless they are fired upon first.' He leaned towards them and lowered his voice. 'But once you are out there in the desert, that's up to you and the guys in the Chinook,' he said. 'No one is going to be second-guessing you. If you say you came under fire . . .' He shrugged. 'Well, you'd be defending yourself and that does fall within the UN protocols.'

Shepherd nodded. 'Fair enough,' he said. 'Thank you.'

'So what do you need from me?'

'You have surveillance drones?'

'We do, but there's a no-fly order on the drones, courtesy of the junta.'

'But that doesn't apply to the Chinook?'

'They need the Chinook for the jobs that they can't do. They have some smaller helis, but nothing like the Chinook.' He grinned. 'But as far as they're concerned, both our remaining Chinooks are undergoing maintenance and are unavailable for UN use at the moment.'

'Thanks for that,' said Shepherd. 'So we'll need the Chinook to get us out there. But other than that, I think we're good to go.' He looked across at Standing. 'And I think we've got all the hardware we need, right?'

'We'll need to fully charge the quad bikes,' said Standing. 'I didn't have time to do that before we left.'

'You brought quad bikes with you?' said the Major.

Standing nodded. 'We use them a lot in Syria and Afghanistan. They're perfect for terrain like this. We'll need five power points. And you can never have enough ammunition, of course.'

'Sergeant Needham has set you up with a couple of containers, and they all have power sockets,' said the Major. He looked over at the sergeant. 'Am I right, sergeant?'

'Yes, sir. All the sockets they need. And I'll grab some extension cables.'

'Excellent.' The Major looked back at Standing. 'What weapons do you have?'

'Glocks,' said Standing. 'Heckler & Koch 417 assault rifles. And we've an M16 with the M203 grenade launcher attached.' He grinned over at Shepherd. 'Paddy insisted.'

'I'll inform the quartermaster that you are to take whatever you want,' said the Major. 'What about comms?'

'We brought our own,' said Standing.

'Sounds like you're good to go.'

'We're getting there,' said Shepherd.

'Sergeant Needham can take you to your quarters, and he'll link you up with the Chinook crew.'

'Do you need any updates from us?' asked Shepherd.

'Providing you follow UN protocols, I don't think that's necessary, do you?'

'Don't ask, don't tell?'

'Exactly.'

The sergeant opened the door. Shepherd and Standing led the way out. 'I notice you didn't tell the Galloping Major that the Wagner Group are out there,' said Standing once they were outside. 'I'm guessing he'd have been singing from a different hymn sheet if he'd known.'

Shepherd grinned. 'Don't ask, don't tell.'

. . .

L iam looked over at Mobile. He couldn't see the man's chest moving. 'Mobile!' he hissed. 'Mobile!'

'I think he's gone, Liam,' said Smithy quietly.

'Shit,' said Liam. He was fairly sure that Smithy was right.

The cell had been in darkness throughout the night, but dawn was breaking now and he could see that Mobile's eyes were closed and there was dried saliva down the side of his face.

'The bastards should have got a doctor for him,' said Smithy. 'This is against the Geneva Convention and everything.'

'These people don't follow the Geneva Convention,' said Liam. 'They don't follow any rules. If they did, we wouldn't be chained by the neck like this.'

· 'I swear to God, Liam, the first chance I get I'm killing these fuckers.'

'You and me both, Smithy.'

Liam stood up and reached for the bar across the window above his head.

'What are you doing?' asked Smithy.

'It's light outside. I need to pull the watch back in or they might see it.'

'But you said it might not work inside?'

'It should work, just not as well.' He began pulling at the wire. 'We can't take the risk of them seeing it. If they know we've activated a transmitter, they'll move us for sure. Then it'll all have been a waste of time. The battery should be good for forty-eight hours so we can put it out again tonight.'

They both jumped as they heard footsteps outside the door. Liam cursed under his breath and quickly pulled up the watch. He thrust it into one of the pockets of his flight suit and tried to untie the antenna from the bar. The knot had tightened during the night and he struggled to loosen it.

'Come on, come on,' whispered Smith anxiously. He looked over at the door. The bolt rattled back.

Liam managed to get his fingernail into the knot and loosen it. He pulled at the wire and it came away from the bar.

The door began to open. Liam pulled the antenna, turned to face the door and slid down the wall. He shoved the antenna into his pocket as the door opened. It was Youssouf. Liam's heart was pounding as if it wanted to burst out of his chest, but he took a breath, smiled, and wished Youssouf a good morning in French.

Behind Youssouf was another jihadist, a tall, thin man with a waist-length beard wearing a long grey robe and cradling an AK-47. He stepped around Youssouf and pointed the weapon at Liam.

'*Se lever,*' said Youssouf. Stand up.

'*Qu'est-ce qui ne va pas?*' said Liam. What's wrong?

'Just do as you're told.' He gestured at Smithy and Mobile. 'And tell your friends to stand up.'

'You don't have to do this, Youssouf,' said Liam, his voice trembling.

The man with the AK-47 pointed it at Liam. His finger was on the trigger. Liam got to his feet. 'He wants you to stand up,' he said to Smithy. Smithy did as he was told.

Youssouf went over to Mobile and kicked him savagely in the ribs. When Mobile didn't react he kicked him harder, then bent down and examined his face.

'Is he dead?' asked Liam.

Youssouf straightened up and spoke to the jihadist with the gun who grunted, nodded, and left the room. He hadn't spoken in French so Liam didn't know what had been said.

'You fucking bastards!' shouted Smithy. He took a step towards Youssouf, his hands bunched into fists, but the chain held him back. 'When I get out of here, you're dead!'

'Leave it, Smithy,' said Liam.

'Mobile's dead and they didn't do a bloody thing about it!'

'Screaming at him isn't going to bring Mobile back. We need to keep it together.'

'They're going to kill us, Liam!'

'If they were going to kill us, we'd be dead already,' said Liam.

Youssouf reached into his tunic and took out a phone. It was a brand new iPhone, Liam realised. The last thing he'd expect to see in the hands of a jihadist in the desert. 'I need your picture,' he said. 'To show you are safe.'

Liam stared sullenly at the phone as Youssouf took several pictures. Youssouf turned the phone towards Smithy. 'Why don't you make it a video so I can tell you to go fuck yourself,' said Smithy.

'Smithy, chill,' said Liam.

Smithy glared at Youssouf as he took several pictures.

Two men came in through the door. They were teenagers wearing tunics, baggy pants and white kufi caps. The jihadist with the AK-47 came back with them and stood in the corner, his gun again pointing at Liam. Youssouf gave one of the boys a key and he used it to unlock the padlock that kept the chain around Mobile's neck. Then the two of them grabbed a leg each and started pulling the body to the door. Smithy pointed at them and began screaming abuse. 'Pick him up you bastards, don't drag him like that. What are you, animals?'

Liam explained to Youssouf what Smithy was saying and Youssouf barked at the young men. One of them lifted Mobile's arms while the other grabbed his ankles, and they carried him out.

'What is wrong with these people?' said Smithy, shaking his head.

Youssouf undid the padlock that kept the chain fastened to

the wall, and he gathered it up. 'I am sorry about your friend,' he said to Liam. 'We will bury him now.'

'Can't you send the body to the UN base?' asked Liam. 'They will return the body to England and he can be buried there.'

Youssouf frowned. 'We bury our dead within twenty-four hours.'

'Yes, I know. But he has parents. A mother and father. And a brother. They would want to bury him in England.'

Youssouf stared at him for several seconds and then slowly nodded. 'I will see what can be done,' he said.

Another young man appeared in the doorway, this one holding a tray on which were three bottles of water and three clay plates of food. Youssouf gave one of the plates and a bottle of water to Liam. There was a rice pancake and a piece of fish on the plate. Liam thanked him.

Youssouf picked up the other plate and offered it to Smithy but Smithy just folded his arms and glared at him. Youssouf put the plate on the floor within his reach, along with a bottle of water.

'Please, Smithy, just thank him,' said Liam. 'He doesn't have to feed us. He could let us starve.'

'Fuck him,' said Smithy.

Youssouf looked at the remaining plate, then picked it up along with the last bottle of water and put them on the floor close to Liam. 'I am sorry about your friend,' he said.

'Thank you.'

Youssouf left the room followed by the jihadist with the gun. He closed the door and bolted it. Smithy sat down and glared at Liam. 'What is he now, your new best friend?'

'Don't be ridiculous,' said Liam. 'It's not about being his

friend, it's about getting him to treat us as human beings. He's going to be asking the British government to pay a ransom and we both know that they won't. The moment that he realises they're not going to pay he's going to have to decide what he's going to do with us and if he thinks of us as people he's less likely to . . .' He grimaced. 'You know what I mean, Smithy.'

'He's going to kill us anyway, Liam. You know it as well as I do.'

Liam picked up one of the bottles of water and sat down with his back to the wall. 'My dad told me about his time on Selection. One of the things they do is interrogate them for a couple of days. They get put in stress positions, they get shouted at and treated really badly. Dad said the way to survive it was to become what they call a grey man. You just shut down. You show no emotion and offer no resistance.'

'Yeah, but they know it's just a test,' said Smithy. 'This is the real thing.'

'The principle is the same,' said Liam. 'We mustn't provoke them. In fact, it's the opposite. We have to build bridges with them. Dad was only allowed to tell them his name, rank, serial number and date of birth. We have to tell them more than that. They have to know that we have families, that we have a life to go back to.'

'You think that will stop them killing us?' Smithy sneered, shaking his head.

'Maybe, maybe not,' said Liam. 'But if we provoke them and make them hate us, they're not going to care, are they? If we've shared personal information with them, if they know who we are, then it's more likely they'll give us a break.' He picked up the plate. 'They're feeding us. They wouldn't be wasting food on us if they were planning on killing us. I just want to keep it that way.'

Smithy leaned over and grabbed his plate. 'You're right,' he said. 'It just sticks in my throat being nice to them when they've got us chained up like dogs.'

Liam drank some of his water. 'My dad's on the way,' said Liam. 'I can feel it.'

'I hope you're right.'

Liam smiled. 'Don't worry,' he said. 'I know my dad.'

. . .

The sergeant brought the Ridgback to a halt in front of a white-painted container with a union flag painted on the door, next to a crest of the Royal Anglian Regiment. 'The Major says you can use this for as long as you're here,' said the sergeant. 'There are bunks and a rec area in the container next door.'

The truck with their equipment pulled up behind them.

'We won't be here long enough for a kip,' said Standing as they piled out. 'What about the quartermaster?'

The sergeant pointed ahead. 'Down there, turn left at the Queen's Head and it's on the right.'

'The Queen's Head?' repeated Shepherd.

The sergeant grinned. 'It's just a container filled with cans of beer, but it's the social hub of the camp. They do barbecues at the weekend, if you're still here.' He pointed at the truck. 'Do you need help unloading your gear?'

'We'll be fine,' said Shepherd. 'Can you ask the Chinook crew to pop over?'

'Speak of the devil,' said the sergeant, pointing at four young men in green flight suits heading their way. 'I'll leave you to it.' He gestured at the driver of the truck, who had lit a cigarette and was blowing smoke through an open window. 'The driver there is Corporal Sean Moody, the Major says he's to keep himself available until you leave.'

'Thank you, Sergeant.'

'Good luck, sir. I hope it works out for you.' The sergeant climbed into the Ridgback and drove away as the four airmen walked over. The one on the left was the oldest and he was probably in his mid-twenties. 'Mr Shepherd?' he said. He was looking between Shepherd and Lane, clearly figuring that one of the oldest members of the group would be Liam's father.

'That's me,' he said.

'Peter Chambers,' said the man. 'We're so sorry about what's happened. Anything you need, we're here for you.'

'Thanks guys.'

Chambers introduced the three other airmen. The co-pilot was Simon Farrant, the crew chief was John Topey and the gunner was Richard Haines. Shepherd could see the look of concern on all their faces. They had all worked closely with the men in the downed helicopter and knew it could just as easily have been their heli that was shot down.

'I'm sorry to hear about the gunner who died,' said Shepherd. 'I gather he's being flown back to the UK later today.'

Chambers nodded. 'I know the family so I called his parents this morning. They'll be at the airport to collect him. It's madness. We're supposed to be peacekeepers, we're here trying to help, and they set up an ambush like that.'

'Yeah, well we'll be teaching them a lesson, don't you worry about that,' said Standing.

The Ellis twins nodded in agreement. 'Damn right,' said Joe.

'Our Chinook is fuelled up and ready to go,' said Chambers. 'Just say the word.'

'That's great, Peter, thank you. Come inside and I'll show you where we're headed.'

The airmen headed into the container and Shepherd and Standing followed them.

Shepherd took the two maps from his backpack and unrolled them. Standing used bottles of water to keep them flat. The four airmen peered at the maps.

Shepherd pointed at the crash site on the satellite map. 'This is where the Chinook went down,' he said. He ran his finger along the highway. 'The jihadists drove this way with our guys. And turned off here.' He tapped near the village of Dana. 'They left the road here and headed east.'

Chambers nodded. 'Yeah, there's a lot of jihadist activity out that way. So is that where they're holding our guys?'

'That's where the drone lost contact. But I've got a grid reference that I think is their location.' He read out the numbers and Chambers switched his attention to the general reference map. He ran his finger to the right of Dana, then switched his attention to the satellite map. He stabbed his finger at a group of half a dozen buildings, surrounded by a low wall. Chambers looked over at Shepherd. 'Where did you get the coordinates from?' he asked, then he grinned. 'That watch of Liam's, right?'

Shepherd nodded. 'It was activated last night.'

'We used to tease him about that thing,' said Chambers. 'If there was ever going to be a search and rescue operation we'd be the ones doing it. You bought it for him, didn't you?'

'For his last birthday, yes.'

'Brilliant,' said Chambers. 'The beacons run for up to forty-eight hours, so once we're in the air we should be able to track his signal on our radio. It should take us straight to him.'

'It's a bit more complicated than that,' said Shepherd. 'The Wagner Group are active in the area and they were at the crash site. They were last seen heading after the jihadists.'

Chambers nodded thoughtfully. 'That makes things . . . awkward.'

'I'd say so,' said Shepherd. 'The Wagner Group are hunting down jihadists and killing them. The danger is that Liam and the guys get caught in the crossfire.'

'Which means we need to get over there now,' said Chambers. His three colleagues nodded enthusiastically.

'Hell, yeah,' said Farrant.

Shepherd held up his hand. 'We can't go charging in, we need a game plan.' He pointed at the satellite map. 'The terrain around their compound is flat, they'd see the helicopter coming from miles away.'

'Okay, yes,' said Chambers. He stared down at the map. 'During the day you can hear us from five to six miles away,' he said. 'Bit further at night.'

'What if you come in low?'

Chambers shrugged. 'If the wind is in the right direction, three miles maybe.'

Shepherd leaned over the satellite map, then back at the general reference map. 'There's a plateau six miles behind the compound.' Chambers moved to stand next to him. He stared at the map for several seconds, then went to look at the same area on the satellite map. 'Okay, we can fly up to Dana, head further north and then circle around behind the plateau. We could wait there while you do what you have to do. But then you'd have to cross six miles of desert.'

'Piece of cake,' said Jack Ellis.

'We've got quad bikes,' said his brother.

'They'd hear you coming,' said Chambers.

'Our quads are electric,' said Standing. 'We wouldn't be heard beyond a few hundred metres.'

'Night-time would be best,' said Ireland.

'Agreed, but I'm reluctant to wait that long,' said Shepherd. 'If it was just the jihadists, maybe, but not with Wagner Group in the area.'

'What about a HALO in?' asked Lane. 'We've got the chutes.' The SAS had perfected high-altitude low-opening skydiving, which allowed them to avoid radar and being spotted by enemy personnel on the ground.

'The Chinook's ceiling is what, twenty thousand feet?' said Ireland. 'That's four miles. More than enough for a half-decent HALO drop.'

'The drop is fine but we'd be sitting ducks once the chutes opened,' said Standing. 'There's not a cloud in the sky.'

'I'm for using the quads,' said Ireland. 'Is there any way we can wait for nightfall?'

'If we knew for a fact that the Wagner Group weren't in the area, we could hold off,' said Shepherd. 'But the UN people have been told not to fly drones in the area so we've no intel on what they're up to.'

'But we could set up an OP on the plateau,' said Ireland. 'Keep eyes on the location and wait. If we see Wagner activity we go in guns blazing. If they stay away, we move in at night.'

Shepherd nodded. 'That makes sense.'

The rest of the team nodded. 'Works for me,' said Lane.

'What about you, Peter?' Shepherd asked. 'Can you get us there without us being seen?'

'No problem getting there, but we can't sit on the ground waiting for you. Not with jihadists and the Wagner Group in the area. We'll have to drop you and go.' He looked over at Farrant and the co-pilot nodded in agreement.

'Is there anywhere close by you could wait?' asked Standing.

'I'm afraid not,' said the pilot. 'Wherever we land, all it needs is one jihadist pick-up truck with a machine gun and it's thank you and good night. We'll drop you but then we'd have to come back here. If you were planning on a quick in and out, we'd hang around, but you're talking about an open-ended OP. If you do wait for nightfall, we'll be on the ground for eight hours or so, and that's not a risk we can take.'

'Understood,' said Shepherd. 'So you drop us behind the plateau and fly back here. Penny can liaise on frequencies so if we're ready for a pick-up we'll call you.'

Lane nodded. 'No problem.'

Shepherd looked around the table. 'So are we all good?' Before every SAS mission every member of the team, no matter their rank or seniority, was given the chance to make suggestions and express reservations. Known as a Chinese Parliament, it meant that everyone played their part. It was a stark contrast to the way the regular army operated, where officers took decisions and their men followed orders.

'I worry about the quads,' said Standing. 'It's a long way back. And electric is all well and good, but it's not like we can carry spare fuel.'

'They've got a range of just over a hundred kilometres,' said Joe Ellis.

'That's theoretical,' said Standing. He looked at the general map. 'We're looking at close to ninety kilometres. That's cutting it fine. I'd hate to run out of power ten kilometres away. And that's not smooth terrain. The range figures are based on roads, right?'

'I'll make sure they're fully charged while we're getting the gear ready,' said Joe.

'Okay. But we've got five quads and we'll be bringing back three hostages. That means most of the quads will be two up.'

'I think it'll be okay,' said Joe.

Shepherd nodded and looked over at Chambers. 'We'll stay in contact. If we need a pick up, you'll be what, fifteen minutes away?'

'Fifteen or twenty.'

Shepherd looked over at Standing. 'I have to say I'd prefer a ride on the Chinook to driving a quad ninety kilometres in the dark,' said Shepherd.

'If we take out the jihadists, we can use their transport,' said Jack Ellis. 'Two pick-up trucks would do it. Might even get one with a machine gun.'

'Yeah, we can keep our options open,' said Shepherd.

'And a lot depends on the condition of the hostages and whether we have any casualties,' said Standing. 'We don't want to be driving long distances with wounded.'

'Don't jinx it, Sarge,' said Lane.

'Just putting the options out there,' said Standing. 'I'm as keen as anyone to do this, but if it kicks off we're a long way from home.'

'If we're needed, we'll be there,' said Chambers.

'Let's take it one step at a time,' said Shepherd. 'Have you guys come across the Wagner Group?'

'We see them around from time to time, but there's never

been an issue,' said Chambers. 'They know that we're not allowed to interact with them.'

'Hopefully it'll stay that way,' said Shepherd. 'I just wanted you to be aware that it might be a problem. The ones that you've seen, what equipment do they have?'

'They run around in their Wagner Wagons,' said Farrant. 'But we've seen them with utility trucks and Tigrs.'

Shepherd nodded. The Tigr was the Russian equivalent of the Humvee, a multipurpose 4x4 wheeled vehicle, nineteen feet long and weighing more than seven tons. Like the Humvee it could be used as a runaround or adapted to carry various types of machine guns.

'Any ground-to-air capacity?' asked Shepherd.

'Not that we've seen,' said Farrant. 'The thing is, they don't need to pick a fight with us, they know we're on the way out.'

Shepherd looked at his watch. 'Joe, how long will it take to fully charge the quads?'

'They were all more than seventy five per cent charged when I picked them up from Stirling Lines. An hour's top-up should do it. Two hours at most.'

'Let's say two hours,' said Shepherd. 'Better to be on the safe side. Jack, can you and Paddy visit the quartermaster and collect what ammo we'll need? Let's not go crazy – the more weight on the quads the more we'll drain their batteries.' He looked over at Chambers. 'Can you be ready for take-off in two hours?'

'We're ready now,' said Chambers. 'Once you start loading your gear we'll start the preflight checks. How many men?'

'Just us,' said Standing. 'Six in all.'

'The dirty half-dozen,' said Topey with a sly grin.

· · ·

S hafiq Ali Rafiq arrived at Leeds-Bradford Airport just before midday. The Gulfstream jet taxied to the general aviation terminal and parked. The door stayed closed until two Border Force officers dressed all in black with their trousers tucked into their boots came on board. The officers checked the passports of everybody, even though Rafiq was the only one staying in the country. The older of the two Homeland Security agents, Bill, had Rafiq's passport and he handed it to one of the Border Force officers. She flicked through the pages, compared the photograph to the man, then handed it back to Bill. He shook his head. 'He's yours now,' he said.

The younger Homeland Security agent produced a clipboard and a pen. 'If you could sign this, please,' he said.

The Border Officer frowned. 'Sign what?'

'It's just protocol to say that he is now in your jurisdiction.'

'I can't sign that. I just check passports.'

'Well someone has to sign this or he's coming back with us.'

Harry Hamad got out of his seat and smiled at the two Border Force officers. 'If I may, the people who will be taking Mr Rafiq into custody will be outside. Is it okay for them to come on board? They can collect Mr Rafiq and sign any paperwork.'

'They're not allowed on the plane,' said the male officer. He looked over at his older colleague and she nodded in agreement.

Hamad looked over at Bill. 'Can we sign the paperwork outside, Bill? Does that work for you?'

'He can't leave the plane until the form has been signed,' growled Bill, looking over the top of his bifocals. 'That's the protocol.'

Hamad's smile tightened a little, but he was well aware of the pitfalls of trying to circumvent American bureaucracy.

'How about we take him to the bottom of the steps? Not on the tarmac, he stays on the steps. They can sign for him when he is still officially on the plane.'

Bill nodded. 'That will work.'

'Let me get that arranged,' said Hamad. He nodded at the two Border Force officers. 'Thank you for your help, officers, and you have a nice day.'

Hamad followed the Border Force officers down the steps. There was an ambulance waiting, along with two West Yorkshire Police armed response vehicles and a Mercedes Sprinter van containing eight uniformed policemen wearing hi-vis jackets.

As the Border Force officers came down the steps, six armed officers fanned out, carbines at the ready. They were wearing Kevlar helmets and vests and had handguns holstered on their thighs. The hi-vis police stood around as if they weren't sure why they were there or what they were supposed to be doing.

Hamad realised that the armed cops had assumed that he was Shafiq Ali Rafiq, so he raised his hands and addressed them in a loud voice. 'Gentlemen, my name is Harry Hamad and I am assisting Mr Rafiq. Could I please speak to your senior officer?'

One of the uniformed cops stepped forward. 'Inspector Hargreaves,' he said, raising a gloved hand.

'Inspector Hargreaves, pleased to meet you. We have a small problem with the handover that I hope you can help resolve. Homeland Security won't hand over Mr Rafiq without someone from your end signing a form to accept delivery. But you're not allowed on the plane. I have suggested that we bring Mr Rafiq down the steps, from where you sign the form and take him into custody.'

'A bit like FedEx,' said the inspector.

'Exactly like FedEx,' said Hamad. 'You don't get the parcel until you sign for it.'

'That's fine,' said the inspector. 'I'm happy to sign on the dotted line.'

There was a middle-aged man in a sharp suit standing by the ambulance, tall with slicked-back greying hair and gold-framed spectacles. Hamad recognised him from several Zoom meetings they had had over the past year. His name was Elliott Atkinson, a partner in a leading London law firm who specialised in terrorism cases. Hamad waved at him, then headed back up the stairs. He reappeared a few seconds later with Rafiq, holding him by the arm as he guided him down the stairs. The younger of the two Homeland Security agents followed them down the steps, holding the clipboard and pen.

Hamad and Rafiq stood on the bottom step while the agent gave the pen and clipboard to the inspector. The inspector read the form slowly and thoroughly, which took several minutes, before signing it and handing it back.

'Trey, would you be so good as to remove his shackles?' asked Hamad.

The agent took out a set of keys and bent down. He unlocked the chains and pulled them away.

'And the cuffs?'

'The cuffs have to stay on,' said Trey. 'Protocol.'

'Then they will need the key,' said Hamad.

Trey shook his head. 'The key stays with me.'

Hamad tried to keep smiling, but it was an effort. 'I understand that, Trey. But you can see the quandary. When Mr Rafiq arrives at Bradford Prison they won't be able to remove the cuffs, will they? Because the key will be thirty thousand feet in the air, heading back to the US.'

Trey frowned as if he had been asked to solve a complicated equation. 'He has to remain cuffed,' he said. 'It's protocol.'

'How about the Brits cuff him now? Would that work?'

Trey thought about it for several seconds and then nodded. 'Sure. Yes.'

Hamad waved at the inspector. 'Would you mind hand-cuffing Mr Rafiq?'

'It would be a pleasure,' said the inspector. He took a set of cuffs from a nylon pouch on his belt and attached them. Once they were on, Trey removed the American handcuffs.

'There we are,' said Hamad. 'Now everyone is happy.' He held Shafiq Ali Rafiq by the shoulders and kissed him on both cheeks. '*Hafidaka Allah*,' he said. May God protect you.

'Thank you for everything you have done for me,' said Rafiq.

'It has been a pleasure,' said Hamad. 'And I wish you good luck with what is to come.'

As Rafiq stepped on to the tarmac and Hamad went back up the steps with Trey, the solicitor walked over. 'If I could just have a quick word with my client,' he said to the inspector.

'Go ahead,' said the inspector. 'But please keep it short. Most of my guys are on overtime and the clock is ticking.'

The solicitor shook Rafiq by the hand, gave him a business card and explained that he wasn't allowed to travel in the ambulance or enter the prison with him, but that he would visit him the following day.

Rafiq thanked him, then the inspector nodded at his men who surrounded Rafiq and took him to the waiting ambulance.

• • •

The Chinook lifted off and turned to the right as it climbed into the air. Shepherd was wearing desert-pattern fatigues and a Kevlar helmet and cradling his HK 417. He had a Glock strapped to his right thigh. Sitting to his right was Paddy Ireland. Ireland was wearing similar fatigues but he was holding an M16 with the M203 grenade launcher attached and had three nylon pouches containing the high-explosive dual-purpose grenades on his belt. The HEDP grenades had shaped charges that allowed them to penetrate armour up to two and a half inches thick. The launcher could send them as far as 400 metres and they were capable of causing casualties within a 130-metre radius, with a guaranteed kill radius of five metres.

Standing was to Shepherd's left. He winked at Spider. 'Okay?' he said, patting Shepherd on the leg.

Shepherd nodded. 'All good,' he said. They had earpieces connected to radio sets clipped to their belts so they could hear each other over the roar of the massive turbines.

Running down the middle of the cargo hold were the five quad bikes they would be using to cross the desert.

The Ellis twins were sitting opposite Shepherd. Andy Lane had strapped himself into a seat next to John Topey, the crew chief.

The side door was opened and Richard Haines, the gunner, had positioned his 7.62mm M60D machine gun to get a clear view of the desert below.

'We'll get your boy back, Spider,' said Standing.

Shepherd forced a smile. He appreciated Standing's words of comfort, but they had no way of knowing if Liam was alive or not and he had a cold feeling of dread in the pit of his stomach.

The Chinook continued to climb until the desert below

became a flat brown nothingness. Shepherd turned around in his seat and squinted through a window. The river was at his back, twisting its way through the desert, its life-giving water producing a swathe of vegetation that cut north and south.

The Chinook levelled off at 10,000 feet. Generally pilots needed oxygen when they flew above 12,500 feet for more than thirty minutes, and passengers were usually given it at above 15,000 feet. The Chinook was equipped with oxygen masks and was capable of flying as high as 20,000 feet, but for this mission 10,000 feet worked just fine. The RPG that had taken down Liam's Chinook had been a fluke, and the rockets were ineffective beyond an altitude of 3,000 feet. Intel suggested that, so far at least, surface-to-air missiles had not been used in the conflict.

Lane was talking to the crew chief, Topey, listening and then nodding. Then he sat back and looked over at Shepherd.

'Spider, according to the pilot we're about forty miles from the coordinates where the watch was activated,' said Lane.

Shepherd nodded. 'Okay.'

'The bad news is that he's not picking up any signal on the aviation distress frequency.'

Shepherd nodded again. The watch's transmitter was powerful enough to be picked up by a plane at up to a hundred miles away. The fact that the pilot wasn't getting a signal meant that the watch was either now out of range or it had stopped transmitting.

'He's going to continue monitoring the frequency and he'll let us know if he gets a hit.'

'Cheers, Penny,' said Shepherd. He folded his arms and stared down at his feet. There was a chance that whoever was holding Liam prisoner had found the watch and deactivated it. If that had happened, then his captors might have moved him. Shepherd's heart began to pound and he took deep breaths to calm himself down. There was no point in worrying about what might have happened, he'd know soon enough when they were on the ground. He looked out through the doorway where the gunner was continuing to scan the ground below them. All Shepherd could see was the clear blue cloudless sky. He flashed back to the drone footage that Fischer had shown them, the RPG rocket streaking through the air and hitting Liam's helicopter, sending it spiralling to the desert floor. His stomach lurched at the thought of what his son had gone through.

Shepherd had flown in helicopters hundreds of times during his SAS career – they were often the quickest and most efficient way of moving around, especially in conflict zones – but he had never been a fan. It was the lack of control that made him uncomfortable. If anything went wrong, there was nothing he could do to change the outcome – only the pilots could do that. He was just along for the ride.

Lane waved over at Shepherd, snapping him out of his reverie. 'We're about to start our descent, Spider,' said Lane over the radio.

Shepherd flashed him a thumbs up. Within a few seconds the turbines throttled back and the helicopter banked to the left. Shepherd felt pressure building up in his ears and he moved his jaw until they popped. The Chinook continued to bank and descend, then it levelled off and Shepherd saw sand and rocks through the open door. The helicopter slowed and its nose rose into the air as dust whirled around it. The helicopter's wheels touched the ground and the crew chief pressed the button to lower the back ramp. Lane and the Ellis boys unclipped their harnesses and began unclipping the straps that were holding the quad bikes in place.

The gunner was moving his gun from side to side as he scanned the surrounding terrain but there was no opposition to be seen.

Shepherd and Standing got to their feet. They slung their carbines over their shoulders and got to work unfastening one of the quad bikes. It took the men just a few minutes to free the quads and push them down the ramp, then they grabbed their rucksacks and dropped them on to the ground. Ahead of them was a long slope that led to the plateau. The rotors continued to turn slowly above their heads – the pilots wanted to be back in the air as soon as possible.

The moment the last quad bike was out of the Chinook, Topey waved and the ramp began to rise up. The Ellis boys began to pull camouflage netting over the quads, keeping it in place with small rocks.

Standing shaded his eyes with his hands as he looked up the incline. 'I don't see any cover up there,' he said. 'It's going to be hot.'

'It'll give me a chance to work on my tan,' said Ireland, shouldering his rucksack before clasping his M16 to his chest.

Once they were satisfied that the quads were concealed, they picked up their rucksacks and headed up the slope in single file. The ground was a mixture of rocks and sand and they all trod carefully as they worked their way to the top. A sprained ankle would put the whole mission in jeopardy.

The turbines of the Chinook roared and the rotors began to spin, throwing up clouds of choking dust. Shepherd kept his back to the helicopter, closed his eyes and clapped his hand over his mouth. The Chinook lifted off the ground and flew away from the slope, keeping low for several hundred yards before climbing and turning south.

The men waited for the dust cloud to die down before they continued to climb. Shepherd's legs were aching and his chest was burning as he sucked in the hot desert air but he kept going, pushing himself through the pain barrier.

Standing slowed as he neared the summit. He dropped down on to his knees and then began to crawl forward. The rest of the team followed his example until they had all reached the top.

Standing pulled a pair of binoculars from his rucksack and surveyed the terrain ahead of him. Shepherd did the same. The compound was about six miles away, a waist-high stone wall surrounding six stone cottages with flat roofs. There were three pick-up trucks parked in the compound, two of them with machine guns mounted in the back.

'See the guards, second from the left,' said Standing.

Shepherd focused on the cottage that Standing was referring to. There were two men standing on the roof, smoking. Both had AK-47s on their backs. Shepherd gritted his teeth. It was a good sign that the armed men were there – that suggested there was someone to guard. If they had discovered the watch and moved Liam, the guards would probably have gone too. Liam's watch needed to be outside to be most effective, but during daylight hours it could be spotted. Liam had probably activated the watch at night and had hidden it once the sun had risen. 'What's the plan, Matt?'

'We dig in, set up some shade, and we watch. You can see the terrain there, they'd see us coming even if they didn't hear us. As soon as it gets dark, we'll drive over. We'll use the night vision gear, they won't know what's hit them.'

Lane patted Shepherd on the side. 'Pilot wishes us luck and says that there's still nothing on the emergency frequency. He'll keep monitoring it and he'll let us know if anything happens.'

'Thanks, Penny.'

Shepherd handed his binoculars to Lane, who scrutinised the compound. 'Not much in the way of guards,' he said. 'They're clearly not expecting company.'

'Yeah, well they've got a surprise coming,' said Standing.

• • •

The ambulance drove into the prison through a metal gate that rattled open. The two ARVs went with it, followed by the Mercedes van. Prison officers checked under all the vehicles with mirrors on poles before a second metal gate opened and they drove into a courtyard surrounded by walls topped with razor wire.

The armed officers piled out of their SUVs and stationed themselves around the perimeter of the courtyard, carbines at the ready. The uniformed police climbed out of the van and circled the ambulance. The inspector was talking into his radio, updating his bosses on their progress.

The ambulance doors opened and a paramedic climbed out, followed by Shafiq Ali Rafiq. Rafiq looked up at the razor wire and sighed. A second paramedic followed.

Two prison officers came through a door, followed by a young man wearing a brown suit. One of the prison officers was pushing a wheelchair. The man in the suit walked up to Rafiq and smiled. 'Mr Rafiq, I am Deputy Governor Mark Baker and I'm here to explain what's going to happen over the next few days,' he said. He had a soft West Country accent and a nervous tic at the side of his left eye. He gestured at the prison officer who was standing behind the wheelchair. 'This is Mr Hardwicke, who will take you from here to our admissions centre where you will be processed and admitted.' He nodded at the second prison officer. 'This is Mr Evans, who will be accompanying you. You'll then be taken to the Close Supervision Centre. There will have to be armed police guarding you until you are within the centre itself.'

'I am not a risk to anybody,' said Shafiq Ali Rafiq. 'I am old man. And I am dying.'

'Mr Rafiq, I hear you and believe me I am as unhappy as you are at the prospect of having armed police officers in my prison, but the decision had nothing to do with me.'

'And you have to follow orders?'

Baker smiled thinly. 'You have been in the prison system long enough to know that it's all about following orders, Mr Rafiq.' He waved at the wheelchair. 'Would you like to sit down? It's quite a walk and I'm told you are not in the best of health.'

Rafiq nodded and lowered himself on to the wheelchair. 'When can I talk to my solicitor? He was at the airport to meet me but he wasn't allowed to travel here with me.'

'I am sure we can arrange for you to see your solicitor tomorrow.'

'I would prefer it to be today. There is much I need to discuss with him.'

Baker looked at his watch. 'I will see what I can do. But our priority at the moment is to get you processed and decide what your medical requirements are.'

'Thank you.'

'From the reception centre we will move you to the Close Supervision Centre, and you'll be placed in what we call a designated cell.'

Rafiq frowned. 'I understood that I was to be placed in the general population.'

'That might well happen in the future, Mr Rafiq, but my instructions are that you are to go to the Close Supervision Centre.'

'But that means that my activities will be restricted, correct? You are effectively putting me in solitary confinement.'

'Initially yes.'

'But that was not what was agreed. I was told that I was being returned to England so that I could spend time with my family before I die.'

'Mr Rafiq, there are several agencies involved in the transfer, and I am afraid that we all have our own protocols.'

'This is why I need to see my lawyer as soon as possible.'

'And as I said, I will do my best to expedite that.'

'I am dying, Mr Baker,' Rafiq said quietly. 'I don't have much time.'

'The sooner we get you processed, the sooner we can get you what you want,' Baker said. He looked at the prison officer who was standing behind the wheelchair. 'Please take Mr Rafiq to the reception centre, Mr Hardwicke.'

Hardwicke pushed the chair towards a door at the side of the building. Evans went ahead to open the door for them. Three of the armed police moved with them. They seemed relaxed but their eyes were watchful and they kept their carbines at the ready. The rest of the armed police climbed into the ARVs and the uniformed cops filed back into the van. The gate rattled back and the ambulance, ARVs and Sprinter van drove out.

Baker watched them go. 'What a fucking palaver,' he whispered to himself.

Hardwicke pushed the wheelchair through the door and into a corridor with a tiled floor and walls painted a pale blue. At the end of the corridor was a barred gate which Evans unlocked. They went through and turned right to the reception area, with a wall dotted with posters and printed notices, most of them about the dangers of drugs and how to deal with bullying. The armed cops filed in after them, sweeping the area with their carbines as if they expected to be attacked at any moment.

Rafiq was wheeled into a side room where a uniformed officer holding a clipboard gruffly told him to remove his clothing. Rafiq gave him a tight smile and raised his cuffed hands. The officer sighed and looked at Hardwicke. 'If you wouldn't mind, Mr Hardwicke.'

Hardwicke took out his keys and unlocked the handcuffs, then helped Rafiq out of his orange jumpsuit and plastic shoes.

'If you would change into those, please,' said the officer with the clipboard, pointing at a plastic bag on a chair. The bag contained socks, underwear, a grey sweatshirt and long grey tracksuit bottoms.

'When can I wear my own clothes?' Rafiq asked.

'Once you are on enhanced privileges.'

'How long will that take?' He took off his underwear and ripped the plastic bag open. The clothes looked new, which was a relief. He hated the idea of wearing clothes that someone else had worn.

'It depends on how well behaved you are.'

'The doctors say I only have three months to live.'

'You had best behave then, hadn't you?' said the prison

officer. 'Do you want to keep those plastic shoes or do you want a new pair?'

'By new pair do you mean they're new?'

'Newish,' said the prison officer.

'I will keep these until I can have my own shoes brought in,' said Rafiq. He finished dressing. The trousers were loose but they were wearable.

'Suit yourself,' said the prison officer. He held out the clipboard. 'Can you sign for the clothing please?'

Rafiq signed the form.

The prison officer pointed at a boxy wooden seat, white with black trim. 'I will need you to sit there, Mr Rafiq,' he said. 'This is what we call our BOSS chair. Body orifice security scanner. It allows us to make sure that you're not carrying anything you shouldn't be.' He flicked over the signed form and showed him the form underneath it. 'If you could sign here to show that you understand why the scan is necessary.'

'I know what it is and I know what it does,' said Rafiq disdainfully. He had used the BOSS chair hundreds of times in America. He signed the form and handed back the pen.

'It carries no risk to you or to the operators, it is totally safe.'

'Of course it is,' said Rafiq. He turned around and lowered himself on to the machine.

The operator studied the screen and gave him a thumbs up. 'All good, Mr Rafiq. You can get off now.'

Rafiq pushed himself to his feet. For a moment he lost his balance and he fell to the side. Hardwicke moved quickly and held him up. 'Are you okay, Mr Rafiq?'

'I feel weak,' he said.

'Just a few more minutes and we can get you into a cell and

you can lie down,' said Hardwicke. He helped him over to the wheelchair, put the handcuffs back on, then pushed him into a side room. Another officer was there with a digital camera. He took a photograph of Rafiq's face, then sat down at a desk and busied himself at a computer.

Hardwicke pushed the wheelchair down a corridor towards a barred gate which Evans unlocked. The three armed cops followed.

The door opened into a room with a reception desk. There was a man in a white coat at the desk, looking at a computer screen, and a nurse writing in a file. 'Customer for you, Dr Vines,' said Hardwicke. 'Mr Rafiq.'

'Thank you, Mr Hardwicke.' The doctor looked over the top of his glasses at Rafiq. 'So, Mr Rafiq, do you need that chair all the time?'

'I can walk.'

'I'm afraid I haven't been given your medical file so I shall have to start from scratch.' He nodded at the nurse. 'My colleague here will take your blood pressure and a few measurements, then we'll have a chat.'

The nurse took Rafiq into a side room, weighed him and measured his height, then took his blood pressure. Then she took him to another side room where the doctor was waiting. 'I understand that you are in the late stages of pancreatic cancer,' said the doctor.

Rafiq nodded. 'I am.'

'What painkillers are you taking?'

'At the moment, none. They stopped giving me medication once I boarded the plane.'

'What were you on in the US?'

'Ibuprofen and naproxen.'

'No opioids?'

'The American prison system does not approve of giving its inmates opioids.'

'Are you in pain now?'

'I am always in pain.'

'On a scale of one to ten, ten being the worst, how would you rate your current pain level.'

'Six or seven,' said Rafiq.

'Well, I can give you ibuprofen and codeine now and we'll carry out a full assessment of your needs at a later date. I am not able to deal with any long-standing problems or issues you may have, my role today is to make sure that you will be okay overnight.'

'I am dying, Dr Vines.'

'Yes, I understand that. But your long-standing health issue will be dealt with by the medical centre staff, not here at reception. I can assure you, though, that the British prison system is far more sympathetic to the benefits of opioid medication than our American cousins. We will do everything that is necessary to alleviate your pain as your condition worsens.'

Rafiq nodded. 'Thank you.'

The doctor went over to a cupboard full of medicines and unlocked it. He took out two bottles, opened them, and took four tablets from each which he put in two small plastic bags. The two small bags went into a bigger bag. He tapped on his computer and a printer whirred into life, printing a small label which he stuck on to the bag.

The doctor gave the bag to Rafiq. 'One of each tablet, every eight hours,' he said. 'Take them with water, before or after food, it doesn't matter.' He looked over at Hardwicke. 'So, Mr Rafiq is good to go,' he said.

Hardwicke pushed the wheelchair out of the office. The prison officer who had taken Rafiq's photograph came over with a plastic ID card. It showed his name, photograph, date of birth and prison number. 'You need to keep this with you at all times,' he said.

Rafiq took it and thanked him.

'You are allowed a phone call, Mr Rafiq. Maybe there's a family member you would like to talk to?'

Rafiq shook his head. The prison authorities recorded all phone conversations so he would have to choose his words with care, and if he spoke to his wives or children they might well say something that could cause him problems. He would rather wait. 'There is no need,' he said.

'Do you know what a Listener is, Mr Rafiq?'

'I do.' The Listeners were prisoners who had been trained by the Samaritans to deal with people who were depressed or suicidal.

'Would you like to talk to a Listener?'

'Do you think I'm suicidal?'

'I wouldn't know, Mr Rafiq. I am required to ask you if you wish to talk to a Listener. I'm doing my job.'

'I am dying,' said Rafiq quietly. 'I have no wish to hasten the process.'

A prison officer appeared with a clipboard and pen which he gave to Hardwicke. Hardwicke offered them to Rafiq. 'Could you sign this form to say that you don't require a Listener?'

Rafiq sighed and signed the form.

'Do you know what an Insider is?'

Shafiq Ali Rafiq nodded. 'Yes, I do.' An Insider was a trusted inmate, one of the so-called red bands. They were different from the Listeners. They weren't trained to deal with potential suicides, but they knew everything about the prison and how it ran and could offer support and advice. They knew all the prison rules, often better than the prison officers, plus any local regulations that might apply.

'If you don't want to see an Insider, please sign the form below the one you have just signed.'

'No, I would like to see an Insider.'

'Then tick the appropriate box and sign the form please.'

Rafiq did as he was told and handed back the clipboard to Hardwicke who passed it on to the other prison officer.

'Right,' said Hardwicke. 'Let's get you to your cell.'

• • •

L iam heard footsteps outside the door, followed by the rattle of the bolt being drawn back. He was sitting with his back to the wall, his knees up against his chest. The watch was in his pocket.

Smithy was on his feet but he sat down as the door opened. Youssouf appeared in the doorway. He looked at Liam, nodded, and then stepped to the side. A young boy who couldn't have been more than ten years old walked in, holding a tray. Youssouf waved at the boy to move into the cell. '*Dépêche toi*,' he said.

The boy carried the tray over to Liam and put a plate on the floor. There was some cheese and a chunk of flat bread on the plate, along with some dates and grapes. '*Merci*,' said Liam and the boy grinned.

The boy put a plate of food on the floor next to Smithy, then hurried out of the door.

'Youssouf, I need to go to the toilet,' said Liam. Youssouf frowned and Liam repeated the request.

Youssouf shook his head. 'No toilet,' he said.

'I have to go,' said Liam.

'Wait,' said Youssouf. He hurried out. An older man stepped into the doorway, holding a Kalashnikov across his chest. He stared sullenly at Liam and Smithy until Youssouf reappeared with a metal bucket. He put the bucket down next to Liam.

'Seriously?' said Liam.

'It is the bucket or nothing,' said Youssouf.

'Okay. Thank you. Youssouf, what happened to our friend?'

'We buried him.'

'You had a funeral for him?'

'We buried him, that's all. He was a kafir, he's in hell now.'

Liam gritted his teeth. 'He was a good man, Youssouf. He deserves a proper burial.'

'He was here to kill Muslims.'

'He was here to keep the peace, Youssouf. We're here to save lives, not take them.'

Youssouf opened his mouth to reply but before he could say anything they all heard the sound of shots smacking into concrete outside, followed by shouts and screams.

'What's happening?' shouted Smithy.

The man at the door shouted something in rapid French and hurried away.

There were more shots outside, the crack-crack-crack of automatic fire.

Youssouf ran to the door and out into the corridor. He slammed the door shut and bolted it, then they heard his sandals slapping on the concrete as he ran away.

'Do you think this is our rescue?' asked Smithy.

'I don't know,' said Liam. 'The first shots sounded like heavy machine gun fire. Then the return fire was Kalashnikovs.'

'Would the SAS use heavy machine guns?'

'Not for a hostage rescue. They usually user Hecklers. But they can use what they want so maybe . . .' Liam shook his head. 'I'd just be guessing but it sounds to me as if someone is firing machine guns at the compound.'

'Well it's not the UN, that's for sure. So another rebel group maybe?'

Liam shrugged. He had no idea who they might be, but whoever it was they were getting closer. Off in the distance they could hear the thud-thud-thud of the machine guns interspersed with the crack of Kalashnikovs. He stood up and took the watch from his pocket. 'I'm putting the watch outside,' said Liam.

'What if someone sees it?'

'I think we're running out of time,' said Liam. He grimaced. 'No pun intended. Them spotting the watch is the least of our worries.' He threaded the watch through the window and tied the aerial to one of the bars. The sound of machine gunfire was louder now, and there were shots from close by that must have been Youssouf's people shooting back. Liam was fairly sure it wasn't a rescue, which could only be bad news.

. . .

Shepherd and Standing had watched the six-wheeled trucks drive across the desert, leaving behind vast clouds of dust and sand behind them. There were seven of them, powering towards the compound in a V formation. The Chekan driving point had a machine gun turret, as did the vehicles in the middle of the two wings. They began firing when they were almost half a mile away from the compound and through the binoculars Shepherd and Standing could see the rounds kicking up puffs of dust on the concrete buildings.

Al-Qaeda fighters appeared on the rooftops and began firing back, using whatever cover they could find.

'Idiots,' said Standing. 'The Russians are well out of range. They should be waiting and conserving their ammunition.'

'The Russians are trying shock and awe,' said Shepherd. 'They'll be hoping the Islamists will turn and run.'

'Run where?' said Standing. 'There's nothing between their compound and this plateau. If they don't stand and fight, they'll be mown down out in the open. But the Russians have fucked up doing a frontal assault like that. They should have come in with a pincer movement.'

'The Russians have never been great on military strategy,' said Shepherd. Lane was crawling up towards them. Shepherd waved for him to hold short. The Russians were probably too focused on the compound to see them on the plateau, but it was better to keep out of their line of sight.

'Penny, can you get the heli back?' said Shepherd. 'Tell them that the Wagner Group are attacking the compound.'

'Roger that,' said Lane. He reached for his radio.

'Do you think they'll fire on the Russians?' asked Standing.

'It'll be their call,' said Shepherd. 'If nothing else they can lay down covering fire.' He crawled back down the slope and then got to his feet. Standing joined him. The Ellis boys and Ireland jogged over.

'What's going on?' asked Ireland.

'A Wagner Group unit is attacking the compound,' said

Shepherd. 'Seven Wagner Wagons, three of them with machine guns. Fifty or so men on board, I'd guess. They're about three hundred metres from the compound and going in guns blazing.'

'That's not good,' said Jack Ellis.

'We're calling the heli back but their rules of engagement are that they can't attack unless they're fired on,' said Shepherd. 'If the Wagner unit takes the compound there's every chance they'll kill everyone, including the hostages.' He looked over at Standing. 'I want to go in now,' he said. 'If we wait, we might be too late.'

'I'm okay with that,' said Standing. 'Just be aware that it might put us head to head with the Russians.' He looked around. 'What do you think, guys? We're outnumbered but then we usually are, right?'

'Let's do it,' said Ireland.

'Hopefully they'll be too busy shooting at each other to see us coming,' said Joe Ellis.

Lane came down the slope towards them. 'Heli's on the way,' said Lane. 'ETA fifteen minutes, they'll fly direct to the compound.'

'You told them about the machine guns?' asked Standing.

Lane nodded. 'They'll stay high.'

'Are you okay for heading over on the quads?'

'All for one and one for all,' said Lane.

'Let's do it,' said Shepherd, jogging down the slope towards the quads. The SAS team followed him.

• • •

The prison officers had to unlock and lock eight sets of gates and doors to get from the Reception Centre to the Close Supervision Centre. The Close Supervision Centre was a separate, newer building, a two-storey brick cube with a flat roof and narrow windows that were no more than a few inches across. It was surrounded by two fences topped with razor wire and two gates had to be opened to get to the entrance. A middle-aged senior prison officer was waiting for them, flanked by six regular officers, three on each side. Another officer was holding back an Alsatian dog which was straining at the leash as it barked at Shafiq Ali Rafiq.

The three armed cops kept pace with Hardwicke as he pushed the wheelchair towards the waiting officers. Evans followed close behind. The prison officer spoke to the most senior armed cop, a grey-haired sergeant. 'I'm told that you and your colleagues are to deliver Mr Rafiq here and then stand down, is that your understanding?'

The sergeant nodded. 'Aye, that's right.' He had a gruff, Scottish accent.

'Then consider your job done, guys. Do you want to hit the canteen on the way out? They do a decent fish and chips.'

The three armed officers nodded. 'That'd be great,' said the sergeant.

'I'm sure Mr Evans and Mr Hardwicke will show you the way.'

'No problem,' said Hardwicke. He looked down at Rafiq. 'Will you be needing the chair here?' he asked.

'I can probably manage,' said Rafiq. He slowly stood up.

Hardwicke took the chair and he and Evans led the armed cops back to the gate.

The six regular prison officers folded their arms, trying to look as intimidating as possible. They all had radios clipped to their right shoulders and bodycams attached to their chest pockets. Red lights were blinking on all the bodycams. The dog was growling now, and baring its teeth.

'My name is Mr Gregson, I'm the duty officer here today,' said the senior officer. 'Are you okay to walk?'

'I can walk short distances, but then it hurts.'

'The medical centre gave you medication?'

Rafiq held up the plastic bag. 'Painkillers.'

'Let me take you to your cell,' said Gregson. 'Can I see your prison ID card?'

Rafiq handed over his card. Gregson studied it and returned it. Five of the six guards surrounded Rafiq while the sixth unlocked the door to the centre. Gregson went in first, followed by Rafiq and the five guards. Once they were all inside, the sixth guard locked the door. They were in a reception area with a counter facing three doors. Ahead of them was a barred gate that led to the cells.

There was a female officer standing behind the counter. She had blonde hair tied back in a ponytail, and bright red lipstick. 'This is Mr Rafiq, he'll be in cell number five,' said Gregson.

'Five it is,' said the woman. She smiled at Rafiq and he looked away, unwilling to make eye contact with her.

'This is Miss Owen, she's on the desk here most days,' said Gregson, but Rafiq continued to stare at the tiled floor and didn't reply.

'Right, the cell is this way,' said Gregson. The guard with the key opened the barred gate and the other five guards ushered Rafiq into the cell area with six doors on either side. There were stairs to the right which Rafiq assumed led to the upper floor, where there would probably be more cells.

'This is where you'll be staying,' said Gregson, stopping outside one of the cells. The door was already open. Rafiq walked inside. It was about six feet wide and twelve feet long. There was a fluorescent light buried in the ceiling and two thin vertical windows about six inches wide that looked out at a wire fence and featureless brick wall behind it. The bed was a concrete block with a one-inch-thick plastic mattress on it, a two-inch-thick plastic pillow and two green polyester blankets. There was a combined toilet and washbasin near the door and above it a piece of polished metal set into the concrete wall that could be used as a mirror. There was no light switch and no power socket. Home sweet home.

The six guards lined up behind Gregson and folded their arms as they stared impassively at Rafiq. It was intimidation by numbers, a technique the Americans also favoured.

'You'll be allowed out of the cell for fifteen minutes in the morning to shower and we have our own exercise area which you can use for half an hour in the afternoon,' said Gregson.

'What about prayer?'

'You have to do that in your cell, I'm afraid.'

'How will I know which way Mecca is? I do not have a Qibla compass.'

Gregson smiled. 'We get a lot of Muslims here, Mr Rafiq. You will see a Qibla pointer on the ceiling.'

'I would like a copy of the Koran. My copy was taken from me when I left America.'

'I shall arrange for you to be given a copy. Now, how do you feel, Mr Rafiq?'

'How do I feel?'

'Your state of mind. Are you depressed? Angry? Confused?'

Rafiq shrugged. 'Resigned.'

Gregson frowned. 'Resigned?'

'I have been in an American supermax prison for twelve years. Twenty-three hours a day in a concrete box much like this. So I am resigned, Mr Gregson. Resigned to my fate.'

'You have no suicidal thoughts?'

Gregson's bodycam was showing a red light. Rafiq knew that his answer was being recorded.

'No, Mr Gregson. I have no suicidal thoughts. But thank you for your concern.'

'I do understand how stressful prison can be,' said Gregson. 'I spend most of my life in one.'

'Except of course every night you can go home to your wife and family.'

They heard footsteps in the corridor outside the cell and a small man weaved his way between the six guards. He was barely five and a half feet tall, wearing a long pale blue tunic and baggy grey pants, with plastic sandals on his feet. He was in his forties, his head shaved and topped with a small skullcap. Gregson greeted him with a smile. 'This is Mr Farooqi. He is one of the prison Insiders. I was told you requested an Insider.'

'I did yes.'

'I will leave the two of you alone so that he can assist you with any queries you might have. Actually, he can arrange for a copy of the Koran for you, I'm sure.' Gregson flashed him a tight smile and closed the cell door.

'That kafir is such a prick,' said Farooqi, speaking in Urdu. He gave Rafiq a small bow. 'It is a pleasure to make your acquaintance, sir. Malik Abid Qadeer wishes you well and says that he hopes to meet you soon. He says that if you need anything you have only to ask.'

'Please give Malik Abid Qadeer my thanks,' said Rafiq. 'Is everything prepared?'

'I am told it is, sir. Obviously I do not know the details but Malik Abid Qadeer told me to tell you that your instructions have been followed to the letter.'

'And when?' asked Rafiq. 'When will it happen?'

'I only know that it will be soon. Very soon.'

Rafiq smiled. At last, some good news.

· · ·

The quads made a loud buzzing noise as they cut across the desert towards the compound, but there was no disguising the plumes of dust and sand they left in their wake. In the distance the SAS team could hear the thud of the Russian machine guns and the crack-crack-crack of the return fire from the Islamists.

Shepherd and the team had spread out so they were at least fifty metres apart. Standing was in the middle, Joe Ellis to his left and Jack Ellis to his right. Shepherd was between Joe Ellis and Ireland, Lane was next to Jack Ellis. They all had their weapons on their backs. Firing while driving a quad over rough ground was a physical impossibility, which made them easy targets for the Russians with their machine guns or the Islamists on the rooftops. So far the two groups were so focused on each other that they hadn't spotted the quads racing towards them. Shepherd hoped that their luck held, because if they came under fire they had nothing in the way of cover.

The Russian vehicles came to a halt about a hundred metres from the compound. Their machine guns continued to pour a hail of lead into the buildings, concentrating their fire on the rooftops.

Shepherd had to concentrate on the terrain ahead of him. They were powering along at close to forty miles an hour and even with the oversized wheels, a stray rock could easily tip a quad over. The suspension wasn't great – every bump rattled Shepherd's teeth and the handlebars were twisting as if they had a life of their own. He had wrapped a scarf around his nose and mouth and was wearing protective goggles but he could still taste the desert sand.

'The heli has the Russians in sight,' said Lane in Shepherd's earpiece. 'And good news, Spider, the watch is transmitting and the signal is coming from the compound.'

Shepherd took his eyes off the ground for a second and glanced up. All he saw was blue sky. He swerved to the left to avoid a suitcase-sized boulder, then straightened up and accelerated to keep pace with Standing. He risked another look up at the sky, this time to his right, and he saw the Chinook high overhead, flying towards the compound. It was always hard to judge distances in the air but he figured the heli was at about 2,000 metres, close to being out of range of the Wagner Group machine guns.

'Penny, are they going to lay down fire? It'd be a big help.'

'I'm talking to them now, Spider.'

The quads continued to race across the desert. Shepherd took a quick look over his shoulder. There were huge clouds of dust and sand behind them now – if the jihadists on the rooftops looked in their direction they'd be spotted immediately. But the Islamists were still focused on the attacking Russians. And the buildings in the compound would hopefully block the Russians from seeing the quads. So far, so good.

The compound was just over a kilometre away, two minutes at most at the speed at which they were travelling. Facing them was a waist-high wall with no gates that Shepherd could see. They would have to climb off the quads and proceed on foot, but at least the wall would provide cover.

'Gully to my left, guys,' said Standing in Shepherd's ear. 'Watch out.'

Shepherd, Joe Ellis and Ireland slowed. Shepherd stood up on his footrests to get a better look. There was a deep crack in the ground ahead of him, about two feet wide, zig-zagging through the desert floor. 'I see it,' said Shepherd. The quad would have flipped over if he'd driven into the gully and that could have been fatal at speed. Joe Ellis had stopped and was looking left and right. The gully stretched off to the left as far as they could see so they had no choice but to head right and follow Standing. That meant driving through his dust and within seconds Shepherd was coughing and spluttering, unable to see anything through the cloud of swirling sand. He slowed to walking pace until he was sure that he was around the gully, then twisted the throttle and headed left. As soon as his vision cleared he turned right again towards the compound. Joe Ellis and Ireland did the same.

Standing was several hundred metres ahead of them, with Jack Ellis and Lane keeping pace. Shepherd accelerated and the buzz of his electric engine increased in volume. He took a quick look to his left. Joe Ellis and Ireland were already catching up with him.

Lane spoke in Shepherd's earpiece. 'Spider, the pilot says he's going to fire on the Wagner Group.'

'Roger that, Penny.'

The compound was fast approaching now and Shepherd

could see jihadists crouched on the rooftops of several of the buildings. There were puffs of dust as the machine gun rounds blasted into the sandstone rooftops and during any brief lull in the barrage the jihadists would pop up and return fire with their Kalashnikovs. A Kalashnikov was reasonably accurate up to 300 metres but the Russian mercenaries were probably hiding behind their armoured vehicles and Shepherd doubted that the jihadists would be having much success.

'We should take cover behind the wall before the heli starts shooting,' said Standing through Shepherd's earpiece.

'Roger that,' said Shepherd.

. . .

Peter Chambers put the Chinook in a slow turn to the left to give himself a better look at what was going on down below. The Wagner Group armoured vehicles had pulled up a couple of hundred metres from the jihadist compound. Three of the vehicles had large-calibre KVPT machine guns mounted on turrets. They were equipped with fifty-round belts, intended for use against light armoured targets and shelters at distances of up to 3,000 metres, with the capability of hitting targets in the air at up to 2,000 metres. They were blasting the compound with rounds that weighed sixty-four grams – more than two ounces. The barrage was taking its toll on the sandstone build-ings in the compound.

The Wagner Wagons were also equipped with PKT 7.62mm belt-fed machine guns, which were lethal up to a thousand metres. They came with boxes of 250 rounds which could be emptied in seconds when fired on fully automatic. The weapon was built by the people that made the AK-47 assault rifle – PKT stood for Pulemyot Kalashnikova Tankovvi, or Kalashnikov Machine Gun Tank Version.

The Chinook was still at about 2,000 metres which meant it was at the limits of the KVPT machine guns. But the heli would need to go lower for its own guns to be effective.

Chambers took a quick look at Simon Farrant in the co-pilot's seat. 'You okay about this, Simon?'

'Hell yeah,' said Farrant. 'Our guys are in the middle of that, we've got to get them out of there.'

'And just to confirm that we are under fire?'

Farrant grinned. 'Oh yes, happy to confirm that.'

'What about you, Dopey?'

John 'Dopey' Topey was in the cargo hold with gunner Richard Haines. Both were looking out of the starboard side door at the action far below.

'Yeah, we are coming under fire,' said Topey.

Haines grinned. 'I fear for my safety,' he said as he sighted down his M60D machine gun at the Russian vehicles below. The men in the vehicles had piled out and taken cover behind them. Most were wielding what appeared to be RPK-74 light machine guns – a heavy-barrel version of the AK-74, usually fitted with bipod – but there were designated marksmen in the group equipped with SVD Dragunov sniper rifles. Haines did a quick count. Forty-six men. None of whom had yet noticed the Chinook heading towards them.

'Then I think we should return fire,' said Chambers, putting the Chinook into a steep descent. 'In your own time, gentlemen.'

Topey moved to the front of the helicopter and stood by

the starboard 7.62mm M134 Minigun. Despite the name, it was a more powerful weapon than the M60D. It was powered by an electric motor and could fire a hundred rounds a second at a range of more than a thousand metres.

The Chinook continued to descend as it banked to the right, giving the crew chief and the gunner a clear view of the Russian unit. Both men had their fingers on the triggers but held their fire. As soon as they realised they were being attacked, the mercenaries would run for cover, piling back into their armoured vehicles if possible. The 7.62mm rounds were man killers but would bounce off the armour of a Wagner Wagon.

Topey looked over at Haines. Haines winked at him. 'Aim for the whites of their eyes,' he said.

The Chinook was about a thousand metres above the ground now and still descending. 'Rock and roll!' shouted Haines. He pulled the trigger and even with his headset on the sound of the gun was deafening as it burst into life.

Topey sighted his weapon on the mercenaries behind the Wagner Wagon on the far left and pulled the trigger. He fired a short burst and the tracer rounds allowed him to follow the progress of his shots. He hit two of the mercenaries and they fell to the ground, but the rest of the burst went wide. He fired again, a longer burst this time, and took out a further four Russians.

Haines fired his machine gun on fully automatic, a single extended burst that he walked across the back of the armoured cars, hitting more than a dozen of the Russians.

Some of the mercenaries looked up and began firing at the Chinook, but Chambers had levelled off and they were too high for the assault rifles to do any damage to the heli's armoured underside. So far none of the Wagner Wagons had turned their machine guns towards the Chinook.

The M60D's belt feed ran out and Haines slapped in a new one before firing again, sending deadly rounds towards the surviving mercenaries who were now scrambling to get back inside their armoured vehicles.

. . .

Shepherd peered over the stone wall. The Chinook was about a thousand metres above the compound, its machine guns raking the Russian vehicles. He couldn't see how much damage was being done but he was sure there would be dozens of casualties. Standing was to his right, scanning the buildings ahead of them. There were six flat-roofed sandstone cottages and there were armed jihadists on three of them. 'Spider, we've no way of knowing which building the crew are in,' Standing said. 'We're going to have to clear them all. Do you want to ask the heli to strafe the compound?'

Shepherd shook his head. 'Too risky, they might hit the hostages by mistake. But get them to keep firing at the Russians. It'll be a distraction.'

Standing relayed the instructions to Lane who radioed up to the Chinook.

Standing looked over at the Ellis brothers. 'Joe and Jack, take the building on the far left. There are two bad guys on the roof but there could be more inside.'

'Flashbangs it is,' said Joe.

'Then move forward to the building opposite it. I don't see

anyone on the roof but it's nearer the Russians so they might be keeping their heads down.'

'Roger that,' said Jack.

The two brothers began moving to the left, crouching low to stay behind the wall.

'Spider, do you want to come with me? We can take the building directly ahead of us.'

'Sure,' said Shepherd.

'Paddy, you and Penny take the building on the left. At the moment they don't know we're here so let's go softly softly and then move in on my count of three.'

Ireland and Lane both nodded.

'Assume that anyone you come across is a potential hostile, but let's try only to engage with armed contacts. There could be women and children in there so let's keep collateral damage to a minimum. The main aim of the mission is to recover the hostages.'

Ireland and Lane both nodded again, then headed off to the right, keeping below the wall.

'Ready, Spider?' said Standing.

Shepherd forced a smile. 'As I'll ever be.'

'You feeling a little rusty? How many years since you've been in the Killing House?'

'Too many to remember,' said Shepherd. The Killing House was where the SAS men honed their close-quarter battle skills. It was a two-storey building in the Stirling Lines barracks near Hereford, split into four rooms on each floor, the walls lined with rubber to absorb rounds, extractor fans fitted to suck out the cordite and fumes, with video cameras to record the action. There were targets in each room, and figures representing hostages and members of the public. Members of the royal family were put through Killing House exercises to prepare them for the worst that could happen, as were all serving prime ministers and members of the cabinet.

Standing grinned. 'It's like riding a bike,' he said, patting him on the shoulder.

Off to the left, the Ellis brothers vaulted over the wall and lay prone for a few seconds before starting to crawl towards their target building.

Shepherd looked to his left. Ireland and Lane went over the wall and hit the dirt.

'Time to go,' said Standing. He jumped over the wall and Shepherd followed him. High above them, the Chinook continued to rain fire down on the Russians.

· · ·

Smithy looked anxiously over at Liam. 'Can you see anything?' he asked. Liam was standing on tiptoe, peering up through the window. All he could see was blue sky and wisps of cloud. But he could hear the rapid fire of machine guns on fully automatic and he was sure the sound was coming from the sky. 'That's an M60 isn't it? And a minigun.'

Liam nodded. Smithy was right, which meant that the shots were probably coming from a Chinook. And that meant a rescue.

'What's their game plan?' asked Smithy. 'They're not going to get anywhere firing at the buildings.'

'I don't think they're shooting at us,' said Liam. 'It sounds further away.' He frowned, trying to make sense of what was happening. There was a Chinook overhead, firing almost continuously. There was more firing on the ground off in the distance, also from heavy machine guns. And close by was the crack of Kalashnikovs being fired on semi-automatic. Initially he had thought that Youssouf's people were under attack, but as he had said to Smithy, it sounded as if the Chinook was firing at targets some distance away.

He craned his neck to the left and his heart raced when he saw the Chinook, about a thousand metres above the ground, banking slowly as its guns blazed.

'I see them,' said Liam. 'It's a Chinook. This is a rescue, Smithy. We're going home!'

The door to their room crashed open. Youssouf stood there, an AK-47 in his right hand. His eyes were wide and staring and he was breathing heavily. 'Get away from the window!' he shouted in French.

Liam did as he was told. 'What's happening?' he asked.

'The Russians are attacking us.'

'The Russians?'

'They are outside our compound. They want to kill us.'

'I saw a helicopter.'

There was a series of loud thuds as rounds slammed into the building and Youssouf flinched. 'The helicopter is firing at the Russians,' he said.

'Is the helicopter yours?'

Youssouf shook his head. 'It's a UN helicopter,' he said. 'I have never seen them shoot before. I don't know what is happening.'

Liam pulled at the chain around his neck. 'You have to unchain us,' he said. 'We can help you fight.'

'No.'

'Youssouf, I can hear the machine guns firing at us. You're

outgunned. We can help you. You need all the firepower you can get.'

'How can I trust you?'

'If we stay chained here we're going to die,' said Liam. 'The only way Smithy and I can get out of here alive is if we help you. We don't have a choice.'

More rounds thwacked into their building and they heard screams and shouts outside.

'If you betray me, I will kill you,' said Youssouf, stepping into the cell.

'Why would I betray you? I just want to get out of here and that means I have to help you. We both do. We can shoot, Youssouf. Give us guns and we'll help you fight the Russians.'

Youssouf looked at Smithy. 'Can I trust you?' he asked.

'Smithy doesn't speak French,' said Liam. 'But he's with me. We're a team. We'll fight with you, Youssouf. You need every man you can get.'

More rounds hit the building and Youssouf flinched again. He hurried over to the window, groping in his trousers for his keyring. He leaned his Kalashnikov against the wall and flicked through his keys. He frowned when he saw the wire tied to the bar in the window. He reached for it and started pulling at it. 'What is this?' he said. He pulled until he saw the watch and he grabbed it. 'What have you been doing?'

Liam punched him on the chin and he slammed into the wall. Liam grabbed the Kalashnikov, upended it and slammed the butt against Youssouf's head. The man fell to the ground without a sound. 'Sorry, mate,' said Liam. He bent down and picked up the keys as more rounds thudded into the building.

• • •

S tanding reached the door to the building and stood to the side, his back to the wall. Shepherd joined him at the other side of the door. 'Everyone in position?' Standing said over the radio.

'Yeah, ready to go,' said Jack Ellis.

'We're good,' said Lane.

'Okay, on my three. One, two, three.' Standing slipped through the door and went right. Shepherd followed and went left, his Heckler at his shoulder. They were in a square room with a fireplace to the left. There was no furniture to speak of, just cushions on the floor and a stack of threadbare blankets. There were stone stairs to the left leading to the upper floor and in front of them was an open doorway that led to a kitchen.

Shepherd kept his gun aimed at the stairs while Standing moved towards the kitchen. They heard shots off to their right. A Heckler followed by a Kalashnikov, then two bursts from Hecklers.

Standing disappeared into the kitchen. Sandalled feet appeared on the stairs. Shepherd's finger tightened on the trigger but he waited until he saw the Kalashnikov in the man's hand before pulling the trigger and putting two rounds in his chest. The man staggered back as blood spread across his tunic. The Kalashnikov clattered down the stairs as the man slid down the wall and sprawled across the steps. Shepherd kept his gun trained on the stairs.

Standing appeared from the kitchen. 'All clear,' he said.

Shepherd headed up the stairs, his finger on the trigger. Standing tucked in behind him.

Shepherd stepped carefully over the body, his ears straining for any sound from the room above him. He paused, listened, and then continued up. He heard the scrape of a sandal on wood and stopped again. A head appeared, brown-skinned and bearded, and Shepherd caught a glimpse of the barrel of an AK-47. He pulled the trigger and the head exploded in a crimson cloud. As the body slumped to the ground, Shepherd headed up the stairs. A gun roared and a round smacked into the wall by his head. Standing fired twice and a jihadist fell back, two red patches blossoming on the front of his tunic. 'You're welcome,' said Standing.

'I had him covered,' said Shepherd.

They reached the top of the stairs. There was a sleeping area with three stacks of blankets and a doorway to their right. A flight of stone stairs continued up to the roof. They could hear the Chinook's guns continuing to fire down at the Russians.

Shepherd covered the stairs while Standing moved over to the doorway, crouching to make himself a smaller target, his Heckler at his shoulder.

'Building clear,' said one of the Ellis boys in Shepherd's earpiece. He didn't know if it was Jack or Joe, their voices and speech patterns were virtually identical. 'Two bad guys down. Moving on to second building.'

Standing moved through the doorway, tensed, and then swore. 'I've got three civilians here, Spider. A woman and two kids.'

'Roger that,' said Shepherd. 'You going to tie them?'

'They're scared shitless. Let's let them be. What's the French for "stay where you are and you'll be fine"?'

'Let me talk to them,' said Shepherd.

Standing backed out of the room, his Heckler still at his shoulder, then he covered the stairs as Shepherd moved to the doorway. Shepherd stepped into the room. There was a small table with four stools around it. There were plates of rice and meat on the table, along with a jug and four glasses. The woman was crouched in a corner next to a glassless window. She was young, barely out of her teens, with braided black hair and hooped earrings. She had her arms around two toddlers who had buried their faces in her chest. She stared at him fearfully and hugged the children. Outside the machine gun fire from the Chinook dropped from fully automatic to single shots. Shepherd figured they were starting to run short of ammunition. Either that or they were running out of targets.

Shepherd lowered his weapon. 'We're not going to hurt you,' he said, in French. He was far from fluent in the language, but had enough vocabulary to make himself understood. 'Just stay here with your children and you will be all right.'

Tears ran down the woman's cheeks. 'My husband,' she said. 'Where is my husband?'

Shepherd realised that her husband was almost certainly one of the two jihadists they had killed, but there was no way he was going to tell her that. 'Just stay here,' he said. 'And keep quiet. We will be gone soon.'

He backed out of the room. Lane's voice came through his earpiece. 'Pilot says the Russians are pulling back,' he said. 'They've had enough.'

'Roger that,' said Standing. He waited for Shepherd to join him on the stairs and then they went up together, their guns sweeping left and right. The stairs opened on to a flat roof with a small concrete wall running around its perimeter. There were several sheets and towels hanging from a washing line, obscuring their vision, so they split up and kept low as they moved towards the front of the building. The Chinook had stopped firing now and the Russians had also ceased fire. It took them a few seconds to confirm that the roof was clear, then they knelt by the wall and peered over at the neighbouring buildings.

'Building clear,' said Ireland through Shepherd's earpiece. Shepherd looked over at the building to the right. Lane and Ireland were on the roof. Ireland waved and Shepherd waved back.

'What took you so long?' asked Standing.

'Four hostiles,' said Ireland.

Shepherd saw a jihadist on top of the building ahead of them, crouching behind a wall and aiming his Kalashnikov at the departing Russians. The man fired a three-shot burst, then another. Shepherd aimed at the back of the man's head, his finger tightening on the trigger. He took no pleasure in shooting a man in the back, but he knew if the roles were reversed the jihadist wouldn't have the same reluctance to pull the trigger. Standing beat him to it and put two rounds between the man's shoulders. The man's tunic turned red as he slumped to the floor. Shepherd looked over at Standing and Standing grinned. 'Sorry, mate,' he said. 'Was he yours?'

They heard the crack-crack-crack of Kalashnikov fire over to the right. Lane and Ireland had come under fire from the building in front of them. Two jihadists had appeared from the stairway and were both firing as they walked towards the wall that ran around the roof. Ireland and Lane had thrown themselves to the floor and the hail of bullets passed overhead.

Standing turned and aimed at the leading jihadist. Shepherd beat him to it and put two rounds into the man, one in the chest and one in the head. The perfect double-tap. The jihadist fell back and hit the floor, the Kalashnikov still in his hands.

Standing switched his aim to the second jihadist. He fired twice and the man went down. 'All right, Paddy, you and Penny can get up now.'

'I had him covered,' said Ireland.

'Of course you did,' said Standing. 'Okay, our building is clear, we're moving on.' He nodded at Shepherd and then headed down the stairs. Shepherd followed him.

The mother and children had stayed in the room, but Shepherd could hear the kids crying. He wasn't sure what sort of life they had ahead of them, their father dead, their country in a state of turmoil. He blotted out the thought and concentrated on the job at hand.

They reached the ground floor and went into the kitchen, which was a small room with a tap over a bowl, a charcoal stove and a low table. There was a small sack of rice on a wooden shelf and a few bottles of sauces and condiments. Standing pulled open a wooden door and surveyed the next building. Shepherd joined him. They checked the windows and saw no sign of movement. 'Okay,' said Standing. 'Let's go.' He stepped outside and jogged towards the building, his Heckler sweeping from side to side. Shepherd followed.

They heard the boom of a flashbang going off to their left, followed by gunshots. Hecklers. Two double-taps, followed by three single shots. 'Building clear,' said one of the Ellis boys in Shepherd's earpiece. 'And the good news is that the Russians have gone. They've left behind a lot of bodies, not all of them dead.'

'Roger that,' said Standing. He reached the building and stood to the left of the door. Shepherd ran over and stood to the right, the barrel of his Heckler pointing skywards. Standing nodded and ducked inside. Shepherd followed him. A Kalashnikov fired and the round smacked into the floor by Shepherd's foot and ricocheted through the doorway.

Standing raised his weapon, his finger tightening on the trigger as he aimed at the figure at the top of the steps to their left.

'No!' shouted Shepherd. 'Hold fire.' Standing paused, his finger still on the trigger. Shepherd shouted up at the figure on the stairs. 'Liam, it's me!'

'Dad? Oh my God, I almost shot you!' Liam was standing at the top of the stairs, a Kalashnikov in his hands. He was wearing a dirt-streaked flight suit and his hair was in disarray.

Standing lowered his weapon. 'Anyone upstairs?' he asked.

'Three,' said Liam. 'They're dead.'

'Where's the rest of your crew?'

Liam gestured with his Kalashnikov. 'Smithy's upstairs on the roof.' He looked over his shoulder. 'Smithy, it's okay, it's my dad.'

Smithy appeared behind Liam. He was also holding a Kalashnikov.

'Come down here while we check upstairs,' said Shepherd. He heard a noise behind a door to his left and he went over to it. 'Who's in here?' he asked.

'One of the guys who was holding us captive,' said Liam. 'And three kids. I knocked him out.' He held up the Kalashnikov. 'This is his.'

Liam and Smithy came down the stairs. Shepherd transferred his Heckler to his right hand and hugged his son. 'You had me worried,' he said.

'Sorry, Dad.'

'Stay here.' Shepherd released his grip on Liam and followed
Standing up the stairs. There were three dead jihadists on the
floor and a dozen or so bullet holes in the walls. It looked as
if Liam had sprayed the room with rounds – not the most
professional method of clearing an area but it had obviously
worked. Standing grinned at him. 'Chip off the old block,' he
said.

'Pretty good for a heli pilot, I'd say,' said Shepherd. They
headed up the stairs to the roof.

'Building cleared,' said Lane in Shepherd's ear.

Standing and Shepherd reached the top of the stairs. The
roof was clear. There was a stack of empty wooden crates on
one side, riddled with bullets. They looked over at the building
to their right. Lane and Ireland were standing in the middle
of the roof, looking at the Chinook high overhead.

Shepherd walked to the front of the building. Five of the
Wagner Wagons were driving eastwards leaving massive sand
plumes in their wake. There were more than two dozen
Russians lying on the ground and the doors of the two
remaining Wagner Wagons were wide open. Shepherd figured
that the vehicles had been disabled by the Chinook's firepower
and they had been abandoned. He turned to look at Standing.
'Shall we call the heli down for an exfil?' he said.

'Sounds like a—'

He was interrupted by a hail of machine gun fire from below.
He dropped to the floor and rolled over to the wall. Shepherd
dived to the side and sought shelter behind the crates, but a
second hail of bullets ripped through them and bits of wood
showered around him.

Shepherd crawled over to Standing and they peered over
the wall. One of the jihadists' trucks was moving, and there

was a man standing behind the machine gun. He saw them and swung the gun around. They ducked down and a stream of rounds ripped through the air above their heads.

'Machine gun at our two o'clock,' said Standing over the radio.

'I see them,' said Ireland. 'I'm on it.' A second later, Shepherd heard the whoosh of a grenade being fired from Ireland's under-barrel launcher and shortly afterwards the stomach-vibrating crump of an HEDP grenade exploding. 'Job done,' said Ireland.

Shepherd peeped over the wall. The pick-up truck was on fire and the machine gun was a twisted wreck. There was no sign of the jihadist who had been firing it. He had probably been vaporised by the explosion. 'Paddy, how about dropping grenades on the two Wagner Wagons, so we don't get any nasty surprises?' said Shepherd.

'Roger that,' said Ireland.

Within seconds Shepherd heard the whoosh of a grenade, followed by an explosion. It took Ireland just a few more seconds to target the second vehicle. There was another whoosh and another explosion. Shepherd and Standing cautiously approached the front wall. Both Wagner Wagons were on fire with thick plumes of black smoke rising into the air. Shepherd took out his binoculars and scanned the desert to the east. He found the other five Russian vehicles, driving in a wedge formation, a cloud of sand in their wake.

'How about that exfil, Matt?' asked Shepherd.

Standing nodded and asked Lane to contact the Chinook. Thirty seconds later the Chinook began to descend in a slow turn around the compound. Standing and Lane headed down the stairs. Liam and Smithy were waiting at the front door, their weapons at the ready. 'We're out of here,' said Standing.

'This is Sergeant Matt Standing,' said Shepherd. 'One of the good guys.'

'Pleasure to meet you,' said Liam.

'Definitely,' said Smithy.

Standing shook hands with them both. 'You took out the guys upstairs?' Standing asked Liam.

Liam nodded. 'More by luck than judgement. Spray and pray.'

'You should think about joining the Sass,' said Standing. 'You're a natural.'

'I like flying too much for that,' said Liam. 'Though my view on that might change if I get shot down again. That wasn't pleasant.'

'I bet,' said Shepherd.

'We've got to get Mobile,' said Liam.

Shepherd frowned. 'Mobile?'

'Harry Holmes. They call him Mobile. He's a pilot. They took him away.'

Shepherd looked over at Standing. Standing shook his head. 'No other Westerners in the compound.'

'He's dead,' said Liam. 'He had internal injuries and he died in our cell. They took him away to bury him.'

Shepherd's jaw tightened. 'We have to go, Liam. The Russians might well come back with reinforcements.'

'Dad, if it was me, would you leave me buried in the ground here?'

Shepherd gritted his teeth. Liam was right, of course. The dead man would have relatives in the UK who would want their boy back. They couldn't leave him behind. 'Matt, can we find him?'

'Sure,' said Standing. He began talking on his radio to the team, telling them to scout the area for recently dug earth.

Shepherd nodded at Liam. 'See if you can find a spade or a shovel.'

• • •

The Chinook's turbines throttled back and the helicopter began to descend towards Gao International Airport. Liam was sitting next to Shepherd. The quads were in the middle of the hold, tied down with nylon straps. Smithy was sitting next to the crew chief by the ramp. In front of them was the body of Harry Holmes, wrapped in a cotton sheet streaked with dirt. It had been easy enough to find the grave. It had been shallow, barely three feet deep, with several large flat stones placed on top.

'What happens now, Dad?' asked Liam.

'Me and the guys will fly back to the UK,' said Shepherd.

'And you'll take Mobile back with you?'

'I expect so. But I'm not sure who'll be making that decision.'

'And what happened to Gerry Fowler? Our gunner?'

'He died, Liam. Sorry. They flew his body back to the UK on the Herc we flew in on.'

'I guessed something had happened when they didn't bring him with us.' Liam shrugged. 'He was engaged. He was going to get married next month.'

'I'm sorry. What do you think they'll do with you? Send you back to the UK?'

'I dunno. I feel fine. I could fly today if they wanted me to.'

'Well, the shock will probably kick in at some point.'

'PTSD you mean? I don't think so. The crash was traumatic but I don't remember much about the actual impact. I probably passed out.'

'More likely your mind has just blanked it out,' said Shepherd. 'But it's not the crash I was talking about. I meant what happened in the house. What you did.'

'Shot the bad guys, you mean?' He shrugged. 'I didn't even think about it, Dad. They were planning on killing me, it was them or us. I don't regret it.'

'You say that now, but trust me, it's not as easy as that to put it behind you. Taking a life is a big thing.'

'It was kill or be killed, Dad.'

Shepherd patted him on the leg. 'I'm glad it was them that died and not you.'

Liam laughed. 'I should bloody well hope so. Trust me, Dad, I'm fine. And PTSD has never been a problem for you, has it?'

Shepherd forced a smile. It was a difficult question to answer. He knew of former SAS guys who had been crippled by PTSD, who had never been able to settle back into civilian life, and some who had been so damaged by their experiences that they had taken their own lives. Shepherd had never suffered from PTSD, but that didn't mean that he hadn't been affected by the actions that he'd taken over the years. His near-perfect memory meant that he had total recall of every man and woman he had ever killed, and the majority of those kills had been up close and personal. So no, PTSD had never been a problem for Shepherd, and while he could justify every single killing, that didn't make taking lives any easier. 'It changes you, Liam. And not in a good way. Once you've taken a life, you've crossed a line. Even if you took that life for the best of reasons.'

'They would have killed me, Dad. And they killed Mobile and Gerry. They had it coming. And if I hadn't done it, I'm sure you and your guys would have.'

'I know, I get what you're saying. And it's good that you can talk about it.'

'You never talk about the things you've done.'

'True. Because I wouldn't want to burden you with my sins.'

'Is that how you think about it? Sinning?'

Shepherd forced a smile. 'No, I didn't mean it literally. I meant that sharing my experiences wouldn't necessarily help you. And knowing what I've done might change your view of me.'

'You're my dad. Nothing's going to change that. And I've always known you were in the SAS. Everybody knows what that means. You can't be in the SAS and expect to treat people with kid gloves.'

The Chinook settled on the ground and the turbines powered down. The crew chief hit the button to lower the ramp. The Ellis boys stood up and began unclipping the straps that were holding the quads in place.

Shepherd and Liam walked to the ramp. Smithy looked up from his seat. 'What do we do with Mobile?' he asked, gesturing at the body.

'Someone from the squadron will deal with it,' said Liam.

'It feels weird, him being here wrapped in a sheet,' said Smithy. 'It's not right.'

Liam patted him on the shoulder. 'They'll have something more appropriate, Smithy.'

Shepherd and Liam walked carefully around the body and down the ramp on to the tarmac. The Geordie sergeant who had taken Shepherd and the team to see Major Jones was standing by his Ridgback. 'Be with you in a minute, Sergeant,' said Shepherd.

'No problem, sir.'

Two young men in RAF fatigues walked over to Liam and patted him on the back. 'Thought we'd lost you there, Skills,' said one.

'You and me both,' said Liam.

Smithy came down the ramp and the two men hugged him, but their faces hardened when they saw the body lying on the floor. They went up the ramp, unfastened the straps that secured the body, then carefully carried it out and loaded it into a plywood coffin in the rear of an RAF truck. One of the men walked to the cab and returned with a union flag which he draped over the coffin. The Chinook's rotors were still turning and the downdraft ripped the flag away. The airman cursed and tried to use a couple of rocks to weight the flag down, but that didn't work.

Topey came down the ramp with a length of wire. 'Try this,' he said.

Shepherd and Liam watched as the airman used the wire to fix the flag to the coffin.

'He was a great pilot,' said Liam. 'I learned a lot from him. He said I could take the left-hand seat. He was in the right. If he'd taken the left seat . . .' He left the sentence unfinished.

'Give me a hug,' said Shepherd. He stepped forward and hugged his son, squeezing him so hard that Liam gasped.

'Bloody hell, Dad, watch my ribs.'

'You gave me one hell of a fright there,' said Shepherd.

'Thanks for . . . well, you know. Thanks for everything.'

Standing walked over and Shepherd released his grip on

Liam. 'That's a nice father-son moment,' said Standing. 'I feel like I should be taking a picture.' He nodded at Liam. 'You heading off?'

'Yeah, duty calls. Thanks for everything, Sergeant Standing.'

'It's Matt, Liam. We're family now. It's not the first time I've had to rescue a Shepherd, and I'm sure it won't be the last.'

'To be fair, it has worked both ways,' said Shepherd.

Standing grinned.

'So, Liam, do you have the same trick memory as your dad?' he asked.

'It's good, but not as good as his.'

'I'll give you my number. You never know when you might need rescuing again.'

Shepherd laughed. 'You're all heart, Matt.'

'Ignore your dad, Liam.' He gave him his mobile number and Liam repeated it back to him.

'Now in reverse,' said Standing.

'Say what now?' said Liam.

'Give me the number, but in reverse. Your dad remembers things without trying but we mere mortals need help.'

Liam had to concentrate to be able to say the number in reverse, but he managed it.

'There you go,' said Standing. 'You need me, you call.'

'Thanks, Matt. But I promise to be more careful next time.' He shook hands with Standing, flashed a thumbs up at Shepherd, and climbed into the back of the truck. He sat down next to the coffin and put his arm over it. Smithy joined him and the truck drove off.

The Ellis boys began pushing the quads down the ramp. Lane and Ireland helped them. They took them towards a nearby hangar. Shepherd and Standing went up the ramp and grabbed several kitbags. The SAS guarded its kit jealously and they wouldn't be leaving anything behind.

It took almost half an hour to transfer everything into the hangar. 'What's the plan?' asked Lane when they had finished.

'Matt and I'll check in with the Major,' said Shepherd.

'We'll hit the pub,' said Ireland. 'What was it called?'

'The Queen's Head,' said Shepherd. 'Have fun.'

Land and Ireland headed off with the Ellis boys. Standing looked at Shepherd and grimaced.

'Ready to face the music?' he asked.

'Ready as I ever will be,' said Shepherd.

'How's your boy?'

'He seems fine. I just hope he stays that way.'

'He took care of business out there, Spider. You should be proud of him.'

'I am. And I'm glad he's okay. But that's the first time he's ever shot anyone. He's a pilot, not a squaddie. I worry about how it's going to affect him.'

'He's got your DNA.'

'Yeah, but not my training. We train to shoot people, he fell into it.' He forced a smile. 'Maybe I'm overthinking it.'

'You're his dad, it's your job to worry about him.' He nodded at the Ridgback. 'Your chariot awaits.'

They walked over to the Ridgback and climbed into the back. The sergeant already had the engine running and it took him less than four minutes to drive to the Major's container. 'I'll wait for you here, sir,' said the sergeant in his heavy Geordie accent. 'I don't think you'll be long.'

'Is he in a good mood?' asked Shepherd as he climbed out.

'I've seen him in better,' growled the sergeant.

Shepherd and Standing went over to the Major's container.

Standing knocked and pushed open the door. The Major was sitting at his desk, his shirtsleeves rolled up, holding what looked like a Cornish pasty. The Major nodded, chewed, and swallowed. He put down the pasty and picked up a plastic bottle of water. He drank and wiped his mouth with the back of his hand. He didn't offer them a seat so Shepherd and Standing stood in front of his desk, hands behind their backs like schoolboys about to get a dressing down from the headmaster.

Major Jones flashed them a tight smile. 'Congratulations are in order for bringing back the hostages,' he said. 'I just wish you could have done it without going to war with the Russians.'

Shepherd and Standing said nothing. If the Major was about to blow off steam, best to just let it happen.

'The UN are not happy, not happy at all.' He smiled thinly. 'But fuck them, right? If they hadn't turned chicken when the Chinook went down, maybe we wouldn't have needed a rescue mission in the first place. And I've no sympathy for the Russians, they shouldn't even be in the country.' He leaned forward across his desk. 'And just to be clear, the Russians fired first? They shot at the Chinook?'

'No question,' said Shepherd.

'They started it,' said Standing. 'The guys had no choice but to return fire.'

The Major linked his fingers and sat back in his chair. 'That's exactly what the Chinook crew says, so as far as I am concerned they followed the UN protocols. The UN people won't be happy but I won't be losing any sleep over that. So long as everyone sings from the same hymn sheet, there's nothing they can do. There's an RAF Atlas from LXX Squadron heading back to the UK in a couple of hours and there's space on it for you and your men.'

'Much appreciated,' said Shepherd.

'How's your son?'

'Shaken up, but other than that he's fine.'

'He's lucky.'

'That runs in the family,' said Standing.

'Well long may it continue,' said the Major. 'Have a safe flight back.'

'LXX Squadron?' said Standing as they walked out of the Major's office.

'It's 70 Squadron,' said Shepherd. 'Formed back in 1916 with Sopwith Camels. Did a lot of fighting in France in the First World War.'

'Before my time,' said Standing.

Shepherd laughed. 'Ha ha,' he said. 'In 1928 they helped with the world's first large-scale airborne evacuation from Kabul. And it was a hell of a lot better organised than when the Yanks pulled out in 2021. LXX Squadron was there, too, pulling out the British forces. They used to fly Hercs but since 2010 they've been flying the Atlas. Basically the squadron provides strategic air transport worldwide.'

'I can never get over your trick memory. You never forget a thing, do you?'

'Unfortunately no,' said Shepherd. 'There are some things I'd rather forget but that's not how it works. I don't get to pick and choose what I remember.'

The Geordie sergeant was standing by his vehicle waiting for them. 'We'll walk over to the Queen's Head, sergeant. I think we can take care of ourselves from here on in.'

'I'm under orders to be at your disposal so long as you're in country,' said the sergeant. 'I'll be here, just give me a shout if you need me.'

Standing and Shepherd walked along a line of containers until they reached one with a sign on the door that said 'THE QUEEN'S HEAD'. Standing pushed open the door and they heard music playing. It might have been Adele, or Beyoncé, or Taylor Swift. They all sounded the same to Shepherd.

There were half a dozen wooden tables with a mixture of chairs and stools scattered around the container, and a small bar at the far end, behind which was a young squaddie pulling cans of lager from a cardboard box. He was handing the cans to Ireland who was tossing them over to Lane and the Ellis boys, who were sitting at one of the tables. They were stretched out and there were half a dozen empty cans in front of them, along with bowls of nuts and crisps.

'Want one, Sarge?' asked Ireland.

'I'm good,' said Standing.

'Spider?'

'Yeah, go on.'

Ireland tossed a can to Shepherd. He caught it one handed and popped the tab. It was warm but it helped wash the taste of sand from his mouth.

Standing dropped down on to a chair and stretched out. 'Go on, Paddy, you've talked me into it. I'll take one.'

A second can flew through the air and Standing caught it. 'Just so you know, we've got a flight back to the UK in a few hours. It's an Atlas so we'll take all our gear with us. Penny, can you arrange for us to be collected at Brize Norton?'

'Will do,' said Lane.

Standing looked over at Joe Ellis. 'Joe, as soon as we know where the Atlas is, get our gear stowed on board.' He popped the tab of his beer and swung his legs up on to the table. He gestured with the can at the squaddie behind the bar. 'Who's in charge of the music?'

The squaddie raised his hand. 'That would be me, sir.'

'I'm not a sir, lad,' said Standing. 'Can you play something a little less feminine?'

'I've got AC/DC.'

'Bring it on.'

The squaddie changed the CD and turned up the volume. The sound of 'Back In Black' filled the container. Standing grinned and raised his can to the squaddie. 'Perfect.' He took a long pull on his beer and looked over at Shepherd. 'Are you coming back to Hereford with us, Spider?'

'I've got to get back to Bradford, ASAP.'

'What's going on there?'

'We've got an operation running in the local prison. It's a terrorism hot spot and getting hotter by the day.'

Standing pulled a face. 'When will they learn that you can't treat terrorists like regular criminals? The Yanks had the right idea with Guantanamo Bay.'

'Two words, Matt. Human rights.'

'Yeah? And what about the rights of the civilians who were killed and maimed on the London Tube, and the rights of kids to go and see their favourite pop star without being blown to smithereens? When we do catch the bad guys what do we do? Give them three square halal meals a day and a PlayStation. I heard they have prayer mats in their cells, is that right?'

'Yeah, that's true. But yoga mats are okay, too. It's no biggie.'

'Well good luck with your operation. I have to say I couldn't do what you do.'

'I think you'd make a shit-hot MI5 officer.'

Standing shook his head. 'I couldn't abide by all the rules,

Spider. Give me a Heckler and a few bad guys shooting at me and I'm good to go. Your world would drive me around the bend.'

They were interrupted by the door opening. It was Liam with Smithy behind him. They had both showered and shaved and were wearing clean flight suits.

'Come on in, guys,' said Standing, waving his can in the air. 'Grab a beer.'

Liam and Smithy walked in, but Liam shook his head when Ireland offered him a can of lager. 'We're on a tighter leash than you guys,' said Liam. 'I'm still on duty. Smithy, too.'

'More for us then,' said Ireland. He popped the tab and drank.

Liam looked at Shepherd. 'Dad, the CO says that Smithy and I should go back with Mobile's body. He wants us to represent the squadron at his funeral, and at Gerry's funeral. The body's going back on the Atlas and we're to go with you.'

'Sounds like a plan,' said Shepherd.

'We'll meet you at the plane,' said Liam. 'We're only allowed in here when we're off duty. Anyway, we've got to pack.'

Liam and Smithy went outside. Shepherd put down his beer and hurried after them. 'Liam, wait, can I have a word?'

Liam stopped and told Smithy to go on ahead. 'What's up?' he said, as Shepherd walked over.

'Do you want to stay at my flat while you're in the UK? I'll be heading up to Bradford. I'm in the middle of a job there so the flat'll be empty.'

'CO says we're to go straight to Odiham. There'll be transport waiting for us at Brize Norton.'

'So I won't even have a quick drink with you back in the UK?'

'Sorry, Dad. Duty calls.'

'And what about Naomi? You still seeing her?'

Naomi Clarke was Liam's long-time girlfriend. Shepherd had only met Naomi a few times and Liam rarely mentioned her, but he knew that his son had strong feelings for her. 'As much as I can,' he said. 'But switching from the army to the RAF means I'm abroad more often. She wasn't happy about this Mali posting, that's for sure.'

'Does she know what happened?'

'Me being shot down? No. I haven't called her and so far as I know our names weren't released.'

'The press'll get the names eventually,' said Shepherd. 'They always do. You need to talk to her before she reads about it in the papers.'

'I'll call her as soon as we land,' he said.

'Be careful what you say to her,' said Shepherd.

Liam frowned. 'What do you mean?'

'You don't want her worrying. If she knows how bad it was, she'll always be thinking it might happen again.'

'I don't want to lie to her, Dad.'

'I'm not suggesting you lie. Just be careful what you tell her. You were held prisoner and you were rescued. End of.'

'You mean skip over the fact that I killed three men? And that my dad rescued me?'

Shepherd shrugged. 'It's your call, obviously. Naomi is your girlfriend, so you know her better than I do. But I'd appreciate it if you didn't mention my involvement. And in my experience, it's better not to tell civilians about the bad stuff.'

'Not do a Prince Harry, you mean?'

Shepherd forced a smile. 'Soldiers don't generally boast about the number of people they've killed. And they certainly don't make light of it. Harry's going to rue the day he admitted to killing twenty-five Taliban and that it was like removing chess pieces.'

'You think there'll be repercussions?'

'There was a fatwa placed on Salman Rushdie in 1989 and he spent years in hiding but they got him eventually, almost killed him on stage in New York in 2022. So they waited more than thirty years for a writer. How long do you think they'll wait for a prince of the realm?'

Liam wrinkled his nose but figured the question was rhetorical and didn't answer.

'So things are still okay between you and Naomi?' Shepherd asked.

'It's not easy, dating a civilian,' said Liam. 'But she's busy growing her company and the time we do spend together is pretty intense.'

'She's still teaching you to sail?'

Liam grinned and nodded. 'I'm pretty good at it now.'

'I like her, you know that?'

'I do. I like her, too. More than like.' He blushed and looked away. 'You know what I mean.'

'I know. And I know how difficult it is to maintain a relationship when you're in the forces. Your mum hated it. She's the reason I left the SAS, way back when.'

'Nah, I was the reason you left. If I hadn't come along, you'd probably still be in the Regiment.'

'At my age? I don't think so.'

'You left the SAS because you were a dad. Not because you were a husband.'

'A bit of both,' admitted Shepherd. 'Your mum hated me being in the SAS even before you were born. But yes, it's tough on kids to have a dad in the SAS. Maybe tougher than it is for the wives and girlfriends.'

'Yeah, but then you joined the cops and if anything I saw even less of you. After Mum died, I spent most of my time with Grandma and Grandpa.'

'I'm sorry. I wasn't much of a father, I know that.'

'No Dad, you were a great father. You were just never around.' He forced a smile. 'But when I really needed you, you came through with flying colours, right? I doubt anyone else has a dad who could fly around the world and rescue them from murderous jihadists.'

'It was the least I could do,' said Shepherd.

Liam lifted his wrist to look at his watch, then laughed as he realised his mistake. He reached into his pocket and took out his Breitling Emergency watch. He had wound the aerial wire around the strap to stop it transmitting. 'Plus you gave me this,' he said. 'Best present ever.'

. . .

It was a six-hour flight from Gao to Brize Norton in the Atlas, with an hour on the ground refuelling at Gibraltar. Shepherd had changed out of the fatigues and into his regular clothes. He spent most of the flight sleeping, as did the SAS team. Liam and Smithy sat together towards the front of the plane, most of the time lost in their own thoughts. They were both wearing full dress uniform out of respect for their dead comrade.

The Atlas had been designed as an improvement to the Hercules, with a larger cargo capacity and an increased range.

It had a maximum payload of thirty-seven metric tons – compared with the Herc's twenty tons – and could carry six Land Rovers and trailers or a complete Chinook helicopter. Like the Herc, the fuselage was lined with seats, though unlike the Herc it came equipped with a proper toilet, complete with a door and a washbasin.

The quads and bags of equipment were tied down in the middle of the hold, and the coffin was close to the ramp, shrouded in the union flag. The crew chief supplied them with sandwiches, fruit and soft drinks from a stainless steel fridge, and, when he was awake, updated Shepherd on their progress.

They landed at Brize Norton at three o'clock in the morning. The airport was always busy. It was the largest RAF station in the UK with almost 6,000 service personnel based at it. In the fifties the airfield was home to American B-47 bombers with nuclear payloads, but the Americans pulled out in 1964 and handed the airfield back to the RAF. It was now home to the RAF's Strategic and Tactical Air Transport forces, supporting the UK's overseas operations and exercises, and it also provided air-to-air refuelling services for the RAF across the country.

As they taxied off the main runway, Shepherd saw a Boeing C-17 Globemaster, a C-130 Hercules, an Airbus Voyager and an Atlas similar to the one that he was in, along with dozens of smaller jets and helicopters.

They came to a halt in front of a massive hangar and the engines powered down. Shepherd unfastened his harness, stood up and stretched. The ramp slowly came down, revealing half a dozen vehicles waiting for them, including a black hearse. There were four airmen in dress uniform standing by the hearse, all of them barely in their twenties. Behind them was a squadron leader, a man in his early thirties, his face a blank mask.

The SAS team stood up and walked down the ramp, then formed a line, backs ramrod straight, heads up, eyes forward. Shepherd joined them. The four airmen went up the ramp and solemnly shook hands with Liam and Smithy. They exchanged a few words before carefully removing the nylon straps that had been holding the coffin in place. The officer stood at the bottom of the ramp, watching as the men gently lifted the coffin on to their shoulders. They moved slowly down the ramp, past Shepherd and the SAS men, and across the tarmac to the waiting hearse. An undertaker in a black suit opened the rear of the hearse and the airmen gently slid the coffin inside.

The undertaker closed the door and climbed into the driving seat. Liam looked over at Shepherd and gave him a small nod. Shepherd gave a thin smile and nodded back.

Liam and his colleagues climbed into a truck parked behind the hearse, its engine running. The officer got into the passenger seat of the hearse and the two vehicles headed for the exit. Only as the vehicles drove away did the SAS men relax. They headed back up the ramp and began unloading the quads and the rest of their gear. Shepherd helped them, pushing one of the quads down the ramp and on to the tarmac.

Two olive-green six-wheelers were parked at the side of the hangar. The drivers climbed out and began fixing ramps at the rear. One by one, the quads were loaded on to the trucks. Lane and Ireland carried kitbags over to two black Range Rovers and stowed them in the boots. It took the best part of an hour to take all the equipment off the Atlas. 'That's the lot,' said Standing eventually. The drivers were removing the ramps and stowing them in the back of the trucks.

'Thanks for everything, Matt,' said Shepherd.

'I'm just glad we got your boy back in one piece,' said Standing.

'I owe you one.'

'No one's keeping score, Spider. You stay safe, yeah?'

'You, too.'

The rest of the SAS team came over and one by one hugged Shepherd. 'There's life in the old dog yet,' said Ireland, patting him on the back.

'Less of the old,' said Shepherd. 'Thanks guys, have a safe trip back to Stirling Lines.'

As the SAS team headed over to the two Range Rovers, Shepherd went off to retrieve his car. He had a long drive ahead of him. As soon as he was in his SUV, he opened the glove compartment, took out his Tony Swinton phone and switched it on. There were four missed calls from Tariq, and a dozen or so text messages including 'CALL ME', 'FUCKING CALL ME', 'WHAT THE FUCK ARE YOU PLAYING AT?' 'WHERE ARE YOU?' and 'WHERE THE FUCK ARE YOU?' The last message had been sent at just before midnight. He switched the phone off again, put it in his pocket, and started the engine.

. . .

It was almost eight o'clock in the morning when Shepherd arrived in Bradford. He drove to the city centre and parked at the Great Victoria Hotel, an imposing four-storey sandstone building with towering chimneys. He had told Diane Daily that he was on the way and when he arrived at her suite she was dressed and had coffee and bacon sandwiches waiting for him. She didn't know the reason for his absence and she didn't ask, she just brought him up to speed on what had happened while he'd been away.

'The big news is the arrival of Shafiq Ali Rafiq. He's being held in the Close Supervision Centre and the whole prison is buzzing.'

'Has he been examined by a doctor yet?'

'Just the induction medical, which is really only concerned with his risk of suicide. They're not planning to run him out to a hospital, a doctor will be in to see him. But the American doctors are sure he only has months to live. Weeks maybe.'

'How does it impact on our operation?'

'I don't think it does. It's not as if he's going to be allowed into the general population, so I can't see how he can make contact with the emirs that we're investigating. I have to say it would be great if we could engineer a meeting and somehow listen in to it. But that's a pipe dream, obviously. He's been out of the UK for more than twelve years, so it's doubtful that he knows what's going on here. It's an interesting wrinkle but I don't think it affects us.' She sipped her coffee as Shepherd wolfed down a sandwich. He hadn't realised how hungry he was until he'd smelled the bacon. 'We had a funny one with Tariq, Hussain and Khaliq, just before you left. They were in Tariq's Prius, driving around, then they parked up and we lost them. They left the vehicle in Bradford NCP car park. We didn't have eyes on them for five hours, then Tariq collected his car and drove it home.'

'Did they switch vehicles?'

Daily looked uncomfortable. 'If they did, we missed it. It might just be that they went somewhere on foot. I only had two units following them, a bike and a car, and they were slow in getting into the car park. They did a sweep of the area but couldn't find them, but there was a lot of area to cover. There's a cinema that's walkable, a fair number of shops and the magistrates' court.'

'CCTV?'

'There was a camera covering the area where the Prius had parked, but it had been vandalised so there's no footage of it or the vehicles around it.'

'Coincidence?'

'Who knows? It had been smashed a few days earlier. Could have been deliberate, but if it was it'd be the first time we've seen them using counter-surveillance techniques. We do have CCTV of the vehicles leaving the car park after the Prius arrived. There were eighteen in all and we have their registration numbers, but this is Bradford where a high percentage of vehicles aren't insured and a good proportion have out-of-date registered keepers. We're doing what we can but unless we're lucky enough to find a vehicle owned by someone on our watch list, we're just going through the motions. When Tariq did return it was on foot, we've checked CCTV footage in the area but we can't find him being dropped off. It might be nothing, Spider. And there is one silver lining in that we were able to plant a tracker on the car so following it is going to be much easier from now on.'

'What does your gut tell you?'

Daily grimaced. 'That they pulled a switch and were up to something.' She forced a smile. 'But I don't know what it is. You know how it works, Spider. You watch someone for weeks and every day he walks down his road and turns right. It's boring and predictable but you keep doing it. Then one day the guy turns left and everything changes. That's what it felt like when he left the car in the car park. Everything changed.'

'What else has Tariq been up to?'

'He went around to your place twice yesterday. At eight o'clock in the morning and again at half past six. Banging on the door and shouting up at the bedroom window. Nazim Hussain was with him both times.'

'What about Mizhir Khaliq?'

'He wasn't with them and we don't have him under surveillance. I just don't have the manpower.'

'He's the one in charge, I'm sure of that.'

'If I put people on him, I'll have to take them off Tariq.'

'I'll raise it with Pritchard.' He finished his coffee and headed out of the hotel. He drove to the car park where he usually left his SUV, taking a circuitous route to check that he wasn't being followed. He parked and walked back to his house. He checked the road carefully to make sure that no one was watching before he let himself in. He made himself a cup of coffee, sniffing the milk first to make sure that it hadn't gone off in his absence, then he called the prison control centre and spoke to Neil Geraghty, explaining that he was feeling much better and was available for work. Again there were no questions about his days off, it was simply accepted that he had been sick and that he was now well enough to work. 'If you can be in at six, that would be great,' said Geraghty. 'And if you're up for overtime, you could stay until breakfast.'

Shepherd wrinkled his nose. He preferred being in the prison during the day. His main role was to take care of the two MI5 officers and to see they were safely locked up at night.

'I'd prefer days, Mr Geraghty.'

'Wouldn't we all,' said Geraghty.

'I know, but if I'm at home during the day I have to fight the urge to walk down to the betting shop. I know how pathetic that sounds.'

'We all have our vices, Tony. It's good that you're keeping a grip on yours. How about this? Come in at three today, off at eleven unless you want some overtime. Then I'll put you on earlies for the rest of the week. Six o'clock starts, and again you can have as much overtime as you want. Stay until the betting shops shut.'

'You're a star, Mr Geraghty, thanks. I owe you one.'

Shepherd ended the call and then phoned Pritchard on his personal phone. Pritchard answered almost immediately. It sounded as if he was in a vehicle, presumably heading into the office. 'I'm back and I'll be in the prison this evening,' Shepherd said. 'I met Diane this morning so I'm up to speed.'

'Congratulations on getting your boy back,' said Pritchard. 'That must be a weight off your shoulders.'

'It is. It was pretty tense for a while. But he's back with his squadron now, so all good.'

'I'm pleased it went so well,' said Pritchard. 'Though the dead Russians are a worry.'

'They were mercenaries,' said Shepherd. 'I doubt anyone will be shedding any tears for them.'

'There's no way that the Wagner Group would know that you were involved, is there?'

'It was an RAF Chinook that did the damage. We were only active in the compound.'

'I was told that your guys took out two of their vehicles.'

Shepherd frowned, wondering how Pritchard knew that the SAS unit had destroyed the disabled Wagner Wagons. Had he been following the skirmish via satellite? Or had the Chinook crew said too much?

'I'm not interested in the ins and outs of what happened,' continued Pritchard. 'Just be aware that the Wagner Group bear grudges and have long memories.'

'It's not the first time I've come upon against them,' said Shepherd. 'But I hear what you're saying.'

'Just stay safe,' said Pritchard. 'And again I'm glad that Liam's okay.'

'Thanks. Oh, Diane could do with more resources. I'd like her to keep an eye on this Mizhir Khaliq. I'm sure he's the one pulling Tariq's strings.'

'All he did was give you a phone to take in.'

'Yes, and very soon afterwards a prisoner was murdered. I think it was Khaliq who was behind that. I think if we look at him we'll find a connection to the emirs.'

'We did look at him. Nothing is known, he's not on any of our watch lists.'

'So he's a cleanskin. That in itself is a worry, surely? Why would a cleanskin want a phone smuggled into prison?'

'All I can tell you is that he's British-born, got himself a degree in computer science from Leeds Beckett University, lives with his mum and three siblings, never been in trouble. They could just be using him as a runner in which case full-time surveillance would be overkill.'

'As I said, it looked to me as if Tariq and Hussain were deferring to him.'

'Okay, I'll get someone to take a closer look at his background. If we find any red flags I'll give Diane the resources she needs.' Pritchard ended the call. Shepherd went upstairs, showered and shaved and changed into his work clothes, then made himself another cup of coffee and sat on the sofa. He was halfway through his coffee when his Tony Swinton mobile rang. It was Mohammed Tariq. 'Where the fuck are you?' he snapped.

'On the sofa,' said Shepherd. 'Why?'

'You don't answer your phone and you weren't home.'

'What do you mean I wasn't home?'

'We came around yesterday, twice, and banged on your door.'

'I was in bed. Sick. Dosed up on Night Nurse.'

'You could have answered the door.'

'I was dead to the world, mate.'

'But you're okay now, right? You're going in today?'

'Yes I'm going in today. Not that it's any of your business.'

'I need you to take something into the prison for me.'

'What?'

'It doesn't matter what,' snapped Tariq. 'Just make sure you're there when we come around.'

'When?'

'Just fucking be there,' said Tariq, and he cut the connection.

Shepherd put the phone down on the coffee table. Was Tariq guessing that he was working today, or had he spoken to someone inside the prison? Was Neil Geraghty also on Tariq's payroll? Shepherd frowned. No, that wasn't necessarily so, Geraghty would have added Tony Swinton's name to the roster and anyone with access to the prison's computer system would have seen it. But Tariq definitely had someone on the inside.

· · ·

S hepherd's doorbell rang at just after ten o'clock. He opened the door to find Tariq and Hussain glaring at him. They pushed by him and stomped into his living room. 'Please, make yourself at home, why don't you?' muttered Shepherd as he closed the front door.

'You don't look sick,' said Tariq as Shepherd joined them in the sitting room.

'You should have seen me yesterday,' said Shepherd. 'I was throwing up for England.'

'So what was it? You said you were dosed up on Night Nurse. Was it flu or food poisoning?'

'I dunno what it was, I'm not a doctor.'

'So what did the doctor say it was?'

Shepherd laughed. 'Mate, when was the last time you got to see your GP? First appointment was next month. The only option I had was to go and sit in A&E for twelve hours and I was in no fit state to do that. I just took Night Nurse and went to bed. When I wasn't sleeping I was throwing up. I think it was some virus that's going around.'

'You look okay now.'

'I still feel a bit rough. But I have to go into work. I need the money.'

Tariq frowned and took a step closer to Shepherd. 'It looks like you've caught the sun,' he said.

'I doubt it. Haven't been out of the house and the curtains were drawn.'

Tariq gestured at the mirror on the wall above the fireplace. 'Take a look for yourself.'

Shepherd went over to the mirror and saw his reflection. He kept his face a blank mask but he could see what Tariq meant – there was reddening on his nose, cheeks and forehead, the result of being out in the harsh West African sun. He rubbed his nose. 'Nah, that's an allergic reaction, I get it sometimes with paracetamol. I probably took too many tablets.' He looked at Tariq and laughed again. 'Trust me, I wasn't lying on a beach somewhere. Go and have a look at my bedroom, if you want. Smells like a doss house up there.'

Tariq stared at him for several seconds, then nodded and took a step back. He reached into the pocket of his bomber jacket and took out a plastic-wrapped package, about the size of a Mars bar. He handed it to Shepherd. 'You need to give that to a guy called Adil Rashid on A Wing. Today.'

Shepherd weighed the package in his hand. It was five ounces, maybe six. If it was tobacco it could be worth five thousand pounds inside. If it was heroin or cocaine, the sky was the limit. 'I can't guarantee that I'll be in A Wing today.'

'That's already been sorted,' said Tariq. 'Just make sure he gets it.'

Shepherd grinned. 'And my fee?'

Tariq took a roll of fifty pound notes from his pocket and pulled out four of them. He gave them to Shepherd, who wrinkled his nose. He held up the package. 'What's in here?'

'It's none of your fucking business what it is. Just give it to Rashid. He'll be expecting it.'

'It's not tobacco, is it?'

'Maybe it is, or maybe it isn't. What's the difference?'

'About eight bloody years,' said Shepherd. 'If I get caught with tobacco in my pocket, I lose my job and maybe go down for a few months. But if I get caught with a pack of cocaine that size then it's possession with intent to supply and they'll throw the key away.'

'Then don't get caught,' said Tariq.

'I'm just saying, that if you're increasing the risk, you should be increasing the reward.'

Tariq's eyes hardened. 'And I'm just saying that if you don't do as you're fucking told, a couple of the brothers will be paying your mother a visit. Okay?'

Shepherd let his shoulders slump as he stared at the floor, playing the weak man. 'Okay, fine,' he said.

Tariq patted him on the shoulder. 'Get it to him before evening association and there'll be a bonus in it for you.'

Shepherd nodded. 'Okay.'

Tariq nodded at Hussain and the two men left. 'No need to see us out,' said Hussain.

Shepherd followed them into the hall and watched as they left. 'Pricks,' he muttered under his breath. Tariq was a bully and Shepherd would have loved to have shown him the error of his ways, but that wasn't going to happen. Shepherd was just going to have to grin and bear it.

He picked up his phone and called Daily. When she answered he waved up at the smoke detector in the ceiling. 'Did you get all that?' he asked.

'Every word.'

'I've a few hours before I have to go to work, could you send someone around to check on the contents of this?' He waggled the package at the concealed camera.

'Sammy's on her way,' said Diane.

'I'll put the kettle on,' said Shepherd.

The doorbell rang half an hour later. Diane's operative was a young MI5 officer by the name of Samara 'Sammy' Gupta, a recent recruit who Diane had taken under her wing. Shepherd had met her several times and she was obviously going to go far. She carried out any task she was given efficiently and with a smile, and although she was still in her mid-twenties, she was wise beyond her years and nothing ever seemed to faze her. He grinned when he opened the door and saw that she was wearing British Gas overalls and carrying a blue metal tool box. Her long black hair was tied back under her British Gas cap. 'A neighbour has reported the smell of gas,' she said, her brown eyes sparkling.

'Then you must come in immediately,' he said straight-faced.

She walked down the hall to the kitchen, where Shepherd had put teabags in two mugs. As she sat down at the small kitchen table, Shepherd switched on the kettle again while he went to fetch the package that Tariq had given him. He put it on the table in front of her and poured boiling water into the mugs.

Sammy picked up the package and looked at it carefully, turning it over several times. There was an outer layer of clingfilm over what appeared to be a thicker plastic that had been folded around whatever was inside. She took an iPhone from her pocket and photographed the package from various angles, then took a ruler from her tool box and put it next to the package before taking more photographs.

Shepherd added milk to both mugs and two sugars to Sammy's and put hers down on the table.

'I think I'm going to have to open it,' she said. 'If I puncture the bag, even just slightly, they might spot the damage. But it might take me some time.'

'We've got a few hours,' said Shepherd. 'There's no rush.'

Sammy slowly and carefully removed the clingfilm, taking care not to tear it. She laid it flat on the table. It was easier to make out the contents now, a fine white powder. 'I'm almost certain it's cocaine,' said Sammy.

Shepherd nodded. 'I think you're right.'

She took a small digital scale from her tool box and weighed the package. It came in at 140 grams, about five ounces. She took several photographs of the package on the scales.

The drugs were in a small plastic ziplock bag that had been rolled over to form a cylinder and fastened with a strip of Sellotape. Sammy carefully undid the Sellotape, then opened out the bag. She undid the ziplock, then put the bag on the table. She reached into her tool box and took out a small white cardboard box that contained a clear glass ampoule, a small bottle of clear liquid, and a thin wooden spatula.

The ampoule contained white crystals and Sammy tapped it on the table several times to make sure that the crystals were all at the bottom, then she snapped off the top. The small bottle contained a buffer solution, which she carefully poured into the ampoule before shaking it. She then used the spatula to add a small amount of the white powder, and stirred it until it had all dissolved.

'Right, now we wait,' she said, pushing the ampoule into a slot in the cardboard box. She picked up her tea and sipped it. 'What's it like, being in the prison?' she asked.

'Boring, most of the time,' he said. 'With flashes of violence, which means you can never let your guard down.'

'I don't think I could do it,' she said.

'You'd be surprised,' he said. 'The cons often go easy on the female officers. Not as much testosterone.'

'I meant working undercover the way you do. I mean, I've played undercover roles, but only for an hour or so at most. But you're in there for hours at a time. Doesn't it mess with your head?'

'You get used to it.'

'Really? So it gets easier?'

'I'm not sure that it gets easier. Maybe a little less stressful, but then you have to make sure you don't get careless.'

'I guess it's like being an actor, right? You're playing a part?'

Shepherd nodded. 'Yeah, except that if something goes wrong, you don't get a bad review, you get . . .' He grimaced and didn't finish the sentence.

'What if somebody shouts out your real name? Don't you react? If ever I hear someone shout "Sammy" I look around. I can't help myself.'

'It's the reacting to your cover name that's a bigger problem,' said Shepherd. 'My cover is Tony Swinton, but I don't react automatically when someone calls out my name. I have to hear the name and then process that it's me, which can take a fraction of a second. That can be a dead giveaway if somebody notices it.'

'So how do you deal with that?'

'I just keep reminding myself who I'm supposed to be. But yeah, it's a problem.' He took a drink of his tea. 'Are you interested in undercover work?'

'No, not as a career option,' she said. 'As I said, I've done it on various operations, but never on my own, always as part of a team, usually as back-up to a more experienced officer. I actually think I'm quite good at it. I did drama at school and I was never nervous on stage. But career-wise I'd prefer to do what Diane does, organising operations and the like. Behind the scenes.'

'What about surveillance?'

'Again I prefer the organising, rather than being in the field. There's more of a buzz when you're seeing the big picture. Like moving chess pieces on a board.'

'I think we're polar opposites,' said Shepherd. 'I much prefer being at the sharp end.'

'But you're running Kamran and Sayed in the prison.'

'I am, yes. And I worry more about them than I do myself.'

'It's probably about control,' said Sammy. 'Once you start depending on others, you lose control, don't you?'

'Maybe,' said Shepherd. He sipped his tea again. Actually he had no problem trusting others. Being in the SAS was all about teamwork. Lone wolves were a liability on special forces operations, despite what Hollywood thought. But in the SAS he was dealing with men he'd trained with, been in combat with, and gotten drunk with. He knew everything there was to know about the men he'd served with, the good and the bad. He knew much less about the MI5 officers he worked with – often just their name, sometimes not even that – which meant he was never sure just how much he could rely on them.

Sammy looked at her watch, then picked up the ampoule and gave it a shake. She took a colour comparison chart from the cardboard box, held it against the ampoule and showed it to Shepherd. The liquid was a dark brown. 'It's almost pure,' she said. 'Hardly cut at all.'

'So street value would be what, seven thousand pounds?'

'It would depend on your street,' said Sammy. 'On a Liverpool housing estate, maybe five thousand. In Soho, double that. But in prison, cocaine this pure? You could cut it fifty per cent and still get up to a thousand pounds a gram.' She put the ampoule and chart into the box.

Shepherd whistled softly. That meant the package could be worth as much as a hundred and forty thousand pounds once it was inside the prison.

'I'm going to take a small sample for evidence,' she said. 'Do you think they'll weigh it inside?'

'I doubt it,' said Shepherd.

'Just a gram will do,' said Sammy. She took a small glass bottle from the cardboard box and used the spatula to transfer a small amount of the cocaine. She screwed the top back on, then photographed the bottle. There was an evidence bag in the box; she took it out, popped in the bottle and sealed it. She wrote her name, the time, the date and their location on the bag's label, then took a photograph with her camera, including a selfie of herself holding the bag and smiling brightly. She saw him grinning at her and she laughed. 'Not for social media, obviously,' she said. 'I'm just providing a chain of evidence.'

'Obviously,' he said. He watched as she carefully sealed the ziplock bag, rolled it up and used the Sellotape to keep it in place. She checked the photograph she had taken earlier to reassure herself that the tape was in the same place, then rewrapped it in clingfilm.

'There you go,' she said eventually. 'As good as new.' She gave it back to him.

'Nice job.'

'I used to wrap presents in Harrods as a Christmas job when I was a student.' She smiled at him and he had no way of knowing if she was joking or not. The girl was definitely going to go far.

• • •

Mizhir Khaliq unzipped the holdall and smiled when he saw what was inside: a couple of dozen machetes, each in a nylon scabbard. He took one out. 'These are nice, bruv,' he said.

Mohammed Tariq nodded. 'All brand new. Sharp as a razor.'

Khaliq slid the machete out of its scabbard and waved it in the air.

Nazim Hussain grinned. 'You could take an arm off, no bother.'

'How many have we got?' asked Khaliq.

Tariq pointed at a line of five identical holdalls. 'Six bags in all, mostly machetes but we've got flick knives, carving knives, a few axes, some zombie knives.'

Khaliq frowned. 'What's a zombie knife?'

'You know, they use them in the movies for killing zombies. Big knives with a jagged edge, great for taking heads off.'

'And how many knives in all?'

'About two hundred. Is that enough? You said a couple of hundred.'

'The more the merrier, that's what they say.'

They were standing in a warehouse on an industrial estate on the outskirts of Bradford. A friend of Khaliq's had rented it for six months through a shell company. It had once been used to store cat litter and there were still several boxes of the stuff piled up against a wall. There was a small office cubicle in one corner but it was empty, the dust on the floor spotted with paw prints left by scavenging rats.

They had driven Tariq's Prius into the unit and pulled the shutter down. There was a fourth man, still sitting in the back of the Prius. Khaliq waved for him to get out of the car. His name was Umar Zaman and he was nervous, looking around anxiously as if he expected the police to appear at any moment. 'Umar, chill,' said Khaliq, 'you're among friends here.'

Zaman nodded. 'Okay, okay,' he said.

Khaliq put the machete back into its scabbard and nodded at the van driver. 'Tell me again what they do when the van gets there.'

'We pull up outside. We use an entrance at the rear of the prison that's for deliveries only.'

'Is there a guard outside?'

'No, they see us on CCTV. If they don't, there's an intercom thing. They open the gate and we drive in. The gate closes behind us.'

'You say "us". How many of you are in the van?'

'Me and a mate.'

'Same mate every day?'

'There are three or four who do it. They're basically there just to help with the unloading.'

'And do you have to show ID?'

'Nah. We're supposed to wear company IDs around our neck. I do but the other guys sometimes forget. But nobody checks.'

'What about doing it without a mate? Solo?'

'Never happens. We're always two up.'

'What about Mo here?' asked Khaliq. 'Could you use him as your mate tomorrow?'

'I could swing that yeah.'

'He can turn up at your warehouse, right? And drive here with you?'

'No problem.'

Khaliq looked at Hussain. 'Okay with what?'

'Works for me, bruv.'

Khaliq looked back at Zaman. 'Okay, so the gate then closes. What happens then?'

'A guard will come out and check the vehicle. He has a mirror on a stick thing and he runs it under the van. Dunno what he expects to find.'

'Does he talk to you?'

'Nah. Doesn't even look at us. Just runs the mirror around the van and then goes back inside.'

'He never opens the van doors?'

'They used to. But it's been ages since they bothered.'

Khaliq nodded. 'Other than you, who drives the van?'

'To the prison? Me and a guy called Zaki. One or the other.'

'But you'll definitely be driving tomorrow?'

Khaliq nodded again. 'Yeah, Zaki's on holiday.'

'And there won't be a problem if I'm sitting in the front with you when we get to the prison?'

'I don't see why there would be. Like I said, they don't even look at us.'

Khaliq turned to Tariq. 'So I'll sit in the front seat. You can be in the back with a gun, just in case they do open the door for a look inside.'

'What about me?' asked Hussain.

'You need to drive Mo's car home,' said Khaliq. 'We don't want to leave it here and we won't be coming back.'

'So I'm not coming with you?'

'There'll be plenty for you to do on the outside,' said Khaliq. He looked at Zaman. 'What happens when they've checked under the vehicle?'

'The guard goes back inside and then the second gate opens and we drive through to the kitchen courtyard. The kitchen staff unload the van and carry the stuff inside.'

'What about guards?'

'There are guards there but they usually don't come out.'

'How many?'

'I've only ever seen two.' Zaman frowned. 'Do I have to drive?'

'Why do you ask that, bruv?'

'I've got a family. A wife and kids.'

'We've all got families. Are you a good Muslim or not?'

'I am. Yes, I am. But this . . .'

'I can drive the van,' said Tariq.

'But what if they check us?' said Khaliq.

'They won't. He said they won't. But even if they did, we're already in, right? We can have guns in the cab with us.'

Khaliq frowned as he considered what Tariq was saying. He wasn't happy at the idea of switching drivers, but Zaman was already sweating like a man about to be hanged and he'd be even worse driving into the prison. 'You're sure you can drive it?'

'Bruv, I've got an HGV licence, I can drive anything.'

'Okay,' said Khaliq. 'You drive the van, Mo can take your Prius back to your place.'

'I want to go into the prison with you,' said Hussain. 'I want to be part of this.'

'Nah, bruv, we need people on the outside. People we can trust. You are part of this. A big part.'

'And what happens afterwards?' asked Zaman. 'I'll lose my job.'

Khaliq laughed. 'After tomorrow, a lot of people are going to be losing their jobs.'

Khaliq and Tariq got into the front of the Prius, and Zaman climbed into the back, obviously still unhappy. Hussain pulled up the metal shutter and Tariq drove out of the warehouse and stopped in the loading bay. Hussain pulled down the metal shutter and locked it, before climbing into the back of the Prius.

As they drove out of the estate, they didn't pay any attention to the Openreach van parked at the side of the road.

• • •

Shepherd pushed open the door to the staff entrance. Jim MacLeod was on duty, though he didn't look up from his newspaper as Shepherd walked over to the baggage scanner. Shepherd put his backpack on the conveyor belt along with his watch and keys before walking through the metal detector arch. The plastic-wrapped package was in his trouser pocket.

MacLeod dragged his eyes from his newspaper to look over at the screen. 'What culinary delights are you having today, Tony?'

'Ham and tomato, with oxtail soup.'

'Heinz?'

'Of course.'

'Branston pickle on the sandwiches?'

'Am I that predictable?'

'You should try it with piccalilli. It adds bite.'

'Maybe I will.'

Shepherd picked up his belongings and walked to the staff room to collect his radio, baton and bodycam.

Neil Geraghty had finished his shift and an officer by the name of Caroline Connolly was running the control centre. She was one of the longest-serving officers in the prison, coming up for almost thirty years with no sign of wanting to retire. She was one of the few who actually seemed to enjoy her job, though her experience meant she spent most of her time in the control centre and rarely walked the landings.

'Tony Swinton, reporting for duty,' he said, flashing her a mock salute.

'I was told you were at death's door, Tony,' she said. 'But that the promise of overtime dragged you back in.'

Shepherd grinned. 'I was as sick as a dog, Caroline. Really.'

'Don't kid a kidder,' she said. 'You're here now, that's all that matters.' She checked the computer. 'You're on A Wing tonight,' she said.

'Who's with me?'

She looked at the screen. 'Sheila Jeffries. Andrew George. Nick Durst.'

Shepherd knew all three officers. Jeffries was a bubbly blonde from Wakefield with a gift for diffusing difficult situations with a joke and a wink, George was a decent guitarist who was happy to help inmates improve their musical skills, and Durst was one of the more relaxed officers, a fervent Liverpool fan who would stand and listen to inmates complaining about their lot, nodding and stroking his greying goatee and offering a sympathetic word. He had the patience of a saint. Like Shepherd he brought in his own lunch and they would often sit together in the staff canteen. It was a good team, they were all experienced officers and could be relied on if trouble broke out. Jeffries might have looked as if butter wouldn't melt in her mouth but Shepherd had seen her apply a choke hold worthy of an MMA champion.

'Who did the rota?' Shepherd asked.

Connolly frowned. 'Is there a problem?'

Shepherd flashed her his most disarming grin. 'No, all good. It's just I was on B Wing before I was sick.'

She looked at the screen. 'Neil did the rota. I wouldn't worry about it. It's good to move around, that way you get to know more of the population. It's a quiet wing, too. Very few problems. Linda Wilson has done a good job of calming things down.'

'I'm not complaining,' said Shepherd. 'I was just wondering, that's all. At the end of the day, a wing's a wing.'

'I just wish that were true,' said Connolly. 'There's good wings and bad wings, and A Wing is one of the good ones, so if I were you I wouldn't be looking any gift horses in the mouth.'

'It's the last thing I'd do,' said Shepherd. 'I've never been a fan of horses.'

Shepherd left her office and walked across the octagonal floor to the gate that led to A Wing. There were two officers on the gantries overhead, walking slowly around so that they could see down each of the wings. It was a protocol that had been used since Victorian times, though new prisons being built no longer used the design. It was seen as old-fashioned and authoritarian and modern prisons tended to remove the bars from windows and cluster cells in smaller groups around landscaped courtyards.

Shepherd unlocked the gate to A Wing and stepped inside. The lunch trolleys had been cleared away and a trustee was mopping the floor with broad sweeps of a wide mop. There was a fluidity to the motion that suggested he had been doing it for years, though the guy was only in his early twenties, wearing an Adidas tracksuit and gleaming Nikes. 'Watch yourself, boss,' he said with a strong Birmingham accent. 'That bit's still wet. I wouldn't want you to slip and put in a six-figure compensation claim.'

Shepherd thanked him and walked around the wet patch. From overhead came the thump-thump-thump of a stereo being played with the bass up high, and somebody was kicking his door at the far end of the ones. Two inmates were playing table tennis, shrieking every time they hit the ball. They were being watched by a dozen or so inmates leaning over the railing on the twos. Several of them were vaping.

Shepherd knocked on the door of the wing governor's office. Linda Wilson was a former solicitor who had moved into the prison service after two decades of defending criminals – alleged and otherwise. Shepherd had read her file, which included her original application, where she had discussed her frustration at dealing with the same clients again and again, functioning as a revolving door in a system that had them back in prison almost as soon as they had left. Realising that prison wasn't stopping reoffending, she had decided to try and change the system from the inside. She had done three years walking the landings in Leeds Prison before being promoted to governor at Bradford. That was five years ago, and while she was still as determined as ever to bring about change, she had begun to accept that she was fighting a losing battle. She had the best of intentions but with the number of inmates rising year on year at a time when staffing was being reduced and budgets slashed, her job was almost impossible. Wilson had pushed to start a number of apprenticeships at the prison, teaching prisoners a trade so that they could find a job when they left. But most had been closed within a year for financial reasons and those that were still open depended on there being officers to take them to and from the workshops. If there weren't enough staff on the wing, the work and study details were the first to be cancelled.

She smiled as Shepherd walked into the office. 'Just checking in, ma'am,' he said.

'Good to have you on board Tony. Neil says you're up for some overtime? Can you stay until midnight?'

'Sure, not a problem.' There was a whiteboard on the wall behind her with a series of squares marking the cells on the three landings and the names of the current occupants. Shepherd spotted Adil Rashid's name on the second landing. He was two up with a prisoner called Mohammad Ahmadi. Shepherd ran through his mental filing cabinet. Mohammad Ahmadi was serving three years for dishonestly obtaining Covid loans during the pandemic, buying off-the-shelf companies and applying for money which was never repaid. Ahmadi had popped up on to MI5's radar when he began transferring some of his ill-gotten gains to a friend in Syria, a friend who had left his job in a Leeds kebab house to fight for ISIS.

'It's been quiet today and they've had burgers and chips for lunch which always gets them in a good mood,' said Wilson. 'We've had a few spice incidents today, but they were confined to their cells and we'll let them sleep it off. Seems like there's a really strong batch going around.'

'Any idea how it's getting in?' A common way of getting spice into prison was by soaking it into paper, which would then be written on and sent to an inmate. The paper could then be cut up and smoked in a roll-up, but it was a lot less potent than if the drug was sprinkled directly on to tobacco.

'We've got a few smashed windows on the upper landing and a few days ago the night staff heard drones outside. But who knows? This prison leaks like a sieve.'

Shepherd smiled but felt a twinge of guilt at the fact that he was carrying five ounces of cocaine in his pocket.

Wilson opened her mouth to speak but was interrupted by the sound of alarms going off. 'There's a fight on the twos,' said a male voice on Shepherd's radio, echoed through a radio set on Wilson's desk. 'Assistance required.'

'No rest for the wicked,' said Wilson.

'I'm on it,' said Shepherd. He hurried out of her office and headed for the stairs. Sheila Jeffries was already there. Running on the wings was forbidden for health and safety reasons, but they both jogged up the stairs.

Shepherd took a look over his shoulder. The gate to the control centre was open and four burly officers were barrelling through, wearing protective gear and helmets, wielding batons. They were the Rapid Reaction Team, specially trained officers who were based in the control centre, available to be sent to wherever they were needed. When the unit had first been set up it had been called the Fast Reaction Team before someone in charge realised the unfortunate acronym. The name was changed but it was too late and the unit was still known by the inmates – and some of the officers – as the FART.

Jeffries reached the top landing, with Shepherd hard on her heels. The landing was crowded with inmates shouting and swearing. Jeffries pushed her way through and Shepherd followed her. His instinct was to call out and tell her to hang back, that he'd deal with it, but he knew she would have ignored him.

He took a quick look over the railing and down through the netting. Four more Fart officers were running towards the stairs.

As Shepherd and Jeffries reached the far end of the landing they saw two prisoners had cornered one of the female guards. Her name was Jenny Johnston, a new recruit who had joined at the same time as Shepherd. They had gone on an induction course together and Shepherd had figured she was going to have a tough time on the wings. She was barely out of university with a second-class honours degree in sociology, and for some reason had decided that she wanted to make the prison service her career. It was clear that she wanted to be a governor running her own prison, and she would probably have had the skills to do that and do it well, but to get to that stage she needed to do her time on the landings. She knew all the theory and could recite the various prison manuals by heart, but she didn't have the mental toughness that was required to keep prisoners in order. There were times when inmates had to be faced down and made to follow instructions by sheer force of will, but Johnston had difficulty even making eye contact with prisoners, and rarely spoke above a whisper. The senior officers had done their best to protect her, but at the end of the day guards had to stand on their own two feet.

Today she was alone on the landing and had been pinned against the wall by two inmates. One had his hand around her throat, the other had grabbed at her belt and was either trying to take her baton or her radio, it was hard to tell. Other inmates were shouting and screaming, one was telling them to throw her over the railing, another was shouting 'rip her clothes off'.

Jeffries reached for the baton on her belt. She flicked it out to extend it and held it high in the air. 'Get back!' she shouted at the top of her voice. 'Get away from her now!'

The inmates ignored her. Johnston's eyes were wide and staring and her face had gone red. Shepherd couldn't tell if her attacker was actually trying to kill her or was just restraining her, but either way the end result was that she was being choked to death. His memory kicked in. The inmate holding her was a convicted rapist who was serving seven years for a home invasion in Halifax, where he had tied up a husband and raped his wife in front of him. His name was Dave Ward and his defence, such as it was, was that he had been high on drugs at the time. From the look on his face and the way his eyes were wide and staring, there was every chance he was high now, probably on spice. The inmate who was fiddling with Johnston's belt was another rapist, or rather alleged rapist as he was on remand awaiting trial. His name was Darren Patterson and he had been held without bail for almost a year. Like Ward, he appeared to be high on spice. Shepherd could smell acetone coming from the men, probably from nail varnish remover. Spice was often mixed with nail varnish remover before it was sprayed on to dried herbs or tobacco, to mimic the appearance of natural cannabis.

'Go on, miss, give 'em what for!' shouted one of the prisoners.

Jeffries stepped forward and again shouted for the men to get away from Johnston but they ignored her. Jeffries brought the baton crashing down on the back of Ward's knee but he didn't even register the blow and continued to strangle the guard. Patterson managed to pull Johnston's baton from her belt and he made several attempts to extend it. Inmates began jeering at his efforts. The spice had disrupted his coordination and he stared at the baton and gritted his teeth in frustration. There were sweat stains on his T-shirt and he hadn't shaved in a few days. Personal hygiene was never a priority with spice addicts. He flicked the baton again and this time it extended and he grinned in triumph, showing yellowed teeth.

'Drop the baton!' shouted Jeffries.

'Sheila, be careful!' shouted Shepherd. Patterson was clearly not going to obey any instructions.

'I've got this!' hissed Jeffries, taking a step closer to Patterson.

Patterson used the baton like a rapier and prodded it at her face. Jeffries yelled at him to get back, then struck him on the side of the neck with her baton. Patterson didn't even seem to feel the blow.

Shepherd reached for his PAVA spray but realised that if he sprayed Patterson he'd hit Jeffries, too.

The inmates were screaming at Patterson, telling him to hit Jeffries. He grinned and raised his arms as if accepting applause at a concert. Jeffries hit him again, this time on his left knee, but the blow was as ineffective as the first. Patterson lashed out with his baton, narrowly missing Jeffries, and he began to laugh maniacally.

Shepherd stepped forward and waved his hand to get Patterson's attention. 'Hey, pick on someone your own size!' Shepherd shouted. As Patterson hit out with the baton again, Shepherd twisted to the side, caught the man's wrist and twisted his arm back. Patterson roared, more in anger than pain, and struggled to free himself. Shepherd pulled one of Patterson's fingers away from the baton, then pulled harder until he heard it crack. The baton fell to the floor. Jeffries quickly bent to pick it up and began shouting at Ward to let go of Johnston.

Patterson was cursing at Shepherd, spittle flicking from between his lips as he tried to claw at Shepherd's eyes with his free hand. Shepherd kept the pressure on Patterson's wrist, twisting him around so that his stomach was pressed up against the railing. Patterson wasn't giving up, it was clear that he was so drugged up that he wasn't feeling any pain.

The Rapid Response Team had reached the top landing and were pushing their way through the crowd of baying inmates. Shepherd swung Patterson around so that his back was to the guards, then he kicked him in the stomach and sent him sprawling backwards.

Jeffries was screaming at Ward and hacking at this leg with her baton, but her blows were having no effect and he was now strangling Johnston with both hands.

Shepherd took two quick steps towards Ward, grabbed his hair and pulled his head back. Ward's hands stayed around the guard's neck. Shepherd punched him hard on the right temple. Ward grunted and Shepherd hit him again, this time with his elbow, slamming it into the inmate's head. Ward finally released his grip on Johnston, who slid down the wall, gasping for breath.

Shepherd span Ward around and pushed him against the wall. The inmates were screaming at the top of their voices now, full of hatred and loathing, in the grip of a blood lust that would only be satisfied with either Shepherd or Ward out for the count.

Shepherd heard boots pounding on the landing and knew that the Rapid Response Team was only seconds away, but Ward was already moving forward, his hands forming claws that were reaching for Shepherd's face. Shepherd formed a fist with his right hand, knocked Ward's hands away with his left and then punched him on the chin. Ward's head twisted to the right and his whole body span around. His eyes rolled up and he fell like a stone, crashing into the landing floor so hard that Shepherd felt the vibrations through his feet.

The inmates burst out cheering and yelling and Shepherd realised that they were actually on his side. Or maybe they just wanted to see violence and didn't care who was at the receiving end. He stepped back, then glanced over at Jeffries. The red light wasn't blinking on her bodycam, and he hadn't switched his on. With any luck the nearest CCTV camera's view would have been blocked by all the inmates crowding around to get a look at the action. He looked down at Ward, who was still out for the count.

'Nice one, Tony,' said Jeffries, appearing at his shoulder. 'Personally I'd have PAVA'd him.'

'I figured he was so high it wouldn't have affected him.'

One of the officers from the Rapid Reaction Team patted Shepherd on the shoulder. 'Nice right hook,' he said. 'But next time wait for us.'

'I had it in hand.'

The man chuckled. 'Damn right you did. But a punch like that could have killed him if he'd hit his head on the floor. I'd hate to see you on a manslaughter charge.' Two members of the Rapid Reaction Team had picked Patterson up and were marching him to his cell.

Shepherd nodded. The man was right. He'd reacted instinctively, exactly as he would have done in combat, but the prison wasn't a war zone and if the prisoner had been badly hurt there would have been consequences, with Shepherd being suspended at the very least. 'Sorry,' said Shepherd.

'Hey, no need to apologise. I've been more than tempted to deck one or two of these morons myself, but we've got protocols in place for a reason.'

Ward was still on his back, his eyes closed, a dribble of saliva running down the side of his face.

'Right,' said the officer, 'let's get sleeping beauty back into his cell.' He looked at Shepherd. 'I'll do the paperwork. We'll say he was restrained by the Rapid Reaction Team. Not that I'm trying to steal your thunder, just best that we forget about you going all Mike Tyson on him.'

'Fine by me,' said Shepherd. He looked around the landing and spotted Rashid leaning on the railing with half a dozen other inmates, obviously watching what was going on. One of them was Kamran Zaidi. They were all wearing Islamic clothing and most had skullcaps. Rashid had a long light blue tunic and dark blue baggy pants, and was holding a set of prayer beads. He was in his thirties with a long straggly beard and black-framed spectacles and was smoking an e-cigarette. The smoke smelled of apple.

Shepherd walked over to them. Four of them moved away as he approached, like sheep scattering from a dog, but Rashid and Zaidi stayed where they were. 'Gentlemen, if you could go back to your cells, that would be great,' he said.

'I'm waiting to go to work,' said Rashid. He sucked on his e-cigarette.

'I know, but in view of what happened, we'd like everyone safe in their cells until everything is under control.'

Rashid blew a cloud of vapour at Shepherd. 'Looks like you had it well under control,' he said. 'You fucking laid into him, innit.'

'I was defending myself,' said Shepherd. 'So please, guys, can you just pop into your cells until the heavy mob are gone. No need to close the doors, you can keep them open. Just until everything has been sorted.'

'This is a liability,' said Rashid. 'We didn't do nuffing.'

'I know, and I appreciate it,' said Shepherd. He gestured at the door to Rashid's cell. 'Please. You're not supposed to be vaping on the landing anyway.'

Rashid groaned and walked into his cell. Shepherd followed him in. As he sat down on his bunk, Shepherd slipped the package out of his pocket and gave it to him. 'Tariq sent this,' said Shepherd.

Rashid nodded and slipped it under his pillow. 'Well aren't you the dark horse,' he said.

'Mum's the word,' said Shepherd.

Rashid shook his head. 'Nah, man, bent screw is the word.'

'That'd be two words, actually,' said Shepherd. He backed out of the cell. 'Be lucky.'

'Fuck off, kafir,' said Rashid.

'You have a nice day,' said Shepherd. He walked down the landing to Zaidi's cell. He wasn't sure if he was alone or not so he knocked on the door. 'You decent?' he asked. He popped his head around the door. Zaidi was alone and sitting on his bunk reading a paperback. Shepherd stepped into the cell. 'You okay?'

'Sure, yes, all good.'

Shepherd kept his voice down to a whisper. 'Listen, I need you to keep an eye on Rashid for me. I've just delivered him a package, plastic-wrapped and about the size of a Mars bar. I'm pretty sure he'll be passing it on to someone else later today, I need to know who.'

Zaidi nodded. 'No problem.'

They heard a noise on the landing outside the cell. Zaidi looked over Shepherd's shoulder and his jaw tensed. 'If I wanted advice from a fucking kafir I'd ask for it!' he shouted. 'Now get the fuck out of my cell!'

Shepherd looked around to see that Zaidi's cellmate, a middle-aged man wearing a long grey robe and a skullcap, was standing in the doorway. He looked back at Zaidi and raised his hands defensively. 'There's no need to get upset, I was just trying to help.'

'Yeah? Well I don't need no help from a fucking kafir. So fuck off.'

'Okay, okay,' said Shepherd, keeping his hands up as he backed out of the cell. The cellmate slipped inside.

Shepherd walked back to the stairs. Hopefully Zaidi's quick thinking had worked and the cellmate would be none the wiser. Shepherd did a slow circuit of the landing, nodding at those inmates who made eye contact with him, and avoiding the hate-filled glares of those who were looking for a confrontation. The wing had gone quiet when the Rapid Reaction Team had stormed in, but now the noise levels were building again. Sound systems were switched on, televisions were blaring and there were shouts and curses from the inmates playing pool and table tennis. Doors and gates clanged shut and radios crackled. The wings were rarely quiet, and what noise there was became intensified by the thick stone walls so that often when he went home Shepherd's ears were aching.

He headed down the stairs to the first floor landing. Two men were blocking his way, deep in conversation. They looked so similar that they could have been brothers, but Shepherd knew from their files that they weren't related. Josif Dhana and Mihal Nushi were Albanian gangsters, serving eight years apiece for a vicious attack on a Leeds cocaine dealer. The Albanians had hacked off four of the dealer's fingers before he'd told them where his stash was and another two before he gave up his bank details. Once they'd taken his drugs and money they had dropped him outside Bradford Royal Infirmary with his mutilated fingers sandwiched between two packs of frozen chips.

The drug dealer had at first refused to give evidence against the Albanians, making the not unreasonable observation that if he did his entire family would likely end up dead. His wife, though, was made of sterner stuff and once she told the police that she would give evidence that they had broken into her house and abducted her husband at gunpoint, her husband agreed to cooperate. They were now in witness protection up in Scotland with their two young children. A search of the homes of the Albanians had turned up a number of weapons, including assault rifles and ammunition, which had added another five years apiece.

Both men were short and squat with barrel-like chests and thick necks, with shaved heads and matching tattoos of back-to-back Glocks on their forearms. They wore matching blue tracksuits and Nike trainers.

'Excuse me guys,' said Shepherd.

The two men turned to look at him scornfully, then turned their backs on him as they continued to speak in their own language.

'I need to get by, guys,' said Shepherd, louder this time.

They carried on ignoring him so Shepherd tapped Dhani on the shoulder. 'I need to get down the stairs, Mr Dhani,' he said.

Dhani whirled around and glared up at Shepherd. 'Don't you dare fucking touch me!' he shouted.

His voice carried down the landing and heads turned to see what was going on. Shepherd held his hands up. 'I apologise for touching you, but I need to get down to the ground floor.'

Dhani sneered at him, then cleared his throat and spat on the stair in front of Shepherd. He muttered something in Albanian and Nushi laughed. The two men moved apart, giving

Shepherd just enough space to squeeze through. He could smell their fetid breath as he passed between them. 'Thank you so much,' said Shepherd sarcastically. He hated having to play the power games that went on in the prison, but he had no choice. If the two Albanians had attacked him, the worst that would happen to them would be a few months in solitary and a couple of years added to their sentences. Shepherd was reasonably certain that he could take on either of them individually, but not the two of them, which meant that at some point he would have gone down and they would have almost certainly kicked him to a pulp before the Rapid Reaction Team could reach him. He'd face months in hospital, with injuries that he'd probably never recover from. And for what? Because they wouldn't move out of his way? It simply wasn't worth it.

In what many of the older officers would have referred to as the good old days, the guards ruled with violence. Any inmate who stepped out of line would be dealt with quickly and aggressively, often by a gang of officers with the cell doors closed. Prisoners learned quickly where the power lay and knew the consequences of behaving badly, especially when it came to using violence – even threats of violence – against the officers. Retribution would come hard and fast and no questions would be asked, no reports filled in. Those days had long gone, and if anything the pendulum had swung the other way.

CCTV and bodycams meant that almost everything officers did was seen and recorded, and inmates were much more aware of their rights. A prisoner could simply refuse to obey an officer's request, knowing that there was no way the officer could use force to make them comply. They could be punished by losing privileges – no television, no PlayStation, fewer visits, less money to spend on luxuries – but the days of being punished by a baton to the head or a knee in the groin were gone. In the three months that Shepherd had been in Bradford Prison he had seen officers verbally abused, spat at, pushed, shoved, kicked and had urine and faeces thrown at them. In most cases the inmates weren't even put on report. Retaliation just wasn't possible, partly because it would mean instant dismissal but also because the prison officers were hopelessly outnumbered. If all the inmates acted together, even the Rapid Reaction Team would be powerless. The power had passed from the guards to the prisoners and it looked as if it would stay that way for the foreseeable future.

Shepherd reached the ground floor. Four old timers were playing pool. They were in their early sixties and all serving long sentences. Billy Holgate and Tommy Plant were armed robbers, old-school villains who had used sawn-off shotguns to raid post offices across Yorkshire. They had been fairly successful during the eighties when they had started out as teenagers, but technology and digital money meant that the risks had increased as the potential profits had fallen. Between them they had served more than twenty years already and were both midway through fifteen-year sentences. Shepherd doubted that even a reformer like Linda Wilson would be able to get them to change their ways. Crime was in their blood and neither of them had anything in the way of a pension to look forward to.

The other two were older. One, Jeremy Billingham, had smothered his wife with a pillow before trying to end his own life by swallowing a bottle of paracetamol. Billingham had survived, albeit with major liver damage, and while he had explained that his dementia-ridden wife had begged him to end her misery during one of her brief moments of lucidity, a jury had found him guilty of murder and he had been sentenced to life with a minimum of twelve years. He would almost certainly die behind bars. The final member of the foursome was a retired doctor, Ralph Spencer, who was in his seventies. He had taken money from patients to invest in what he promised would be a rock-solid property development in Spain and instead spent the money on drugs, high-class prostitutes and tickets to the world's top sporting events. 'In the famous words of George Best, I squandered the rest, your honour,' Spencer told the court, before accepting his twelve-year sentence with a smile.

'You want to watch yourself with those two, Mr Swinton,' said Spencer, whispering from the corner of his mouth. 'They're nasty pieces of work.'

'Thank you for your concern, Mr Spencer.'

'He's right, Mr Swinton,' said Plant. 'They'll kill you as soon as look at you. They're Albanian, they don't give a fuck.'

'I'll bear that in mind, Mr Plant.'

Holgate potted a ball and looked up at Shepherd. 'You need to show them who's boss, Mr Swinton.'

'I'll take that on board, Mr Holgate.'

Holgate straightened up and walked over to Shepherd. He tapped his cue on the floor. 'It never used to be like this, Mr Swinton.'

'In what way?'

'Allowing the inmates to run the asylum. Back in the day, if a couple of twats had tried a stroke like that, they'd have been shown the error of their ways.'

'Times have changed, Mr Holgate.'

'Yeah, and not for the better.' He waved the cue at the far end of the wing. 'You know the emir, right? Mohammad Al

Camel Fucker. Has a cell all to himself and gets his meals delivered by a lackey.'

Holgate was referring to Mohammed Kamil, an elderly Muslim cleric who was serving a six-year sentence for urging people to support Islamic State. He was actually a very pleasant man, always respectful to the prison officers, and at least once a day Linda Wilson would pop into his cell for a chat. But Shepherd had seen undercover footage of the man where he assumed he was speaking to the converted. Kamil had a vitriolic hatred of the West and in particular the British, despite the fact that he had held British citizenship for more than fifty years. Shepherd had heard him heaping praise on the 7/7 London Tube bombers and the Syrian refugee who had killed twenty people – most of them children – in the Manchester Arena suicide bombing. Kamil was trying to persuade the wing governor to allow him to teach religious classes but MI5 had already advised against it. Even so, there would often be up to a dozen young men crowded into his cell listening to him talk.

'I'm not sure that's his actual name, but yes, I know the emir.'

Holgate lowered his voice and looked around to make sure that no one was listening. 'Look, I'm not a grass, and I'm not telling you anything that isn't common knowledge, but the emir uses the Albanians as enforcers. Has done for the last couple of years. I don't understand why the governor allows it.'

Plant nodded in agreement. 'It's an open secret, that's what it is.'

'The world is going to hell in a hand basket,' said Holgate. 'First time I went inside, it was the Faces who kept order on the wings. Ordinary decent criminals, you know? There was respect because they walked the walk before they talked the talk. Prison was a safer place back then. The only drug anyone was interested in was nicotine, and maybe cell hooch. Now you've got every drug known to man in here: coke, smack, crack, meth, spice, you name it you can buy it. And who's running the drugs? The Muslims and the Albanians. They're in bed together, splitting the profits between them. And if there's a problem, they use the Albanians to sort it out.'

'It's true,' said Plant, nodding furiously.

'We had a thing a couple of years back, long before you arrived. The number of Muslims has been growing every year. Back in the nineties, there'd only be a couple on the wing. These days it's what, thirty or forty per cent?'

'Closer to half,' said Plant.

'So, you know they pray five times a day. The last time is when the sun goes down.'

'The Maghreb, is what they call it,' said Shepherd. 'And as the Islamic day starts at sunset, it's actually counted as the first prayer of the day.'

Holgate frowned. 'What's that you say?'

'Nothing, it doesn't matter.'

'Right, okay. But they pray when the sun goes down, that's the important thing. And they all do it. They get out their little prayer mats and bow towards Mecca. Anyway a couple of years ago, the lads thought they'd have a bit of fun, so as the sun went down they'd turn up the volume of the TV and stereo, maybe start singing the national anthem or a football song. The noise was something, I can tell you. The whole wing would be shaking.'

'And you were doing it to interfere with their prayers?'

Holgate shrugged. 'It was just a bit of fun, Mr Swinton. But the emir had a word with the Albanians and half a dozen guys ended up in hospital. Now as the sun goes down, you won't hear a peep on the wing.'

'I'm not sure of the point you're making,' said Shepherd.

'The point, Mr Swinton, is that the Albanians are the enforcers on this wing, and you showing weakness like that on the stairs . . .' He shrugged. 'It's none of my business, I suppose.'

'Let me ask you a question, Mr Holgate. Suppose it had got physical on the stairs, and suppose they had started kicking the shit out of me. Who would have stepped up to help me? You? You, Mr Plant?'

Both men looked away.

'That's what I thought,' said Shepherd. He walked away. The terrible thing was that the two career criminals were right. The power was in the hands of the inmates and Shepherd couldn't see how that was going to change any time soon. His main mission in the prison was to put an end to the recruitment and training for terrorism that was going on. The emirs would almost certainly be charged with terrorist offences and see their sentences lengthened, but all that did was keep them behind bars even longer. No doubt they would no longer be allowed to hold teaching sessions and they would be more tightly controlled, maybe even sent to a stricter Cat A prison, but would anything really change? And prosecuting the emirs wouldn't change the corruption that was so endemic within the prison. MI5 guarded its intelligence closely and its officers rarely if ever appeared in court to give evidence. So while the MI5 operation had exposed corruption within the system, it would be down to the police gathering the evidence to present to the CPS, and they were as starved of resources as everyone else. Shepherd had a horrible feeling that nothing was going to change.

• • •

There were more than thirty men seated cross-legged on the floor, and Malik Abid Qadeer knew them all by name. Good Muslims, all of them, men who were prepared to fight and to die for their religion. Qadeer taught his Islamic Studies course every day, and his lessons were always well attended. A good part of his time was indeed spent teaching from the Koran. The Koran was the word of God but sometimes the words could be confusing and needed explanation. Muslims needed guidance, especially the younger ones, and that was why Qadeer was there, to provide guidance. But he gave them deeper guidance too, about the importance of *jihad* – struggle – and the way that good Muslims could take part in it.

The course was in theory open to all, but there were two men in the corridor outside who kept all non-Muslims away. His teachings were not for them.

Malik Abid Qadeer closed the copy of the Koran he had been reading from, and placed it reverently on to the stool next to him. He removed his thick-lensed spectacles and began polishing them with a soft cloth.

'I have something very important to tell you, brothers,' he said, his voice a low whisper that had them straining to hear his words. 'Something that must stay within these four walls.' He spoke in Urdu, his first language, and the first language of most of the men there, even the ones that'd been born in the UK.

Qadeer knew everyone in the room, who they were and where they had come from. They were all to be trusted. But there were others in the prison – Muslims and kafirs – who could not be trusted, and what he had to tell them could under no circumstances be relayed to the authorities. In a perfect world no one would be told until the last minute, but plans had to be made and once things started to move they would move quickly and it would be too late then for explanations.

'Tomorrow, your world is going to change. I have explained how it is the duty of all good Muslims to fight for their religion, and to die, if necessary. Tomorrow you will get that chance. I cannot give you the details now, but all will become clear to you tomorrow. When your cell doors are opened before lunch, all will be explained to you, and you must follow all instructions to the letter. For those of you on B Wing, I will be there to tell you what needs to be done. For the brothers on the other wings, you will follow the orders of the emirs there. You must follow all instructions given to you, even if the reason behind those instructions is not clear to you. You must trust us. And we will trust you. And together we will change this world forever.'

His audience nodded earnestly, hanging on his every word. '*Allahu Akbar*,' he said. 'God is the greatest.'

'*Allahu Akbar*,' they replied, their eyes burning with enthusiasm. '*Allahu Akbar*.'

. . .

Shepherd left the prison at midnight. He had wanted to leave at eleven but he'd promised the wing governor he'd do the extra hour and it made sense to take Geraghty up on his offer of overtime. It was only an hour but it showed that he was still short of money. He had managed to grab a few words with Zaidi just before he was locked in for the night. Zaidi's cellmate had hurried away for a last-minute shower and Zaidi was standing on the landing, looking down. Shepherd had joined him. There was no one within earshot but even so Zaidi had whispered from the side of his mouth. 'Fairly sure Rashid passed the package to Mihal Nushi, the Albanian.'

Shepherd nodded but didn't say anything as he'd walked away. So Tariq had given drugs to the Albanians, drugs worth as much as a hundred and forty thousand pounds inside? That had to have been payment for something. But for what?

The night bus service was irregular at best but he was lucky and one turned up within minutes of him arriving at the stop. By half past midnight he was walking in through his front door.

He tossed his backpack on to the kitchen table and threw a Marks & Spencer shepherd's pie into the microwave. He took a bottle of lager from the fridge, opened it and took a long drink, trying to get the taste of prison out of his mouth.

He sat down at the table and phoned Diane Daily. It was Donna Walsh who answered. 'Diane's grabbing some sleep,' she said. 'I'm in the hot seat.'

'It's about the cocaine that I took into the prison today. The guy I gave the package to passed it on to an Albanian prisoner. Guy by the name of Mihal Nushi. Nushi is in for torturing a rival and for a weapons cache that they found at his house.'

'What do you think the cocaine is for?'

'To get high, I assume.' Walsh didn't say anything. 'Bad joke,' said Shepherd. 'Sorry. It's been a long day.'

'That much coke will get a lot of people high,' said Donna.

'I'm assuming Tariq isn't giving it to them out of the goodness of his heart. And aren't the Muslims and the Albanians rivals, when it comes to the prison drugs trade anyway?'

'They have different ways of bringing the drugs in but they sell to the same market. I think the demand is always greater than the supply so there isn't much animosity between the two groups. The Muslims control the corrupt officer route, the Albanians use drones, mainly, for their hard drugs. But the drones aren't guaranteed, they lose as many consignments as they get through. The Albanians have pretty much cornered the market in spice, which is much easier to get in, but if they're having problems getting harder drugs in, maybe they've done a deal with Tariq. But I think there's more to it than that.'

'What are you thinking?'

'It's payment for something. Either in advance or after the event. Tariq needs something – or needed something – from the Albanians, and the coke is payment.'

'And what do you think that something is?'

'Absolutely no idea,' he said. 'My theory is very much a work in progress. But I'll keep you posted.'

Shepherd ended the call just as the microwave dinged to let him know that his shepherd's pie was ready. He decided to call his son before eating. Liam answered almost immediately. 'You okay?' asked Shepherd. 'Sorry it's so late, I've only just got in.'

'I'm fine. Not even tired. I think I'm still fired up on adrenaline.'

'Did you call Naomi?'

'I did. Had a long chat. They still haven't released our names so I was able to give her a heads-up. I'm going to see her at the weekend.'

'How much did you tell her?'

'I took your advice, Dad. Told her about the crash and the rescue, but I didn't tell her that it was my dad who busted me out. Or what happened in the house. Maybe one day I'll tell her, but at the moment it's better she doesn't know the details.'

'Good lad. What about the funerals?'

'Mobile is being buried in Exeter on Monday. Gerry's going to be cremated on the Wednesday. Smithy and I will go to both, along with as many members of the regiment as can make it. The wing commander will be at both.'

'I'm sorry, Liam. I know how difficult it is to lose a comrade.'

'I keep thinking that it could so easily have been me.'

'They call it survivor's guilt,' said Shepherd. 'You should talk it through with someone.'

'With you, you mean?'

'No, a professional. Someone who knows about survivor's guilt and PTSD.'

'Dad, I don't have PTSD.'

'You were shot down and nearly died. And two of your colleagues did die. You don't think you have PTSD and maybe you don't, but it never hurts to explore your feelings.'

'I didn't realise you were so touchy-feely.'

'I just wish we could sit down and have a chat about it,' said Shepherd. 'But I'm stuck in Bradford for the foreseeable future.'

'Undercover?'

'Yes.'

'How are your stress levels?'

Shepherd chuckled. 'They've been better. But I'm coping. Seriously, though, undercover work can take its toll and I used to spend time with a psychologist.'

'You saw a shrink?'

'I don't think they like being called that,' said Shepherd.

'Psychiatrist, then.'

'Actually the ones I spoke to – there were several – were psychologists.'

'What's the difference?'

'Between a psychiatrist and a psychologist? The main difference is that psychiatrists are medical doctors and psychologists aren't. So a psychiatrist can prescribe medication but psychologists concentrate on psychotherapy – basically talking.'

'And this was because you had problems?'

'I had to be psychologically examined every three months when I was working undercover, really just to nip any problems in the bud. But I learned a lot about stress and how a person reacts to it.'

'But you're undercover now, right? Does that mean you have to see him again?'

'Usually they're women, the ones that I've seen, anyway. And yes, I probably will have to check in. Sometimes stress can manifest itself in ways that you're not aware of, but an outsider can see.'

'I'm fine, Dad. Really. Thanks for your concern. I'm lucky to have you as my dad.'

'And I'm lucky to have you as a son. I'm proud of you. You wouldn't believe how proud.'

'Thanks, Dad. Stay safe.'

'You too.'

There was a brief pause. 'Love you, Dad.'

Shepherd smiled. It had been a long time since Liam had said that. Years.

He opened the microwave and steam billowed out. Dinner was served. The microwave pinged before Shepherd made the call!

. . .

One of Shepherd's phones rang and he rolled over, rubbing the sleep from his eyes. It was his personal phone. He didn't have any numbers stored in the phone's memory. He blinked his eyes and focused on the screen. It was five o'clock in the morning, he'd been asleep for barely four hours. It was Diane Daily and it wouldn't be a social call. 'Hello Diane,' he said. 'What's up?'

'Sorry about the wake-up call,' she said. 'But I thought you'd want to hear this straight away. We were following Tariq in his Prius yesterday. He spent most of the day working, so you can imagine how much fun that was. Anyway, he finished mini-cabbing at about six and picked up Khaliq and Hussain, and a third guy that we haven't yet identified. They drove to an industrial estate on the outskirts of Bradford and parked inside a unit there. They were there for the best part of an hour and then left. They dropped the new guy in the city centre and we lost him. The remaining three went for a curry and then home.'

'You woke me up for this?'

Daily chuckled. 'Bear with me, Dan. Long story short, we sent a team into the industrial unit a few hours ago and found an Aladdin's cave of weapons.'

'What sort of weapons?'

'Kalashnikovs, Glocks, and several hundred machetes and knives.'

'How many Kalashnikovs?'

'Fifteen. And fifteen Glocks too.'

Shepherd sat up and ran his hand through his hair. 'Who does the unit belong to?'

'An offshore company. The Virgin Islands. We're trying to pin it down but I'm not holding my breath.'

'Anyone else in the unit? Was it a meeting? Or a buy?'

'They had a key and they let themselves in. We didn't have enough manpower to keep the unit under observation, we could barely keep tabs on the Prius.'

'What are you thinking, Diane? They're planning an MTA?' A marauding terrorist attack was where lone wolves or multiple groups of attackers went on the rampage, often with guns. There had been MTAs in the UK before, like the one at Westminster Bridge in March 2017 when six civilians were killed and 50 injured, and the one at London Bridge in June the same year, when eight people were killed and 48 were injured. An MTA was one of the security service's worst fears, as the attacks tended to come out of the blue.

'Too early to say, Dan. We don't know if the guns belong to our guys, or if they belong to someone else and they were there for a buy. We've got serial numbers so we're chasing up consignments as we speak, but at the moment we're none the wiser. I woke Giles Pritchard from his beauty sleep and he's given me the green light to put a surveillance team on the unit, and we'll go in again tonight to fix trackers to some of the weapons. This could take the investigation to a whole different level, obviously.'

'Obviously,' said Shepherd. The investigation into terrorist recruitment and grooming at Bradford Prison was major, no question, but it was a long-term operation and there were no immediate lives in danger. A marauding terrorist attack, especially an imminent one, was a very different matter. If the weapons did indeed belong to Khaliq and his terror cell, then whatever they were planning was big. Fifteen Kalashnikovs alone could cause hundreds of deaths in a few seconds. As Daily had suggested, it was possible that Khaliq and his team were only there as buyers, in which case they needed to know who the sellers were and who else they were selling to. There was every chance that Giles Pritchard would now regard the weapons cache as the priority and put the prison investigation on the back burner. Busting a weapons cache of that size, and ideally the people behind it, would be an intelligence coup, no question.

'You'll still be following Tariq?'

'Oh yes, of course. He's led us to this arms cache so who knows what else we'll find by tailing him. And Pritchard wants me to put a team on Khaliq as well. Turns out that he's the son of Shafiq Ali Rafiq. He's an illegitimate son. Shafiq Ali Rafiq has two legitimate families with registered marriages and they're all in the system. But he has other families, some that we know about and others that we don't. We pulled Khaliq's birth certificate and Shafiq Ali Rafiq is listed as the father.'

'That can't be a coincidence.'

'That's what Pritchard said. Anyway, I'm liaising with our Birmingham office. Or at least I will once we get to a decent hour. Speaking of which, I'll let you go back to sleep.'

'Ha, too late for that,' said Shepherd. 'I start work at six.'

'Then consider this your early-morning alarm call,' said Daily. 'You stay safe.'

'You too, Diane,' said Shepherd, and he ended the call.

He rolled out of bed, shaved and showered, then pulled on his work trousers and a clean white shirt. His prison tie was a clip-on, designed to tear away from his neck if grabbed by an inmate. He went downstairs to the pokey kitchen and switched on the kettle. He opened a can of Heinz tomato soup, poured it into a pan and put it on a hob. While it was heating up he made himself two ham sandwiches. He was out of cheese but he had plenty of Branston pickle, so he spread it thickly across the ham.

The kettle boiled and he made himself a cup of coffee which he drank as he waited for his soup to heat up. It had been his ritual for almost three months, done solely to back up his cover as a cash-strapped officer who was saving pennies whenever he could.

The bus was on time and he was in the control centre five minutes before his shift was due to start. Neil Geraghty was in charge and he nodded a greeting at Shepherd.

'B Wing again today, Tony.'

Shepherd smiled. 'Thanks.'

'Figured better to keep you off A Wing for a while, just in case you get the urge to chin anyone again.'

'You heard, yeah?'

'I heard you saved Jenny Johnston from a strangling, so more power to you,' said Geraghty. 'The Fart boys are covering for you, so there'll be no repercussions.'

'Good to know.'

'Just be careful with your fists,' said Geraghty. 'You can belt them as much as you want with a baton if you're under threat and it's justifiable force, but once you start punching an inmate they see that as brutality.'

'Message received and understood, Mr Geraghty. It won't happen again.'

Geraghty grinned. 'If it does, just make sure nobody sees you.'

'Who am I on with today?'

'Stephen Underwood. And I've moved Jenny to B Wing, too.'

'I would have thought she'd have been off sick today.'

'She didn't want to go sick. She's a trooper.'

'It's not my place to say, Mr Geraghty, but she's a bit out of her depth.'

'We were all green once. She'll learn.'

'I hope so. But I'm not sure she can be left on a landing on her own.'

'We don't have enough staff to have her shadow another officer,' said Geraghty.

'I know, I know.' Shepherd shrugged. 'But she was in serious danger yesterday.'

'But you saved the day, so all's well that ends well. Maybe you could keep an eye on her.'

Shepherd forced a smile. The last thing he needed was to be babysitting an officer who wasn't up to the job. 'I'll do my best, Mr Geraghty.'

'And are you up for overtime today?'

'Always.'

'If you could stay on the wing until after association tonight, that would help me out a lot.'

Underwood and Johnston arrived. 'Great, so that's three of you,' he said. 'And you'll be glad to hear I have two more bodies on the wing today. Derren Griffiths and Sandra Shakespeare.'

'Finally,' said Underwood. 'We've been understaffed every day this week.'

'The flu that's going around isn't helping,' said Geraghty. 'But at least you shouldn't have any problems moving them around today.'

Underwood led the way to the gate. 'Thanks for yesterday,' Johnston whispered to Shepherd.

'Pleasure,' said Shepherd.

'It happened so quickly,' said Johnston. 'One moment they were laughing and joking, the next minute I was up against the wall and he had his hand around my throat.'

'You have to try to keep your distance,' said Shepherd. 'I know it's hard, but you need to protect your personal space. And where you were was a bit of a blind spot. The CCTV is some distance away and when the landing is busy they can't see you from the control centre.' He shrugged. 'But at the end of the day, if an inmate attacks you there's not much you can do. If at any time you do feel threatened and you're on your own, best to radio in straight away.'

'I didn't want to seem like a wuss.'

'Better safe than sorry,' said Shepherd. 'As soon as you've called it in, they'll know that they're being watched and they're unlikely to try anything.'

'I'll remember that,' she said.

Underwood opened the gate and Shepherd and Johnston went through.

'Hold the door!' someone shouted and they looked over to see two officers walking away from Geraghty's desk. Derren Griffiths was in his thirties and had worked as a nurse before joining the prison service. He wore oblong-framed spectacles and was always flicking his fringe away from his eyes. Sandra Shakespeare was the more experienced of the two, with more than twenty years' service under her belt. They were capable officers and Shepherd had seen both of them get physical when necessary.

'Hi Sandra, written any good plays lately?' said Underwood.

'You say that every single time you see me, Stephen.'

Underwood grinned. 'And it never gets old.'

They all went through to the wing and Underwood locked the gate. It was barely six thirty but the wing was already noisy. Televisions and stereos were blaring and prisoners were banging on their doors and shouting to be let out. A couple of red bands were cleaning the ground floor. He saw Mary Garner looking over the railing of the twos and he waved up to her. She waved back.

They filed into the wing governor's office. Maria Crowley was sitting behind her desk. She took off her glasses and smiled. 'Well finally we have a halfway decent number of officers,' said Crowley. 'I can't remember the last time I had five bodies on a day shift. Things aren't looking so good for the night shift. Sonny Shah has called in sick and we were already short-handed. Tony, Mr Geraghty says you're up for some overtime?'

'I'll take whatever you can give me,' said Shepherd.

'Anyone else?'

Griffiths raised a hand. 'I can stay until six or seven.'

Mary Garner and Nick Durst arrived and stood at the back of the room. They both looked tired.

'Seven would be great, thank you,' said Crowley. 'Just so you know, Supervising Officer Blackhurst has some issues at home and will be in late. He's hoping to get in before lunch.' She looked over at Garner and Durst. 'So, any issues over-night?'

'We heard drones again,' said Garner. 'I went up and checked the cells with broken windows but didn't see anything.'

'It could have been a dry run,' said the governor. 'I'll talk to security and see if we can get a team outside tonight.'

'Also Sake Nazir's cell still reeks of cannabis. I had a look around but I couldn't find anything. He says it was someone else who came in his room to smoke but he can't remember who it was.'

'At least it's only cannabis,' said the governor. 'All they want to do is sleep or snack after cannabis. It's spice that's causing all the problems at the moment.' She looked over at Shepherd. 'Did Mr Macdonald say anything to you about showering?'

'He said he'd had trouble getting to the showers, that's all. He was grateful that I'd taken him. But no issues, no.'

'He's raised a COMP1, and I'd like to nip it in the bud, so make sure he gets a shower today. All the morning shower slots are filled and he's got an Alcoholics Anonymous meeting after breakfast so get him a shower after that. See if anyone else wants to join him.'

A COMP1 was an official complaint form and could be used to raise any issue that a prisoner was unhappy with. The prison authorities had five days in which to reply. In the bad old days, written complaints from prisoners would go straight in the bin, but now any COMP1 complaint was taken seriously and prison staff had to use what was referred to as a 'problem-solving approach' when responding. That meant they had to work out what the cause of the problem was, look at possible solutions, and then implement an agreed solution.

'Prison Rule 28 says that he's only required to have a bath or a shower once a week,' said Shepherd. There were eighty-five rules that prisons had to follow, and Shepherd had memorised all of them. A knowledge of the rules was often the quickest way to diffuse an argument with a prisoner.

'Well, that's true, but the governors are supposed to decide what access to washing facilities is reasonable. The problem is that the Muslim prisoners have been pushing for more shower time for religious reasons and it's hard to argue with that. That cuts down the shower time for everybody else.'

'Maybe Mr Macdonald could consider converting?' said Shepherd.

The governor flashed him a tight smile. 'Perhaps you could suggest that to him,' she said. 'The problem is that his COMP1 isn't just about shower time. He's raised what he claims are a number of breaches of the rules about showering. The showers and toilets should be cleaned daily, which they aren't, unfortunately. The communal washing areas and toilet areas should be part of the deep cleaning schedule and it has been months since that was done. There is no receptacle for discarded clothing and no one seems to know where it has gone. And there are no slip mats. So far as I know there have never been slip mats in the showers but they should be there. And he says that the privacy screening hasn't been maintained as it should be.'

'The rules aren't that specific,' said Shepherd.

'I know, but he is using the Prison Reform Trust's guidelines. I think he's just using the COMP1 to achieve his aims, which is more shower time. So let's just give it to him and hopefully he'll drop his COMP1.'

'The squeaky wheel gets the grease,' said Underwood.

'Sadly that's the way of the world,' said the governor. 'So, he showers after his AA class, and we'll see about getting him a daily shower thereafter.'

'No problem, ma'am,' said Shepherd.

Crowley looked at her watch. 'Right, let's get the cells open. As we're decently staffed today, let's get as many as we can out in the exercise yard.' Each wing had its own exercise yard at the far end of the building, accessed from the ground floor.

The yards were the size of two basketball courts and were surrounded by double wire fences topped with razor wire. There was some outdoor exercise equipment and a row of wooden benches, but usually inmates just walked around in small groups, and always in an anti-clockwise direction. It was one of the first activities to be closed whenever there was a staff shortage, and so far as Shepherd was aware the yard hadn't been used for more than a week.

The officers filed out. 'I'll do the threes,' said Shepherd. 'It'll give me a chance to chat with Macdonald.'

'I could do the showers,' said Johnston.

Underwood shook his head. 'No you won't,' he said. 'I get that you don't want to be on a landing, but the showers would be out of the frying pan into the fire. You've got to get landing experience, it's the only way you'll learn to control them. You can do the ones, they won't give you any trouble.'

'Okay,' said Johnston. She bit down on her lower lip, clearly worried.

'Just be firm, and polite,' said Underwood. 'But at the first sign of any bolshiness call it in on your radio and we'll be there. Once they know you won't stand for any messing they'll be as good as gold. I'll take the twos. Mr Griffiths, you take care of the showers. Then can you start working on a rota for the exercise yards? Let's say twenty at a time. For an hour. You could squeeze two in before lunch and two after. That'll help with the exercise quotas. You can take Miss Johnston with you.'

'I've had requests for gym time, too,' said Griffiths.

Underwood nodded. 'Maybe this evening, during association. Let's see how the afternoon goes. We can get more out in the yard than we can in the gym.'

Shepherd headed up the stairs to the threes. He went straight to Willie Macdonald's cell and opened it. Macdonald had the lower bunk and the top bunk was taken by another Scot who was also on remand, though Robbie Mitchell had been caught with a kilo of heroin in his car and was facing a much longer sentence. Mitchell was already wearing a blue tracksuit and he climbed down off his bunk, grabbed a plastic bottle of water, and headed out. He was presumably anticipating exercising in the gym, which meant he was going to be disappointed. Shepherd didn't bother bursting the man's bubble, he'd find out soon enough.

'Morning, Mr Macdonald,' said Shepherd. 'I'm told you'll be having a shower after your AA meeting. Head to the gate as soon as you're back on the wing.'

'Why can't I have a shower now, Mr Swinton?' He swung his feet off his bed. He was wearing grey joggers and a matching sweatshirt, presumably his sleeping gear.

'The list is full.'

'Yeah, and we know why, don't we? Morning showers are only for the Mussies, right?'

'Please stop the Islamophobic comments, Mr Macdonald. You're getting your shower. Just be grateful for that. We both know that you're only entitled to one a week.'

'I am grateful, Mr Swinton. You're a prince among men.'

'It's nothing to do with me. Your COMP1 got the governor fired up.'

Macdonald grinned. 'I thought it might.'

'I think she's hoping that you'll withdraw it if she shows willing.'

'Yeah, I probably will. Let's see how it goes.'

'How long have you been off the booze?'

'Three months since my last drink.'

Shepherd frowned. 'How long have you been on remand?'

'Five months.'

Shepherd raised his eyebrows. 'Prison hooch?'

Macdonald chuckled. 'Gave me a hangover like a bitch. That's one of the reasons I'm off the sauce.'

Hooch was brewed by mixing fruit, water, sugar and bread in a ziplock plastic bag. Pretty much any fruit worked, including oranges, apples, even fruit juices or fruit cocktail, and the yeast in the bread kickstarted the fermentation process after it was warmed. Then it was just a matter of keeping the bag hidden of a few days, at which point the mixture could contain anywhere from 2% to 15% alcohol.

'Well good luck with that.'

'Do you drink, Mr Swinton?'

'I've been known to.'

'Maybe when I'm on the out, I could buy you a pint.'

'I'll look forward to that.'

Shepherd walked along the landing opening the rest of the cells. A dozen inmates had gathered at the gate leading to the basement. They were all carrying washbags and towels and were all wearing Islamic clothing. Griffiths was checking names against a clipboard, then he unlocked the gate and they all filed down.

Robbie Mitchell approached Griffiths and began pointing at the gate. Griffiths shook his head, obviously explaining to Mitchell that there wasn't going to be any gym time that morning. Mitchell began shouting at Griffiths, calling him every name under the sun, but Griffiths just stood stony-faced and let the insults wash over him. Mitchell eventually calmed down. Griffiths said something and Mitchell nodded. Shepherd figured he was probably telling him he could use the exercise yard later. That was a better deal because the downstairs gym was pokey and badly ventilated – most inmates preferred to exercise in the open air.

Once Shepherd had unlocked all the cells, he took the stairs down to the twos, where Underwood was leaning on the railing looking down. 'Threes are done,' said Shepherd.

Underwood nodded at the men heading down to the showers with Griffiths. 'They seem a bit agitated today.'

'Really?'

Underwood nodded. 'A lot of talking going on. Back and forth. Did something happen on another wing?'

'Not that I'm aware of.'

Underwood gestured at the far end of the ones. The door to Malik Abid Qadeer's cell was open and a line of men were waiting to go inside. 'And look at that. The emir doesn't usually receive visitors until the evening association. I wonder if it's to do with the arrival of Shafiq Ali Rafiq? He came in yesterday and they've put him in the Block.'

'Could be that, I suppose,' said Shepherd.

'Big mistake bringing a man like that here,' said Underwood. 'They should have taken him to Belmarsh.'

'Apparently it's so he can be near his family.'

'London's only a few hours away,' said Underwood. He pushed himself away from the railing. 'Anyway, those problems are all above our pay grade. Do you want to do classes or workshops?'

'Classes, I guess.'

'Do you want to take Jenny with you?'

'Sure.'

'What do you think of her?'

'We were all green once,' said Shepherd, echoing Geraghty's words.

'Yeah, well it's sink or swim in here, we can only keep her head above water for so long.'

• • •

Jamie Donaldson sighed and stretched, and wondered what he was going to do to relieve the pressure on his bladder. He was sitting in the driving seat of an Openreach van parked a hundred metres from the front door of the house where Mohammed Tariq – AKA Tango One – lived. Tariq's Prius – AKA Victor One – was parked in its usual spot in the driveway, directly under a CCTV camera mounted on the corner of the house.

Tariq usually didn't get out of bed until nine but he was watched twenty-four hours a day. Donaldson preferred to be on the move. Sitting and watching a house in darkness was boring beyond belief. But the job had to be done.

He had an empty bottle in the back of the van but he hated pissing into it. He looked at his watch. It was just after seven and he was due off at nine. Could he wait two hours?

A light came on in the upstairs bedroom where Tariq slept. Donaldson smiled. Tango One was just getting out of bed. It had been light for almost an hour and Donaldson had heard the early morning call to prayer from the three nearby mosques. 'Naughty boy,' Donaldson muttered to himself.

The fact that Tariq was up meant that there was a reasonable chance he'd be leaving the house soon, so Donaldson decided he would have to use the bottle. He clambered around his seat and knelt on the floor to pee into it. When he'd finished he screwed the top on and wrapped it in a Tesco carrier bag. He made a mental note to take it with him when his shift was over. There was nothing surveillance teams hated more than reporting for duty and finding a bottle of pee waiting for them. Well, solids were worse, obviously, but you would have to be very desperate to shit into a carrier bag.

Donaldson climbed back into the driving seat and used a wet wipe to clean his hands. He was alone on the surveillance job. Now that there was a tracker on Victor One he had plenty of leeway. He looked down at the tablet on the passenger seat. The red dot that marked the position of the Prius was clearly visible. It meant he could follow the car even when it was out of sight, though there was always the possibility that the tracker might suddenly stop transmitting. Donaldson had been in the surveillance business long enough to know that equipment had a tendency to go wrong at the worst possible time. Sod's law.

Twenty minutes after the bedroom light had gone on, Tariq appeared at the front door, wearing blue overalls and a blue baseball cap. Donaldson frowned. He'd never seen the man dressed like that before. As Tariq climbed into the Prius, Donaldson called up Donna Walsh on his radio. 'Tango One is on the move,' he said. 'Foxtrot One has eyes on Victor One.'

'The early worm,' said Walsh in his earpiece.

'He's dressed differently,' said Donaldson. 'Overalls and a cap.'

'Maybe he's got a job.'

'Maybe,' said Donaldson.

Tariq reversed the Prius out of the driveway, heading away from the Openreach van. Donaldson followed.

• • •

S hepherd and Johnston took the B Wing prisoners to their classes in the admin block. Shepherd let Johnston do most of the work, but stayed close by in case she had any problems. She seemed buoyed by the fact that Shepherd was there, shouting for the men to keep together and telling them to keep the noise down. She had some authority in her voice and the second time she shouted for quiet, she actually got it.

Underwood let them go first so there was quite a bit of catcalling from the prisoners heading to the workshops. They were paid by the hour so being delayed cost them money. It might only be a few pence, but behind bars a few pence mattered.

Willie Macdonald was in their group and he stuck close to Shepherd. 'You're serious about my shower, Mr Swinton?'

'Dead serious,' said Shepherd. 'I tell you what, you can put together another five prisoners to go with you.'

Macdonald's eyes narrowed. 'Are you pulling my chain, Mr Swinton?'

'Why would I do that, Mr Macdonald?'

'You're telling me I can choose five guys to get a shower? Before lunch?'

'Soon as we get back to the wing, I'll take you down.'

'You really are a prince among men, Mr Swinton. A prince.' His eyes narrowed again. 'This isn't a wind up, is it?'

Shepherd couldn't help but grin. 'No, it's not a wind up. The governor wants you to drop that COMP1, and if getting you squeaky clean is the price for that, then so be it. And there's no point in me taking just the one of you. And I can't be bothered getting another five names. So go for it.'

'Yes!' said Macdonald, clearly elated. He hurried away, pushing his way through the crowd with mumbles of 'excuse me' and 'sorry' and 'coming through'. He was clearly planning on leveraging his shower list into whatever perks and cash he could get and he didn't have long.

Once they had delivered the prisoners to their classes, Shepherd and Johnston headed back to B Wing. Johnston still had to fill out her paperwork on the previous day's attack and she wasn't sure exactly what to say. So far Shepherd hadn't been asked to submit a written report, everyone appeared happy to accept the Rapid Response Team's version of events. Shepherd wasn't sure how much guidance he could give her because paperwork had never been one of his strengths.

Luckily Supervising Officer Blackhurst was in the office when they arrived on the wing, and he waved for them to join him. 'I hear you're now the Mike Tyson of A Wing,' said Blackhurst.

'News travels fast,' said Shepherd.

Blackhurst flashed him a tight smile. 'Be careful using your fists,' he said.

'I hear what you're saying, Mr Blackhurst. I should have used my baton, I realise that.'

'I always find a knee in the nuts is a far more efficient way of getting someone down,' said Blackhurst, lowering his voice. 'The thing about fists is that if you use your fist you can graze your knuckles so there's evidence that you've then got to explain.' He tapped the side of his nose with his finger. 'Word to the wise.'

'Much appreciated, Mr Blackhurst.'

'And you, young lady,' said Blackhurst, smiling at Johnston. 'Don't ever be afraid to call for help if you feel a situation is getting out of control. We've all had to call for help at some point, it's nothing to be ashamed of. Better safe than sorry.'

He nodded at a table and chair. 'Sit yourself down and we'll get stuck into the paperwork. Miss Wilson on A Wing has been chasing me for it.'

'Thank you, Mr Blackhurst,' said Johnston.

Blackhurst gave Shepherd a print-out of twenty names. 'Can you take these guys out to the exercise yard for an hour before you collect the prisoners from their classes?'

'No problem,' said Shepherd, taking the list. 'Did Miss Crowley tell you about Willie Macdonald and his extra shower?'

'She did. He's a chancer, that one. His COMP1 is a total try-on.'

'I'll take them down just before lunch,' said Shepherd.

'Good man. Make sure they wash behind their ears.'

. . .

Jamie Donaldson was half a mile from the industrial estate when he realised that was where Victor One was heading. Ten minutes earlier, he had stopped in front of a supermarket and picked up Tango Three, AKA Mizhir Khaliq. Khaliq was also wearing blue overalls and a peaked cap. Donaldson had radioed Donna Walsh to let her know that there were now two Tangos in the Prius and that Tariq and Khaliq were both dressed in overalls.

'Any idea what's going on?' Walsh had asked.

'None at all,' Donaldson had replied.

He had promised to keep her posted, and called her again once he realised where they were heading.

'I can't see them loading Kalashnikovs into a Prius,' said Walsh. 'But let's keep an open mind.'

Donaldson held back when Foxtrot Three called in to say that he had eyes on Victor One. Foxtrot Three was another Openreach van parked by the wire fence that ran around the industrial estate. From there it had a good view of the unit that Tariq had visited the previous day. The Openreach vans were perfect for surveillance purposes and MI5 had a fleet of them. There were more than 29,000 genuine Openreach vans across the UK, and they were often parked up for hours at a time as their technicians carried out maintenance work on phone and broadband cables. No one ever paid them any attention. Personally Donaldson would have preferred to have been behind the wheel of a high-powered BMW, but discreet surveillance would have been out of the question and that was what mattered. People noticed BMWs but Openreach vans blended into the background.

Foxtrot Three reported that the Prius had driven up to the unit and that Tango Three had got out to open the shutter. Donaldson pulled up at the side of the road and radioed in his position, though his van had a GPS tracker and Walsh would know exactly where he was.

• • •

Shepherd spent an hour in the B Wing exercise yard over-seeing twenty prisoners. He was as grateful as they were to be outside, if for no other reason than it provided a break from the foul prison air. There were half a dozen fitness-conscious inmates working out on the exercise machines, though from the look of their bulging biceps and thick necks their physiques had more to do with steroids than physical exertion. Steroids were smuggled into the prison on a large scale and commanded a high price. Shepherd had never seen the advantage of a bodybuilder's physique. He had never seen anyone in the SAS who wasn't lithe and trim. Big muscles might look impressive but they slowed a man down and just because a guy had big biceps didn't mean that his punches had any power. Big muscles meant an increase in body mass, and in a firefight the smaller your body mass, the better. Not that Shepherd would ever say that to any of the steroid brigade – their whole sense of self-worth was tied up in the way they looked and they took any criticism to heart.

A few of the older inmates were sitting on wooden benches, just happy to feel the sun on their faces. Everyone else walked around the perimeter of the yard, all going anti-clockwise. One of the inmates had changed into shorts and a singlet and was jogging, taking care not to bump into anyone. It was Mick Walker, the former Para. He nodded at Shepherd as he went by. 'Good to be out, boss?'

'Certainly is,' said Shepherd.

Walker kept up a brisk pace, his arms pumping, his head up. He had a good fluid pace and looked as if he could run for hours. It was funny how life worked out, sometimes. If Walker had made different decisions, he could possibly have joined the SAS and become a pal of Shepherd's. Maybe even left to join the police, or even MI5. And if Shepherd had made just a few wrong decisions, he could well have been the one serving a long prison sentence. It was funny, and tragic. Shepherd had killed for his country and had been treated like a hero. Walker had chinned a few coppers defending his dog, and was serving nine years for GBH.

Shepherd looked out over the razor-wire-topped fences at the clear blue sky. He hated prisons, hated everything about them, and the sooner he was out, the better. He couldn't imagine how it would feel to know that he couldn't leave and that he would be inside for years. He shuddered at the thought.

. . .

Behind the wheel of the Openreach van tagged as Foxtrot Three was an MI5 surveillance veteran, Janet Rayner. She had spent a year with the Metropolitan Police's surveillance team before being headhunted by MI5, and was one of the best followers in the country. In the back of the van, sitting on a plastic stool and looking at a bank of video monitors, was another surveillance long-timer, Matty Clayton. He was in his fifties and had spent more than half his life working for MI5. The monitors showed views from the concealed cameras around the vehicle, and there was a screen showing a GPS plan of the area with a flashing red light showing the position of Victor One. There was also a laptop running the Met's automatic number plate recognition software. Clayton had bluetacked photographs of Tango One, Tango Two and Tango Three to the side of the van, along with several snaps of the Prius, AKA Victor One. He was drinking a can of Fanta as he studied the screens.

'You see that, Janet?' he asked. 'White van pulling up outside the unit. Peugeot Boxer.'

'I see it,' said Rayner. It was a large square-sided van with the name of a food distribution company on the side. 'Does it check out?'

Clayton studied the laptop. 'Belongs to a company in Leeds. Taxed and insured, all good.' He watched a screen showing a view of the unit's loading bay. The shutter opened and the van disappeared inside. 'Wish we had cameras in there,' he said. 'Do you want to call it in, or should I?'

Rayner held up the Marks & Spencer salmon sandwich that she was halfway through. 'Be a shame to interrupt my breakfast, wouldn't it?'

'I'll do it then,' he said, reaching for his radio.

. . .

Tariq and Khaliq grunted as they swung a box of Kalashnikovs into the back of the van.

Hussain and Zaman brought over the last of the holdalls containing the knives and machetes.

'I wish I was going with you,' said Hussain.

'We need men we can trust on the outside,' said Khaliq. He helped them stack the holdalls in the back. The fifteen Glock cases were already in the van.

Tariq went over to the cardboard box filled with AK-47 ammunition. He tried to lift it but realised immediately that he wasn't strong enough. Hussain hurried over to help him. Together they carried it over to the van and Khaliq helped them heave it inside. 'Who knew bullets were so heavy?' said Hussain.

'They're lead and brass, innit,' said Khaliq. 'Squaddies have to carry kilos of ammunition around with them. That's why they're so fit.'

They loaded the rest of the ammunition into the van, then

Tariq went over to the Prius and opened the boot. He took out two large nylon holdalls. Hussain took one off him and together they took them over to the van and loaded them. 'That's the lot,' said Tariq, rubbing his hands together.

Khaliq looked at his watch. 'Good to go,' he said.

Tariq nodded at Hussain. 'Watch my Prius, bruv,' he said. 'As if it was my own.'

'Yeah, but it ain't yours, it's mine,' said Tariq. He tossed him the keys. 'So drive carefully.'

Hussain grabbed Tariq in his arms and kissed him on both cheeks. '*Hafidaka Allah*,' he said. May God protect you.

'He will,' said Tariq. 'Now get the fuck off me.'

● ● ●

Matty Clayton's voice came over Donna Walsh's radio. 'Foxtrot Three, Victor One and Victor Two are leaving the unit.' Walsh put down her coffee and looked over at the screen map of the area. There were three red dots – Foxtrot One, Foxtrot Three, and Victor One, the Prius. The dot representing the Prius was moving away from the unit, towards the entrance to the industrial estate. 'Victor Two is following.' Victor Two was the food wholesaler van. 'Please advise.'

Walsh sat back in her chair as she tried to rank priorities. The unit had to be kept under constant surveillance because of the weapons it contained. But what if the weapons were now in the Prius or, more likely, the van? She had only Foxtrot One to follow two vehicles, so if they split up they could only follow one. Victor One had the tracker, which they could follow remotely, so it made more sense to keep eyes on the van.

'Foxtrot Three, just to let you know that Tango One and Tango Three are now in the van. Tango Two and Tango Four are in the Prius.'

Walsh frowned. Tango Four was the unknown male who had been at the unit the previous night. 'Please confirm that, Foxtrot Three.'

'It's the big switcheroo. Tango Four drove the van into the unit. But he's driving the Prius. Tango Two is in the front passenger seat of the Prius. Tango One is driving the van. Tango Three is in the passenger seat of the van. That probably explains the overalls they're wearing.'

Walsh's mind whirled as she tried to understand what was going on. 'Are Victor One and Victor Two staying together?' she asked.

'So far,' said Clayton.

'Foxtrot One, do you have eyes on Victor One and Victor Two?'

'Foxtrot One, affirmative,' said Donaldson.

'Okay, Foxtrot Two, stay in position and keep the unit under observation. Foxtrot One, follow Victor One and Victor Two. In the event that they part company, stick with Victor Two.'

'Sticking with Victor Two,' said Donaldson.

Donna phoned Giles Pritchard and quickly explained what had happened. 'This van, how big is it?' he asked.

'It's a Peugeot Boxer. It can carry over a ton, up to eight cubic metres.'

'So big enough to be carrying the whole weapons cache?'

'Comfortably.'

'But just the two Tangos, correct? Tariq and Khaliq?'

'Yes.'

'So if the weapons are on board, they could well be on their way to a MTA scene.'

'That was my worry, yes.'

'Or they could just be moving the weapons. Or the van could be empty. If we send in armed police and the guns are still in the unit, we show our hand and get almost nothing in return.'

'We take the guns off the street, but yes, we're no closer to knowing what they have planned.' It was a tough call, and one that Walsh was glad would be made by Pritchard. Bad calls had a way of ending careers.

'And who owns the van?'

'A food distribution company in Leeds. Nothing known. They distribute food supplies to restaurants, school cafeterias, corner shops.'

'Rob Miller got into the unit last night, correct?'

'Correct.' Rob Miller was one of MI5's top locks and alarms specialists. He had spent a decade as a burglar alarms technician and the rumour was that he had been recruited after he had installed a security system at the house of a former MI5 director general. There wasn't a lock he couldn't defeat given enough time, but usually twenty seconds was all he needed.

'Where is he now?'

'He's still here. In the hotel.'

'Get him out there and get him to check if the weapons are still in place. If they are, he can take the opportunity to place a few trackers and surveillance cameras. If they're not, we'll consider our options. We've still got eyes on the unit?'

'Janet Rayner and Matty Clayton are there.'

'Perfect. Matty can go in and help. He's good with cameras. As soon as you know the status of the weapons cache, let me know. Do we have any idea where the van is headed?'

'Just that it's heading south.'

'So it could be heading for London?'

'It could be, yes. But it could also be driving to any town or city in the south. Once they get to the M62 and M1 they can get anywhere.'

'Keep me posted, Donna.' Pritchard ended the call.

. . .

It took Shepherd the best part of fifteen minutes to clear the exercise yard on his own, but eventually he got everyone inside and locked the gate. Johnston was waiting for him. She clearly didn't want to go and fetch the men from the classes on her own but he didn't say anything. 'Good to go?' he asked and she nodded gratefully.

This time Shepherd shared the unlocking and locking. He opened the gates and Johnston relocked them after she'd gone through. They arrived at the classes block a few minutes late and the prisoners were already lined up. There was a mixture of jeers and cheers when they spotted Shepherd and Johnston, then they began a spontaneous chant of 'Tony and Jenny, sitting in a tree, K-I-S-S-I-N-G.'

'Looks like we're a couple,' said Shepherd. He was only joking but he saw the look of concern that flashed across her face. He smiled. 'They're only teasing,' he said. 'It shows they like you.'

'I wish that were true,' she said. She unlocked the final gate and the B Wing prisoners began to file through. Willie Macdonald was at the front. 'I'm still on for the shower, right, Mr Swinton?'

'Yes you are, Mr Macdonald. Did you drum up a posse to join you?'

Macdonald nodded enthusiastically. 'Yes, boss.'

'Soon as we're back, get them together at the gate and I'll take you down. How was the AA meeting?'

'It was good. Fewer people than usual.'

'Yeah? Why was that?'

'None of the Mussies were there today. Not one.'

'Please don't call them that, at least not when I'm around. I have to report any racist comments I hear.'

'Islam isn't a race, boss. It's a religion. Lots of Muslims in here are white.'

'Islamophobic, then. Either way, it's reportable.'

'No problem, Mr Swinton. I hear and obey.'

'And getting back to the subject, Muslims don't drink. Why would they be going to AA meetings?'

Macdonald laughed. 'They don't, but it gets them out of their cells if they can't get in on one of the Islamic classes. But today, none of them turned up. It's not Ramadan is it?'

'Ramadan is March the twenty-second until April the twentieth. And it wouldn't stop them going to meetings.'

'Then I don't know what happened. But it meant more biscuits for me.'

'Biscuits?'

'We always get tea and biscuits at the meetings,' said Macdonald. 'It's one of the perks.'

. . .

Jamie Donaldson had the Peugeot van in his sights but the Prius was slowing and he didn't want to attract attention by overtaking so he had no choice other than to turn back. The Prius indicated a left turn.

'Foxtrot One, Victor One is turning left, left, left,' he said over the radio.

'I saw that,' said Walsh. 'Stick with Victor Two.'

Donaldson accelerated and got closer to the van. There was no tracker on it and he didn't want to risk losing it.

The van stopped at a set of red traffic lights and Donaldson pulled up behind it. Following one on one was never a good idea, it was all too easy to be spotted.

'Foxtrot One, any chance of some support?' he asked over the radio. 'We're stopped at lights and if he checks his rear-view mirror he'll be looking right at me.'

'I'm working on it,' said Walsh.

'A couple of bikes would be nice,' said Donaldson.

'It's on my wish list.'

The lights changed and the van moved off. Donaldson followed. They were heading south on Wakefield Road now. They crossed an interchange and Wakefield Road became Tong Street which then curved to the east. Donaldson wasn't too familiar with the geography of Bradford but he knew that they were heading towards Bradford Prison. After a few minutes he saw the brick turrets of the prison in the distance. Donaldson frowned. Was it a coincidence? He wrinkled his nose. Two decades of surveillance work had proved to him that genuine coincidences were few and far between. He called upon Walsh on the radio.

'Foxtrot Three, I think they're heading to the prison.'

'Are you sure, Foxtrot Three?'

'I'm not sure, but we're on Tong Street heading east and the prison is in that direction.'

'Victor One is parked outside Tango Two's house,' said Walsh. 'We backed the right horse. But I need to know where that horse is going. Tong Street also leads to the M62 and that's one of the busiest roads in the country.'

'But if they are headed for the prison, what does that mean?' said Donaldson. 'You can't just drive into a Cat B prison, can you?' Realisation dawned and he sighed. 'What if they deliver to the prison? Is that possible?'

'I'll check,' said Walsh.

'We're only minutes away,' said Donaldson.

'Roger that.'

The van indicated left, taking them off the main road and away from the main entrance to the prison. 'Foxtrot Three, Victor Two is left, left, left off Tong Street.' That meant the van wasn't heading for the M62. Donaldson frowned. He knew it was a rookie mistake to make assumptions about where a target was going, but it was becoming increasingly likely that Bradford Prison was Victor Two's destination. But if that was the case, why were they driving away from the entrance?

Donaldson's question was answered when the van drove up to a large metal gate set into the razor-wire-topped wall. There was a sign that said 'HMP Bradford' and another that said 'DELIVERIES ONLY'.

The area around the gate was covered by two large CCTV cameras. The van pulled up in front of the gate, and as Donaldson picked up his radio it rattled back and the van moved forward.

'Foxtrot Three, Victor Two is now inside the prison,' said

Donaldson over the radio. 'I repeat, Victor Two is inside the prison.'

The gate closed.

.   .   .

'Relax, Mo,' said Khaliq. 'You're gripping the steering wheel so hard that your knuckles are going white.'

'Sorry, bruv,' said Tariq. He opened and closed his hands.

The metal gate had closed behind them with a loud clang. Ahead of them was an identical gate. Two CCTV cameras were looking down at their van. There was a brick wall to their right and a black metal door set into the wall on their left. There was a small glass panel in the door and they saw movement on the other side.

'Why don't we just pull out the guns now?' said Tariq.

'Because we're not actually in the prison yet.' He nodded at the gate ahead of them. 'We're not in until we get through that.'

The door opened and a guard appeared. He was holding a long white stick with a mirror attached. He didn't even look at the cab, he just stuck the mirror under the van and slowly walked around it. When he'd finished, he walked back to the door and disappeared inside.

The gate stayed shut.

'What's happening?' said Tariq.

'Chill, bruv. These things take time.'

'Maybe they know there's something wrong.'

'They don't know nothing. Relax.'

'This is taking too long,' said Tariq.

There was a loud metallic clicking sound from the gate and Tariq flinched as if he'd been shot. He laughed nervously as the gate rattled back. 'We're in,' he said. 'We're fucking in.'

'Stay cool, bruv,' said Khaliq.

'I'm cool, I'm cool,' muttered Tariq. He pressed his foot on the accelerator and they moved forward into a courtyard. There were wheelie bins of different colours stacked against the wall to the left. There was a razor-wire-topped fence to their right now, through which they could see a two-storey flat-roofed modern building surrounded by more fences.

'That's the Close Supervision Centre,' said Khaliq. 'That's where they're keeping Shafiq Ali Rafiq.'

'I can meet him, right?'

'Of course. He's going to want to thank us for everything we've done.'

There was a set of double doors at the end of the line of wheelie bins and a large man with a shaved head wearing chef's whites appeared. He flashed them a thumbs-up and disappeared back inside. Tariq pulled a Glock from the side of his seat and held it in his lap.

'Take your finger off the trigger, bruv, I don't want you blowing your nuts off.'

Tariq's cheeks flushed red. 'Sorry,' he muttered.

Khaliq patted him on the leg. 'You're doing fine, bruv.'

The chef reappeared with two bearded men wearing aprons. Behind them was a female guard. She was in her thirties, with dyed blonde hair tied back in a ponytail. She was holding a clipboard and a pen. 'The kafir's here to check the delivery,' said Khaliq. 'I'll deal with her. You get out first and walk to the front of the van.'

'Do I shoot her?'

'You don't shoot anyone, bruv. Keep the gun behind you.'

Tariq nodded and opened his door. He climbed out. 'You're early,' said the woman. 'Where's Umar?'

Tariq frowned. 'What?'

'I said where's Umar? I thought he was on today.'

Khaliq opened his door and stepped out. He levelled his Glock at the guard's chest. 'Don't say a word,' he said.

'What the f—' she began, but Khaliq rushed towards her and put the gun to her throat.

'I said shut the fuck up,' he hissed. 'Don't make a sound.' He gestured with his chin at Tariq. 'Open the back.'

Tariq hurried around to the back of the van. Khaliq looked over at the chef. 'How many guards inside?'

'Two. But there'll be another five along in half an hour to escort the trolleys to the wings.'

Khaliq pushed the guard to the rear of the van. She was trembling with fear and her face had gone white. Tariq opened the doors.

'Get the tape and stuff,' said Khaliq.

Tariq pulled out one of the holdalls he had taken from his Prius, dropped it on to the ground and unzipped it. He pulled out a polythene bag filled with black plastic zipties, ripped it open with his teeth and used one to bind the guard's wrists behind her back.

'Please don't hurt me,' she said.

'Shut up, bitch,' hissed Khaliq.

Tariq took a roll of duct tape from the holdall, ripped off a piece and used it to blindfold the guard.

Khaliq pressed his lips close to her ear. 'Listen, bitch,' he hissed. 'If I have to use duct tape to gag you, there's a good chance you'll suffocate. So keep your kafir mouth closed, okay?'

The guard nodded fearfully.

Khaliq took her over to the wheelie bins and forced her to sit down.

The chef walked to the rear of the van and his eyes widened when Tariq opened one of the crates and took out a Kalashnikov. The chef held out his hands and Tariq gave it to him.

'You've handled an AK?' asked Khaliq.

'I was in Syria, three years ago,' said the chef.

'Okay, it's yours. But no firing unless we have to.'

Khaliq shoved his Glock into his pocket and opened the box of Kalashnikov ammunition. He handed the chef a full magazine. The chef slotted it into his weapon and nodded.

'Right,' said Khaliq. 'Call the guards out, say there's a problem with the delivery.'

 * * *

Diane Daily opened the door and saw that Walsh was on the phone. She had a tray with two Starbucks coffees and she closed the door and put one down in front of Walsh before dropping down on to an armchair. Walsh mouthed her thanks. 'Yes, Rob Miller and Matty Clayton are just about to go in. I'll call you as soon as I know what's what.'

Walsh ended the call. 'Tango One and Tango Three have just driven into the prison with what might well be a van load of weapons,' she said.

Daily's jaw dropped. 'What? How?'

'They were at the unit and a van turned up. Then the van and the Prius left. But Tango One and Tango Three were in the van. The van drove into the delivery area of the prison a few minutes ago.'

'So we send in armed cops?'

Walsh grimaced. 'But if there are no weapons in the van there'll be hell to pay and we'll blow the whole investigation.'

'Can't we at least phone the prison and tell them to hold the van?'

'We're to wait until we've got confirmation that the weapons are no longer in the unit. Matty and Rob are on the case as we speak.'

'How did they get to drive into the prison?'

'They're in a food delivery van.'

'Donna, this could be really bad.'

'Yes. I know.'

'What about calling Dan?'

'The staff aren't allowed to take mobile phones into the prison. If we call the main office and ask to talk to him, we risk blowing his cover.' She forced a smile. 'Let's just keep our fingers crossed and hope that the weapons are still in the unit.'

• • •

Rob Miller took out the small leather wallet from the inside pocket of his jacket. He unzipped it to reveal a dozen small picks. 'You know, a monkey could do this, and he probably wouldn't need training either.'

'I think the monkeys were needed elsewhere,' said Matty Clayton.

Miller selected a pick. 'The point I'm making is that I came all the way from London to open a lock that a five-year-old could pick.'

'A five-year-old monkey?'

Miller inserted the pick into the lock, brushed it against the tumblers and then twisted. The lock opened. Miller put the pick back into the wallet and pushed up the shutter. 'It wouldn't have been so bad if they'd had some sort of alarm. But this is a total waste of my time.'

Clayton walked into the unit. It was empty, except for the boxes of cat litter. 'Well, now we know,' he said.

'Giles Pritchard isn't going to be happy,' said Miller. 'Can you break the bad news to him?'

Clayton shook his head and took out his mobile phone. 'I'll tell Donna, she can do the honours.'

. . .

Shepherd stood at the gate leading down to the showers. Three prisoners had already lined up, holding their washbags and towels, and Willie Macdonald was hurrying down the stairs leading from the threes.

'Boss?' said a voice behind him. It was Mick Walker, still wearing his exercise gear and dripping sweat.

'Mr Walker,' said Shepherd.

'Boss, Willie says there's an extra shower session going.' He held his arms out to the side. 'I really need to get clean, boss, a wipe down in my cell isn't going to cut it.'

'Did Mr Macdonald put you on the list?'

Walker screwed up his face. 'The price was too high,' he said.

'What did he want?'

'A five-pound spend in the canteen. I'd pay, but I'm flat broke this week. Please, boss, just a minute or two is all I need. I can't stay like this.'

Shepherd was going to say no, but he could see that Walker was genuinely distressed. 'Okay, go and get your stuff.'

Walker beamed. 'God bless you, boss,' he said, and hurried off to his cell.

Shepherd looked over at the area where meals were served. There were two long tables against the wall. There were six hotplates on the tables which were usually switched on half an hour before the food trolleys arrived from the kitchen but there was no red band there and the hotplates were switched off.

Macdonald arrived with a towel over his shoulder and his shower things in a net bag.

'Mr Walker will be joining us,' said Shepherd.

Macdonald opened his mouth to say something, but then obviously realised he had already been given more than his fair share of favours, so he just smiled and nodded.

The rest of the inmates on Macdonald's list arrived quickly, no one wanted to miss the opportunity of a shower. Shepherd unlocked the gate and the prisoners streamed down. Walker jogged over, a towel in one hand, a small black net washbag in the other. 'Thanks for this, boss,' he said.

Shepherd just nodded. As Walker headed down the steps, Shepherd closed the gate and locked it. He could already hear the water running in the showers.

When Shepherd got to the shower room, Willie Macdonald was singing 'Flower of Scotland' as he lathered himself up and this time nobody shouted at him to shut up. Shepherd wondered how much prison hooch the Scotsman had earned by selling spots in the shower run.

Walker was standing by the sinks, patiently waiting.

'First one out, you take his place,' said Shepherd. 'And take as long as you want.'

'Thanks, boss,' said Walker.

Shepherd looked at his watch. Lunch was about twenty minutes away, so they had time.

      •   •   •

Giles Pritchard's mobile rang. He grabbed it and looked at the screen. It was Donna Walsh. 'Yes Donna?'

Walsh got straight to the point. 'The weapons and ammunition are no longer in the unit,' she said.

'That's not good,' said Pritchard.

'Only two vehicles left the unit, the Prius and the van. We have eyes on the car and I can get it searched but in volume terms alone, it has to be the van.'

'I think that's pretty clear,' said Pritchard.

'I'm sorry.'

'You've nothing to be sorry about, Donna,' said Pritchard. 'Okay, well let's keep an eye on Victor One. And keep Tango Two under surveillance. You can tell Rob Miller to get back to Thames House.'

'Do we still install CCTV in the unit?'

'I think the horse has bolted, Donna. I've got a few calls to make and then I'll get back to you.'

He ended the call. He tapped on his computer and searched for the phone number of HMP Bradford. He called the number and it began to ring, but it wasn't being answered. He went to the prison's website and got the name of the governor, Jonathan Blunt. He was just about to hang up when the call was answered. 'HMP Bradford,' said a woman. 'How may I direct your call?'

'Can you put me through to Jonathan Blunt's office. The governor.'

'Who's calling please?'

Pritchard frowned. Was this all a huge mistake? Was he worrying about nothing? 'If you could tell him it's the West Yorkshire Police on the line,' he said.

'Putting you through.'

There was a ringing tone for about thirty seconds before the call was answered. 'Yeah?' It was a man's voice.

'Could I speak to Mr Blunt please?'

'You the cops?'

'This is West Yorkshire Police. Can I speak to the governor?'

The man laughed. 'The governor's tied up at the moment,' he said. 'Literally. Who are you?'

'This is Superintendent Taylor,' said Pritchard. 'Can you explain to me what's happening there, please?'

'I ain't explaining nothing,' said the man. 'You just listen and listen good. You'll be told what you have to do on Instagram and TikTok and YouTube. Hashtag FreeTheBrothers. Got that?'

'Hashtag FreeTheBrothers, yes.'

'And tell everyone that anyone who tries to get inside the prison will be met with deadly force. Do you understand?'

'Yes, I understand. Can you tell me, who am I talking to?'

'Hashtag FreeTheBrothers. And the deadline will be six o'clock tonight.'

The call ended. Pritchard sat back in his chair. No, he wasn't worrying about nothing. He clearly had a lot to worry about.

. . .

Khaliq put the phone down and looked across at Malik Abid Qadeer. 'That was the police. They're aware of the situation.' Khaliq was sitting at Blunt's desk, almost dwarfed by the huge black leather chair.

Qadeer was sitting in a winged chair by a window that overlooked the Close Supervision Centre, fiddling with Islamic prayer beads. He frowned. 'How? We have made no announcement.'

'I don't know. And it doesn't matter. We already have control over the kitchen, the admin block, the classrooms and the workshops. Within minutes we will have the wings and the control centre. There is nothing they can do.'

Qadeer nodded. 'I hope you are right, brother.'

Khaliq looked over at the corner of the office where the governor was huddled on the floor with three members of staff, two men and a woman. Tariq was standing over them with his Glock aimed at the governor's face. 'Come here, Mr Blunt,' said Khaliq.

The governor stood up and walked over to the desk. 'You don't have to do this,' he said.

Khaliq waved his hand. 'It's already done,' he said. 'Once the food trolleys have been taken to the wings, we will control the entire prison.'

'Please do not hurt my staff,' said the governor. 'Or the prisoners. Nobody needs to be hurt.'

'That depends on what the authorities do in response to our demands.'

'And what are they? Your demands?'

'That's not for you to concern yourself with, Mr Blunt,' said Khaliq. He pointed at the computer in front of him. 'What I need from you is your password so that I can access the prison computer system.'

Blunt shook his head. 'I can't do that. You know I can't do that.'

'But you can, Mr Blunt, and you will. You and your people are totally in my power now. I can do anything I want to you. How would you feel if I began removing your fingers, Mr Blunt? One at a time. With a knife.' He waved at one of the men by the door. He was holding a long carving knife. He spoke to the man in Urdu and the man grinned and waved the knife in the air. 'How many fingers do you think you could stand to lose before you broke down and gave me the password?'

'Please don't do this,' said Blunt, his voice shaking.

'Who is the woman?' asked Khaliq, gesturing towards the group huddled on the floor.

'That's Miss Maguire,' said Blunt.

'She's your secretary?'

'My head of security.'

Khaliq smiled. 'Well she didn't do a great job, did she?' He laughed and spoke to Qadeer in Urdu, who also laughed. The smile vanished from Khaliq's face. 'Or suppose I throw Miss Maguire to the brothers. Many of them have been without female company for years.'

Tears ran down Maguire's cheeks and she turned her face away.

Khaliq stared at Blunt, and lowered his voice to a threatening whisper. 'You are the number one governor at HMP Bradford. You make all the decisions here, so I will give you the choice. We can start removing your fingers, or we can deliver Miss Maguire to the brothers downstairs. You decide which. Or, you can simply tell me your password and avoid any unpleasantness.'

Blunt gritted his teeth, but then the fight went out of him and his shoulders slumped. Khaliq put his fingers on the keyboard and waited.

. . .

Supervising Officer Ed Blackhurst looked down from his vantage point up on the thirds. From where he was standing he could see the gate that led to the control centre, the pool table and table tennis table, and the serving area where meals were delivered to the inmates. Most of the inmates were in their cells and the sounds of the TVs and stereo systems echoed around the wing.

Stephen Underwood was on the ground floor, walking by the pool table. The officers were carrying out a roll call, checking that all the prisoners were present and accounted for. Those prisoners who hadn't been to classes or work were locked in their cells; those who had been out were in their cells but their doors were unlocked.

Jenny Johnston was also on the ones, more relaxed now that she wasn't having to deal with prisoners. Blackhurst didn't think that Johnston had what it took to be a prison officer, but he could see that she'd be a decent enough governor. The problem was there was no short cut, she'd have to spend at least a couple of years walking the landings and he just hoped that she could stick it out. Something like one in seven prison officers quit every year and more than half lasted less than three years. He had Johnston down as a quitter but he'd be happy if she proved him wrong.

Swinton was down in the showers. Swinton was a strange one, no question. He had a quiet authority about him, and he was what Blackhurst called a watcher. Swinton was constantly on the alert, always aware of what was going on around him. Most prison officers reacted to what was happening around them but watchers were able to see trouble brewing. Swinton had been a prison officer for more than twenty years, mostly in Liverpool, but he had none of the cynicism that most long-timers had. The prisoners respected that, and the fact that he tended to treat them as human beings rather than numbers. But Blackhurst couldn't help wonder why the man seemed to be so relaxed at his job. He was in debt up to his eyeballs, brought his own packed lunch to work every day, and didn't seem to have any friends, but he never appeared to take out his frustrations on the prisoners.

Blackhurst heard the rattle of trolleys coming down the wing. He frowned and looked at his watch. Lunch was early. And the red bands hadn't prepared the hotplates. The inmates would express their unhappiness if their food was cold.

Three prisoners walked towards Johnston and he saw her tense. They surrounded her, invading her personal space. Blackhurst frowned, wondering what was happening.

Three more prisoners approached Underwood. One of them pushed Underwood against the wall and another held something to his throat. Blackhurst straightened up. What the hell was happening?

A figure appeared to his left. 'Don't touch your radio, Mr Blackhurst,' said a voice. Blackhurst turned to look at the man. It was Atif Mahmood. His cell was on the twos. Blackhurst's eyes widened when he saw the shiv in Mahmood's hand, a razor blade that had been melted into a plastic toothbrush handle. 'I will cut you, Mr Blackhurst. I swear it.'

Another man appeared on Blackhurst's right. He was from the threes and he was also holding a shiv.

'What's going on, guys?' said Blackhurst, trying to keep his voice from trembling.

'Just don't touch your radio and everything will be fine,' said Mahmood.

The two heated trolleys appeared. Four red bands were pushing the trolleys, watched by a guard. The guard didn't seem to have noticed that Underwood and Johnston were being assaulted. Blackhurst stared at the guard. He didn't recognise him and the man's uniform didn't fit him either, it was a couple of sizes too big.

The red bands bent down and opened the side doors of the trolleys. One of them took out a rifle and began walking towards the control centre. The rest of the red bands began pulling out machetes which they handed to a queue of prisoners that had formed in front of the trolleys. Johnston began to scream and one of the prisoners slapped her, hard, the sound echoing like a pistol shot.

· · ·

Neil Geraghty looked up from his computer screen as he heard a scream and footsteps running towards B Wing gate. Running was against health and safety regulations. When it did happen, it meant that something was wrong. There was a man standing at the gate and it took Geraghty a second or two to process what he was seeing. The man was holding a gun. A big gun. A rifle. And he was pointing it directly at Geraghty. 'Put your hands in the air!' the man shouted.

There were dozens of prisoners standing behind the man, most of them holding machetes or knives.

A second man appeared at the C Wing gate. He was also holding a rifle. 'Hands in the fucking air!' he screamed. Geraghty recognised the man. Saeed Ghani. He was one of the C Wing red bands who worked in the kitchen. What the hell was he doing with a gun?

Two guards came out of the office behind Geraghty and they froze when they saw the guns.

'Touch your radios and you're dead!' shouted Ghani.

A prison officer appeared next to Ghani and he unlocked the gate. Geraghty didn't recognise the officer. As the man stepped into the control centre, Geraghty realised he was wearing trainers and that the trousers were several inches too long. And he was holding a handgun.

Ghani kept his weapon trained on Geraghty's chest as he walked across the tiled floor towards him.

Another fake guard opened the gate to C Wing and prisoners with machetes rushed in. For the first time the guards up on the gantries realised there was a problem and they began shouting down to Geraghty, asking what was happening.

Ghani aimed his rifle up at the gantries and shouted for them to come down.

The prisoners with machetes surrounded the guards on the ground floor and began ordering them to remove their uniforms.

'You too, Mr Geraghty,' said Ghani, gesturing with his weapon.

Geraghty began to take off his shirt.

One of the guards started to protest but he was clubbed across the face with a machete handle and fell to the floor, blood pouring from his broken nose.

Geraghty held up his hands. 'Everybody just do as they say!' he shouted. 'Whatever instructions they give, just follow them!'

Ghani nodded. 'Exactly,' he shouted. 'You all listen to Mr Geraghty!'

. . .

Shepherd heard shouts from upstairs and he frowned. Had they started serving lunch early? Nothing was ever early, prison time meant that almost everything ran late. He went down the corridor to the stairs. There were more shouts now. And screams. And the pounding of running feet. He walked slowly up the stairs, trying to make sense of what he was hearing. There was always noise on the wings, but this was something else.

He reached the top of the stairs but he stayed back from the gate. He hit the light switch to turn off the lights. He saw a prison officer running away from the direction of the control centre. It was Sandra Shakespeare, a look of panic on her face. Shepherd peered to the side and saw a prisoner in the middle of the landing, waving a machete. He was joined by another prisoner, this one carrying what looked like a carving knife. There were more shouts now, and screams.

Walker appeared at Shepherd's shoulder. 'What's going on, boss?'

'Stay back,' hissed Shepherd.

A third prisoner came into view, a bearded man in his fifties wearing a dark blue robe and cradling a Kalashnikov. Shepherd's eyes widened.

'That's an AK-47,' hissed Walker.

'Get down the stairs now,' said Shepherd.

'What the fuck's going on, boss?'

'Now!' Shepherd pushed Walker down the stairs and headed after him.

．　．　．

Khaliq sat back in the high-backed chair and sighed in disbelief. 'I don't believe it,' he said. He looked over at the governor, who was back on the floor sitting next to his staff. The door was guarded by a large man holding a Kalashnikov across his chest. 'Seriously? You allowed MI5 to put undercover officers into your prison?'

'I had no choice,' said Blunt, his voice little more than a whisper.

'What has happened?' asked Malik Abid Qadeer, who was still fingering his prayer beads.

'Mr Blunt here has three MI5 officers working in the prison. Two as inmates and one as a guard.' His fingers played over the keyboard and his eyes narrowed as he stared at the screen. 'The guard is on the books as Tony Swinton. He's one of the guards we've been using to get contraband into the prison. He's the one who got the phone to Mir, and who gave the cocaine to the Albanians.' He shook his head angrily. 'How could I have been so stupid?'

'You know him?'

'Tariq introduced me. The guy has a gambling problem and a mother in a nursing home. That's what I was told. But he's been playing us. Bastard.'

'Does it say what his real name is?'

Khaliq shook his head. 'Just Tony Swinton. The guy is good. I met him a couple of times and I never even suspected that he was a plant.'

He tapped on the keyboard again. 'The two officers under-cover as prisoners are Kamran Zaidi and Sayed Khan. Zaidi is in A Wing under the name Adil Rauf and Khan is D Wing as Nadeem Choudhury. Do you know them?'

Qadeer shook his head.

Khaliq nodded at the man by the door holding the Kalashnikov. 'Tell Tariq I want to see him, now!'

The man nodded and left the room.

'Does this change anything?' asked Qadeer.

'It means they have been watching everything we have been doing,' said Khaliq. 'They must know who we are. And if they were following us, they must have known about the guns.'

'Were they following you?'

'I didn't see anybody, but MI5 are professionals.'

'Then why didn't they stop you?'

'I don't know.' He sat back in his chair and put his hands up to his face, his mind in a whirl. 'I only met Swinton a few days ago,' he said eventually. 'They can't have known about me before that. And I only went to the weapons yesterday.

Tariq had never been to the unit where we're storing them. Maybe they didn't know we had guns, or if they did know it was only last night when they found them.' He grinned. 'They found out too late to do anything.'

The door opened and the man with the Kalashnikov re-appeared with Tariq. 'What's up, bruv?' asked Tariq.

'I'll tell you what's up, bruv. Tony Swinton is an undercover MI5 officer.'

Tariq's jaw dropped. 'No fucking way.'

'It's on the computer. He was a plant, sent in to investigate terrorism at the prison. Him and two other officers posing as prisoners.'

'Bruv, it's not possible. We approached him. We used Tommy Warner to get him to bring in Rizlas and stuff before you gave him the phone. He's got a mother in a nursing home. Lives in a shithole, doesn't have two pennies to rub together.'

Khaliq shook his head. 'He's MI5, bruv. Everything he told you was a lie.'

'You are fucking kidding me.'

'Straight up, bro.'

'The fucking bastard!'

'I need you to go to B Wing and get Swinton. Bring him here. And you need to get the two prisoners. That's Adil Rauf on A Wing and Nadeem Choudhury on D Wing.'

'I will, yeah. Fucking hell.'

Tariq left the room. Qadeer looked over at Khaliq. 'Does this change anything?' he asked.

Khaliq smiled thinly. 'It works to our advantage,' he said. 'It gives us three high-value hostages that we didn't have before.' He stood up and walked over to a black holdall on the floor by Qadeer's chair. He bent down, unzipped it and pulled out a bright orange jumpsuit. He tossed it at Blunt. 'Put this on,' he said. 'We're going to make a video.'

. . .

S hepherd squinted through the bars of the gate. Muslim prisoners were throwing non-Muslim prisoners into cells and locking the doors. They had stripped Underwood and Griffiths of their uniforms, then handcuffed them with their own rigid cuffs before binding their legs and blindfolding them with duct tape. They hadn't stripped Johnston, but they had handcuffed her and bound her legs. Tears were running down her cheeks. One of the prisoners patted her on the face, then plastered a strip of tape across her eyes.

Two prisoners dragged Maria Crowley from her office. They forced her to the ground and began binding her with duct tape. She protested until they used a strip of tape to gag her.

All around there were shouts and cheers and cries of '*Allahu Akbar!*'

A group of Muslim prisoners approached the man with the Kalashnikov. He screamed at them and waved the weapon threateningly. They backed away, their hands in the air. He screamed at them again and they backed into a cell. The man pulled the door shut.

Shepherd backed down the steps and went along to the shower room where the prisoners had huddled together against one wall.

'What's happening?' asked Walker.

'They've tied up the officers and they're locking up some prisoners.'

'They're going to kill us all, aren't they?' said Macdonald.

'All they're doing is locking them up,' said Shepherd.

'They're going to kill us,' said Macdonald. 'I know they are.'

'Listen, Willie, I need your phone PIN number.'

'You what?'

'I need to call out and I don't have a phone. I'm going to try to get to one of the landing phones but I'll need a PIN to use it.'

'That's your plan?' said Walker. 'Do you seriously think they're going to let a guard wander down the landings and pick up a phone?'

'I was planning on checking out the other wings first,' said Shepherd. 'They might only have taken B Wing.'

'I've a better idea,' said Walker. He nodded at one of the prisoners, Angus Meade, who was serving a six-year sentence for fraud. 'Give him your phone, Angus.'

'Fuck off,' said Meade. He was a short man, just over five feet six tall, and overweight, bordering on obese. His towel barely stretched around his waist and he had to hold it in place with one hand.

'We need it if we're going to get out of this alive, Angus.'

'I'm not giving up my phone to a screw,' said Meade. 'It cost me six hundred quid.'

'I'm sure Mr Swinton will reimburse you,' said Walker.

'Do you have a phone on you?' asked Shepherd.

Walker laughed harshly. 'Not on him. In him.'

'Fuck off, Walker. Snitches get stitches, remember?'

'I'm not grassing you up, Angus. I'm trying to save our lives here. Willie's right, these fuckers want us dead and your phone could save our lives. Hand it over.'

Meade looked at Shepherd. 'If I did have a phone, and I'm

not saying that I do, but do I have your word that I won't be on a charge for having it? There's no way I'm having a year or so added to my sentence just for helping you out.'

'You have my word,' said Shepherd. 'It'll be our little secret.'

'And I want reimbursing. I want a grand added to my canteen account.'

'Not a problem,' said Shepherd.

'A grand. You swear?'

'On my mother's grave.'

Meade's eyes narrowed. 'I was told your mother was in a nursing home.'

'Angus, I will look after you, I swear,' said Shepherd. 'But if you don't hand it over willingly, I will bend you over and pull it out with my bare hands.'

Meade muttered under his breath, then shuffled over to the toilets, his flip flops slapping on the concrete floor. He disappeared into a cubicle.

Walker grinned at Shepherd. 'I wouldn't want to be a fly on that wall,' he said.

'How did you know he had a phone?' asked Shepherd.

'I used to share a cell with him,' said Walker. 'Bloody nightmare. Every time he moved, the beds would shake like there was an earthquake. And you can't squeeze by him in the cell, can you? Also he has a serious BO problem.'

The toilet flushed and Meade reappeared, holding a brown package in his right hand. He waddled over to the washbasins and ran it under the tap, then shook it dry and wiped it in his towel. He peeled off the condom and tossed it into a bin, then held out his hand. 'Help yourself,' he said.

Shepherd looked at the phone. It was a twin of the one he had brought in for Javid Mir, though it was grey instead of

Stephen Leather

black. He blotted out where the phone had been hiding and took it. Walker laughed at his obvious discomfort. 'Stay here,' growled Shepherd.

He walked down the corridor to the gym and tapped in Giles Pritchard's number. Pritchard wouldn't recognise the number so there was every chance that he wouldn't take the call, but he answered on the third ring. He didn't say anything, just listened.

'It's Shepherd. Can you talk?'

'Bloody hell, Dan. Where are you?'

'The basement of B Wing. All hell has broken out here. They've got guns and they've taken over the wing.'

'They have the governor, too. They took fifteen Kalashnikovs and fifteen Glocks in. And a stack of machetes. What's happening there?'

'They don't seem to be rioting, it's more organised than that. They've stripped the uniforms off the guards and they're locking up the non-Muslim prisoners and the Muslim prisoners who aren't in on it. It looks as if they're planning to negotiate using hostages as leverage.'

'What's your situation?'

'I'm unarmed and I'm with seven prisoners. I can move from here to the other wings, but I'm not sure how much help I can be.'

'Is there any way you could get to the governor?'

'I can get to the admin block, that's not a problem. All the basements are linked. But as I said, I'm not armed and there's a lot of them. I'm going to need help.'

'I'm working on it,' said Pritchard.

'Do you know what it is they want?'

'They're preparing to go public on social media,' said Pritchard. 'Hashtag FreeTheBrothers.'

'That's not good,' said Shepherd.

'No it's not,' said Pritchard. 'Do you think you'll be able to keep below their radar?'

'I'm not sure,' said Shepherd. 'The basements contain the showers and the gyms and the gates are locked, so there's no reason for them to come down. But if they do, I've got nowhere to go.'

'I have to attend a COBRA meeting and I'll have a better idea of what our options are after that. I'll call you.'

'Understood,' said Shepherd.

'Stay safe.'

'I'll try.'

• • •

The governor stared at the iPhone that had been fixed to a tripod on the desk. He was wearing a bright orange jumpsuit and they had handcuffed him with a set of bar cuffs that they had taken from a guard. 'My mouth is dry,' he said. 'I can't swallow.'

Khaliq passed him a bottle of water and waited impatiently while he drank. Blunt's hand was shaking and he spilled water down the front of his orange jumpsuit. He apologised and gave the bottle back to Khaliq.

'All you have to do is to read the message on this sheet of paper,' said Khaliq. 'Nothing else.'

Blunt nodded. 'Okay.'

Khaliq gave him the sheet of paper and nodded at the man who was standing behind the phone and he pressed the screen to start the recording. Blunt cleared his throat. 'My name is

Jonathan Blunt, I am the governor in charge of His Majesty's Prison Bradford. At least I was in charge, now the prison is being run by Islamic State of the United Kingdom. The prison has been seized in the name of Islamic State in retaliation for the way that the British government has treated Muslims, both here in the UK and elsewhere around the world.'

Blunt cleared his throat again. 'The Islamic State of the United Kingdom has a list of demands. The demands are not unreasonable. They are all within the government's gift. If those demands are not met . . .' Blunt hesitated as his eyes scanned the words he was to read. He looked over at Khaliq and shook his head. 'No . . .' he implored.

Khaliq stabbed a finger at the sheet of paper. 'Read it!' he mouthed.

The governor took a deep breath to steady himself. 'If those demands are not met by six o'clock tonight, I will be killed, live, on camera. And then the hostages will be killed, one an hour, until the demands are met. They will start with the prison guards, then the civilian staff, and finally the non-Muslim prisoners. In all they have eight hundred and thirty-seven hostages. Islamic State of the United Kingdom is prepared to kill each and every one of them.'

Tears were welling up in the governor's eyes. He looked over at Khaliq, who again jabbed his finger at the sheet of paper.

'In the event that the authorities try to storm the prison, a lot of people will die. The Islamic State of the United Kingdom does not want anyone to die. They only want justice. The following are their demands. First, they demand the release of the following twenty-six Muslim brothers who are being held in Belmarsh Prison on trumped-up charges. The brothers are . . .'

Blunt then read out the names slowly, occasionally apologising when he stumbled over the pronunciation.

'They are to be taken from Belmarsh Prison to Gatwick Airport, and from there they are to be flown to Syria. The Islamic State of the United Kingdom also wants free passage from Bradford Prison for any Muslim prisoner who requests it. It is up to the individual prisoners if they stay in the country or leave, but any criminal offences they are claimed to have committed are to be expunged from the record.'

Blunt's hands were trembling now and tears began running down his face. 'These demands must be met by six o'clock tonight, or I will be executed. There are to be no negotiations. The demands are non-negotiable. *Allahu Akbar.* God is great.'

Khaliq pressed the button to end the recording, then took the piece of paper from the governor. He pointed at the cowering staff. 'Go back to your people,' he said.

He took the phone from its tripod and emailed the video to Blunt's email account, then sat down at the desk and waited for it to arrive. Once it was on the office computer he cut off the first few seconds and the last few seconds, then watched it all the way through. He nodded his approval. 'Nice work, Mr Blunt,' he said. 'Just the right amount of fear and trepidation, but not enough to spoil the delivery.'

Khaliq posted the video on YouTube, Instagram and TikTok, then sent copies to the country's main newspapers and news websites. As he was sending the last email, the door opened. A heavy-set man in a grey tunic and baggy pants appeared, holding a Kalashnikov. 'He is here,' he said.

'Excellent,' said Khaliq. 'Just in time to see me post the video.'

The man opened the door wide and Shafiq Ali Rafiq walked in. He smiled when he saw Khaliq. 'My son,' he said.

'Father,' said Khaliq. 'It has been a long time. Far too long.'

He stepped forward and embraced his father, kissing him on both cheeks.

. . .

Shepherd motioned for Walker to join him. The man still hadn't showered and his singlet and shorts were stained with sweat. The rest of the men had changed into their clothes and were sitting on the floor in the corridor outside the gym. All the lights were off but there was just enough light filtering in from the ones for them to see each other.

'Mick, I'm going to head down the tunnel and try to get to the admin block. That's where they're holding the governor.'

'What, you have another cunning plan, do you?' Walker shook his head dismissively. 'You've got nothing but your baton and a can of PAVA, they'll see you coming a mile away and you won't get the chance to use either.'

Shepherd couldn't help but smile. 'You're a regular ray of sunshine, aren't you? Did you carry on like this in the Paras?'

'If an officer gave me a crap order, I'd make sure they knew how I felt, yeah.'

'And what about when you were a warrant officer? Did your men talk back to you?'

Walker grinned. 'Not if they knew what was good for them, no. So tell me about your cunning plan.'

'There's nothing I can do here, clearly. The wing is full of prisoners with machetes and I saw an AK-47 and a Glock. But all the prisoners were returned to the wings from their classes and the workshops so it should be quieter.'

'And the tunnel leads to the admin block?'

Shepherd nodded. 'All the basements are connected. The tunnels aren't used any more, but they should be serviceable.'

'What's going on?' asked Macdonald, coming up behind Shepherd.

'Bloody hell, Willie, don't creep up on me like that,' said Shepherd.

'You're up to something. What?'

'I'm going to head to the admin block. They've got the governor hostage.'

'You're not leaving us here.'

'I don't have any choice, Willie,' said Shepherd. 'You'll be okay. They're not killing anybody. They're not even rioting. This has been well organised.'

Macdonald shook his head fiercely. 'You can't leave us here.'

'I can move faster on my own.'

'But you're taking him with you, aren't you?' He gestured at Walker.

'He's got military experience. He was a Para.'

'Yeah, well I had more than my fair share of punch-ups in Sauchiehall Street back in the day,' said Macdonald. 'I can fight.'

'I'm sure you can, Willie. But this won't be a punch-up.'

'You're not leaving me here.'

Walker held up a hand. 'This is your call, Mr Swinton, obviously,' he said. 'But if you do leave them here and they're discovered, the first question they'll be asked is where the officer went. And they're going to say, obviously. Which means they'll be coming after you. But if there's no one here to ask, there's no one to tell. If they do come down to check and there's no one here, well then that's the end of it, right?'

Shepherd considered what the man was saying, and realised that he was right. He nodded. 'Okay. We move together,' he said.

He went over to the group huddled across from the gym. 'Right, we're moving out, down that tunnel there.' He pointed at the locked gate. 'Stay together and no noise.'

'Where are we going?' asked Meade.

'Just putting some distance between ourselves and the wing,' said Shepherd. 'No noise, no questions, just stay close.'

The men got to their feet. Shepherd headed back to Walker. 'I'll have to lock and relock the doors, but when we move, you're tail-end Charlie. Make sure we don't lose anyone.'

Walker threw him a mock salute. 'You were in the military, weren't you? You can tell me.'

Shepherd ignored him and pulled out his keys.

* * *

Pritchard used the back entrance to get into Number 10. Politicians loved to be photographed entering and leaving the building, unless they were there to be sacked, but Pritchard had no wish to see his face in the papers.

The Deputy Prime Minister was already seated at the head of the table when Pritchard arrived at the Cabinet Office Briefing Room. The PM was off on a junket to see his Silicon Valley friends, though it had been billed as a fact finding mission. He wasn't expected back for another twenty-four hours, though Pritchard was fairly sure that the man would be hastily rearranging his schedule.

Also at the table were the commissioner of the Metropolitan Police, the Justice Minister and the Home Secretary. The great and the good, but from the looks on their faces they were clearly all out of their depth.

The Deputy PM greeted Pritchard and waved for him to take a seat. More bodies filed in and took their places. The Secretary of State for Defence and the Director General of HM Prison Service were the last in before the doors were closed.

'I'm going to hand this straight over to Giles Pritchard,' said the Deputy PM. 'I'm assuming he's more up to speed than the rest of us. Please, everyone just listen to what he has to say, I'm sure there are going to be a shed load of questions but they can wait. Giles?'

Pritchard nodded. 'Basically, a group of armed terrorists have taken over HMP Bradford and are threatening to kill the governor at 6pm this evening if their demands are not met. Those demands included releasing twenty-six prisoners from Belmarsh Prison and free passage from Bradford Prison for all Muslim prisoners who want it. The hostage takers have made their demands public on social media so there is no way of keeping a lid on what has happened. By way of background, I can tell you that we had a small terrorist cell under observation outside the prison, but earlier today they moved into the prison and took weapons with them. So the hostage takers are armed and so far as we know have complete control of the prison.'

'How many weapons and what sort?' asked the Home Secretary.

The Deputy Prime Minister sighed. 'Can we leave the questions until later, please,' he said.

'I'm happy to answer,' said Pritchard. 'And to be honest, briefing-wise I don't have much to add. This has only just happened and we're low on intel. But we know that they have fifteen Kalashnikov assault rifles, fifteen Glock handguns, and a substantial amount of ammunition.'

'That seems very specific, considering that you are low on intel,' said the Home Secretary.

'We had the weapons under observation,' said Pritchard.

'So you're telling us that MI5 was already aware of the weapons cache, but you allowed it to be taken into the prison?' said the Home Secretary. 'How does that happen?'

As always the Home Secretary was keen to apportion blame, but on this occasion it was a valid question, albeit not one that Pritchard was comfortable answering.'

'We only found out about the weapons last night. We had the building they were in under observation, but they were moved first thing this morning. We didn't intercept the vehicle they were in for operational reasons, and by the time they reached the prison we were too late.'

'And whose decision . . .' began the Home Secretary, but the Deputy PM raised a hand to silence him.

'We need to confine ourselves to looking forward at this point,' he said. 'We're looking for solutions now, not explanations. There'll be time enough for that later.' He looked at the Police Commissioner. 'How do they stand policing-wise in Bradford?'

The commissioner linked his fingers together. 'They have cordoned off the streets around the prison and have two dozen uniformed officers in place. More are arriving by the hour. The police have tried to make contact through a negotiator but have had no success so far. They have three armed response vehicles outside the prison and are looking for more. We've promised them any assistance as and when they need it, but West Yorkshire Police seem to have everything in hand. Obviously they're not in a position to go in. Prisons are designed to keep people in, but they do an excellent job of keeping people out.'

'How good are their negotiators?'

'The head of their team was with the Met for the best part of ten years. He's good.'

'I presume the media are all over this?'

'Unfortunately, yes. But they are being kept away from the prison itself.'

The Deputy PM looked over at the Minister for Defence. 'I presume we can send in the Army if needed?'

'Without question,' said the Minister. 'But sending in soldiers to put down a prison riot isn't going to play well. Especially if people die. And especially if the majority of those people are Muslims.'

'This isn't a riot, Minister,' said Pritchard. 'This is a terrorist incident. There is no rioting as such. It has all been organised, and planned. This isn't random.'

The Deputy PM looked over at the Director General of the Prison Service. 'What resources can the prison service put into play?'

The Director General grimaced. 'If it was a normal riot - and I accept that this is far from that - then we would send in a Tornado team. They're specially trained officers who are organised regionally and sent in to trouble spots. Usually between fifty and a hundred men with protective equipment, tasers, PAVA spray, everything short of firearms. If necessary we could bring in men from other regions and get up to two hundred officers.'

'The heavy mob,' said the Home Secretary.

'Indeed. And they are used to dealing with knives and the like. But in this situation the prisoners have guns. Handguns and assault rifles. We couldn't send in Tornados to handle firearms.'

The Deputy PM nodded. 'So that brings us back to the Army.' He looked over at the Minister of Defence. 'What resources do you have available?'

'Well, in theory we're spoiled for choice,' said the minister. 'Catterick Garrison is just ninety minutes away, the largest British Army garrison in the world. We have the 1st Battalion Yorkshire Regiment, the Royal Lancers, the 1st Battalion Scots Guards, and the 4th Infantry Brigade, among others. But if we are serious about sending in troops then really you'd want the Paras. First Para are based at RAF St Athan in South Wales, Two Para and Three Para are based in Colchester. So we could have Paras in Bradford in four or five hours, depending on traffic. But I really must counsel against any idea that involves using armed troops to put down a prison riot.' The Defence Minister saw that Pritchard was about to speak and put up his hand to stop him. 'I absolutely accept that this is not a riot in the traditional sense, but that is how the media will portray it. We will be seen as a government that is prepared to use armed troops to quell a prison riot. And how many will die? Ten? A hundred? Two hundred? If we could guarantee a low level of casualties then perhaps, just perhaps, we could justify it. But we have prisoners with Kalashnikovs and Glocks and our troops will have no choice but to return fire if they are fired upon. It could be a blood-bath. A bloodbath in which, as I already said, most of the victims would be Muslims.'

'I hear what you're saying,' said the Deputy PM. 'But at some point we are going to have to put an end to the situation.'

'Then negotiate,' said the Home Secretary. 'Talk to them.'

'We know what they want,' said the Deputy Prime Minister tersely. 'They want us to release twenty-six leading ISIS figures currently being held in Belmarsh Prison. And to provide safe passage from HMP Bradford for anyone who wants it.' He sighed and shook his head. 'Madness.'

'We are going to negotiate, aren't we?' said the Home Secretary.

'We can talk to them,' said the Deputy Prime Minister. 'But I don't see that we can possibly agree to any of their terms.'

'We can't let them kill the governor,' said the Director General of the Prison Service. 'Especially not live on the internet.' He shuddered.

'How many of the prisoners in HMP Bradford are Muslims?' asked the Deputy Prime Minister.

The Director General looked down at a printed sheet of paper on the table in front of him. 'As of today, there are just over twelve hundred prisoners, serving sentences or on remand. Of those twelve hundred, four hundred and twenty three are Muslim. Now, that doesn't mean they are all actually Muslim. Some prisoners claim to be Muslim for various reasons.'

The Deputy Prime Minister frowned. 'Why would anyone claim to be Muslim when they weren't?'

'More religious holidays. More time out of their cells. More time in the showers. Better food. Lots of reasons.'

'And not all Muslims are radicalised, not by a long chalk,' said Pritchard. 'There are plenty of Muslims behind bars who just want to serve their time and get back to their lives. This isn't a riot by the Muslim population, this has been organised by a hard core of radicals. They'll be the ones running the show.'

'And how many of them do you think there are in Bradford?'

'Hard core?' Pritchard shrugged. 'It'd be a guess, but I'd say somewhere between fifty and a hundred.'

'What about the number the governor gave in the video?' asked the Justice Minister. 'Eight hundred and thirty seven hostages,' he said.

'We think that number is plucked from the air,' said Pritchard. 'But including prison officers, civilian staff and non-Muslim prisoners, that's probably a ballpark figure.'

'And who is behind this?' asked the Deputy Prime Minister.

'We think that a man called Mizhir Khaliq is the prime mover. He is the illegitimate son of Shafiq Ali Rafiq. He's been under the radar until now.'

The Deputy Prime Minister sighed. 'I knew that letting Rafiq back into the country was a mistake. I told the PM as much.'

'Do you have any assets in HMP Bradford?' asked the Home Secretary. 'Agents or officers?'

'I'd prefer not to divulge operational matters,' said Pritchard. He could have told the meeting that he had two officers under-cover as prisoners and that Dan Shepherd was still in play, but he didn't trust the Home Secretary, the minister had close links to several journalists on left wing newspapers and websites, and if news of the undercover officers was made public, their lives would be at risk.

'Quite right,' said the Deputy Prime Minister. 'So how do we move forward? The clock is ticking.'

Pritchard realised that everyone was now looking at him.

He cleared his throat, straightened his shoulders and tried to look more confident than he felt. 'The hostage-takers have given us a deadline of six pm. Just after sunset. That may or may not be connected to Maghrib prayers. I'd suggest we get into conversation with them, tell them that their demands are being met, and try to buy us a little time.'

'How does that help us?' asked the Deputy Prime Minister.

'We can move in under cover of darkness,' said Pritchard. 'I'm proposing that we send the SAS in to end the siege.'

The Director General of the Prison Service nodded his approval. 'There is a precedent for using the SAS,' he said. 'They were sent in to end a siege at HMP Peterhead in 1987 and did a first class job. From what I recall they went in with wooden batons and had Browning pistols as back up.'

'Yes, they had flash bangs and tear gas, too,' said Pritchard. 'And they blew their way in with explosives. But you have to remember that it was only one wing that was rioting and they weren't facing prisoners with Kalashnikovs.'

'How do you plan to get in to the prison?' asked the Director General.

'That has to be decided,' said Pritchard. 'We'll be taking advice on it.'

'Well, you'll need good advice. There are only two ways in to HMP Bradford for vehicles, plus the main entrance for pedestrians. The walls are high and topped with razor wire and there are locked doors and gates everywhere. There are no keys outside the prison so even if they get in they'll be blowing door after door to move around. I can't see how they'll be able to get in without being seen which means there'll be an immediate fire fight.'

Pritchard nodded. 'We're working on it. It would be helpful if you could get the Tornados ready to go at some point. There'll be a lot of mopping up to do.'

The Justice Minister held up his hand. The Deputy Prime Minister nodded at him. 'I know this might sound a little off the wall,' said the Justice Minister, 'but is there any way we could use some sort of knockout gas, similar to the one the Russians used a while back. Knock everyone out so that no-one gets hurt.'

Pritchard forced a smile. 'I'm afraid there is no such thing as a safe knockout gas,' he said. 'You can incapacitate a person with a rag soaked in chloroform or the like, but taking down a group of people is next to impossible. The incident you're referring to is the Dubrovka theatre hostage crisis of October 2002. Chechen terrorists took 850 people hostage in a Moscow theatre and demanded that Russia pulled its forces out from Chechnya. They had a huge bomb rigged up in the centre of the theatre and an assault was ruled out. The Russians pumped a chemical agent into the ventilation system, probably based on fentanyl. The agent worked and the 40 terrorists passed out. All were shot dead while unconscious. But 130 hostages also died. That's the official figure, the one that the Russians released. We believe that more than three hundred civilians were killed. The problem is that any agent capable of incapacitating people quickly, is probably also going to be fatal in a lot of cases. There isn't going to be an easy solution, I'm afraid.'

'So the SAS it is,' said the Deputy Prime Minister. 'Can I leave it to you to liaise with Hereford?'

'Absolutely.'

• • •

Kamran Zaidi looked around the wing, his mind in a whirl as he tried to get to grips with what he was seeing. More than fifty men were milling around on the ground floor, waving machetes and a range of knives. Zaidi was holding a wooden-handled machete, the blade almost two feet long. The gate to the control centre was open and three men with Kalashnikovs were standing in front of a line of prison officers who had been stripped of their uniforms and handcuffed with their own cuffs.

It had all happened so quickly that Zaidi kept thinking that he was trapped in a nightmare and that any moment he would wake up. The two heated trolleys had been pushed in through a door at the far end of the wing. There were four red bands pushing the trolleys and a uniformed guard watching over them. But there hadn't been food in the trolleys, the red bands had begun pulling out knives and machetes.

Two of the red bands had pulled out Kalashnikovs and charged towards the control centre. Linda Wilson had appeared from her office, a look of confusion on her face. Two prisoners had grabbed her and taken her back into her office. Another prisoner had thrust a machete into Zaidi's hand. 'Get the kafirs in their cells,' he said. 'They're all being banged up.' The prisoner had hurried away.

Zaidi looked over at the stairs. A group of machete-wielding prisoners were dragging Andrew George and Nick Durst down from the twos. They threw the guards on to the ground and told them to strip off their uniforms, then used their own handcuffs on them and used duct tape to bind their feet and blindfold them before dragging them into a cell.

Zaidi saw the wing's emir standing at the doorway to his cell, his upper lip curled back in a snarl. Zaidi had been at

Wajid Rabnawaz's Islamic Culture class that morning, and there had been no clue that something like this was going to happen. Zaidi went over to him. 'What's happening?' asked Zaidi.

'It is the time of reckoning,' said Rabnawaz. 'Today we get the kafirs to do our bidding.'

'By rioting?'

'This is not a riot, brother. This is a military operation, by Islamic State of the United Kingdom.'

'Why didn't you warn us? Why didn't you prepare us?'

Rabnawaz grabbed Zaidi by the shoulder. His eyes were burning with a fierce intensity. 'Only those who needed to know were told, brother,' he said, peppering Zaidi's face with spittle. 'But now the whole world will know, and you, brother, are part of it.' He waved his hand at the wing behind them. 'Help to lock up the kafirs, they are our hostages now.' He grinned and shouted '*Allahu Akbar!*' at the top of his voice.

There were echoing shouts of '*Allahu Akbar*' all around them.

A man in blue overalls appeared at the doorway at the far end of the landing, the one that the trolleys had come through. He was flanked by two men carrying handguns. Glocks. The man in the overalls grabbed a prisoner by the arm and said something to him. The prisoner looked around and pointed in Zaidi's direction.

'That man, the man in overalls, who is that?' asked Zaidi.

Rabnawaz looked over at the men. 'I don't know them,' he said.

The men were walking towards them now. The two with the Glocks had their fingers on the triggers, which was not a good sign. Zaidi had a bad feeling about what was happening but there was nowhere to run and nowhere to hide. He swung the machete at his side, even though he knew it would be useless against men with guns.

'You're Adil Rauf?' asked the man in overalls. He was in his twenties, maybe a few years younger than Zaidi, with a neatly trimmed beard and eyes that were so brown they were almost black.

Zaidi nodded. 'Yeah, that's me. What's up?'

'You're needed in the governor's office.'

'Why? What's wrong?'

Something slammed against the side of Zaidi's head and everything went black.

• • •

There was a gate ahead of them and Shepherd waved for the men to stop. Macdonald was so close to Shepherd that he almost bumped into him. Shepherd looked back along the tunnel. There were fluorescent strip lights overhead that he had switched on as they entered the tunnel. They illuminated the bare brick walls, curved brick ceiling and dusty concrete floor. There were large patches of black mould on the ceiling and walls and the floor was cracked and uneven. Just inside the gate was a double light switch.

'I'm going to switch the lights off,' Shepherd hissed.

Walker flashed him an 'okay' sign from the rear. Shepherd hit the switch closest to him and the lights went out. There was a soft glow ahead of them, enough to see by. There were stacks of boxes against the walls, and a row of old metal filing cabinets.

Shepherd made his way to the middle of the group. 'I need

you to all stay here while I go ahead and scope out the area,'
he said.

'We should stay together,' whispered Macdonald.

'Yes, you guys stay together while I check out the tunnel
ahead of us. We don't want to bump into trouble.'

'You're dumping us.'

'No I'm not. Just stay here with Mick.' He went back to the
gate and opened it. It grated and he winced. He tried pushing
it slowly but it still made a noise. He pushed it just enough so
that he could slip through. He decided against locking it, partly
because he might need to make a quick escape, and partly
because he was sure that it would freak Macdonald out if he
locked it.

He took the PAVA spray from its holster. It would be better
than nothing if he came across one of the prisoners.

The basement area of the admin block was clearly being
used for storage, but it looked as if it had been months if not
years since anyone had been down there. There were two gates
ahead of one that led to stairs heading up, and another leading
to a tunnel. Shepherd had memorised the plans of the prison
and knew that the stairs went up to the admin block and the
tunnel went to the prison's electrical substation and on to
C Wing. Light was coming down the stairwell but Shepherd
couldn't hear anything. He unlocked the gate and eased it
open, then moved slowly up the stairs.

● ● ●

Maria Crowley looked over at Ed Blackhurst and flashed
him a sympathetic smile. He had been hit on the side

of the head and his left eye was half closed. They had taken his shirt, trousers and shoes so he was sitting against the wall in a vest and Y-fronts. 'Are you okay, Ed?'

'I've been better,' he growled.

There were two men holding machetes at the door, facing the wing, so they kept their voices to a low whisper.

'Jenny, are you okay?' said Crowley.

Jenny Johnston and Sandra Shakespeare were sitting next to Crowley's desk. Thankfully they hadn't forced the women to strip, but Johnston was still clearly in shock, staring down at the carpet. Shakespeare was made of sterner stuff and kept glaring at their captors whenever they walked by.

'Jenny? Look at me, Jenny,' said Crowley.

Johnston slowly lifted her head and looked blankly at the governor.

'It's going to be all right, Jenny. Don't worry.'

'They're going to kill us,' said Johnston. 'We're all going to die.'

Crowley forced a smile. 'No we're not. They're not rioting, they're not hurting anyone. They'll be talking to people on the outside. They'll be negotiating. It'll just take time.'

'They have guns,' said Johnston. 'They're going to shoot us.'

'Trust me, Jenny. That will not happen.'

A man appeared in the doorway. He was wearing blue overalls and holding a gun. Crowley frowned. She knew most of the prisoners by name and all of them by sight, but she didn't recognise this man. He was in his late twenties with a neatly trimmed beard and hair that glistened under the over-head lights. 'Where the fuck is Tony Swinton?' he shouted. He had a Birmingham accent.

No one replied.

The man pointed his gun at Johnston. 'Tell me where Tony Swinton is, or I'll shoot this bitch in the leg.'

'He's not here,' said Crowley quietly.

'I can see he's not fucking here,' said the man. He pointed the gun at her. 'Are you the governor?'

Crowley nodded. 'The wing governor, yes.'

'So if he's not here, which wing is he on, then?'

'He's supposed to be on this wing. But I don't see him.'

The man jabbed the gun at her face and she flinched. 'Where the fuck is he?'

'He went down to the showers,' said Blackhurst. 'He took a group of prisoners down to shower just before . . .' He grimaced. 'Just before you lot went crazy.'

The man pulled a flick knife from his overall pocket and pressed the button to eject the blade. He used it to cut the duct tape binding Blackhurst's ankles and dragged him to his feet. 'Show me,' he said, pushing Blackhurst through the doorway.

'Over there,' said Blackhurst, gesturing with his chin towards the gate that led to the showers.

'Did he come out?'

'I don't know.'

The man pushed Blackhurst back into the office and on to the floor. 'If you're lying, I'll come back and put a bullet in your head myself,' he said. He looked over at the prisoners with the machetes. 'Tie the kafir's legs again,' he said. 'And watch them closely.'

• • •

Matt Standing's phone rang and he pulled it from his pocket. He didn't recognise the number but he took the call anyway. 'Is that Sergeant Standing? Matt Standing?'

'Yeah. Who's that?'

'Matt, it's Liam Shepherd. Dan's son. Look, this thing at Bradford Prison. That's where Dad is, right?'

'That's what I'm told.'

'They'll send the SAS in, right?'

'I think it's being discussed as we speak,' said Standing. 'Where are you, Liam?'

'I'm here at RAF Odiham in Hampshire. I'm with 7 Squadron. I've just seen it on the news.'

'Okay,' said Standing. 'Then you probably know as much as I do.'

'Here's the thing. You guys are definitely going in, right?'

'Well, as I said, that's still to be decided.'

'Well no one else can, can they? It's a prison. Fortified walls, razor wire. And the bad guys have guns, right?'

'That's pretty much the situation as I understand it.'

'Well, I've spoken to my CO and there's a Chinook available if you need it. All it needs is for your CO to talk to my CO and it's a done deal. And he's happy for me and Pete Chambers to fly it. Obviously we can't go in guns blazing like they did in Mali, but other than that, we're good to go.'

'I hear what you're saying, Liam, but the Chinook is as noisy as hell and they'll hear us coming for miles. And even if we get inside the walls, every gate and door is locked.'

'I wasn't planning on landing,' said Liam. 'But what about a HALO? My dad has often talked about his HALO jumps, back when he was in the Regiment. The Chinook could drop you from twenty thousand feet.'

Standing narrowed his eyes. A HALO might work, though there was always a risk in an urban environment.

'We could pick you guys up at Hereford with all your gear and half an hour later be dropping you into the prison.'

Standing smiled. It sounded like a workable plan, though a lot depended on how Colonel Davies felt about it. 'Liam, stay by your phone, I'll raise it with the head shed and call you back.'

· · ·

Shepherd reached the top of the stairs. There was a locked gate and beyond it a corridor. He listened but heard nothing. He was tempted to open the gate, but if he came across a group of prisoners all he had was his PAVA spray and his baton. If he came across a prisoner with a gun, it would all be over. He stood staring down the corridor as he focused on the blueprints lodged in his memory. It led to three gates. The gate to the left led to the classrooms, the one to the right led to the workshops, and a gate straight ahead led to a stairway that would take him all the way up to the top of the building.

They were the stairs he would have to use to get to the governor's office. But there was no way he could make that journey unarmed and wearing a prison officer's uniform. Shepherd flinched as his phone buzzed. He shoved his PAVA spray back in its holster and hurried down the stairs to answer the call. It was Pritchard. 'Can you talk?' asked Pritchard.

'Just about,' said Shepherd.

'Okay, I'm just out of the COBRA meeting, and as you can

imagine everyone is spooked. Headless chickens comes to mind. The bad guys are refusing to negotiate, all they are doing is putting videos on social media. The top hostage negotiator in Bradford used to work for the Met and knows his stuff, but they're just refusing to pick up the phone. The local cops have sealed off the area but they don't have the ability to retake the prison. And the PM has ruled out using the army. What the PM has agreed to is using a Tornado team, and they're putting one together as we speak.'

'The Tornados aren't armed,' said Shepherd. 'Tasers and PAVA spray is the best they've got. They'll be up against Kalashnikovs and Glocks, it'll be a massacre.'

'I understand that,' said Pritchard. 'But we are going to have to do something. They want the release of twenty-six leading ISIS figures currently being held in Belmarsh Prison. And they want safe passage from HMP Bradford for anyone who wants it. If their demands aren't met, they say they will kill the governor, live on the internet. With more deaths to follow.'

'So what's the plan?'

'How easy would it be for an SAS team to HALO into the prison when it gets dark and for you to meet them?'

'The drop would be easy enough, but the yards are all floodlit at night so they'd be seen. They'd be mowed down before they'd even taken their chutes off.'

'Could you cut the power? We can't from outside, I've already checked, but I'm told that you could if you could access the substation there.'

'Yes, I can get there. It's in the basement below the admin block.'

'So you could cut the power just before they jump. Then meet them at the drop zone and unlock gates for them. We're told that there should be enough moonlight for them to see the drop zone from the air.'

'That might work. If they could drop into the B Wing exercise yard, I could take them from there.'

'The one problem I see is that the SAS will have night vision gear but you don't. Will you be able to move through the prison in darkness? I'm hoping your trick memory will kick in.'

'It's doable, yes,' said Shepherd.

'So the plan would be for the SAS team to move through the prison with night vision gear and take out the guys with guns. We're assuming thirty in all. Fifteen Kalashnikovs and fifteen Glocks, according to our intel. Once the guns are out of the equation, you can open the doors and let the Tornado team in. We have a hundred prison officers ready to go with another hundred on the way. They can clear the prison wing by wing.'

'That should work,' said Shepherd.

'It had better,' said Pritchard. 'Because we don't have a Plan B. Let me make some enquiries and I'll call you back.'

*   *   *

Tariq strode over to the gate that the prison officer had said led to the showers. He looked through the gate. The stairs were in darkness. 'Get me a fucking key, now!' he barked at the taller of the two red bands who were with him.

The man nodded and hurried off to the control centre.

Tariq looked down the wing to where a group of four prisoners were standing guard over the two MI5 officers. The one who had been using the name Adil Rauf was unconscious, the other, Nadeem Choudhury from D Wing, had been bound and gagged with duct tape. Tariq waved the men over and they dragged the captives with them.

'Take them to the governor's office, Mizhir Khaliq will deal with them. Tell Mizhir I am still looking for the guard, Tony Swinton.'

The prisoners nodded and dragged the two men towards the control centre.

The red band returned with a key. Tariq grabbed it and unlocked the gate. 'Stay with me,' he said.

'Let me get a knife,' said the unarmed red band.

'Use this,' said Tariq, taking out his flick knife and giving it to the man. He stepped through the gate and switched on the light.

· · ·

Shepherd walked slowly back down the tunnel. There was enough light coming from the stairs behind him to illuminate the prisoners gathered together at the gate. 'I think we're okay, the stairway ahead is clear and I don't hear anything.'

'So what's the plan?' asked Walker.

'I need a weapon,' said Shepherd. 'Ideally a gun.'

'Guns, plural,' said Walker. He saw the frown that flashed across Shepherd's face. 'One gun against dozens of inmates isn't going to cut it,' he said. 'At the very least they've got machetes. I need a gun, too.'

'Me too!' said Macdonald.

'You daft Scots bastard,' said Walker. 'Have you ever fired a gun?'

'I went to a firing range in Pattaya once.'

'I meant fired a gun at a living, breathing human being,' said Walker. 'One that has every chance of shooting back at you. That's a whole different experience, right, boss?'

Walker looked over at Shepherd, a sly look in his eyes. Shepherd could see the game he was playing and he just shrugged. 'You're the former soldier, Mr Walker,' he said. 'I'm just a humble prison officer.'

'Yeah, right,' said Walker. He was about to say something else when the overhead lights flickered on.

Shepherd looked over at the light switches by the gate but no one had touched them. 'Someone's coming,' he said.

'We've got to leave now,' said Walker.

Shepherd shook his head. 'Out of the frying pan,' he said. 'We've no idea what we'll face up there. Besides, this might be our chance to get weapons.' He pulled his PAVA spray from its holster and gave it to Macdonald. 'Use this on them Willie, but be careful. No friendly fire. Keep it behind your back until you're ready to use it.' He pulled his baton from his belt, flicked it open, and gave it to Walker. 'Make it look like you've got me prisoner. Keep talking so they don't have time to think. As soon as they're in range, we rush them.'

There were three men coming down the tunnel towards them.

'They've got guns,' said Meade.

'Yeah, but you're prisoners, you're not the enemy,' said Shepherd. Two of the men coming towards them were wearing Islamic tunics and baggy trousers. The man in the middle was wearing blue overalls and holding a gun. Shepherd realised it was Mohammed Tariq. Tango One. The man on the right also had a handgun, the one on the left was holding a knife.

Walker moved quickly, stepping behind Shepherd and

thrusting the baton under his chin. 'We've got the bastard!' he shouted. 'We've got him!'

Shepherd pretended to struggle as Walker pushed him down the tunnel towards the three men.

'Fucking screw!' shouted Macdonald. 'Fucking bastard screw!'

'He tried to run!' shouted Walker. 'But we've got the bastard!'

The three men were about twenty metres away now. Shepherd could see the look of triumph on Tariq's face.

'Let me go!' Shepherd shouted. 'They'll kill me, you know they'll kill me!'

'Who gives a fuck?' shouted Macdonald. 'You're a dirty fucking screw and you deserve everything you've got coming to you!'

Tariq had his gun down at his side. 'Where was he taking you?' he shouted.

'He wasn't taking us anywhere, the bastard was running,' said Walker, keeping the baton tight against Shepherd's chin. 'He tried to lock us in but we weren't having it.'

The men were ten metres away now. All three were grinning.

'Yeah, fucking bastard screw thought he was better than us!' shouted Macdonald, who was clearly enjoying the role playing. The Scotsman kicked out at Shepherd, catching his shin. Shepherd yelped in genuine pain.

'We'll take him,' said Tariq. 'Use his handcuffs to cuff him behind his back.'

'I'll do that,' said Macdonald.

Tariq frowned. 'Where's his spray?'

'It's here!' shouted Macdonald, pulling the PAVA canister from behind his back and pressing the trigger. A jet of the toxic chemical hit Tariq in the chest and erupted over his face. He immediately staggered back, coughing and spluttering.

Macdonald kept his finger on the trigger and aimed the spray at the man on the right. He too was immediately incapacitated and his gun rattled to the floor.

Walker released his grip on Shepherd and lashed out with the baton, hitting the knife away with one blow and then whipping it back to strike the man across the side of the head. The man whirled around and the knife slipped from his hand. Walker hit the man again and this time he fell to his knees and then slumped forward.

Shepherd nodded his approval. 'Nice,' he said.

Macdonald was standing over the man in overalls, screaming obscenities as he played the jet of PAVA fluid over the man's face and chest.

'Willie, mate, ease off!' shouted Shepherd. 'You'll kill him.'

'And us,' said Walker, whose eyes were already watering from the fumes.

Macdonald finally stopped spraying. He was gasping for breath and his face was glistening with sweat. He kicked the man in the chest and he rolled over.

The man that Walker had hit was out for the count, but the other man who Macdonald had sprayed was curled up into a foetal ball, coughing and retching.

Shepherd pointed at the unconscious man who had been wielding the knife. 'Get his clothes off,' Shepherd said to Walker.

Shepherd started taking the tunic off the man who was curled up on the floor but he started resisting. 'I don't have time to mess about, mate,' said Shepherd, and he punched him in the side of the head. The man went still.

Shepherd pulled off the man's tunic and pants, then he stripped off his own shirt and gave it to Macdonald. 'Willie, cut my shirt into strips and tie and gag them.'

Macdonald picked up the flick knife and began to hack at the shirt.

Shepherd took off his trousers and pulled on the tunic and pants. They were a reasonable fit. He caught Walker looking at him with an amused smile on his face. 'Yeah, now you'll pass for a Muslim,' he said, his voice loaded with sarcasm.

Shepherd pointed at the other unconscious man. 'You use his clothes,' he said. 'Close up we won't pass, but at a distance it might stop us getting shot.'

Walker nodded and started undressing the man. Shepherd patted down Tariq's pockets and found a set of keys. 'And keep these in case we get separated,' he said. He tossed them at Walker who caught them one-handed.

Shepherd picked up Tariq's Glock and ejected the magazine. It was full. Fifteen rounds. He slotted the magazine back into the grip.

Walker finished dressing and picked up the second weapon. He checked the magazine and nodded at Shepherd. 'Good to go.'

Macdonald had finished slicing Shepherd's shirt and was using the strips to tie up the unconscious men.

'Go where?' said Meade.

'I need to check the electricity substation,' said Shepherd.

'Why?' asked Meade.

'That's need to know,' said Shepherd. 'You guys stay here until we get back.'

'You're leaving us?' said Meade.

'Trust me,' said Shepherd. 'You'll be a lot safer here.'

• • •

B ecause of the short notice, Standing could only grab eight guys from Air Troop, but Andy Lane, Paddy Ireland and the Ellis brothers were keen to sign up for the mission, especially when they learned that Spider Shepherd was trapped in the prison, and all were HALO certified.

The 22 SAS regiment had four squadrons – A, B, D and G, each with about sixty troopers and each commanded by a major. Each squadron was subdivided into four troops, each troop overseen by a captain. There were usually sixteen men in each troop, divided into four-men patrols.

The troops each had their own specialisation. Air Troop were the freefall specialists, Boat Troop had maritime skills, Mobility Troop were vehicle specialists and trained to fight in the desert, and Mountain Troop specialised in Arctic combat and survival. The Air Troop captain had agreed to act as head shed, and had obtained a map of the prison, a set of blueprints, and a satellite photograph of the prison and the surrounding area, and downloaded photographs of the prison from the internet. He had stuck the maps and photographs on the wall of the briefing room and Standing and the team sprawled on plastic chairs as he briefed them.

There were surprisingly few interruptions. Officers were only attached to the SAS for short periods, generally just a few years, so they were usually regarded as transient by the troopers, and treated less than respectfully. But Captain Tony Parrott had come from 3 Para with whom he had done three tours in Helmand Province, Afghanistan. He had been involved in countless firefights with the Taliban and had been shot twice. He was in his early thirties and the rumour was that he would be promoted to major after his stint with the SAS was over, so the troopers listened to what he had to say.

The captain explained that the men were to jump from 20,000 feet from the side door of the Chinook, rather than off the ramp. 'The landing point is the exercise yard attached to B Wing which isn't huge,' he said. 'It's going to be a tight fit landing thirteen men in such a small area, but it's doable. The heli can hover so we're not worried about dispersing you across a wide area. You can take your time, three or four seconds apart. As soon as you're on the ground, gather up your chute and move to the side. MI5 has a man inside, Dan Shepherd, and hopefully he'll be there to meet you.'

'Spider!' said Lane.

'Spider?' repeated the captain.

'He's one of ours,' said Standing. 'Or was, anyway. Bit of a legend. They call him Spider because he ate a tarantula on the jungle phase of Selection.'

'Okay, right. Good. Now the plan is for Spider to kill the power to the prison just before you jump. There should be enough moonlight for you to see what you're doing, but not enough for the men inside the prison to see you coming. You'll all have night vision gear with you, and a spare set for Spider. He will also have the keys you'll need to move through the prison. He will take you through to B Wing. We have no real idea of what you'll be facing, there could be up to two hundred bad guys, mainly armed with knives and machetes. I am told that there are fifteen Kalashnikovs and fifteen Glocks in the prison. Everyone else will have blades. Your mission is to neutralise the men with guns and at that point to open the main gate to allow in the prison service Tornado team. There will be up to two hundred of them, with helmets, shields, tasers, batons and PAVA spray. They're used to dealing with prisoners carrying knives.' He smiled. 'Guns, not so much.'

He looked around the briefing room to make sure that he had their undivided attention. Joe Ellis was looking at the screen of his smartphone but he nodded an apology and put it away when he realised the captain was glaring at him. 'Sorry, boss,' he mumbled.

'I can't stress enough that this is not a shoot-to-kill mission,' said the captain. 'I know it goes against all your training, but unless it's absolutely necessary there must be no head shots or double taps. You need to be incapacitating rather than killing.'

'You know some of these guys will have had ISIS training out in Syria and Pakistan?' Lane said.

'I understand that,' said the captain. 'But the world's media are watching and they'll see this as a prison riot. We can argue until we are blue in the face that we're up against terrorists, but the BBC and the *Guardian* won't have it. They'll see it as the SAS killing British Muslims on British soil. If you are fired upon then of course you fire back. But just because they are carrying a weapon doesn't give you carte blanche to shoot them.'

'Cart what now?' said Ireland.

The captain opened his mouth to reply but then realised Ireland was pulling his leg and he just shook his head.

'This is worse than Mali,' said Lane.

'Mali?' repeated the captain.

'The UN peacekeeping forces there pretty much have their hands tied behind their backs,' said Lane. 'There are all sorts of rules about when they can and can't return fire, but the bad guys don't have any rules.'

'Again, I understand. And no one is going to complain if you shoot dead a guy with an AK-47 who has you in their sights. But the vast majority of the guys in there will only have knives or machetes. You need to choose your targets carefully. And if you can, put a round in a shoulder or a leg.'

'The thing is, boss, there are how many bad guys in there?' asked Standing.

'We'd estimate between two and three hundred. The majority of the prisoners will be in their cells, either locked up or keeping out of the way.'

'So call it three hundred.' Standing pointed at the map of the prison. 'There are five wings, the admin block and the control centre. So seven areas in all. If the bad guys are spread equally, that means forty or so in each area. That means when we move into B Wing there could be forty armed men there.'

'Yes, those numbers make sense,' said the captain. 'But hopefully there will only be four or five guns at most on the wing. More likely two or three. And they'll be in the dark and you'll have night vision gear. Thirteen of you in all, you move through the wing and disable the men with the guns. Break the guns apart and toss them. From there you move to the control centre. Same again. Take out the men with the guns. Then you can move to the wings, with a four-man team heading straight to the admin block to rescue the hostages there. The governor is being held in his office, probably with his senior staff.' He nodded at Standing. 'I was assuming you could lead the four-man team?'

Standing nodded. 'Sure. I'm just worried that there's a lot to do and not much time to do it in.'

'It's not going to be easy, I get that,' said the captain. 'And in a perfect world we'd have five times as many men. But the world isn't perfect and we have to make do with what we have. I understand that it looks daunting, it's a big building and there are a lot of people in there. But if you take it step by step, it's all achievable.'

'How do we decide the order we clear the wings?' asked Lane.

'You'll be going in through B Wing, so obviously that's the first. That will take you to the control centre. From there, the four-man team can move into the admin block. As I said, the governor is being held captive in his office, so presumably the ringleaders are there. I think we can worry less about headshots in that room. The remaining nine troopers can split into four groups to do the remaining four wings. Three twos and a three. Or they can stick as one group and go through the wings one at a time. You can make that call when you're there.' He looked around the room. 'Any questions?'

'Flashbangs?' said Standing.

'Definitely,' said the captain.

'Can I take my M203 grenade launcher?' asked Ireland, hopefully.

'Definitely not,' said the captain.

• • •

Shepherd unlocked the gate and waved Walker through. 'Why do we need to go to the substation?' whispered Walker.

'Like I said, it's need to know.'

'If it kicks off down here, you'll be relying on me,' said Walker. 'I think that's earned me the right to know what the hell we're doing.'

Shepherd closed the gate and locked it. 'The SAS are going to mount a rescue operation,' he said.

'I knew it!'

'They're going to parachute in, but we need to kill the power before they land.'

'But how will they see what . . .' He grinned. 'Night vision gear. Of course.'

'The plan is to jump as soon as it gets dark. Which is about the time they say they're going to kill the governor. So it'll be against the clock. I have to kill the power and then get to the B Wing exercise yard to meet them.'

'They're jumping into the yard? That's going to be tight. It's surrounded by razor wire.'

'They're trained to jump into difficult places.'

'I hope they're wearing steel underwear, that's all.' Walker narrowed his eyes. 'Who are you, Mr Swinton? You're definitely not a prison officer.'

'I'm just a guy trying to get out of here alive, Mick.'

'Me too,' said Walker. 'The difference is that when this is over, I'll be back in a cell.'

They heard a noise behind them and they turned and looked through the gate. 'Sounded like a rat,' said Walker. 'This place will be full of them.'

'Come on,' said Shepherd. 'Let's not hang about.' He headed down the tunnel. Shepherd knew that Walker was right. When it was over, Shepherd would be back home, back with his friends, back to his real life. But Walker would still be behind bars with the smell of piss, bleach and stale cabbage, the constant noise and the ever-present threat of violence. Sometimes life was so damn unfair.

They passed a row of pipes, each as wide as a man's waist, running along the side of the corridor, and walked over two metal inspection hatches that led to the sewers. The further they got from the gate, the darker it became. Shepherd didn't want to turn the lights on in case anyone came down the stairs but now he could barely see a few feet ahead.

Eventually he reached a set of metal doors with ventilation panels, festooned with signs warning of high voltages and electrical discharges. He gingerly touched one of the handles, half expecting a shock, but he turned it and pulled open the door without a problem. Beyond the doors was a concrete room lined with wiring and fuse boxes. In the centre of the room were two large waist-high metal boxes with more high voltage warnings.

'Are you going to kill the power now?' asked Walker.

'It's too early,' said Shepherd. 'We have to do it just before they jump.' He looked at his watch. 'That's in about four hours.'

'And what do we do until then?'

'Keep from getting caught,' said Shepherd. 'I don't know, staying down here is probably our best bet.'

'And how do you plan to kill the power? Or are you actually an electrician, working undercover as a prison officer?'

Shepherd grinned. 'I'm not an electrician, but I can see from here that all the fuses are labelled.' He pointed at one of the fuse boxes on the wall. 'That's the admin wing, all the offices, the power circuits, the lights.' He pointed at the box next to it. 'That's the control centre. All we have to do is to flick the trip switches into the off position.'

He closed the door and turned the handle. 'We should check on the guys,' he said. 'They're likely to panic if we leave them on their own.'

'The man who came down, the one in the overalls with the gun. He's not a prisoner, is he?'

'No, he's one of the men who planned it.'

'Can't you use him? As a hostage, I mean. Do some sort of swap?'

'I think he's pretty low down the food chain,' said Shepherd.

'You know who he is?'

'Let's go,' said Shepherd.

'I hate the way you treat me like a mushroom,' said Walker. 'It's not fair the way you keep me in the dark and feed me bullshit.'

'Need to know,' said Shepherd. 'Come on.'

He took Walker back to the gate and unlocked it. They both walked through and Shepherd pulled it closed. He flinched as someone shouted, then there were rapid footsteps on the stairs, followed by more shouts. Men were running down the stairs, waving machetes. Walker cursed, elbowed Shepherd out of the way, pushed the gate open and ran through it, his trainers slapping on the floor and echoing off the walls of the tunnel as he disappeared into the darkness.

'Mick, no!' shouted Shepherd. He brought his gun up but as his finger tightened on the trigger a machete spun through the air and smacked into his arm. Luckily it was the handle that hit him but it was enough to deflect his aim and the round sparked off the floor. There were men screaming all around him now. His legs were kicked out from underneath him and he went down, and his attackers continued to rain kicks and blows on him. He tried to protect his head with his hands but the beating was relentless and at some point he passed out.

• • •

When Shepherd came to he was sitting in a chair and
his hands were zip-tied in his lap. He could taste blood
in his mouth and it hurt when he breathed. At least one of his
ribs was fractured. He blinked and tried to focus his eyes. He
was wearing an orange jumpsuit, he realised. His ankles were
bound with duct tape.

He looked around and his heart fell when saw Kamran Zaidi
and Sayed Khan, similarly bound and wearing orange jump-
suits. Strips of duct tape had been fastened across their mouths.

'Wakey, wakey,' said a voice. Shepherd looked to his right.
Mizhir Khaliq was sitting behind the governor's desk. He was
wearing blue overalls, similar to the ones that Tariq had been
wearing. Sitting next to Khaliq, wearing a long grey robe, was
a bearded man in his sixties or seventies. Shepherd recognised
him from various files he had seen over the years. It was Shafiq
Ali Rafiq.

'What's going on?' asked Shepherd, playing the innocent
but knowing that he was wasting his time.

Khaliq laughed. 'I'm sure you can put two and two together
and get something approaching the correct answer.' He waved
at the computer terminal on the desk in front of him. 'The
governor was stupid enough to leave emails referring to the
MI5 operation on his computer,' he said. 'So I know everything. I have to give you credit, it never crossed my mind
that you might be an MI5 plant. You are very good at what
you do.'

Shepherd averted his eyes and said nothing. There was
nothing he could say that would change the situation or its
outcome. He stared down at the ziptie. It was white plastic
and about half an inch wide. He had practised breaking his
way out of similar ties, it was more about timing and technique

than it was about brute strength. But even if he freed his wrist his legs were still bound with duct tape and there were three weapons in the room that he could see – two Kalashnikovs in the hands of large men guarding the door and a Glock on the desk by the computer keyboard.

He looked over at Zaidi and Khan. Both were terrified but managing to hold it together. He flashed them a reassuring smile but it was an act, they were in big trouble and they all knew it.

'Who was your target, that's what I want to know?' asked Khaliq. 'Did you know about me and my father when you started your investigation? Or were you just fishing, casting your bait to see who would bite?'

Shepherd stared at the door. Father? Did Khaliq mean that Shafiq Ali Rafiq was his father? That was news to Shepherd, and presumably news to MI5. Khaliq had supposedly been checked out and had come back as a cleanskin, with no terrorist affiliations. Shepherd flashed back to the last file he had seen on Rafiq. He had two families, one in Bradford and one in Leeds. Two wives, fifteen children and eight grandchildren, all supported by the state. His first wife was British-born, the second was from Pakistan. Shafiq Ali Rafiq had travelled to Pakistan for the marriage, and as soon as she was pregnant had applied for her to join him in the UK. The authorities knew that she was his second wife, and that bigamy was still technically illegal in England, but her application was approved and five years later she was granted British citizenship. But nowhere in the file had there been anything about having a son by the name of Mizhir Khaliq.

Khaliq stood up and reached for his Glock. He walked around the desk and stood in front of Shepherd. He put the barrel of the gun against Shepherd's forehead and tightened his finger on the trigger. 'I should kill you now,' he said.

Shepherd stared back at him. The orange jumpsuit suggested that Khaliq had plans for him and so it was unlikely that he would pull the trigger. But plans could be changed. Khaliq's lazy eye had swivelled all the way to the side but the good eye burned with a fierce intensity. 'And then when you thought you were going to be caught, you hid behind a brother's clothes,' sneered Khaliq. 'You stripped them off a brother and wore them as a disguise, like the coward you are. If I pull the trigger, I'm not executing a man, I'm putting down a dog.'

Shepherd gritted his teeth. He wasn't going to beg or plead, he wasn't going to say anything. If his life was going to end at that point, so be it. He'd had a good run.

Khaliq's smiled tightened and Shepherd realised that he was going to do it, he was going to pull the trigger. Part of him wanted to close his eyes but he resisted the urge because that would show weakness and that was the one thing he wasn't prepared to do.

'Fuck you, kafir,' said Khaliq.

Shafiq Ali Rafiq said something in Urdu, his voice low and measured.

Khaliq replied, keeping the gun pressed against Shepherd's forehead.

Rafiq spoke again, this time with more urgency. Khaliq listened, and then slowly took the gun away.

A mobile phone buzzed on the desk and Khaliq went over and picked it up. Shepherd realised it was the tiny phone that he had been using. Khaliq took the call with a sly smile on his face. 'This is your worst nightmare speaking,' he said. There was no reply and Khaliq let the silence stretch out. He was in control, he didn't have to speak to anybody.

'Who am I talking to?' said a voice.

It was a man, and Khaliq recognised the voice. 'So it's Superintendent Taylor, is it?' said Khaliq. 'West Yorkshire Police?'

The man didn't reply.

'Cat got your tongue, Superintendent?' said Khaliq. 'Or are you trying to work out how you can explain the fact that a police superintendent is phoning an undercover MI5 officer?'

'Can you tell me your name, so that I know who I am talking to,' said the man.

'I told you last time. This is the Islamic State of the United Kingdom. And if our demands are not met, we will be killing the governor at six o'clock tonight. And then we will start to execute your men, Superintendent Taylor or whatever your name is. Yes, that's right. Your men, plural. We have the traitorous Muslims Kamran Zaidi and Sayed Khan, and we have the kafir who calls himself Tony Swinton. And if the BBC does not show our brothers leaving Belmarsh Prison and arriving at Gatwick by six o'clock this evening, your men will die. They are your men, aren't they? You're very keen to know my name, so why not give me a quid pro quo and tell me who you are? Talk to me like a man, a real man, not a bitch who has to hide behind a fake name.'

'We need to talk.'

'No, we don't. I will talk to you through social media so that the whole world can follow our conversation. I will tell you what to do and you will obey, and if you don't, your men will die. There is nothing left to say.' Khaliq ended the call.

'Who was that?' asked Rafiq.

'MI5, pretending to be the police,' said Khaliq. 'He wanted to talk.'

Rafiq smiled. 'The time for talking is over,' he said.

Khaliq grinned. 'Exactly.'

• • •

Pritchard put his phone down. So now they had Dan Shepherd and the two undercover officers? How had that happened? And how did they know that the men were in the prison undercover? It had been a closely guarded secret known only to the governor and the prison's head of security. Realisation dawned and Pritchard cursed under his breath. The hostage takers were in the governor's office which meant they had access to his computer. Khaliq had studied computing at university, he'd presumably have the skills necessary to access the governor's records and email accounts.

He picked up his phone and called Colonel Davies at the Stirling Lines barracks in Hereford. 'Colonel, we have a problem,' said Pritchard. 'Our man Shepherd has been captured, which means we can't kill the power to the prison. That means the floodlights will be on when your men land. Which obviously isn't good news.'

'It means they'll be sitting ducks,' said the Colonel. 'Also, Shepherd was planning to let them in to the wing. If he's not there, they'll have to blow their way in which means there'll be no element of surprise.' The Colonel sighed. 'This is bad, Mr Pritchard. This is very bad.'

'Under the circumstances, this has to be the call of the men involved,' said Pritchard. 'Whether it's a go or a no-go, it has to be down to them. We can't order them to take part in what might well turn out to be a suicide mission.'

'Understood,' said the Colonel. 'Let me talk to them. I'll get back to you.'

The Colonel ended the call and Pritchard put down his phone. He paced up and down his office, rubbing the back of his neck. He had a headache building and he was out of paracetamol. The fact that Khaliq was the son of Shafiq Ali Rafiq explained a lot. Presumably Rafiq had been in contact with his son, probably through his lawyers. What was happening at the prison had obviously been well planned. Was it Rafiq's last hurrah? One final display of power before he met his maker, a chance to go out in a blaze of glory? Pritchard went to his door and opened it. His secretary looked up expectantly but before she could say anything, Pritchard's phone burst into life. Pritchard hurried over to his desk and answered it. 'It's a go,' said the Colonel. 'An unequivocal go.'

. . .

'You will read what is written, or I will kill you,' said Khaliq, thrusting the sheet of paper at Shepherd's bound hands.

Shepherd refused to take it. 'You're going to kill me anyway,' he said.

'Not if the authorities bow to our demands,' said Khaliq.

'That's not going to happen,' said Shepherd. 'They're never going to release convicted terrorists.'

'They can and they will, once the bodies start piling up,' said Khaliq. 'We have a lot of hostages. Hundreds. And believe me, we will kill them all if we have to.' He shoved the paper at Shepherd again. 'Now read it.'

Shepherd shook his head. He was sitting on a chair facing an iPhone that had been placed on a tripod stand on the governor's desk. Kamran Zaidi was sitting on Shepherd's right and Sayed Khan was on his left. Both were terrified and Khan had wet himself. Shepherd understood their fear and sympathised. No MI5 training could possibly have prepared them for what they were going through. SAS training was much more physical and rigorous, but all the training in the world couldn't erase the fear that came from having a loaded weapon pointed at your face.

The duct tape gags had been ripped from their mouths but neither man had said anything as their chairs were dragged over to the desk. Zaidi was physically shaking, his eyes wide and fearful.

Khaliq shouted in Urdu at the men by the door. One of them walked over to the prison staff who were all cowering against the wall, bound and gagged. The man pointed his Kalashnikov at Liz Maguire. She flinched and began grunting through her gag.

'You have a choice,' Khaliq said to Shepherd. 'You read the words on this sheet of paper, or you condemn the kafir woman to death. It is your choice. Your call. Her life is in your hands. If you want her to die, then continue to refuse to do as you are told.' He shrugged. 'It's up to you.'

Shepherd looked over at Maguire who had brought her knees up against her stomach and turned her head to the wall. The governor was staring at Shepherd, pleading with his eyes. Shepherd nodded. 'Okay,' he said.

'Good call,' said Khaliq. He held out the paper and Shepherd took it with both hands. He scanned it. It was gibberish. Nonsense. The ranting of a religious fanatic. Shepherd knew that it wouldn't make the slightest bit of difference, the government were never going to release the Belmarsh prisoners. And they were never going to allow the Bradford prisoners free passage after what they had done. This was only going to end one way, and that was violently. But there was no point in trying to explain that to Khaliq.

Khaliq went over to start the recording. He pressed the button on the iPhone and nodded at Shepherd to start speaking.

• • •

Andy Lane peered up into the darkening sky. 'There it is,' he said, pointing to the east.

Matt Standing squinted and shook his head. 'That's a bird.'

'It's a plane,' said Joe Ellis.

'Nah, it's Superman,' said his brother.

'You all need glasses,' said Lane. 'It's a Chinook at about eight thousand feet.'

Standing narrowed his eyes and then nodded as the twin-motored helicopter came into focus. 'I see it.'

The Chinook was descending, still several minutes away. Standing was on the edge of the Stirling Lines helicopter pad with the twelve SAS troopers, all kitted out with the equipment they needed for the HALO jump. Most HALO jumps were from 30,000 feet and above and the jumpers needed to wear special helmets attached to oxygen bottles. The Chinook's ceiling was 20,000 feet, which was about the maximum height for breathing without additional oxygen, so the plan was only to fly up to that height when they were close to the prison. Jumping was much easier without oxygen masks.

They had their weapons on slings, and nylon pouches containing their night vision gear. From what Captain Parrot had said, the power at the prison wasn't going to be cut and the chances were that Shepherd wasn't going to be at the exercise yard to meet them. The captain hadn't been told what had happened to Shepherd, but clearly the change in plan meant that it wasn't good. No Shepherd meant no keys, so they were going to have to blow their way through any locked gates and doors. Two of the Air Troop guys were explosive experts and had each been issued with a dozen small C4 explosive charges. If the men had any reservations about the change in plan, they kept them to themselves. Spider Shepherd was in trouble and they would do whatever it took to rescue him. He was one of theirs.

. . .

K haliq stared at the computer screen and frowned. 'Nothing,' he said. 'There is nothing on the BBC, nothing on the *Guardian*'s website, nothing on the *Mail*'s website.'

'Nothing at all?' said Shafiq Ali Rafiq.

'They're calling it the "Bradford Prison Siege", and they're reporting on the videos we posted, but there is nothing about the government agreeing to our demands. There was a COBRA meeting earlier today and the prime minister is flying back from the United States, but there is nothing about the prisoners being released or a plane being made available at Gatwick Airport.'

'We have time,' said Rafiq. 'We have all the time in the world.

We have hundreds of hostages, there is no way they can allow them all to be killed. They cannot get into the prison, we have the entrances covered. And we have food and water to last for weeks. Possibly months if we don't feed the kafirs. They do not believe that we will kill the hostages. Once we start showing them that we are serious, once they see the blood, then they will give us what we want.'

'You need to talk to them,' said Shepherd. 'You need to negotiate.' He was still sitting on the chair facing the desk, with Khan and Zaidi either side of him.

Rafiq shook his head. 'There is no negotiation,' he said. 'Our demands will be met or people will die.'

'Then you need to explain that to them,' said Shepherd. 'You need to open a dialogue.'

'We've opened the dialogue through social media,' said Khaliq. 'They can reply through social media. That way the whole world can follow the conversation.'

'What, you think the prime minister is going to talk to you through Tik Tok? You need to pick up the phone. Next time they call, answer the phone and talk to them.'

The sky was darkening outside and the clock on the wall behind the desk said it was a quarter to six. Fifteen minutes to the deadline. Shepherd had no idea if the SAS were coming. Presumably Pritchard would have told them about Shepherd's capture, and that he wouldn't be able to cut the power. Would they still jump? Shepherd figured they would, which meant they would be putting their lives on the line.

Khaliq stood up, walked around the desk and opened the door. There was a red band from the kitchen standing there with a large machete. Khaliq took it from him and closed the door. 'It is time,' he said.

'You said six o'clock,' said Shepherd.

'I said sunset, and the sun has gone down.'

'No, the deadline was six o'clock. There's still fifteen minutes.'

'Nothing is going to happen in the next fifteen minutes,' said Khaliq as he walked back to the desk. He put down the machete and picked up a black ski mask. He pulled on the mask and then looked over at Rafiq. 'Father, do you want to do it?'

Rafiq smiled. 'I do, but I am not sure I have the strength. You should do it, my son. And you do not need a mask. There is no need to hide your face. You are carrying out the will of Allah.'

Khaliq nodded and took off the mask. He tossed it on to the desk. 'Will you start the recording?' he asked.

'It would be my honour.'

Khaliq swung the machete from side to side, getting a feel for the blade.

'You don't have to do this,' said Shepherd. 'You can talk to them.'

Khaliq walked behind the three chairs, swinging the machete.

Rafiq leaned over and pressed the button on the phone to start the recording.

Khaliq raised the machete in the air and addressed the phone. 'I take no pleasure in doing this,' he said. 'But the government has given us no choice. The Islamic State of the United Kingdom has only asked for justice for its Muslim brothers. We want only to be allowed to live in peace. But it has become clear that the British government only understands force. They used force in Afghanistan and Iraq and Syria and they have used force to repress our brothers and sisters in the United

Kingdom. It is time for change. *Allahu Akbar!'* He stepped forward, placed the blade against Khan's throat, and sawed at the flesh. Blood spurted down Khan's chest and he tried to scream but his throat was already wide open and all he could do was gasp. He thrashed his head from side to side as Khaliq continued to cut. Khaliq screamed *'Allahu Akbar'* again as he sawed at Khan's neck.

Shepherd looked away and blood splattered over his cheek. The prison staff began to scream and shout.

Shepherd gritted his teeth. He knew there was nothing he could say that would stop what was happening, he just had to ride it out. Hopefully there wouldn't be too much pain. And at least it would be quick.

There was a loud bang from behind him. A shot. A handgun. He twisted around in his chair just in time to see one of the men with a Kalashnikov stagger back. Then there was a second shot and the man's skull exploded and he fell to the floor. The door was open and Mick Walker was standing there, both hands on his Glock.

The second man with the Kalashnikov swung his weapon around but Walker was already squeezing the trigger again. One shot hit the man in the shoulder and as he span around, Walker fired again, two quick shots that both hit the man in the chest.

Khaliq had stepped away from Khan. He was holding the machete in the air and it was dripping blood on to the floor. Walker took a step into the room, sighted on Khaliq's face and pulled the trigger. The round ripped off the top of Khaliq's skull but it wasn't a killing shot and he stood where he was, a look of surprise on his face until Walker put two rounds into his heart.

Shafiq Ali Rafiq put his hands in the air and shuffled backwards until he was against the wall. He stared at his dead son with tear-filled eyes and began muttering in Urdu.

Walker kicked the door shut, then hurried over to Khaliq's body and picked up the machete. He used it to sever the ziptie binding Shepherd's wrists and then cut the duct tape around his legs. 'No need to thank me,' he said.

'I thought you'd done a runner,' said Shepherd.

'He who fights and runs away . . .'

'Usually doesn't come back,' said Shepherd. 'I'm glad that in this case you did.'

'Pretty good shooting, right?'

'Three clean kills,' said Shepherd. 'Can't ask for better than that.'

'Yeah, you never lose the knack,' said Walker. 'Are you still going to the substation?'

Shepherd looked at the clock on the wall. It was five to six. He nodded. 'If they're coming, I'll need to kill the lights.'

'If?'

'They might have had a change of heart. I'm not sure.'

'What do want me to do?'

'Stay here. Cut the hostages loose but make sure that they stay in the room. If I get to the substation all the lights will go off so you need to keep everyone safe.'

'I have torches,' said the governor. He nodded with his chin at a cupboard by the window. 'Top left.'

Shepherd hurried over to the cupboard and opened it. On a shelf were four black Maglite torches. He put three on the desk and checked the fourth. It worked. He picked up the tiny mobile phone and slipped it into his pocket. His prison keys were also on the desk and he gathered them up.

Walker used the machete to set Zaidi free. Zaidi wrapped his arms around himself. He was shuddering and close to tears. Shepherd went over to him. 'Kamran, are you okay?'

Zaidi nodded but he was clearly not okay. Hardly surprising as he had just seen his friend and colleague practically beheaded.

Walker began cutting the rest of the hostages free.

'Have you ever fired an AK-47?' Shepherd asked Zaidi.

Zaidi shook his head. 'No.'

'But you've fired a Glock, right?'

'Yes. On the range.'

Shepherd went over to the desk, picked up Khaliq's Glock, and gave it to Zaidi. 'You need to support Mick if anything happens, okay? He's a former Para, you can trust him.'

Zaidi nodded.

'Kamran, you understand what I'm saying, right?'

'Yeah, yeah, yeah,' said Zaidi, but there was a faraway look in his eyes as if his mind was elsewhere. He was in shock, which was understandable, but Shepherd needed the man to focus. He went over to him and grabbed his shoulder. 'Kamran, snap out of it. There are people here who need your help, okay?'

Zaidi took a deep breath, and nodded. 'I'm okay,' he said.

'Good man.' He pointed at Shafiq Ali Rafiq. 'Tie him up, gag him, and make sure that it's MI5 who take him into custody. Don't let the cops take him.'

Kamran nodded. 'Who is he?'

'That's Shafiq Ali Rafiq, who I am fairly sure planned this whole thing.'

Walker finished releasing the hostages, then picked up one of the Kalashnikovs. He gave it to Shepherd who checked the action and confirmed that the magazine was full. Walker picked up the second Kalashnikov and slung it over his shoulder. 'If they do try anything, they'll discover they've bitten off more than they can chew,' he said.

'You might want to think about changing your clothes,' said Shepherd. 'If the SAS come charging in, they might well jump to the wrong conclusion.'

Walker grinned. 'Message received and understood,' he said.

The governor had stood up and was massaging his wrists. 'This man is a prisoner,' he said, nodding at Walker.

'He is,' said Shepherd. 'But he's also the man who probably saved all our lives, so I plan to leave him in charge here until the authorities have regained control. Do you have any problem with that?'

The governor shook his head. 'I'm good.'

'I'm glad to hear it,' said Shepherd. He looked over at Walker. 'Stay safe, yeah?'

'You too.'

Shepherd nodded and headed out of the door.

• • •

Liam Shepherd twisted around in his seat. 'We'll be over the prison in about two minutes,' he said over the radio. 'Climbing to twenty thousand feet now.'

Matt Standing nodded. As the Chinook started to climb, he unbuckled his harness and made his way over to the side door where the crew chief was peering out. Off to the right was a golf course. That had been designated as an alternate drop zone in the event of any problems, and was also suitable for landing the Chinook in an emergency. The prison was about a quarter of a mile from the golf course. Standing could clearly see the prison wings radiating from the control centre. At the end of each spoke was an exercise yard surrounded by flood-lights.

'I thought the plan was to kill the lights,' said the crew chief.

'Plans change,' said Standing.

The SAS troopers were all standing up now and checking each other's gear. They all had ram-air chutes, and no reserves. If anything did go wrong, there wouldn't be time to deploy a reserve. They would be reaching terminal velocity – 120 miles per hour – just five seconds after jumping. They would be heading straight down, and the chutes would be opened auto-matically at 800 feet. Standing and his team had all packed their own parachutes at Stirling Lines – that way if anything went wrong, they only had themselves to blame.

Standing peered down at the floodlit exercise yard. The lights meant that the drop zone was much easier to spot from up high, but anyone looking out of the windows of the wing would see them land.

Lane appeared at Standing's side. 'You think Spider's okay?' he asked.

'I hope so,' said Standing.

'The lights are still on?'

'Yup.'

'That's not good, is it?' said Lane.

'Not great, no.'

• • •

S hepherd hurried along the corridor away from the governor's office, cradling the Kalashnikov against his chest.
They had taken off his boots when they'd dressed him in the
orange jumpsuit and his bare feet made no sound on the tiled
floor.

He heard voices ahead of him and he slowed. He took a
quick look at his watch. He didn't have time to go softly-softly.
He moved forward quickly, his finger on the trigger, and turned
the corner that led to the stairs. There were two men standing
in the corridor, both wearing long robes and skullcaps. One
had a machete, the other a Kalashnikov that matched Shepherd's
own. Shepherd fired once, shooting the guy with the Kalashnikov
in the chest. The sound of the shot was deafening in the
confined space and Shepherd's ears were ringing as he moved
towards the man with the machete. The man he had shot fell
to the floor, his chest soaked in blood, his lips moving sound-
lessly, just seconds away from death.

Shepherd took no pride in using a gun against a man with
a knife, but the decision was taken from him when the man
raised the machete and charged towards Shepherd. Shepherd
shot him in the face and he slammed against the wall and slid
down, the machete falling from his lifeless fingers.

Shepherd ran towards the stairs, his left foot slapping into
a pool of blood and leaving a trail of prints on the tiles.

The gate to the stairs was locked and Shepherd allowed the
Kalashnikov to hang on its sling as he fumbled with the keys.
He opened the door and ran down the stairs.

The gate to the tunnel leading to B Wing was locked. He
peered through the bars and could see Tariq on the floor, along
with the two other men, bound and gagged. There was no sign
of Willie Macdonald and the other prisoners but they weren't

a priority, he had to get the lights off before the SAS jumped. And he was rapidly running out of time. He turned away from the gate and ran towards the electricity substation.

．　．　．

The air felt like a living thing under Matt Standing's outstretched arms and legs as he fell to the ground at 120 miles per hour. Terminal velocity occurred when the drag force of falling was the same as the force due to gravity. At that point there was no acceleration. He could fall forever and never go any faster.

He glanced at the altimeter on his right wrist. Nine thousand five hundred feet. Halfway. He didn't feel as if he was falling at 120 miles per hour, the perspective was barely changing. As always it would be the final thousand feet that would rush at him.

His breathing was slow and even and he knew that his pulse would be barely above eighty. Heights had never bothered him, and neither had falling. He began to drift to the left so he corrected his posture and almost immediately the drift stopped. Free falling from a hovering helicopter was always much easier than from a plane. It was straight down all the way.

He glanced at his altimeter again. Five thousand two hundred feet. He looked back at the prison. One of the wings went dark. Then another. The B Wing exercise yard floodlights went off. Standing smiled. 'Nice one, Spider,' he muttered to himself.

．　．　．

The tunnel Shepherd was in went black. He switched on his torch so that he could see the rest of the fuses that still had to be clicked into the off position. He did them all, then hurried back down the tunnel, using the torch to light his way, his bare feet making almost no sound.

He ran down the branch of the tunnel that led to B Wing, unlocked the gate and stepped over Tariq and the two men. They all appeared to be unconscious. He reached the B Wing showers less than a minute after killing the power. He switched off the torch before making his way slowly up the stairs to the ground floor.

The gate at the top of the stairs was closed but not locked. Shepherd eased it open. The wing was in complete darkness. Prisoners were shouting and cursing, and banging into things. Shepherd kept the AK-47 across his chest and his finger off the trigger. He stepped through the gate, listening intently, but there was so much shouting going on that he couldn't hear if anyone was close by or not. He let the gun hang on its sling and put both hands out in front of him. He knew where the table tennis table was, and the pool table, and he moved around them. His fingers touched something soft and a man cursed at him.

'Sorry,' said Shepherd.

'What the fuck's happening, why are the lights out?'

'Dunno,' said Shepherd, moving around the man and heading for the far end of the wing. He bumped into three more prisoners on the way but none were threatening, they were all scared and confused. Finally he reached the gate that led to the exercise yard. He ran his fingers over the metal bars until he found the lock, then he used his key, as slowly as possible. There was a loud click as the key turned and he waited several seconds before slowly easing the gate open.

He padded across a paved area and opened a second gate, which led to the outside. He unlocked it and stepped into the open air. As he did, he heard the crack of a canopy opening high overhead. His heart pounded. They'd done it, they'd jumped. There was enough moonlight to see by, but he could only make out vague shapes in the night sky.

He groped for his torch, switched it on and pointed the beam down at the ground, playing it across the surface of the yard. Then he heard a whoosh and a dark shape whizzed by him, then there was the pounding of boots on tarmac and the rustle of a canopy deflating and scraping along the ground.

Shepherd shone the beam at the figure and grinned when he saw it was Matt Standing. Shepherd quickly shone the beam on his own face so that Standing could see who it was.

'Bloody hell, Spider, what have you come dressed as?' said Standing, as he rolled up his chute and removed the harness.

A second figure hit the ground running. Then a third. And a fourth.

'Don't ask,' said Shepherd. 'The good news is that the hostages in the admin block are safe. So we only have to clear the wings and the control centre.'

'You've been busy,' said Standing. 'And the Kalashnikov is now your weapon of choice is it?'

'I had to take what I could get,' said Shepherd. He switched the torch off and shoved it into one of the pockets of his jumpsuit.

More figures hit the ground running and gathered up their chutes. Five. Six. Seven.

Shepherd and Standing moved to the side of the yard. Standing took a pair of night vision goggles from a nylon pack attached to his belt and gave them to Shepherd, then took another pair for himself. They fitted them and switched them on. The units buzzed softly and within seconds Shepherd was able to look around and see everything in shades of green.

Eight. Nine. Ten.

Two figures moved towards them. Shepherd grinned when he recognised Jack and Joe Ellis.

'Is that what you secret squirrel boys wear these days?' asked Joe Ellis. 'Suits you.'

The Ellis boys had their night vision goggles on and were carrying Heckler & Koch 417 assault rifles.

More dark shapes hit the ground. Eleven. Twelve. Then a gap of a few seconds before number thirteen hit the ground running.

'What's the new plan then, Spider?' asked Standing.

Andy Lane and Terry Ireland walked over, cradling their carbines. They both nodded at Shepherd.

'The admin block is now under our control,' said Shepherd. He pointed at the gate behind him. 'We go through there to B Wing. We can clear it of weapons and then go through to the control centre. I've just been through the ground floor and there's a lot of shouting but no one can see anything. I suggest we clear all three landings, then hit the control centre. Then we can split up into two groups, seven apiece. We clear A Wing and C Wing. Then D Wing and E Wing. Then back to the control centre. We can then move to the entrance and once we've cleared that we can let the Tornados in.'

'How many guns did you take out?' asked Standing, gesturing at the Kalashnikovs.

'Six,' said Shepherd. 'Three AKs including this one and three Glocks. Which means we have twelve AKs and twelve Glocks to account for.'

'Let's do it, then,' said Standing. Shepherd led the way to the gate.

. . .

T here were more than two dozen prisoners on the ground floor of B Wing, most of them walking slowly with their hands out in front of them. Shepherd went left and Standing went right. It was tough to pick out faces with the night vision goggles, but going by the clothing there were only Muslims walking around. More than half the cell doors were shut, so Standing assumed that the non-Muslim prisoners had been locked away. There was so sign of the staff, either.

There was a group of prisoners huddled together ahead of Shepherd, but they had no weapons so Shepherd moved silently around them. He took a quick look over his shoulder. The Ellis boys were directly behind him, and Lane was behind them. More troopers were filing through the gate, Hecklers at their shoulders.

Shepherd looked over at Standing. Ireland was directly behind him, with a line of four more troopers in his wake.

Shepherd moved forward, his gun at the ready but with his trigger finger outside the guard. This was a very different situation to when he was in the SAS's Killing House in Hereford. There it was always about despatching targets as efficiently and as quickly as possible, but the last thing he wanted to do was to start shooting civilians, even if they were armed prisoners.

He stopped when he saw a man in a long robe clutching a Kalashnikov to his chest, a twin of the one that Shepherd was holding. Shepherd held up his hand to attract the attention of the troopers behind him, then tiptoed over to the man and slammed the butt of his AK-47 against his head. The man went down and the weapon clattered on to the floor. Several prisoners turned to look in his direction, but he knew that they couldn't see him. Shepherd let his own weapon hang from its sling as he picked up the AK-47 and quickly pulled out the magazine, tucking it into one of the leg pockets of his jumpsuit. He pressed a button to eject the dust cover of the weapon, then pulled out the carrier spring and tossed it away. He put the disassembled gun back on the floor and cradled his own weapon as he started moving down the wing again.

They reached the stairs that led up to the twos. Shepherd pointed at the Ellis boys and then at the stairs. They both nodded and headed up, guns at the ready. Shepherd pointed at Lane and signed for him to go with them. Together they could check the twos and threes.

Shepherd reached the table tennis table. There was a bare-chested man by the pool table holding a Kalashnikov. One of the SAS team moved ahead of Shepherd and knocked the man out. The trooper disassembled the assault rifle and tossed the parts away.

There was the sound of a scuffle on the other side of the wing. Standing had hit a prisoner with the butt of his Heckler but the prisoner was a big man, well over six feet six, and he had taken the blow in his stride. He was holding a kitchen knife and he was waving it around in the darkness, grunting aggressively. Standing stepped back and aimed his Heckler at the man's chest. Shepherd grabbed a ball off the pool table and threw it at the man's face. It smacked into his mouth and the man staggered back. His hands went up to his face and the knife fell to the floor as blood streamed down his chin. 'You're welcome,' said Shepherd as Standing looked over at him.

'I had it covered,' said Standing.

'Of course you did.'

The man was still on his feet so Standing stepped forward and hit him again with the stock of the Heckler. The man still didn't go down and Standing kicked him between the legs. Finally the man collapsed in a heap.

Shepherd drew level with Maria Crowley's office. The door was open and he peered inside. The governor was sitting on the floor, her hands behind her and her legs outstretched. Sitting next to her was Ed Blackhurst. The governor was fully clothed but Blackhurst had been stripped of his uniform. His left eye was half closed. As Shepherd moved into the office he saw Jenny Johnston and Sandra Shakespeare sitting against another wall. They had been allowed to keep their uniforms, which was something, but their hands were behind their backs and their ankles were bound with duct tape.

A prisoner was sitting on Crowley's desk, a Glock in his hands. He was wearing a tunic and baggy pants and swivelling his head from side to side as if that would help him see better. Shepherd stepped across the threshold. There were two more men to the right, both with machetes. The last time he had seen them they had been standing guard outside Malik Abid Qadeer's study group in the education block. One of them said something to the prisoner with the Glock, in what was probably Urdu. The prisoner shook his head and replied.

Shepherd raised his gun and moved silently towards the desk. He was about six feet away when a light flickered off to his right. He looked across and saw that one of the men had just struck a match. The light from the burning match was enough to disrupt the night vision goggles and the man disappeared in a pool of green.

Shepherd looked back to the desk. The man with the Glock could clearly see him now and was bringing the weapon up, his eyes wide and fearful. Shepherd had no time to try for a wounding shot, he just aimed at the centre of the man's body and pulled the trigger. The shot was ear-splitting in the confines of the room and the tang of cordite made Shepherd's eyes water. The man fell back, his chest a light green mass. Johnston screamed at the top of her voice. As Shepherd turned away from the desk, the two men with machetes rushed towards him. The lit match went out. Shepherd took two quick steps to the right and slammed the butt of his AK-47 against the chin of the man closest to him. The man slumped to the floor and got tangled in the legs of the second man who stumbled and fell. Shepherd stood over him and brought the butt of the assault rifle down on the man's face, breaking his jaw and smashing several teeth.

Johnston continued to scream in terror. Shepherd hurried over to her and knelt down beside her. 'Jenny, it's okay,' he said, but she continued to scream. Shepherd grabbed her shoulder and shook her. 'Jenny, it's Tony Swinton,' he hissed.

'Tony?'

'Look, the SAS are here, it'll all be over soon. Just stay quiet. It's going to be all right.'

'Untie me, please,' she sobbed.

'I can't. There's too much to do. But you're safe now, just stay quiet.'

Shepherd went over to the governor. She flinched as he approached her. 'It's me, governor. Tony Swinton. The SAS are gaining control of the prison, but you need to keep everyone quiet. Stay put and you'll be released as soon as it's safe.'

Shepherd could see the confusion on the governor's face, but she nodded. 'Okay,' she said.

Shepherd straightened up and headed to the door where two troopers were waiting for him, Hecklers at the ready. 'Okay, now we move into the control centre,' said Shepherd.

The troopers followed him towards the gate. Standing and his team were already there. 'You okay?' asked Standing.

'I had to shoot one of them,' said Shepherd.

'Yeah, the gunshot's got them all fired up,' said Standing. 'But they're not sure where it came from.'

Through the bars they could see a couple of dozen or so prisoners milling around. Two had AK-47s, one had a Glock and several had machetes. Shepherd recognised one of the men with a Kalashnikov. He was Saeed Ghani, one of the C Wing red bands who worked in the kitchen. Both the men with the Glocks were also from the kitchen.

The prisoners were shouting at each other, some in Urdu, some in English. Everyone was confused, they had no idea what was happening.

'What the fuck's going on, bruv?'

'Who fired the gun?'

'Can anyone see anything?'

'What the fuck, man.'

Then a cigarette lighter flicked into life. Standing cursed and took aim at the prisoner holding the lighter. He fired once and the man fell back, hit a wall and slid to the floor. The light went out.

A group of prisoners waving machetes ran towards the gates screaming and shouting despite the fact they could no longer see. Standing slammed the gate shut and the men ran into it, hard. One fell to the floor, unconscious, one was bleeding from his arm where he had been cut with his own machete and another had a broken nose.

Standing pulled the gate open. Ireland took out a flashbang grenade. 'Flashbang, fire in the hole!' he shouted.

Shepherd and the SAS team turned away as Ireland ripped the pin out and tossed the grenade into the control centre. A second later the grenade went off, first with a blinding flash of light, followed by seven loud bangs, each as deafening as a jet engine.

As soon as it was over, Standing headed through the gate. Shepherd and Ireland followed him. The prisoners in the control centre had all been disorientated by the explosions. Most had slumped to the floor or against the walls, and all had dropped their weapons.

The SAS troopers moved quickly, gathering up the knives and machetes and breaking down the guns.

Shepherd looked around for Neil Geraghty but there was no sign of him. There was a line of prison officers sitting against a wall, stripped of their uniforms and bound and gagged with zipties and duct tape. Shepherd quickly pulled the tape away from their mouths. He didn't release them, they were safer on the floor than they would be walking around while the SAS were still active.

The Ellis boys and Ireland arrived. 'All clear upstairs,' said Ireland.

'I'll take A Wing,' Shepherd said to Standing. 'You do C Wing. Meet back here and then we'll do D and E.'

Standing nodded and headed to the C Wing gate. Shepherd went on to A Wing with Standing, the Ellis boys, Lane, Ireland and one of the Air Troop guys.

Again, most of the non-Muslim prisoners were locked in their cells. Another six prison officers had been stripped of their uniforms and had been bound and gagged and left sitting against a wall. A man in a tunic and baggy trousers was standing next to them, a Kalashnikov in his hands.

Ireland went over to the man and slammed the stock of his Heckler against his head. He slumped to the ground. Ireland quickly pulled out the magazine and threw it away before breaking the weapon down to its parts and scattering them.

They found two prisoners with Glocks on the wing. In a matter of seconds, the men were knocked out, the weapons were disabled and the magazines tossed.

Shepherd and his team cleared all the landings in A Wing within five minutes, then went back to the control centre. The second SAS team had finished clearing C Wing, with no shots fired.

They moved silently into the final wings, D and E. They disabled three more Kalashnikovs and four Glocks before regrouping in the control centre.

'We're missing some guns,' said Standing.

'Probably in the main entrance area, or the kitchen block,' said Shepherd. 'There's a delivery gate there for kitchen deliveries, that's how they got the guns in. It would make sense to have firepower there.'

'How do you want to handle it?' asked Standing.

Shepherd pointed at the gate that led to the main entrance. It was open and they could see prisoners moving in the corridor behind it. 'The staff changing rooms are that way, then there's a control room that overlooks the main entrance. They'll have put guns there, for sure. That's the main way into the prison and it's a choke point. I can take Jack and Joe to the kitchen entrance and deal with whatever they have there. Meet you back here in ten minutes?'

Standing nodded. 'Go for it.'

Shepherd waved the Ellis boys over. 'Stick with me,' he said, and headed through the B Wing gate.

Most of the prisoners had simply given up and were either in the cells or sitting on the floor. There was some shouting and yelling but the majority were just sitting in silence, waiting for it all to be over. Shepherd led the way and the Ellis boys tucked in behind him. They crossed the wing to the gate at the far end that led to the path that wound its way around the exercise yard to the kitchen block. The gate to the kitchen block was open and there was a man standing there. There was enough ambient light for him to see them and he raised his Kalashnikov. Shepherd fired and hit the man in the chest and he went down. Another man appeared in the doorway and this time it was Joe Ellis who put two rounds into the man's chest. The man was holding a Glock and it tumbled to the ground as he fell back into the kitchen.

They reached the doorway and Jack Ellis went first, heading right. His brother followed, moving left. Shepherd heard shots as he ducked through the doorway. Jack Ellis had shot and killed another gunman who was standing by the door that led to the delivery yard. Shepherd looked around the kitchen. There was no one else around. He motioned for the Ellis boys to check the yard. They went through the door, Hecklers at the ready, but were back within seconds. 'All clear,' said Joe Ellis.

On the way back to the control centre they picked up the thirteen chutes and harnesses from the B Wing exercise yard. In the distance they heard the sound of a flashbang going off. And another. Then brief bursts of fire from Hecklers.

Shepherd made his way to the main entrance. Standing and the rest of the SAS team had gathered in the main entrance area. Standing flashed Shepherd a thumbs up. 'Area cleared. Three AKs and two Glocks, two fatalities.' There were two dead prisoners on the floor, blood pooling around their heads. Their Kalashnikovs had been stripped. 'That's pretty much it, Spider,' said Standing. 'The prison is ours.'

Shepherd and the Ellis boys dumped the chutes on the ground and Shepherd took out the tiny mobile phone and called Pritchard, who answered almost immediately. 'It's done,' said Shepherd. 'The governor and the staff hostages are safe. The weapons have been cleared from the wings and we are in control of the main entrance. A few casualties on their side, but only a few.'

'Music to my ears, Dan. Are you okay?'

'Other than a cracked rib and a few bruises, I'm fine. But they killed Sayed Khan.'

'Damn,' said Pritchard.

'It wasn't pretty,' said Shepherd. 'Khaliq killed him, but Khaliq's dead, too.'

'You killed him?'

'Long story,' said Shepherd. 'We can play catch-up later. I'm at the main entrance now and am able to open the main gate. Are the Tornados ready?'

'Champing at the bit, all two hundred of them,' said Pritchard.

'Get ready to unleash them,' said Shepherd. 'All the guns

have been taken care of and the fight has gone out of most of the prisoners. Do you want me to put the lights back on?'

'Negative on that,' said Pritchard. 'I've spoken to the head of the Tornado team, they'd prefer the lights to stay off. They're equipped with super-bright LED strobe flashlights, so shock and awe.'

'No lights then. I'll open the gate in thirty seconds.'

'Roger that.'

Shepherd ended the call and realised that Standing was shaking his head in confusion. 'What is that?' asked Standing.

'A prison phone,' said Shepherd.

He gave it to Standing who stared at it on the palm of his hand. 'Why is it so small?'

Shepherd grinned. 'Concealment.'

'Concealment?' Standing realised what Shepherd meant and he laughed out loud. 'That's disgusting,' he said.

. . .

The first wave of Tornado officers were carrying plexiglass shields and had helmets with visors but they met no resistance as they ran through the prison gate and into the yard beyond. Shepherd had opened the gate that led to the control centre. It was a bottleneck as it was only wide enough to allow two men through at a time, but they had practised entering confined spaces and they barely slowed as they rushed through.

The control centre was empty other than for the SAS men. Most of the prisoners had retreated in the dark to what they saw as the safety of the wings. The SAS team headed for the main entrance as the Tornados charged into A Wing. They cleared the ground floor in less than two minutes, then moved up to the twos and threes. What few prisoners were up there were dealt with within minutes.

They kept up the momentum, moving back to the control centre and entering B Wing. By now most of the prisoners realised what was happening. Most of them threw down their weapons and groped their way in the darkness to a cell where they sat and waited. The Tornados mopped up the few prisoners that were left on the landings and locked them up. B Wing took less than five minutes to clear.

Within half an hour the Tornados had secured all the wings and moved into the admin block. One of the team went down into the basement and turned the power back on.

As the floodlights came on in the entrance yard, Shepherd and the SAS team took off their night vision goggles. The gates were open and behind the prison a line of uniformed police were holding back dozens of reporters, photographers and TV news crews. Paramedics rushed forward carrying their kit and they hurried into the building.

Lane was on the radio. 'Exfil in two,' he called over to Standing.

'Do you want a lift?' Standing asked Shepherd.

'I've got to stay,' he said. 'My boss will want to debrief me.'

'And give you a bloody medal,' said Standing.

'Not sure about that,' said Shepherd. 'One of our people died in the governor's office.'

'That wasn't your fault.'

'I know. But it shouldn't have happened. And they'll want to make sure it doesn't happen again. Lessons will be learned, as they always say.'

Standing nodded. 'They say that, but our betters seem to make cock-up after cock-up, don't they? Oh, by the way, your boy asked me to say hello.'

'My boy? Liam?'

'Who do you think was flying the heli?' said Standing. 'He did a bang-up job, too.'

'Seriously?'

'The HALO was his idea.'

Shepherd grinned. 'I'll make sure to buy him a drink,' he said.

Four black Range Rovers roared through the open gates. Standing and his SAS team loaded their gear into the vehicles and climbed in. 'We need to get the hell out of Dodge before the inquisition starts,' said Standing.

'You were never here,' said Shepherd.

'Exactly.' Standing grinned. 'Glad to have been able to pull your nuts out of the fire, again,' he said.

'I thought we weren't keeping score.'

'We're not,' said Standing. 'But if we were . . .' He punched Shepherd on the arm and climbed into the front passenger seat of the lead Range Rover. Shepherd waved as the convoy roared back out through the prison gates, and watched them go. There would be no black Range Rover convoy coming to pick him up, but hopefully Pritchard or one of his people would collect him, sooner rather than later, because he had no ID and a lot of explaining to do.

He smiled as an Openreach van drove in through the gates. Diane Daily was driving, with Sammy Gupta in the front passenger seat. 'Best we could do at short notice,' said Daily through the open window.

'I'll take what I can get,' said Shepherd.

She smiled at his jumpsuit. 'Orange suits you,' she said. 'Climb in the back. Giles Pritchard is on the way up from London as we speak. He'll debrief you at the hotel. But he told me to tell you, job well done.'

Shepherd climbed into the van and pulled the doors closed behind him. Job well done? Maybe. But it would be a long, long time before he'd be able to blot Sayed Khan's gruesome death from his mind. Not that his trick memory would ever let him forget the last few seconds of Khan's life. Those images would be with him until the day he died.

• • •

Shafiq Ali Rafiq stared up at the narrow slit in the wall that passed for a window. All he could see was the night sky. The door banged shut behind him and the lock clicked. There were no keys where he was, all the doors were opened and closed electronically from a control centre. The men who had brought him to the cell had said nothing to him. There had been no induction, no medical, no questions about how he was feeling, no explanation about where he was or what would happen to him.

The cell they had placed him in was a bare box. Four paces long, three paces wide. There was no inspection slot in the metal door, just a hatch that was locked. There was no bed, no chair, no furniture of any kind, no toilet and no washbasin. Just four bare walls.

He knew where he was. Belmarsh Prison. There had been a sign on the gate that had rattled back to allow the police van inside. Belmarsh had a one-mile-long high wall surrounding it, but unlike HMP Bradford it was made from smooth concrete and was topped with rotating cylinders. It was only when Rafiq had passed through the gate that he had seen the wire fences topped with razor wire. The true horror of Belmarsh was kept hidden from the public.

Six men had escorted him from the police van. Three wore prison officer uniforms, three wore dark suits. Security service personnel, obviously, but they had not shown any identification or said who they were. The name of the place they had taken him to had been stencilled on the wall above the entrance – 'HMP BELMARSH, HIGH SECURITY UNIT'. It was possibly the most secure prison unit in the United Kingdom. Rafiq knew that the HSU had originally been used to hold IRA prisoners, but now that the IRA was a spent force, it was where the authorities punished jihadists. It was where they kept Hashem Abedi, the brother of the Manchester Arena suicide bomber; Ahmed Hassan, who tried to detonate a home-made bomb on a packed commuter train at Parsons Green; the Buckingham Palace sword attacker Mohiussunnath Chowdhury; Michael Adebolajo, who beheaded British soldier Lee Rigby; Ali Harbi Ali who murdered MP David Amess; and the ISIS supporter Muhammed Saeed. Rafiq was proud to be in their company. They were all good Muslims who would one day be rewarded in heaven.

Rafiq sighed as he looked around the tiny cell. If he was to spend the rest of his life in a featureless concrete box, then so be it. It was the will of Allah and Allah was great. Everything that happened in the universe flowed from Allah. The Koran said that the will of Allah prevails in shaping the destiny of man, letting the light of guidance shine in a heart to make it understand the divine reality. Rafiq had not been the recipient of the light of guidance, but he trusted Allah and was happy enough to follow his destiny. If Allah wanted this to be Shafiq Ali Rafiq's fate then there had to be a reason for it. The fact that he was not party to the reasoning made no difference. His fate was his fate. *Allahu Akbar.* God is great.

He looked up at the ceiling and smiled. There was a small metal disc set into the concrete, with an arrow pointing to the side. It was a Qibla pointer, showing the direction of Mecca. It was a sign, literally and figuratively. It showed him where he should be facing when he prayed, but it also showed that despite all the hatred the kafirs had for Muslims, they acknowledged the power of Islam. They were fighting a battle they could never win.

Shafiq Ali Rafiq dropped to his knees, placed his forehead against the cold concrete floor, and began to pray.

. . .

Shepherd looked at his watch for the hundredth time and wondered what was taking so long. He had been sitting outside the prison for the best part of two hours and he was starting to think that there might be a problem, even though Giles Pritchard had promised him that everything was running on schedule. Shepherd was sitting in his BMW SUV listening to BBC Radio 5 Live. The main story all day had been the clearing of Bradford Prison and the dispersal of the prisoners, who were being placed in high-security units around the country. As the keys had been compromised, every lock in the prison would have to be changed, a job that would take weeks and cost millions of pounds. There was no mention of the

SAS and the role they had played. And no mention of Shepherd and the two MI5 officers.

A wooden door opened and Mick Walker appeared, carrying two black plastic bags. He was wearing a brown leather jacket over a black polo neck sweater and blue jeans, clearly the gear he had been wearing on the day he was sent down. Walker grinned when he saw that Shepherd was waiting and he did a soft-shoe shuffle as he walked across the tarmac to the car. Shepherd popped the boot open and Walker tossed in the bags and climbed in to the front passenger seat. 'I wasn't sure you'd be here,' he said.

'Yeah, well I've been there, that's for sure,' said Shepherd.

'You really thought I'd run out on you? Back in the basement?'

'Mate, I knew you'd run out on me. The question was, were you going to come back or not? And you did, so all's well that ends well.'

Shepherd put the car in gear and drove away from the prison.

'Where to?' asked Walker.

'I was going to ask you the same question,' said Shepherd. 'What plans do you have?'

'To get a few pints down my neck and tuck into a full English,' said Walker. 'Other than that, no plans. No family. Most of my pals are long gone. No one came to visit all the time I was inside.'

Shepherd headed towards the M1. 'London it is then.'

'What's in London?'

'A job, if you want one.'

'What sort of job?'

'Plenty of time for that, Mick. But we might have to work on your fitness.'

'You're going to take me to the gym?'

Shepherd grinned. 'I was planning on doing some running with you,' he said. 'Carrying a rucksack filled with house bricks.'

Walker turned to look at Shepherd, his brow furrowed. 'Are you serious?'

'You'll find out soon enough,' said Shepherd.

THRILLINGLY GOOD BOOKS
FROM CRIMINALLY
GOOD WRITERS

CRIME FILES BRINGS YOU THE LATEST RELEASES FROM
TOP CRIME AND THRILLER AUTHORS.

SIGN UP ONLINE FOR OUR MONTHLY NEWSLETTER AND BE THE FIRST
TO KNOW ABOUT OUR COMPETITIONS, NEW BOOKS AND MORE.

VISIT OUR WEBSITE: WWW.CRIMEFILES.CO.UK
LIKE US ON FACEBOOK: FACEBOOK.COM/CRIMEFILES
FOLLOW US ON TWITTER: @CRIMEFILESBOOKS